THE HYMN OF ALL

A Dark Fantasy Adventure

THE SPLINTERED LAND
BOOK VI

RICHARD PARRY

The Hymn of All

The ancients call all debts due. **Evanne refuses to pay.**

Half-Vhemin, half-human, and bound by a gods-promised destiny, **Evanne has never walked an easy path.** Her music has sparked revolutions, her blade has cut through legend, and her name has become a beacon of hope.

But hope isn't enough against **Wild Sur**, the master of the Vide—**an order of assassins with a perfect record of death.** From his Vhemin fortress, where a portal to the demon realm yawns wide, **he's set his sights on Evanne**. And this time, he means to finish what the ancients started.

She doesn't stand alone. **Myryntir, a resurrected wild blue dragon**, soars at her side. **Tarragon, her heart's love, fights beside her.** And in the shadows, the newly **empowered Raven Queen** weaves her own brand of magic.

But the demons are endless. The battle ahead isn't just futile. **It's unwinnable.** Their only hope may lie beyond the portal itself, where **Geneve, Saviour of Ravenswall, is lost to time and legend.** Evanne's ancient armor may shield her body, but **can it protect her from the despair** of an impossible mission?

Wild Sur holds the key to the end of the world. If Evanne can't stop him, the fortress will fall, the demons will rise, and this time, **there will be no song left to sing.**

The final battle has begun. Read *The Hymn of All* today.

You're Awesome

You could have picked any book, but you chose this one. That means a lot.

Your support keeps independent authors like me forging ahead, writing the stories we love (and hopefully, the ones you love too). Whether you're here for the characters, the worldbuilding, or just a little escapism, thank you for being part of this journey.

You. Kick. Ass.

Roll for Narrative

WHERE WORLDBUILDING AND OVERTHINKING COLLIDE

Love stories that linger in your brain long after The End? Ever wonder why some books hit like a natural 20 and others critically fail their way into the 1-star abyss?

Join *Roll for Narrative*, my hub for sci-fi and fantasy lovers. I explore storytelling like a rogue casing a dungeon, review movies, books, and games, and dish out writing tips like a chaotic-good bard with a grudge against bad prose. No spam, just good stuff.

Join the quest:
https://rollfornarrative.parrydox.com

For my Rae, always.

A Day Like Any Other

A mir was no fan of rain, cold, or halitosis.

He stood in the middle of a corpse farm. Bodies were scattered. Most of them were in pieces. It spoke volumes of the past few moments, but the slimy rodent of a man before him did not seem to care. They stood, too close for Amir's comfort because of the weevil's halitosis, in a tavern. The tavern was in a blasted shithole named Wandermere. It seemed most had left, following music true, a melody that called the heart. Some say the dawn goddess sang it, her eyes violet. Others claimed it was a monster, teeth sharp, always parched, seeking to slake her thirst on the blood of villains. A vampire lord, they said, had fallen at her feet.

Amir contacted a fence, who said a local man of action knew the hero's location. They would meet in the pride of the town: this tavern. The storm outside hurried them in, armour slick, boots muddy, which meant Amir was pissed off before the ruckus started. The man of action turned out to be the weevil, who had been late to his assassination at the hands of the Vide. The Vide forgot their manners, and died against Amir, Faust, and Larochette's steel. Which left the three of them in the middle of a shitty tavern, Amir talking to the weevil, because Faust said *You're the one who's good with people.*

Vertiline had arrived after the ruckus but before the weevil. She'd pressed her lips into a line at the mess, and made a noise that sounded like *hmm*, which was the kind of noncommittal nonsense that made Amir fear a future sparring 'lesson' at the Justiciar's hand. She'd walked to a scorched patch on the floor, touched it with her metal hand, sank back in thought a moment, then settled herself in a dark corner, eyes hooded.

And that was when the weevil arrived, looking at the corpse farm as if this was the kind of thing Wandermere's tavern produced on a daily basis. He'd demanded coin for information, which Amir expected, but more than the fence agreed, which Amir didn't. It left them at an impasse, the weevil with information, and Amir with bared blade and stirring resentment.

When the weevil spoke, he sounded like an old, blocked-up drain. "The problem is the amount of solars. There are none."

"Friend," Amir lied, "you will note the number of corpses around me. These men and women did not accidentally fall. They tried to kill me, my friends," he gestured with his sword toward Faust and Larochette, who were rummaging through the dead, "and would have dispatched you, if you had not been late."

"So you say." The weevil's face was so punchable Amir almost gave it a shot, but he didn't want slime on his gloves. "Everyone knows you don't turn up first to a meeting when you're outnumbered. You want to make an entrance, casual like, hand over information, all without breaking a sweat, and still collect your solars." He jingled the pouch Amir had given him. "There are no solars here."

The wave of foul breath that arrived with the use of the word *solars* made Amir pale. He slicked cold water from his hair, a parting gift from the deluge outside the tavern. *Truth, but inside isn't much better. They could have at least put a fire on.* The roof was in bad need of repair, puddles of water spotting the floor in ways that dragged the steps and mired the patterns. Amir braced himself. "That is because we made no agreement for platinum. The offer was for sovereigns with a smattering of barons."

"I'm rounding up, see?" The weevil squinted up at Amir. "Cost of business is high. Was difficult to wrangle the information. I'm a businessman. Got expenses."

"Sir, are you aware you address a Knight of the Tresward?"

The weevil squinted harder, eyes almost screwing shut. "Tresward known for their business acumen?"

"Not our true calling, I'll admit."

"Then why does it matter?" The creature attempted a smile, the result ghastly. "Solars for satisfaction. I'll hear it no other way."

Amir felt the weight of the blade in his right hand, and imagined how it could be inserted underneath the weevil's ribs, living for a brief moment in his heart. It was a sorely tempting thought, and he felt the blade tremble in anticipation. *A small bending of the truth, first.* "A child's life is at stake."

The weevil pushed out his paunch and brushed an imaginary speck of dust from it. "Children are everywhere. Lose one? Plenty more where that came from."

Amir was moments from sticking the pig with his blade when strong fingers enclosed his wrist. "Sirrah." Vertiline, calm as the sky before a storm. She'd arrived from behind the weevil without sound, despite the bodies and muck on the floor. It was a trick Amir would have to learn. He hadn't even marked her moving, which was the kind of lapse that would get you killed. "It is *my* child."

"Then *you* can pay the solars." The weevil's squint turned into a glare. "We're still talking, which means you're not going to knife me with that pretty blade. You want your child back? Cross my palm with heavy platinum."

Vertiline cocked her head, hand still on Amir's arm. *How did she make it here so quietly? She breathes urgency to our cause but didn't charge the weevil.* He wondered why they weren't beating the weevil into submission. "Is it a matter of true cost, wretch, or is this a play for more coin?"

"Here, now." The weevil straightened. "First, I ain't no wretch. Businessman, see? Better than. Higher up than the likes of you." He looked down at Vertiline, or made the attempt. "Second, does it matter? The cost is the cost."

"It is difficult to extract information from a corpse," Amir murmured.

"I know a way." Vertiline didn't let him go, still facing the weevil. "I knew a man, once. He said—"

"We all know men. What of it?"

Amir noticed Vertiline's jaw muscles clench. "This wonderful man laid his life down before a demon gate so the likes of you could keep breathing. He told me there's always a reason. The reason, Meri said, was important. If it's a simple play for more coin, with you holding the knowledge but unwilling to part with it, then we can kill you now and leech the answer from your soul. If it's a cost of business matter as you suggest, then we can still kill you now. We will simply pay the people you are beholden to, avoiding middle-man fees."

The weevil paled but stood firm. "Here now. Ain't no way you know who they are. They're my people, not yours—"

"They will come looking for their platinum," Amir said. "We need but wait."

"And you have confirmed it is a true cost of business." Vertiline glanced to Amir. "Insert the blade as you were going to but mind the lungs. The corpse will have trouble speaking if he's missing a lung." And she let his hand go.

The weevil noticed, backed away, voice rising as he said, "The Tresward are good. You're no necromancers. You're—"

//DO YOU DOUBT ME?// Vertiline's voice cracked like the breach between worlds. The tables in the bar shook, and lamps flickered as a wild wind surged among them.

The weevil sank to his knees. "Holy Cophine, please—"

//DO NOT PROFANE THE GODDESS.// She relaxed, the lamplight rising again, the wind dying down. "I am not her. I am her ... sometime servant."

"Sometime?" Amir looked to his blade. "You still want me to stick him with the sharp end, boss?"

"Wait," the weevil pleaded again. "Just *wait*."

She crouched before the horrid little man, cupped his chin, and tilted his head so they locked eyes. "It is *my* child, creature. There is no force on this world that will keep me from her. I will raze cities and destroy armies if they stand in my way. Remember this as you give Knight Adept Amir what he's asked for. Because if you treat us false, I will come back. I will come here, find you, and make your soul cry for mercy. Do you hear me?"

The weevil's frantic nod tugged his head free of her grip. She eyed him a moment longer, then stood, turning to Amir. "Pay the man."

"But—"

"Adept, he is a businessman. He will remember the fairness of our offer as he remembers a future of pain. If more Vide come, he may be ... circumspect."

Amir sheathed his blade, counting coins into his palm as he watched the Knight Champion walk to the tavern's exit. As her hand touched the door, he called, "Could the Sway do that? Call his soul back from beyond to account for his crimes?"

"The Sway can shatter reality. It can do whatever we need but we must mind the price." She didn't turn. "And I will pay *anything*."

Chapter One

Tarragon prowled the corridors of *Dancing in the Storm*. There was an ache just below her heart, and she couldn't rub it away. It was odd; she'd spent so long fighting Vhemin and now she'd fallen for one. *And now, every minute of every day, I worry for her.*

Evanne had not been herself.

How do I know what she's like? I spent mere weeks at her side.

Being Big meant Tarragon was ... *different.* Big, sure, that was obvious to anyone with eyes or a seismometer. But her mind seemed larger, like she had more room to think about things like, *What are we going to do next,* maybe *what is up with the Raven and all those people we saved,* or the big one, *how did I fail my exams?* That was a bother that wasn't going away, because she was sure it was a test impossible for fairies to fail. They had a *Manifest.*

She knew lots of other things too, many from before the world fell, because she'd lived here. The ship was her home. She knew what this ship held, where to go to get the good booze, the great threads, or how to start the kitchen's fabricators so they at least had plenty of oatmeal. What with all the people from Hollyhead, there were a lot of mouths to feed.

Evanne wasn't by the liquor stores, nor was she eating. That was a rare thing, because the maybe-Vhemin always seemed to need calories. She'd hungered for more and more after her fight with Dancing Stars. Tarragon drifted past the fabricators, smelling oatmeal and honey as starveling villagers ate, then shored up at the middle deck's best faux leather store. *No Evanne.* If she wasn't where all the cool clothes were, it left one place.

The only training room still working was a modest football field in size. There were fencing sabres alongside racks of jousting armour, and weight cages for making the weak strong. A central stage took up a good third of the room where the battles were fought. Back in the day —a thought that made Tarragon feel as ancient as her eight-hundred-and-mumble years—glimmering Artifices made of illusory light would battle against dragons and warriors on that stage.

Now, one warrior panted, sweat dripping. Her jacket and guitar rested against a wall by her scattergun. A rapier was in the woman's hand, a tiny weapon for one whose shoulders were broad and strong. Tarragon fancied Evanne more of a match for the broadsword, but the maybe-Vhemin looked magnificent either way.

She turned and parried a flickering warrior of light and rainbow. The stage's projectors must be damaged like so much else, but it got the job done. Evanne grunted, turned, parried, and thrust. She was no Tresward, but her skill grew faster than any Tarragon had seen.

Perhaps she was her mother's daughter.

With a spin and thrust, Evanne dispatched her opponent, then raised the épée in a salute before offering a short bow. Tarragon frowned. "They're not real, love."

Evanne puffed out a breath, not facing Tarragon. "All things are real. This ship is the master of all the make-believe we see. I salute *him* as much as those I vanquish. It's only polite." Her voice was husky, with an odd, flat edge. "Besides, it's good practice."

"When have you ever practiced politeness?" Tarragon stepped closer, head cocked, because something wasn't quite right.

"Oh," Evanne waved a well-muscled arm but *still* didn't turn, "since forever."

"Dear heart? What is wrong?"

"Nothing." Evanne slumped a little. "I'll be up in a minute."

Tarragon stepped on the stage, ignoring all protocols against entering a live training environment. No one who cared was left. She padded before Evanne. The maybe-Vhemin's face was lowered, sweat slicking her rust locks. Tarragon touched Evanne's chin, raising her face. Evanne's lavender eyes were red-rimmed and bloodshot. Tarragon wanted to hug her, to say whatever it was would *be all right*, but she held back the impulse. Evanne wasn't her child, and the set of her jaw said she was in no mood for coddling. "What wind blows?"

"A fell one," Evanne admitted. "I have wasted my life."

Tarragon felt her mouth open and closed it with a snap. "You are sixteen summers. There was precious little time to waste."

Evanne pulled away, flourished her sword, then laid it carefully aside. Standing, she ran a hand through her hair. "Mama wanted me to learn the blade. I should have listened. This world cares little for mongrels and strays. There are many who would see our lifeblood spilled because of how the fates made us. The terrible trouble is knowing who the 'us' and 'them' are. I've been too much in my cups, singing songs, and wasting thought on fripperies and notions of no consequence."

Each word was laid like a brick made of doom. Carefully, with a mark of self-loathing beneath. Tarragon hugged herself. "You have saved the villagers of Hollyhead and Wandermere. You have—"

"I destroyed the village of Hollyhead, more like. Brought an ancient hulk from beneath the lake's depths and killed their livelihood."

Tarragon frowned. "You released those in thrall to a vampire lord. You saved the Raven from a life of servitude. Bent hordes of spectres at an ancient temple into a fighting force. Freed those still in thrall." She pressed her lips into a line. "You have raised this ship from below. By song and heart, and no other way would do it." She almost put a hand on Evanne's shoulder but left it trembling at her side. "I see no wasted life."

"I got rinsed by a cat!" Evanne snarled. "I fell and fell again. And fell some more, and at first I wanted it, I wanted you to get free, to run. But then I didn't want it. I wanted you back, and I wanted to stop hurting, and I couldn't *die*, Tarragon. I couldn't even die."

"Ah," Tarragon said. "I think it's time for you to meet the oracle."

"The what now?"

Tarragon sighed. "I don't know if he still lives. Not like before. But if there is someone he'll speak to, it's you. Come, love."

THE ORACLE'S LOUNGE WAS MUCH AS TARRAGON EXPECTED. SHE'D been here before, just once, when trying to discover the truth as to why she couldn't Build things. Then, it'd had plush chairs for Bigs. The chairs nestled within a wood-panelled room that sported a full bar with expensive liquors and tall, tinted windows that overlooked the clouds and planet below.

That was more or less what was here now, except with eight hundred years of time added. The chairs were faded, some rotted, and the windows were grimed. Merciful Three, but the bar remained, its host of liquor intact. No surprise to anyone, but that's where Evanne gravitated to first.

The oracle wasn't here. Or, he was always here but not visible yet. Tarragon hadn't worked out how the oracle-ship combo worked. The ship saw all, but the oracle was something ... individual. A thaumaturge had explained to Tarragon, his eyes earnest beneath an unruly carrot top, the oracle was a thing of two worlds. The ship and oracle were constructed of magic and science in a bundle.

She rubbed her arms. Fairies were made things too, and it wasn't always good to be a tool of the ancients, no matter how cool it sounded to the young sorcerer.

He's dead now, ash and dust like all the rest. Tarragon's arms had the good grace to show goosebumps at the thought. Evanne rummaged behind the bar, helping herself to spirits of unknown type, the labels long worn with the verdigris of age. She turned striking purple snake eyes on Tarragon. "What'll it be?"

"You don't know what those are!"

"We'll muddle through." Evanne sniffed a bottle, made a face, and recapped it. "Smells like liquorice ass. Where is this oracle, anyway?"

"He's here if he's anywhere." Tarragon cruised to the opposite side of the bar, and settled herself on a stool that didn't look like it would give up on the challenge despite the years. Her Big body still felt weird, but she was getting used to it.

"Do you miss flying?" Evanne splashed something purple into a glass.

"I miss it," Tarragon admitted.

"Me too." Evanne looked at a bottle filled with red liquid. "I miss how you used to hide in the cowl of my cloak."

"I did *not* hide."

"Steal a ride. Whatever." The concoction before Evanne was turning, as all mixed watercolours tended to, a muddy brown. She sipped. "This isn't half bad."

"But is the other half good?" Tarragon took the offered cup, braced herself, and took a chug. It tasted like dark honey and fire. "Okay, that's nice. How did you do it?"

"Dunno." Evanne started mixing into a second glass, then after a moment added a third beside it. "The ancients made so many things. Fruit that turns into whatever you needed it to be. Meat for cats. Sugar plums for fairies." She bit her lip. "Anyway, is it so strange to think this bar is filled with whatever you need?"

Tarragon looked about. Remembered the people here, waiting for their turn at prophecy. Some went away empty-handed, never meeting the oracle. Others were told dire dooms. Still more left hopeful. The fates were not easy masters. "I think that sounds right. It's what you need, but not always what you want."

"Well said." A slender man in his late fifties settled himself beside Tarragon. She could have sworn there was no stool there moments earlier, but he didn't seem overly concerned with reality. His hair was close-cut in a Caesar style, and Tarragon could tell that while he was lean, he was also hard. *Perhaps good enough to swing a blade in times of strife.* "Make mine a double."

Evanne's eyes narrowed. "You the oracle?"

"You the bartender?" The man's voice was mostly smooth, just a hint of the gravel age could bring. Cultured, like he spent time reading and wanted to say the words right.

"No one else was offering." Evanne pushed a glass toward the man. "Try that."

"Oh, great oracle—" Tarragon was cut off as the oracle put a palm out right in her face. He sipped, then nodded. "This is pretty good. I haven't had a drink in eight hundred years."

"Did you lose your manners in that time, asshole?" Evanne bristled, glaring at the oracle's hand.

"It's of no moment," Tarragon said.

The oracle ignored her, staring hard at Evanne. "It's as I thought. You are unruly."

"*I'm* unruly?" Evanne's snake eyes narrowed. "I'm not the one picking a fight with a fairy."

"She's no fairy." The oracle frowned, lowered his hand, then gave Tarragon a glance. "Leastways, not all the way, and not anymore."

"What do you mean, 'all the way'?" Tarragon said.

"This is a waste of time," Evanne said. "We came here because the world's ending, and all we're getting is sass."

"Did I say unruly?" The oracle seemed surprised at his own mistake. "I meant you are a moody teen. You don't understand the structure of the world or how it works."

"Oh yeah?" Evanne's chin jutted. "You're a jacked up faded memory of times that were lost because no one could admit they had no idea what they were doing."

Tarragon's mouth opened, then closed. The oracle was *here*, a rare event, and still *working* unlike so much else on the ship. And there was Evanne, blowing her one chance at understanding the future. "I think she means—"

"You know, I think I like her." The oracle tossed back his drink, then stood. "Here's the deal. Everyone, everywhere, is going to die."

"Of course." Evanne crossed her arms. "That's a natural state for the living when they reach the end of their allotted span." She rolled her eyes, letting them come to rest on Tarragon. "I thought you said this was an *oracle*, not a stater of the obvious."

"He is great and wise—"

"Okay, how's this for oracle-ness?" The old man leaned forward against the bar; his eyes locked on Evanne. "In orbit is a weapons—"

"What's orbit?"

The oracle blinked. "In outer space, there is—"

"What's outer space?" Evanne glared. "Make sense, man. We've no time for wise men too clever by half. Speak plain, or not at all."

The oracle's mouth opened, closed, then he tried again. "Where the sky stops, there is a great void where the stars grow. Each star is a sun like ours. This space between stars is like standing atop a giant cliff, where you can look down on all."

"Well done." Evanne offered a small smile. "Was that so hard?"

The oracle's jaw clenched. "The people who used to rule this world made platforms that floated in the void so they could see the lands below. And sometimes, throw rocks from there upon their enemies."

"Nice," Evanne admitted. "Where are you going with this?"

"When you raised *Dancing in the Storm* from beneath its blanket of water, I could see the sky again. The platforms up there spoke to me."

"That's when you dropped the truth bomb about us losing?" Evanne puffed a rust lock from her face. "Yet we're still here. And we've got a flying city now."

"We're moving really slowly." Tarragon's stomach clenched. The *Storm* had fallen as she rode high in the sky, and now she was a wallowing target. "We don't have height and must navigate around the smallest hills. And we don't control where we're going."

"That's because I'm doing the steering." The oracle favoured the once-fairy with a beatific smile. "We need to get to a confluence point. Once there, we can open a gate to the platforms and get orbital defences, uh," he glanced at Evanne, "the big rocks back online."

"Wait." Tarragon stood, bristling. "A gate? To the demon realm?"

"Not all gates go to bad places." The oracle's smile remained in place. "This one is but a hop to orbit, uh," another glance at Evanne, "the void between stars, where we will get the tools and weapons we need."

"Nah." Evanne started mixing another drink.

"Excuse me?" The oracle blinked.

"We're not going to the space between stars. We've got a boatload of refugees. We need a berth for them. Homes and jobs. Then, vengeance."

"If we wait, the enemies I see amassing in the north will sweep across the land and kill everyone." The oracle shrugged.

"Void it is," Evanne sighed. "Tell me about the amassing force."

"It is a collection of Artifices surrounded by a perplexing mix of Fey Branded, Vehement Systems, and—"

"Feybrind," Evanne corrected, as if to a small child. "They aren't slaves anymore. And we are Vhemin."

"You are a little bit Vhemin." The oracle wobbled his hand *so-so*. "You are mostly human."

"I'm—"

"Anyway," the oracle steamed on, "the perplexing thing is, they have all the tools of the old world. They have Artifices docked at a Vehement citadel. All three races performed together to work the magics of ancient time. We might fight Vehement Systems powers but we can't fight Itikari as well."

"Lucky I'm here." Evanne jerked a thumb to her chest. "I'm a mongrel too."

"Quite." The oracle beamed. "I'm glad that's settled. Now, let's talk about the armour you stole."

Evanne eyed the oracle through narrowed lids. "Make your own drink."

"I can't." The oracle frowned. "I'm not really here."

"I'm glad we understand each other." Evanne strode toward the door. "You need people with hands. We're not your servants. Best not forget it."

Chapter Two

Evanne found Morgan overlooking her people on the foredeck. The Raven Queen wore a pensive mood like a shawl. Men and women bustled about, clearing detritus and doing their best to make the ship habitable. The ship had smelled of drying washing; now it was tasting sunlight, a warm, pleasant smell permeated that was at odds with it mouldering beneath a lake for most of a millennium. The folk on her decks sang to each other, sharing nods and smiles, tossing a little hope between them.

A dark-skinned man with tremendous biceps worked metal not ten meters off, and if Evanne was any judge, he was making the world's largest barbecue. If Tarragon could get the fabricators to make anything other than oatmeal, it would be killer. She sidled up to Morgan. "Ho, Auntie."

Morgan winced. "That makes me sound a hundred years old."

"You're but sixty summers, and don't let anyone tell you different." Evanne offered a grin in return for Morgan's scowl, then sobered. "We must get the Hollyhead refugees to safety. We go to war."

Morgan gave her a sideward glance. "We have ever been at war."

"Sure, but this ship," Evanne stamped the deck, "is going *toward* the enemy."

The wannabe-smith paused his work and stood. He wiped grimy hands on an apron. "Excuse me for interrupting, but I couldn't help but overhear."

Evanne swivelled to him. "Goodman, uh..?"

"Turner, if it please." Turner eyed the deck, then straightened. "The way of the powerful is to make decisions for the little. Often these are good and wise." A slight glance at the Raven for this. "Sometimes they are not. Perhaps it might be wise to see what we want?" He swept an arm to his half-made barbecue. "I'm setting up shop here. Going to make a life aboard a wonderful ship my ancestors built. We'll sail the very sky. Can you imagine it?" He beamed. "I aim to fly this ship to the end, if she'll have me."

"More of a he, this ship," Morgan murmured. "But I understand your point. What would you suggest? The preposterous notion of drawing straws to determine fates?"

"Now that's not a bad idea, your ladyship," Turner said. "I couldn't have thought of better."

Morgan's eyes bulged, perhaps aware she'd been snookered, before turning to Evanne. "This was your doing, wasn't it?"

Evanne laughed, then hugged her. "Auntie, no. I want these people safe." She released the Raven. "But I'll take the willingly damned instead. Cast your lots, Turner, and we'll park those who want off at the next hillock."

THE SHIP COASTED TO A HALT OVER THE TOP OF A SUSPICIOUSLY FLAT plane. Tarragon stood at Evanne's left, Hitch by her right as the three looked over the side railing. The spectre huffed. "It has the look of a jump gate. Bit overgrown, though."

"What's a jump gate?" Evanne frowned.

Tarragon gripped the railing. "What it sounds like. It allows a person to jump between spaces."

"Ah." Evanne nodded. "Like Mama said the hero Geneve and her companions used to get between Or'sen and Imshir."

Hitch turned not-eyes to the sky. "The oracle said this goes up?"

"The oracle was a snide old man well into his dotage," Evanne said.

"Hello." The oracle coasted to join them at the railing. "I see you have found the gate below."

Evanne glanced behind them. "Where did you come from?"

"I've always been here," he said.

"Can you leave the ship?"

"Why would I want to?" The oracle seemed surprised at the notion. "There are dangers out there."

"That's a no, then." Evanne looked down again. "How does it work?"

"You go down. I open it. You go through, appear above," the oracle pointed to the clouds, "grab supplies, and come back. It'll be a cinch. Then we can repair the *Storm*, head north, and rain confusion on our enemies."

"I'm in." Evanne rubbed her arms. "Let me get my guitar."

Chapter Three

Sands Apart felt the metal shackles were a bridge too far but understood the intent. The metal about her wrists meant no one had to watch her too closely, and they also meant the *other* Feybrind with them wouldn't get jumpy and murder her for sneezing. They'd bound both her hands and feet but left her room to speak. It showed the Feybrind wasn't a monster. He didn't want to steal her words from her like so many humans did.

She wished she could talk to him in private. If she could just explain things, she was sure he'd understand. His name was Sight of Day, and he had the most glorious golden eyes. Gold was a rare colour among Feybrind. Most of the People had eyes the colours of gemstones, but a rare few had orbs coloured like metal burnished by the sun. His coat was the perfect length, just long enough to fuzz your fingers through if that was where the two of you were going.

Sands Apart knew he was a mastersmith. He carried his sword like he knew how to use it, but also like hew knew how it'd been born. Perhaps his was the hand that stoked the fires of its cradle before it took adult form. He held it like it was a part of him, and she knew how that worked. She'd made things too, before humans had set fire to her home and killed everyone she ever loved.

They'd stopped to rest in a small clearing. Their band was small; a handful of soldiers playing at learning the patterns, two merchants who looked surprised to be alive, a monster, and the other Feybrind. The sky was clear and bright, and a gentle breeze touched Sands Apart. She felt the world was still kind to her, touching a favoured daughter, even though she'd fallen into captivity through her own carelessness.

Her reverie broke as one of the humans squatted before her. He was a Knight, this one, and if there was someone more dangerous than Sight of Day, it was this muddy, imperfect creature. That the Three had gifted their kind with the Light was another blemish Wild Sur would erase before they were done. The Knight called himself Amir, which wasn't a proper name. It didn't tell her what he did or how he thought about the world. It told her he believed he was important enough to have a made-up sound attached to his person.

"Hello." Amir placed a plate between them. It settled easily enough on the ground. Their camp was near a babbling brook in a thicket of hunchbacked little trees. The winds that coursed through this valley had bent them to their will but they made good enough nesting for birds. She'd watched Sight of Day bring down a brace of them before setting off for other prey. The giant, Faust, had packed the birds in clay and roasted them, their eventual fate to be on the plate before her. "I thought you might be hungry."

She raised her shackled hands between them. *{I'm surprised you can think at all.}*

He raised an eyebrow. "Suit yourself." Before he could leave, she moved with Feybrind swiftness and rescued the plate. He didn't react to her speed, no involuntary twitch, widening of the eyes, or scream of surprise. These Knights didn't *react*; they were trained in patterns. They felt the world was a thing to bend to their will, an extension of all human hubris. He smiled, stood, doffed an imaginary cap with the unbearable arrogance of his kind, and sauntered off to check the horses.

Sands Apart tore a bird to pieces, wolfing it down. They'd fed her well, but you never knew where your next meal was coming from. She had disassembled most of the first bird when she looked up to see golden eyes but an arms length away. The other cat had a half smile.

His hands moved People-fast, as Feybrind did when speaking to each other. *{Do you have worms?}*

She placed the remains of her bird down. Her shackles *clinked* at the speed of her speech. *{Terror gives me hunger.}*

{I don't know why you're afraid. We're the ones doing all the fighting and dying.}

{The bandits?} She rolled her eyes. *{They were sure to come, after the bungle your lot made of the informant in the last town. We watch all and hear more. Wild Sur will defeat you all anyway.}* She looked at her traitorous hands. She hadn't meant to say Wild Sur's name. It fled through her fingertips as if needing release.

Sight of Day sat crossed-legged. *{That is a Feybrind Command name.}*

Of *course* one of the People would know that. Their given names were descriptive, but their Command names were a part of their soul. The words felt ... *different* on the fingers. *{He isn't afraid of you knowing it. He has the powers of the ancients.}*

She met golden eyes gone wide with astonishment. Sight of Day then made a big show of hilarity, silently guffawing as the apes did, slapping his thigh, and wiping an imaginary tear from beneath one of those glorious golden eyes. *{He is terrified, little sister. He hides behind men and machines far from here. His every moment is spent trying to keep his presence from our sight. This is the mark of a man who is concerned for his welfare.}* He sobered. *{Can you keep a secret?}*

Sands Apart blinked. *{Any morsel you'd share with me is valueless.}*

{Perhaps.} A shrug. *{I give it anyway. I, too,}* he touched his chest, *{am terrified.}*

{You should be. He comes for you.}

{You mistake my meaning.} Sight of Day's golden gaze left hers for a moment, and she felt an emptiness at its passing, like clouds had clustered over a sunbeam she'd been napping in. *{There is little left for me here. My mate is gone. My son, taken. My dear friends, lost on the other side of a demon gate.}* He looked about, those golden eyes resting on the platinum-haired leader of their party, and then shifting to one of the hated enemy, a brutish thug larger than any Vhemin had a right to be. *{There are but two left, and their cub. I fear for them, little sister.}*

{Then tell them to stop.} She sliced the air, blade of her hand hitting the palm of the other. *{It is not too late.}*

{It was too late when Wild Sur sent killers for their child. There is no force in creation that will stop them. But I fear for their humanity. I fear for what they will give to win.}

She folded her hands, thinking for a moment. The world moved so slowly for the People, but things could still take time to think through. There was little value in trying to make him cease pursuit, so she tried a different tact. *{Why do you call me little sister? We are the same.}*

He gave her a tired half smile. *{You are much younger than I. But you are also a child in your understanding of the world.}* She could tell from the weight of his hands he was not insulting her, a kindness living in the gentle movement of fingers and hands. *{You have been lied to. And I would give you the truth before the end.}*

{What if it's you that's been lied to?}

He stood, brushing down his pants. *{Like I said, I didn't come down with the last shower.}* His golden gaze sparkled. *{Get some rest. They'll attack before dawn.}*

{Who? Why?}

He gazed at the stars. *{Can't you feel it? The terror that drives Wild Sur. He will want to be sure no one shares his secrets, not even his treasured name. And you, little sister, know too much to be left alive.}*

THE CAMP WAS QUIET. SANDS APART FEIGNED SLEEP, THE TIP OF HER tail twitching every so often, one arm thrown over her face. The human rabble had given her a comfortable enough billet. It wasn't a patch on Feybrind mattresses, but they hadn't given her a flea-infested bundle of rags.

It was almost as if they treated her with respect.

Respect or no, she'd had enough of being a prisoner. She'd found a twist of wire left behind when one of their imbecile companions repaired a dagger. He'd left tools within close reach of a furred hand. She thought his name was Amber. He had a sister, Jade, the devious scullion always watching Sands Apart when awake. All were asleep, except the giant Faust and killer Larochette, who guarded opposite sides of the camp.

The twist of wire unlocked her manacles. She waited until darkness was her shroud. Faust and Larochette might play at guards, but they were only human. Their dim eyes were worthless at the best of times.

Time to go.

She opened one eye, surveying the camp beneath the shelter of her arm. No movement. Snores from Amber's tent. A slight moan as someone yonder turned in their sleep. It was a wonder humans survived at all; they made more noise than a herd of buffalo, even while asleep. She removed her shackles, rose, and threaded her way through the meagre collection of tents.

I must be watchful for Sight of Day.

The other Feybrind was nowhere to be seen. Perhaps he patrolled. *No matter.* As long as he wasn't here, he wasn't a threat.

At the southern edge of the camp, she started to relax. No one raised the alarm. She picked up the pace, careful not to displace much in her passing. Sight of Day might be able to track her through grass, so she headed for the sound of water. Passage through a stream was a reliable trick, and by the time they found her egress from the water downstream she would be gone, smoke lost in a hurricane.

"Nice night for it, isn't it?" Sands Apart whirled at the voice, startled she'd been caught unaware. The too-clever-for-his-own-good Knight Amir sat on a fallen log. His hands were empty, blade sheathed at his hip. His teeth were bright in the night as he smiled. "You've chosen a good time to get away. I pick it perhaps three hours after midnight, when humans are most lethargic."

She crouched, teeth bared. *{You have sealed your death warrant by waiting for me.}*

He shrugged, amiable enough. Damn the human, but she could sense no threat from him. "If you must be away, then be away." He glanced at the cloudless sky, perhaps admiring the stars. "I beg but a moment first."

Sands Apart straightened cautiously, as if any movement would be the one to provoke a snake to strike. *{You will let me go?}*

"Sure. You're another mouth to feed." He stood, brushed down his pants—perhaps not meaning to highlight his curious lack of armour—then arched his back. "That feels good. I've been sitting on this damn log for hours waiting for you. It was even odds if you'd go north or south. Sight of Day awaits the other way."

{You...} She looked at her hands. *{You knew I'd leave?}*

"It was hard enough to leave a piece of wire sturdy enough to use as a lockpick without making it look obvious, but we managed it." This human was too pleased with his own cleverness. "Thing is, our camp is being approached by a collection of assassins disguised as bandits. I'll bet a shiny solar they're here to remove all witnesses. Us, that's understandable. Expected, even. We're inconvenient, and this Wild Sur doesn't strike me as a man large on patience."

So many words to say so little. *{Do you have a point? Do you wish to make a deal for your lives?}*

"Eh, we'll be fine." Amir twisted his torso, then windmilled his arms as if warming up for a fight. "High Justiciar Vertiline is about. Good luck taking her down! Hah." That flash of teeth in the darkness took her by surprise. This human was *enjoying* this. "What I think will happen is they will kill you, too. You're a mistake to be remedied. Wild Sur? That man thinks of you as a failure, and he's going to remove you from his ranks."

{He will not.} Doubt roiled in her gut. *{I am one of his senior lieutenants.}*

"Were. You *were* a senior lieutenant. Now, you're a bottle of secrets waiting to be uncorked. And an unreliable bottle at that. He's no way of knowing if you've spilled your guts already. He might think you've turned coat and accompany us. You are not bound, and we've let you go." That brilliant smile cut the night again. "So, here's the thing. If you make it out to your side and they welcome you with open arms, great. We're back to being enemies and all that entails." His voice lowered and slowed at the end.

{This troubles you?}

"I like cats." Amir tipped his head side to side, working out the kinks. "If your lot try killing you, maybe come back here. See what we've got to offer."

{Why would you do this?} Sands Apart looked at her traitorous hands, because she shouldn't even have asked the question. *{Besides liking cats.}*

"Favour to a friend." Amir pointed north. "Sight of Day said you could be helped, or at least ... *saved*. Said there weren't enough of you left to meet blade on blade and would prefer you free. I get that. Not many Knights left either." He flicked his hand south in a shooing motion. "Now go on, get."

She looked him up and down, then fled. Knight he might be, better with a blade by half than she, but he was only human. He couldn't match her speed. Her legs took her another klick from the camp. She emerged from the low scrub and trees into a small clearing. A large rock brooded in the middle like a crouching dragon. Old lichen patterned its sides in soft greens.

The clearing was populated by waist-high grass that felt soft against her palms. She breathed, sniffed the air, and listened. Her nose told her humans were here, and her ears told her they might be lurking just west of the rock, hunkered low in the grass. Sands Apart rolled her eyes, fetched a stone, and tossed it into the grass.

It hit metal with a *clink*. A soft, *ow, fuck*, came from that direction, with an accompanying, *be quiet you idiot*. She rolled her eyes again, lifted a second stone, and tossed it at the be-quiet-idiot. She got a *gods damned*, at which point a company of men and women in black leather rose from the grass.

She padded to them. *{We've not much time. One of them is behind me.}*

The leader had the look of Vide about him. Sands Apart didn't much like the assassins, but they got the job done. He glanced at her hands, lower face hidden behind a soft cloth mask, then grunted. "I don't do finger painting, and I don't do finger talking either. Just nod. Are you alone?"

She sighed. The People couldn't speak, and cretins like this didn't take the time to learn their language. Sands Apart shook her head. *{There is one.}* She emphasised *one* by raising a digit, then stabbing her hand back the way she came. Moving her hands slowly, carefully, she said, *{He is a Knight.}*

"Just one, hey?" The Vide grunted. "Well, your new allies don't think much of you." Sands Apart felt her stomach grow cold, because this was *exactly* what that too-clever human said would happen.

As if on cue, Amir emerged from the tree line. He offered a cheerful wave and called, "Ho, friends. Don't mind me." He produced an apple from a pocket and took a bite.

The Vide glanced at Sands Apart. "Is this some kind of joke?"

"Could be." Amir gestured magnanimously with his apple. "Be about it, then."

The Vide drew a sword and tried to run Sands Apart through. She sidestepped his slow movement, but barely; these were not fuck about people. She punched him in the throat, but her fingers connected with a gorget. Sands Apart caught movement from her left, stepped around a woman's lunge, and elbowed her in the face.

The Vide surrounded Sands Apart. Five at equidistant spacing, and beyond, another ten waiting to join the fray. She took a glancing blow to her shoulder from a mace and cursed herself for a fool. She turned, accepted a sabre thrust from a short man, disarmed him, and cut off his hand. He grunted, and she smelled copper-bright on the night air. The woman with the mace swung again and she took the hit on the edge of the sabre. The sword cracked, a shard of the blade snicking Sands Apart's face as it passed.

The leader swept in with a low slash, which she jumped, then an upward cut that would have taken her from groin to throat had she not turned. As it was, it took her along the side, a hot wire of pain running along her leg and ribs as she turned away.

She threw the worthless sabre at a man, hoping to startle him, but he slapped it aside with a buckler, then hunkered, dagger held low.

"For pity's sake, it's about time you turned up," she heard Amir say, but she had no time for the fool. Sands Apart jumped, Feybrind agility taking her higher than any human could make. Her spring took her to a woman's shoulders, which she used to springboard out of the death ring. She landed behind the woman, just in time for a man with a rapier to run her through.

She leaned into it, sinking teeth into his shoulder. Leather armour resisted. She elbowed him in the jaw, broke his fingers, and turned in time to take a sword slash to her arm. She sagged, then dropped to her knees. Blood pounded, her life leaking from her middle, her side, her arm. *There are too many. Merciful Three, why did you make us voiceless? We can't even cry.*

Blood pounded more, and she realised the earth shook with it. The man with the sword turned about, surprised, as Armitage arrived like a runaway cart. The monster slammed the human with a fist the size of a human head and the swordsman bounced into the night. The monster roared, arms wide in challenge, then punted the legs of a woman who took him up on it. She landed face-first in the grass, and he followed her down with a vicious punch to the back of the head.

The Vide leader stuck him with a sword and the monster, oblivious to the wound, grabbed the assassin, hefted him, dropped to one knee, and broke the man's back over it. He tossed the broken assassin aside, freed the blade from his side, and cut a woman's head off with it.

A monster comes to help me? Sands Apart felt dizzy from blood loss, sure she was hallucinating. Amir joined the fray, sword a golden arc that cut through weapons, shields, and humans all the same. Where it cut, metal glowed with heat, and flesh charred. He was exquisite to watch, each step a painting of perfection. Five died in as many footsteps.

Armitage grunted. "Stop showing off."

The too-clever human beamed. "Tell your wife to—"

Armitage shoved him aside from the halberd strike coming for his rear, grabbed the weapon, and yanked it and the hapless wielder close. He punched the man in the throat, hit the same style of gorget Sands Apart had, dropped the halberd, and closed both hands about the gorget. Sands Apart saw his shoulders bunch, then metal shrieked as he crushed the gorget about the assassin's throat. The man staggered away, clawing at his neck before toppling into the grass. "Tell my wife what?"

"You know, it's not important." Amir straightened, then rejoined the fight.

In twenty seconds, it was over. Fifteen dead Vide and the Knight wasn't even breathing hard. Armitage buffed like a bellows but he was old for one of his kind. The white scar tissue about his shoulder and neck bunched as he bent, rooting through the dead. "Assassins."

"Of course." Amir ignored Sands Apart, looting the bodies.

She wondered why she was being ignored until golden eyes met hers. Sight of Day crouched before her. *{Are you well, little sister?}*

{I'm dying,} she complained.

He nodded sagely, looked at the rapier through her middle, then yanked it free. She almost passed out from the pain. *{Let's see what we can do about that.}*

{Leave me be.} Her hands didn't want to move. She wanted to be left alone.

{Hush.} His finger pressed against his lips. *{I think it's time to see what you can become. Besides a pincushion, that is.}* He bent, hefted her, and draped her over his shoulder like a sack.

She bled down his fine jerkin but he didn't seem to mind. He padded back to the camp with gentle, soft steps. She faded into black before he made the trees.

Chapter Four

Evanne waited on the deck. The flat, grassy area waited below, *Dancing in the Storm* holding steady above, not shifting even a little in the delicate northern wind. Turner's barbecue was coming along nicely, but the supply of steak wasn't. Evanne saw a woman had set up the beginnings of a still, which was an admirable enterprise, as the ship's stores wouldn't last forever.

Evanne double-checked her kit. Mama would be proud, because the Half-Made's usual style was to jump and work it out on the way down. Guitar? Check. Scattergun? Also check, but the ammunition situation was dire. Sword? Evanne had one of those too, a shiny ship-forged machete Tarragon found. The once-fairy's eyes glimmered as she said, *That has no finesse*, so Evanne hefted it, gave it a twirl, and asked, *What's your point?* She was unlikely to be a good duellist, despite her time in the training room. *But I can make up for lack of skill with enthusiasm.*

The oracle eyed the machete in its sheath. She eyed him in return. "Got something to say, old man?"

"The weapon lacks finesse."

"Got something *original* to say?" She arched an eyebrow. "Tarragon said that already."

"And where is your friend?" The oracle cast about the deck, making a great show of not finding Tarragon there.

"She's getting ready." Evanne looked over the railing. The keel of the ship hovered over a hillock; not a half hour earlier they'd grazed the top, displacing trees and boulders as a great shudder ran through the hull. "You sure this thing will work?"

"Eh." The oracle sighed. "About eighty percent positive."

"This ship isn't even eighty percent operational."

The oracle sighed louder. "This is why we're going up there." He jabbed a finger skyward. "There are delights. Treasures ready for the taking. Perhaps a fairy still waits there. They live a long time. Ah! Speaking of which."

Evanne turned. Her heart stumbled as she saw Tarragon. The once-fairy strode like Cophine herself, shoulders broad and strong, gladiatorial armour covering her left side, atop a simple leather jerkin and skirt. Requiem was belted to her hip. Her golden skin begged for kisses. "Um."

Tarragon joined her at the railing. "Hello, love."

"Um," Evanne repeated.

"You look good, too." Tarragon looked away, as if realising they weren't alone, then turned back quickly and planted a kiss on Evanne's lips.

Evanne closed her eyes. *Is this what happiness feels like?* They broke apart as the oracle cleared his throat. The old man's voice was businesslike but his eyes held a twinkle. "Are we ready?"

"What do you mean, 'we'? You can't leave the ship." Evanne shook her head. "Never mind. Where's Uncle Heser?"

"Other side." The Oracle pointed.

As if on cue, Heser ran from behind a makeshift shelter. He looked angry and out of breath. An executioner's axe was in his hand. "'Ware! Villainy!"

Evanne's machete was in her hand in a moment. Tarragon stood in front of her, Requiem's shining length a brand. Evanne appreciated the sentiment, but it made it hard to see. "Heser? What news?"

The man swung the axe to point behind him. "Assassins scale the hull."

Evanne groaned. "As the living dead did before. We should clear the vines off the ship to make that harder."

"Or, fly higher." Tarragon gave a pointed look to the oracle. "They wouldn't be able to get a grip if we didn't hit hills."

"Don't blame me," the oracle sputtered. "I only work here."

Three black-clad figures came from behind the same building Heser had. They wore masks and a bad attitude Evanne respected immediately. They moved with an oiled precision not unlike Tresward, although with less perfection. She made to go at them, but Tarragon put an arm out to bar her path. The not-fairy hissed, "Vide."

"You know these assholes?"

Tarragon called to Heser, "The queen!" The guardsman nodded, turned, and pelted off toward the conning tower. "They are assassins for hire."

Evanne felt a touch of fear, but also a thrill. *Someone cares enough about us to set hired thugs on our trail.* "You know you've made it by the quality of your enemies."

The Vide came at them, steps sure and quick, no headlong rush evident. Pros, then. "The gate!" the oracle cried. "We must get to the gate!"

Tarragon ignored him, closing with the Vide. She cut one in half without looking, the man landing in two places, his mace clattering in a spray of blood. The leader tried for her neck, but the gorget of her half armour took the thrust with a shriek. She pirouetted back, Requiem going low to high, and claimed the man's arm.

The third paced, eyes locked with Tarragon's. Evanne drew her scattergun, levelled it, and pulled the trigger. The weapon roared, tearing the stomach from the Vide, a crimson spray showering the deck behind the assassin's toppling body.

Tarragon looked at the corpse, then Evanne. "Don't waste the shells."

"You're welcome," Evanne gritted.

"What's that mean?" Tarragon pulled back.

"It means, I don't always need coddling like a newborn—"

"Help!" the oracle cried.

They both turned to see the old man wrestling with two assassins.

Evanne wondered where they'd come from but the old geezer was perilously close to the railing; perhaps they'd come up this side. He was putting in a good fight for a man over eight hundred years old. Tarragon charged, blade held high and back. One assassin let go her prize, drawing a shortsword. Perhaps aware she'd brought a butterknife to a magic sword fight, she held the blade in crossguard. Tarragon swung, slicing the shortsword in half.

The assassin stumbled back, collided with the oracle, who also stumbled, tangling with his remaining assailant. That one's legs fouled in their scabbard, and all three skewed toward the railing.

And over.

Tarragon froze, then stared at Evanne. "He can't leave the ship!"

"He just did!" *Think, dammit.* "What do we do?"

"He is the only one who can open the gate," Tarragon said.

"Can't you do it?" Evanne wiggled her fingers. "You know, ancient know-how. Wizardry. Arcane tricks."

"I never passed my exams," Tarragon wailed.

"Ah, fuck." Evanne felt hot and cold as the revelation hit her. "Well, then. It's time to go." She put a hand on the railing, ignored Tarragon's startled yelp, and slipped over the side.

THAT WAS STUPID! IT'S A LONG WAY DOWN!

Evanne had assumed the handholds on *Dancing in the Storm's* side were strong, perhaps conveniently vine-like. When she'd boarded the other side, the encrusting of barnacles had done a passable job of providing nooks for her fingers.

The first handhold she grabbed lied to her. It said *I am strong*, then it gave way like the bubble of a dream on waking. She fell, flailing, as bits of detritus came away from the hull like lies on a harlot's lips. *If there was a rope...* Nothing like that here. No, wait: there was a handful of Vide climbing toward her. Her hand scrabbled as she dropped, finding very little of anything as the ship's curve left her swinging at air. Then, Evanne's flailing hand found a startled woman's cloak.

It tore, of course.

But while tearing, Evanne acted as the bob on a pendulum, swinging back toward the hull. She slammed into it, the woman falling past her. The woman, clearly not keen on death by the sudden stop at the end of the fall, grabbed Evanne's trailing boot.

They both spun free of the ship's side.

Evanne found the scattergun in hand as if by magic. She pointed it at her assailant, hoping to not hit her foot, and pulled the trigger. The assassin turned into a shower of assassin parts, and Evanne was blasted back into the hull with a *bang*. She grabbed a crevice. Held, cheek to ship.

It gave way.

She dropped another two metres before her flailing hand found a rope. An enterprising assassin had no doubt left it here. She hung, hands burnt from a quick skid down the line, but didn't let go. She glanced up and saw a masked Vide above her. His blade was against the rope. She shook her head. "Don't you fucken *dare*."

His eyes crinkled in a smile, and he sliced her free.

Falling, *again*. If there was a piece of good news in all this, it was that she was closer to the ground. Impact would likely break bones but not leave her dead. Maybe.

She pointed the scattergun away from the ship, somehow now falling head first, and pulled the trigger. It cannoned her into the hull again, and by the Three's grace, another surprised assassin. This man was a hulk, perhaps the reason why he was slower climbing than his companions. She clung, a limpet, breathing into his ear, scattergun against his jaw. It felt awkward but got the point across. "Hi."

He grunted. "If you kill me, we both go down."

"Do you happen to have a rope about your person?"

He—carefully, slowly, clearly nobody's fool—pulled his hand away from the hull. He wore a clever glove with hooks extending from the knuckles. *A kind of portable piton.* "Afraid not."

Evanne glanced down. Where *Dancing in the Storm* nosed the hillock was perhaps a half klick south of her. At this distance from the hillock, the ground was perhaps three storeys. "Why'd you come here?"

"Recover the relic. Kill the targets. Usual." He seemed unfazed. *Perhaps he hangs on the side of ancient ships every other week.*

"Relic?"

"The ship, obviously." She could hear the eye-roll in his voice. "Our eyes above saw it."

Evanne looked up, seeing only the curve of the hull, but imagining the platforms the oracle spoke of. The enemy had these too, then. "Do you have rocks there?"

He paused. "What?"

"Excellent." She kneed him in the ribs, getting an *ooph* for her troubles. He hunched, right on cue, and she swung her legs about him, feet flat against the hull, and *heaved.*

A heartbeat, and then they sailed into the air. They turned as she'd hoped, him going first, with an accompanying scream, cut short as they hit the ground.

The air went out of Evanne. The scattergun roared. The Vide died in a spray of surplus body parts. Evanne gasped, the air knocked out of her. *I think I've lost a tooth.* She spat blood, tongue cut, lip bleeding, head ringing. *Move. Father would have walked this off.* She staggered upright. The world swayed, while she stayed a pillar of strength.

Breathe. Just fucking... breathe, dammit.

The blackness crept on her. She fought it. Held it down, teeth gritted. It wisely walked back, leaving her be.

The wind whispered. She straightened, taking stock. A woman ran at her from the cover of some wooden crates, so Evanne pointed the scattergun, pulled the trigger, and ended that nonsense. Red painted the boxes. *I'll wait until that dries to see what's in there.*

She found the oracle near the crates. His arm was twisted in a manner no arm should be, neck likewise, and his knee was bent the wrong way. Despite that, he seemed in good spirits. "I've never been off the ship!"

"How's it feel?"

"Cold."

"That's the wind." Evanne crouched. "Do you need a hand? Or something?"

"We must open the gate. It's over there." His good hand wavered in the air, pointing in the general direction of a clearing.

"I repeat, do you need a hand? I can get you there. But it's going to hurt."

"Pain is for mortals."

"As you say." Evanne got her arm under his shoulders and hefted. He came with her, screaming all the way. She dragged him toward the centre of the clearing, grasses whispering at their feet. She glanced up, seeing Vide on their way back down. Above, a glimmer of blue-white as Tarragon began a more sensible descent. "We should hurry."

"That's my line." The old man shook his broken arm until it *clicked* back into place, then used both hands to straighten his neck. The grating, graunching sound was one Evanne would never forget. "That's better."

"For who?"

"Hush, child." He shook his leg, the knee popping back the right way. "Good as new."

"You look like shit. Still, that could just be you doing you."

"Hah." He slipped from her helping arm, staggered a few paces, and threw his arms wide. The bung one trailed lower. "*Praecipio tibi aperire.*"

"You what?"

"I'm not talking to you." He glanced up, perhaps worried about the approaching Vide, then roared, "*PRAECIPIO TIBI APERIRE!*"

For a moment, nothing happened, then the ground jumped. It didn't so much rumble as rise and smack her feet from under her. She fell, right along with the oracle. The grass ruptured, grass tearing wide, loamy soil spilling wide. A stone ring erupted. It was as tall as two humans. Strange runes were scribed about its circumference. They glimmered a starlight blue. The oracle jumped about, cackling with joy, clearly healing faster than any Vhemin. He turned to Evanne, arm cast behind him toward the ring. "There! The gate awaits."

"That's a gate?" Evanne stood. "How do we turn it on?"

The oracle snapped his fingers, and the space in the middle of the ring shimmered, flickered, then turned black. Beyond Evanne saw a vast curving arc of blue green, backed by stars. She did a double-take, her perspective shifting, and then looked up. Then back. "Am I looking at... us? At... *here?*"

"Yes." The oracle was all business. "Now get in there. The platform," he pointed at a pale beige walkway extending from the gate, "is quite safe. Follow it to get to the supplies we need."

A woman landed on him. It took Evanne a moment to parse what happened, because one moment the oracle was beneficent, smiling, hand out, then next he was in the dirt, blood everywhere, and a woman crouched in his place, impaling him to the soil with a straight blade, much like an insect to a board.

Evanne swung her scattergun to bear. The woman's eyes widened behind her mask. The moment strained almost to tearing, so Evanne pulled the trigger.

Click.

They both looked at the scattergun, then the woman leapt at Evanne. She was all swift strikes, both hands around the straight blade's hilt. Evanne hacked right back, machete carving steel smiles in the air. Blade against blade, the ring of combat echoing around the glen.

Evanne thought, *I'm finally getting the hang of this*, then the woman gave a swift counter to her lunge, twirling her blade around the machete. The machete flipped from Evanne's hand to land upright in the dirt. Her enemy's eyes widened in delight above the mask.

"I say." The oracle stood between the assassin and the gate. Blood covered his cloak, a nasty rent at the neckline showing where the blade had gone in. Evanne wondered if the coot might be part Vhemin, because he had more spring in his step than anyone had a right to. "That wasn't very nice."

"Ancients' tricks," the Vide spat, and mule-kicked the oracle.

The oracle stumbled back, eyes widening in surprise, and stumbled through the gate.

Lightning arced from *Dancing in the Storm's* hull to the top of the gate. The stone smoked and charred, glowing with heat. The oracle, now on the other side of the gate, switched from surprise to resignation, shoulders slumping, eyes meeting Evanne's. "Well, that's torn it. You'd best flee."

The gate snapped to black with the crack of a whip, cutting the oracle from view. The portal shuddered, then turned in place like a waterwheel. Runes hidden from view beneath the earth shifted into sight, each glowing a sullen ochre. The gate turned clockwise, then counterclockwise. Over and over it turned, coming to rest with another whip crack.

The Vide turned to Evanne. "Is this some kind of trick?"

A creature of horror stepped through the gate. It had the loose approximation of a man, the regular number of arms and legs about its person but it was larger than any Vhemin. It had scaled, blackened skin. Four eyes were set in its face and bat's wings stretched wide as it stood on Evanne's side of the gate.

The Vide didn't fuck about, taking a swift lunge forward as she stabbed it with her sword. Her blade went in, but no blood came out. The creature grabbed her face with a large, clawed hand, and lifted her struggling body from the ground, then tossed her aside.

It faced Evanne, head tipped sideways. *"What kind of creature are you?"*

Evanne bristled, feeling her shoulders straighten in anger. She snarled, "Cute, coming from a creature with four eyes. Compensating for anything?"

It chuckled, then crouched, launching into the sky with a flap of leathery wings. The gate shimmered, a crab-like creature scuttling through. It was followed by a horse with the face of a snake, then a woman with two heads. The trickle turned to a stampede.

Evanne helped herself to her fallen machete then brandished it. Not a single creature paid her any mind, then they were gone. The last was a giant lamprey, by far the least horrific thing to come through. It slithered up the hill and away.

Tarragon ran to her. She was out of breath, eyes wild with panic, sword in hand. "What are you *doing?*"

"I, uh." Evanne looked at her sword, then the gate. "Hang about. There's a man in there."

True enough, Evanne could make out rude details beyond the black disc. No pleasing ancients' beige stone, this. The ground there was scorched as if by a great fire, naught left but rocks and ash.

Perhaps five hundred metres in, a cloaked man was battling a horde of horrors.

"These are *demons*," Tarragon hissed.

"Right you are." Evanne brandished her machete. "We must go to his aid."

The man flourished a whip of pure light and fire, laying about with great strokes. Where the whip landed, demons blew apart like dropped melons. One leaped at him from behind and he cast a hand back without looking. Evanne couldn't see what he did, but the demon struggled a moment, then shattered as if made from glass, shards showering the plain behind him.

Evanne put away her machete. "You know, I think he's fine." She approached the gate, beckoning. "Hey! This way!"

The man turned, then ran toward her. As he got closer, finer details emerged. He was lean, perhaps as old as Uncle Heser, and sported a close-cut beard. His clothes were dirty and shabby, but he jogged sprightly enough. He stepped through the gate, glanced around, saw Requiem in Tarragon's hand, looked up at the ship, then said, "Where's Geneve?"

"Who?" Evanne looked around, then pointed to the Vide the demon tossed aside. "Is that her?"

He laughed. "No. You can't miss her. About her height," he pointed to Tarragon, "used to carry that sword," he pointed to Requiem, "and hair red as fire. She was right *here*. I followed her." His face went slack with realisation. "Wait. Where am I?"

"The Kingdom," Tarragon said.

"*Which* kingdom? Hurry, lass."

Tarragon bridled. "I'm no lass, I'm—"

"Now's not the time for protocol. I'll apologise later. *Which kingdom?*"

"Or'sen." Evanne stepped forward. "I don't know how it's done where you're from, but—"

"*Shit.*" The stranger turned to the gate, then stopped as it winked shut. The wheel creaked, then rolled sideways from its mount, before dropping like a tossed copper baron. When it hit the ground, it landed with a *crump*, then cracked, a gout of grey mist escaping the seam.

Evanne pointed at the crack. "What was that?"

"The magic smoke," Tarragon said. "It won't work now."

"Shit, shit, *shit*," the man said. "And fuck. And double fuck!"

"Hello?" Evanne reached out a hand, remembered the fire whip, and dropped it. "I'm Evanne. This is Tarragon. Are you okay?"

The stranger slumped, then turned to her. "I apologise. I've been stuck in a demon-infested wasteland for sixteen years." Evanne's eyes widened, realising who this man must be. "My manners have slipped. My name is Lord Meriwether du Reeves, and I am the last Holomancer."

Chapter Five

When the dragon arrived, Amir was not ready for it. But really, who is?

He was sitting upright near a clean-burning fire, a pot set atop bubbling with early morning gruel. As much as the savages of this land had no idea what to eat, he didn't mind the butteriness of this. It was, perhaps, also favourable because Armitage mixed more than a flask of whiskey into the mix.

Thus, looking forward to gruel, eyes on the pot, bowl in hand, it was the, "Mother," from Larochette that drew his attention. She, like him, leaned toward the cookfire, but her eyes strayed beyond Armitage's ministrations to their breakfast. Her bowl was now only loosely held, her lips slack, just like that time the Justiciar laid her across the school's floor with a stout blow to the skull. Amir raised an eyebrow, because *Mother* was a curious thing to say about the quantity of whiskey in their breakfast, when she finished, "*Fucker.*"

He swivelled. There, wings wide in a braking glide, was a dragon. No mistaking it for a heron, because it was pretty close. Its body was blue, and the size of—here, his mind scrabbled for a useful yardstick—perhaps seven horses. Speaking of horses, they panicked, which is what Amir should have been doing. He commanded some modest mastery of the Storm, but if legends were true, dragons didn't much *care*. This dragon wore no cloak of caution as it descended, and where Amir expected fire to blaze, the crackle of electricity arced between giant teeth in a wide-gaping maw.

He swivelled further, eyes finding Sands Apart. The Feybrind had spent the rest of the night sulking, which was understandable since her side tried to murder her. They hadn't bound her hands, and now would have been a prime time to leg it. But no, even Feybrind could be stunned. The cat sat, jaw slightly agape, ochre gaze locked on the dragon. Amir glanced about for Faust, expecting the big man to be there, hammer in hand, but he was only half right. The giant was half-way out of his tent, frozen in the act of straightening, weaponless, mouth open.

There's nothing for it. I'll have to get involved.

He dropped his bowl, charging the dragon. He made it perhaps ten metres from it, blade held high and back, yellow glow tinting the steel as his perfect steps shook the ground. The dragon impacted, shaking the ground harder, Amir's perfect steps thwarted. His blade flickered as he stumbled. The dragon's long neck gave it impressive reach as it snaked its head forward, mouth wide.

Amir dived, rolling away from the maw, coming up in high guard, because what else was a man supposed to do when facing a foe that stood—again, his brain fumbled with measurements—three storeys above the ground?

The dragon arched back, inhaling, and Amir figured this for the end.

//HOLD.// Vertiline's Sway gripped his heart, holding all in earshot. The dragon trembled, then turned ponderously toward her. Amir was able to slide his eyeballs, the rest of him locked tight, and he marvelled the dragon was only slowed. Vertiline strode from her tent, and while she must have left in a hurry and thus lack of armour was a given, Amir was astounded she carried no blade. Her hair was unbound, platinum locks tugged in the breeze from the dragon's great wings. "I thought never to see another wonder, and here you are. I am Vertiline, and would know your name, dragon."

The dragon's eyes narrowed as it peered at her. *//LITTLE THING.//*

"Vertiline." She said it slower. "The world has changed much since your kind flew above it. I knew one like you, once. She was mighty. Ormeon the Redeemer."

Lightning crackled between the dragon's teeth. *//ORMEON'S NAME IS CARRIED BY THE WIND. IT IS A MEMORY IN THE EARTH. YET I DO NOT KNOW HER.//*

Vertiline walked closer. "Where do you come from, dragon? Where is your Skyforge?"

Skyforge? Amir managed to blink, muscles trembling with the strain imposed by the Sway. The dragon didn't notice his struggles, lowering its massive head to peer at Vertiline. *//I AM LOST.//*

"Hmm." Vertiline closed with the creature, hands on hips. Amir noticed her metal arm glint in the dawn's light from beneath the billowing cotton of her shirt. "Geneve said you must be *called*. That your names are given things. What does your Manifest say?"

//THERE IS NO MANIFEST.// The dragon looked to the sky, but there was naught there Amir could see. The morning was cloudless. *//THERE IS NOTHING LEFT.//*

"Then I shall name you." Vertiline made no move, but the dragon reared back.

//NAMES ARE FOR BINDING. I REMEMBER SLAVES OF THE COMMAND.// It's blue eyes crackled.

Amir managed to turn his head, and spotted Sands Apart. The woman still hadn't moved, perhaps stuck fast in the Sway's molasses as he was, but her ochre gaze seemed to shift from yellow to an earthier shade. *The dragon remembers Commands but doesn't know they only apply to Feybrind.* He tried to speak, but nothing but a croak came out.

"There is no binding." Vertiline shook her head. "We hold none of that here."

//YET THE PEOPLE ABOUT YOU LIE SUBSERVIENT TO YOUR SINGLE WORD. YOU ARE A SLAVER, AND I WILL END YOU.// It inhaled, great chest widening like the Three's own bellows.

"I wouldn't do that if I were you," Vertiline warned.

The dragon breathed, and where Amir expected cleansing, terrible flame, the blue-white actinic glare of lightning crackled. Vertiline held her metal hand up, energy arcing and spitting as it wound about the hand. When the dragon was done, she held a thunderstorm in her clenched fist. Her arm trembled with strain, and Amir thought he heard the creak of tortured metal. She gritted, "We keep no slaves," pointed her arm at the sky, and relaxed her hand.

A crackling, sinuous whip of light scorched the sky. The sound was all thunderstorms in one, a resonating *BOOM* that made Amir's bowels tremble. The dragon watched the discharge, head tilted to one side like a curious dog, then eyed the High Justiciar. *//YOU ARE A MAGICIAN?//*

"I am lost, too," Vertiline said. "But I'm with people who can help us find the way."

The dragon considered this, then bunched as if to leap. Amir managed to choke out, "A name, Justiciar. Give it a name."

The dragon held a moment, and Amir wondered if it was afraid. Surely something that large could fear nothing. Vertiline walked toward it, bowed her head a moment in thought, then said, "Myryntir the Protector, come back to us when you have need of answers."

The dragon launched; a gust of wind knocked Amir to his backside. He watched it fly away, wings wide against the sky, and thought, *She didn't give it a name. She reminded it of its purpose.*

FAUST WAS UNUSUALLY PENSIVE. AMIR COULD SEE IT IN THE SET OF his shoulders, the cant of his head, and just how damnably hard he swung his hammer. They were embroiled in a round of sparring, because the High Justiciar had noted their inadequate attempts to face a dragon then ordered a rousing round of Three's Bastard before setting up an impromptu fighting ring.

Amir didn't have the heart to call Three's Bastard its correct name of Destiny's Supplicant. His legs hurt too much from squat jumps in full steel plate.

I have not had breakfast, and Khiton's balls but the big man can swing.

Faust's hammer slammed into Amir's blade. It was a blow so ridiculous in the context of most men's wars Amir should have been a nail pounded into the dirt. The one saving grace was the lick of yellow about his steel but it was only the raggedy edge of the Storm. *I am getting tired.*

"Knight Adept, the edge of your blade is not straight." Vertiline's cool voice carried from Amir's right. "In moments, Novice Faust will have the better of you, and it is only perfection and art that stands between you and the bleak other side of death."

Amir felt his jaw clench, because of *course* Faust was beating him like a toy drum. Vertiline had said to win without drawing blood or 'causing undue damage on our limited supplies', which meant Amir couldn't use the Storm to cut Faust's weapon in half. Or, the man himself, and while he loved Faust like a brother most of the time, this was a rare moment he carried true hate in his heart.

They stalked each other, circling like dogs. Sweat dripped from Amir's brow, slicked his palms, and did nothing whatsoever to cool him, because he still wore that damnable plate. If anything, he was basting inside the steel as the sun's bitter brightness smote from on high.

Sands Apart came into view. The Feybrind made a big show of standing back, keeping to her namesake and not mingling, but Amir was sure it was an act from the *swish, swish* of her tail. He glanced to Sight of Day, whose golden gaze rested on him for a moment before returning to Sands Apart. Amir saw no desire there, nothing like lust, just a pure calm as if a golden ocean spread everywhere the Feybrind looked.

At which point he found himself airborne, chest plate ringing like a gong, as Faust's blow inverted sky and earth and set Amir on his ear. He hugged dirt, spat grass, and groaned.

"Well?" Vertiline's call drew his ragged attention. She was partially hidden behind Faust, the man's legs taking most of Amir's limited vision. The giant stood tall, hammer held low, shoulders still bunched as if wrestling with a weight. "Your opponent lies prone. Finish him."

Amir rolled, but Faust's strike never landed. "Justiciar, he is helpless."

"Then he is no Knight." She made a shooing motion with her hand. "Be quick about it."

Faust looked at Amir. Amir looked right back and got an arm under himself. He wished he wore Cophine's summer dress; it would be lighter than all this steel. He had but moments. Knee beneath him, just so. Shoulder held forward. Arm up, palm raised in *Higher Tides*. Faust's blow came down, the hammer blow right on Amir's palm.

A crescent glimmer of yellow ran down Amir's gauntlet. A bare shadow of the Storm's radiance, so he still felt much of the blow through his hand. It numbed right to the elbow. He used the impact to roll, coming upright in a clatter of bitter resentment. "How may I best him?"

Vertiline raised a cool eyebrow. "If you cannot fight a child without hurting him, you are unfit to carry the black."

Amir felt his eyes bulge, a hot retort on his lips. Larochette rested her arms on a pike, a smile on her lips that did not go to her eyes. He didn't understand why. *She* wasn't in this pit with the Bear of Baragor. For some reason he couldn't ken, his gaze was drawn again to Sands Apart. The Feybrind half-smiled, more smirk than anything, but those ochre eyes were dark with curiosity. *You spared me*, they seemed to say. *Can you do the same for a stronger foe?*

Faust swung again. Amir stepped to the side, stuck his foot out, and tripped the giant. Faust was no fool, trained in the same arts as Amir, and staggered only a moment. It was sufficient for Amir to cross to his fallen steel, kick the blade with a toe, and snatch it from the air. He held it cross guard, then pointed the tip at Faust. "You would do well to remember all the tricks of men."

"I know the patterns," Faust rumbled, then croaked to a halt as Amir's foot caught him in the balls. The giant's descent to the ground was as graceful as a toppling tree, as silent as a held breath.

Amir snatched the hammer's hilt from his enemy's nerveless fingers, then placed his steel against Faust's throat. "Do you yield, brother?"

"I want to be sick."

"I'll take that as a yes." He turned to Vertiline, noting her approving smile. "Why do you approve? I didn't beat him with the Storm."

"That was not the lesson," she said.

"Then what was the lesson?" He felt perplexed. "Aside from, 'wear a box'?"

The High Justiciar glanced to Sands Apart. "Knights are more than the Storm, Adept. We are the river that collects the streams of humanity. We are the justice the world needs." She sighed. "And we are its mercy, even when it hurts."

When Amir looked to Sands Apart, he found nothing but empty air.

Chapter Six

This is very confusing. Tarragon stood by Evanne's side, because it made her feel warm. The once-fairy looked with suspicion at the lordling who'd popped out of a demon gate, because he also made her feel warm, just in a different way, like he was an uncle she'd somehow lost along the way but found under the sofa. It made her suspicious because she didn't trust demons, and he smelled like them, but his claims of living in their land for sixteen years would account for it.

It was ridiculous, of course, because no one could live in their world. Especially not a man who held no Storm. And not a very young man at that.

They were in the command room of *Dancing in the Storm*. Heser the Cheg was there, and he and the lordling had pounded each other in a huggy-yet-manly way for some time. The Raven had placed a cool kiss on the lordling's cheek and he'd grabbed her and swung her about in a whirlwind embrace, which—surprise upon surprise—she didn't seem to mind. No one had paid Evanne much mind, which Tarragon could see annoyed the bard no end. Tarragon didn't have fond memories of being sixteen, because she'd spent it locked in a cage underground as everyone above died, but she remembered enough of the confusion about literally everything, so imagined Evanne was in a similar state to her.

Evanne cleared her throat in just the right way. The sound crept under the conversation between three people ignoring her and Tarragon and quietly tugged the rug beneath their feet. They stopped talking, and the lordling looked at Evanne. "Nice."

She blinked. "What?"

"I," he put a hand on his chest, "am a liar, sometime thief, and maker of dreams. I know the tone people use to say they're angry, impatient, and in love. Your throat-clearing was just the right level of aggression and impatience with a salting of boredom. Well done."

Evanne stared at him, so Tarragon stepped in. "You know this sword." She tapped the hilt of Requiem. The blade *tinked*, as if it were happy to be touched.

"I do." The lordling sobered. "It is the blade of my true love. She'll want it back, no mistake."

"Where is the Saviour of Ravenswall?" Morgan put a hand on the lordling's arm. "Where is our dear friend? I admit to missing her these long years and could use her counsel."

"Now hold on." Evanne stepped past Tarragon. "This guy," she jerked a thumb at the lordling, "is supposed to be, what, the Meri of legend? One of the three who dived into the portal, which Mama has guarded for all sixteen years of my life?"

"Legend?" The lordling seemed surprised. "'Mama'?"

Evanne soldiered on. "The man who saved the world by taking his doom into the demon realm?"

"I'm not a legend. I'm barely forty."

"You look sixty," Heser rumbled.

"The doom took it out of me," Meri admitted. "There is always a price. Back to the mother thing. Who's the kid?"

Tarragon felt her suspicion rear. "There is no way a man of any kind could survive in the demon realm for a year, let alone sixteen." She drew Requiem. "Talk, or I put you down, demon."

"Wait," Morgan said.

"Hold," Heser said at the same time.

"What the hell?" Evanne shouted over the top.

"Go for it," Meri said.

Everyone looked at the lordling. Tarragon looked at the sword then the lordling. "What?"

"I said, go for it. I'm either a demon, in which case killing me is absolutely the right call. I'd do it myself in your shoes. Or, and I'm just putting it out there, I'm what I say I am. A man who's survived in the demon realm for years, and who probably has a few Tricks. Like this one." He puffed at Requiem as if blowing out a candle. The sword's light died. Tarragon gawked at the blade, now just exquisite silver-bright skymetal. The lordling clapped his hands, said, "Now that's out of the way," and then he yelped as Tarragon rushed him.

And found herself on the ground, staring at the ceiling. The lordling somehow held the blade, tucked neatly under his arm, hand out to Tarragon. "That's enough of that. Let's grab a drink and talk this out."

Then he went down like a sack of meal as Evanne cracked her guitar over the back of his head.

Everyone shouted all at once. The Raven was screeching at Evanne about how *you don't knock out family* and Evanne was hollering about *he's not family he's a demon-spawned illusion* and Heser was bellowing for *silence, for pity's sake.*

All of that happening up there gave Tarragon a moment to stare at the lordling. He'd fallen quite close to her, his nose perhaps a handspan from hers. He was out, a snuffed candle. His face was an old man's, but well-preserved, like he knew how to eat and live well, starting the morning with grapefruit and yoga. There were smile lines at the corners of his eyes. He sported a close beard, grey about the muzzle, and it suited him well. She believed his face was used to being kind, because that's what it looked like even though he'd been knocked out.

She touched the side of his face. His eyelids fluttered, and he looked at her. His gaze was grey, like her name, and despite being knocked to the floor, he didn't seem angry about it. "You're not used to being a person, are you?"

Tarragon inched her face closer, because everyone up there was still screaming at each other, and there were a lot of angry expressions and pointed fingers. "I was a fairy until recently."

"A Builder?" He seemed surprised. "I knew a Builder. She turned out to be a goddess."

Tarragon took this on faith. "You didn't kill me when you disarmed me."

"I'm not a demon."

"Demons don't kill. They're into the possession game."

"You were here in the last war?" He closed his eyes for a minute. "Some of their rank escaped ahead of me. We rid this world of them, or it all starts again. We must find Geneve."

"She's not here." Tarragon propped herself up, climbed to her feet, then offered her hand to Meri. "But I know someone who can help."

He let her help him up. Evanne, Morgan, and Heser went silent. Meri brushed himself off, then looked to Evanne. "Vertiline."

"You what?" She looked like she wanted to slug him again.

"Your mother is my much-loved companion, Vertiline. Your father is Armitage, the rock that took a dragon from death's door to saviour. I see it in your eyes, your face, and the colour of your soul." He offered her his hand. "I would make peace with you, niece."

Evanne still looked like she wanted to punch him but looked to Morgan. "Auntie, is this the man you know?"

"He is." The Raven nodded. "No one else I know can annoy so many people so quickly."

The bard grabbed Meri's hand and shook it once. "All right, then. But I'm watching you."

"I've no doubt." The lordling seemed amused by the idea.

"This way." Tarragon took Meri by the elbow. "Let's go see the oracle."

"He fell into the gate," Evanne said.

"He's an oracle. You'll see."

TARRAGON LED THE GAGGLE OF BIGS—

Stop it. I'm Big now. It still didn't feel right to think it. Her feet were huge! And her hands were ridiculous. But Evanne hadn't said anything about her enormous dimensions, and Tarragon certainly didn't want to bring it up, but there it was. *I'm Big now.*

Tarragon led them to the top deck. Back behind the broken Skyforge, right above the engines. About where she expected was a collection of human debris, the deck painted in red in a wide area. Evanne gagged. "Merciful Three, what is this, love?"

Love. I'm her love. Tarragon would have dimpled if the occasion were more appropriate. "This is the oracle."

They'd brought the Raven and Heser the Cheg up to speed on the trip up here, but the queen looked doubtful. "You're saying this is the remains of a mythical man who's lived aboard this ship for eight hundred years?"

"He's not mythical. He's right there. Just... in pieces." Tarragon glared at the deck, wishing she'd passed her exams, because she'd know better ways to explain it. "The oracle is magic. He is science. He can see everything and knows the answers to almost everything."

The lordling crouched near a piece of crooked sausage, lifting it for a better view. "This appears to be a finger."

Tarragon pointed up. "He went through the gate up there. Adjusting for air resistance he took about," she *hmm'd*, "twelve minutes to get here."

The lordling dropped the finger with a moue of distaste, stood, and wiped his hand on his pants. "I'm no stranger to falling a long way. When I went through the demon gate the first time, it was a *long* way down. The slightest puff of wind can move you a long way off course. How'd he get back to where he started?"

"I aimed," came a feeble voice.

"That'll be his head," Tarragon said. "We should try getting as many of the parts together as we can. Once they're touching, the rest should take care of itself."

Evanne rummaged under a low wall, returning with the head. "How's he talking without, you know, lungs?"

"Magic," wheezed the head. "Trust me, I've seen worse."

Morgan walked a slow circle around Evanne, observing the head while mindful of where she put her feet. "Could any man learn this trick of endless life?"

"No." The head was pretty banged up, part of the jaw caved in, but Tarragon could see where it had started healing. "Trust me, it's a drag. You get to tell different people the same truths, age after age, and then watch as they ignore you, just like the ones before did."

"I'm not ignoring you." Evanne put the head on the ground near something that looked like part of a ribcage. "I literally followed your instructions."

"You bitched the whole way," the head complained.

"Build a bridge and get over it," the maybe-Vhemin said.

"I've found a foot!" Heser exclaimed, holding his grisly trophy aloft.

"Good work," the oracle said. "Now let's get the rest."

It took some time. Teeth were the hardest to find, but the lordling was surprisingly good at that. Tarragon said, "How are you so good at seeing the little things? Is it because of the fairy you knew?"

He seemed sad. "No, and the loss is mine for meeting her too late in life. Seeing the little things? It's a … gift, of sorts, although I didn't think so when I met her," he jabbed a finger at Evanne, "mother. Before I was a Holomancer, I was a—"

"Thief?" Morgan supplied.

"Rogue and vagabond," Heser supplied in a thoughtful tone.

"Mama said you were a man who made the whole world fall on its ear." Evanne arranged a toe near a foot. "No, wrong side." She put the toe next to the other foot.

"An illusionist," Meri gritted. "To make a thing appear, one must know all its details. Right down to the last tooth." He offered Tarragon an incisor.

She didn't take it. "Yuck. Who was the fairy?"

"A goddess, really, but I didn't know it. Cophine of the Summertime." He gave a small, shy grin. "Yasmine Glittercone. She was a blue-feathered bird when we first met."

"Oh." Tarragon felt her heart trip. "I met her, too."

"Odd." The lordling didn't spout *impossible!* or other nonsense, just took it in his stride. "I saw her die."

"Death is something that happens to other people, when you're a god," the oracle said.

"No, it's not. It's real, and it's horrible." Meri put the incisor in the oracle's mouth, perhaps to shut the old man up. "Yasmine is gone, oracle. Whatever Cophine brought back was a memory. Or a promise. I'm not sure which, but there is no parting the veil without paying the price."

"I've parted the veil," Evanne said, then snapped her jaw shut.

"Odd," the lordling said again. "And what manner of witch are you?"

"I'm a bard." Evanne sounded both evasive and defensive.

"You're certainly good at hitting the beats with your guitar, hey?" No one laughed, and Meri sobered.

"Does anyone know where my ring finger is?" The oracle sounded plaintive.

"I've got it." Heser bussed it over.

"The veil is a place you go once, and never come back from, except at tremendous cost." Meri sounded sad. "I've put a few people there myself, and still others I would have back from the edge. If there were a cheaper way..." He swivelled. "Why is that ghost following you around?"

Evanne gawked. "You can see him?"

"Of course I can see him." He did something complicated with his hands, as if he were pulling together a cat's cradle, but one made of great weight. After a grunt, there was a snap, and Hitch stood there, except ... more blue. "Now everyone can."

Evanne's eyes bugled. "How'd you do that? And don't say," she held up a warning finger, "it's because you're a Holomancer."

"Uh." Meri tugged his ear, then turned to Hitch. "Hello, sir."

Hitch looked down at himself. "I'm ... *real*." The ghost looked as he always did, just a brighter shimmering blue, no hands, pale eyes, but Tarragon thought he looked *solid*. No longer air but ice instead.

"You were always real. Now you're corpo*real*. Hey? Hey?" They stared at Meri. "C'mon, that was a good one."

The ghost poked his own arm with a not-finger. "I don't feel any different."

"You're not. You just look different. Think of it like a snazzy new haircut." The lordling paused. "Say. Is there a barber on this ship? They always talk sense when no one else does."

Tarragon led them to the baths. The ship was coming back to itself by dribs and drabs. One cafeteria now worked but only served oatmeal. The showers had full pressure but most blasted cold water only. It was one such she led the lordling to, because there would be few people to interrupt them.

The room was large, as most were on *Dancing in the Storm*. The showers took up the bulkhead wall, with a long line of mirrors above sinks along the inner. Meri strode up to the wall as if he knew what he was doing and eyed the mirror. His voice took on a sonorous tone, full of mysticism and weight. "Mirror. Attend."

The mirror shimmered, his reflection getting ragged about the edges for a moment before it struck a different pose. Morgan gasped. "What manner of witchcraft is this? A seeming can steal one's soul."

Heser strode beside Meri, his own reflection following his movements more predictably. "Is it magic?"

"The results will be," Meri's reflection promised. It eyed Meri through the glass. "Been a while between visits, has it?"

"I've been stuck in the demon realm."

"We'll include some balm and a moisturising rub," his reflection promised. "Anything else?"

"I need to know what's going on." Meri leaned on the sink. "The love of my life is missing. Her dragon doesn't fly the skies. This ship sails no waves of water. Demons once again escaped into the realm and division and strife haunts the hearts of all."

"You've about summed it up." The reflection pointed at Morgan. "She is the deposed queen. He," the finger tracked to Heser, "is the guard who follows heart not duty. That one," the finger tracked to Evanne, who was sidling behind Tarragon, "shouldn't be here, because she is not possible. And she," it dragged the finger to Tarragon, "has been touched by the goddess."

"Nothing not already known. Spectre, tell me of the gate. The platforms above. The oracle. All of it." Meri crossed his arms. "Leave nothing out, or we will leave without a haircut."

His reflection produced a slender comb and tapped its lips with it. "The gate is broken because the oracle went through it. The oracle can't leave the ship, and when he did, it created a race condition. The ship misfired, altered the gate, switched to the demon realm, and pulled you here. The platforms still function, but you can't get there from here. You'll need another gate. There's another functional gate to the north."

"We can't use that one." Tarragon sidled up to the mirror, her own reflection looking more worried than she thought it should. "If it's by the Great Lake of Ank-Ahn, it's deep in enemy territory. Assuming they're still there."

"They're still there," her reflection said. "Many of Vehement Systems' great works lie in ruins, but enough hearts of iron beat again. We cannot win, as the ship told you. Too many Artifices, all husbanded along from above by their weapons platforms. The ship's magic stops us being seen by them, but if we get close enough to be seen with the naked eye, they will coordinate a strike." She eyed Tarragon. "How about a fringe?"

"If we get close, we die. Got it." Meri frowned. "Why can't we just tell our platforms to throw rocks?"

"We're down here. We need to be up there." The oracle strode in, a remarkable trick for a man who'd been in pieces not twenty minutes past.

"Right. So, we need to get close to use the gate, get up top, and toss our rocks on them. But if we get close, they'll toss rocks on us instead." Meri clenched his fists. "We must do it anyway."

"Are you mad?" Heser the Cheg's reflection goggled.

"I didn't say that," Heser protested. "Although the question seems fair."

Evanne spoke into the silence, her voice calm, even. "We must do it, because on the other side of the gate is—"

"Death," Morgan whispered.

"A horde of monsters," her reflection agreed.

"The Saviour of Ravenswall," Evanne said. "And her dragon. The best swordswoman the world has ever seen, with Sway and Storm at her command."

"You don't need to go." Meri crossed his arms. "I can do it alone."

"You can't," the oracle said.

"No, he probably can," Morgan said. "He is a Holomancer. What he makes becomes real. None can stand against him."

"Do you want to tell her, or should I?" The oracle eyed the lordling.

Tarragon felt her stomach sink. She saw the blank faces of her fellows, Morgan perplexed, Heser confused, and Evanne ready to demand answers. Their reflections, leaning in, waiting, wondering. Meri, looking downcast, but stubborn, and she understood. He was willing to do whatever, for his love. Just as she would, for Evanne. "I will go."

Evanne blinked. "What?"

"I will go to the Great Lake of Ank-Ahn, where the Three were first made. I will travel light and be unseen. I was a spy. I *am* a spy. It will be easy." The lie came out almost painlessly.

Meri nodded, but slowly, because he saw the way she stood by Evanne, or how Evanne stood by Tarragon. Saw the way they looked at each other and was perhaps reminded of how he stood beside another lost soul trapped in the demon realm. "Then we go together."

"What's going on?" Evanne held Tarragon's elbow. "What are you saying?"

"The Holomancer used his power and broke the rules." The oracle didn't sound smug, just tired. "His doom followed him but clearly did not find him. In this world, the Three still hunger for justice. If he uses his power, his doom will find him."

"I saw you make Hitch real," Evanne said.

"That's not power." The lordling looked away. "That's nothing at all."

Chapter Seven

So, they were all going. Evanne didn't like it, but she didn't *not* like it, either. *I wanted revenge for Mama and Papa's deaths, and now it's within my grasp. It just feels ... harder than before. The ancients ended everything and I'm following their path.*

She was hanging out in a workshop. It smelled of clean oil and metal dust. Nothing like the smith's shanty in Imshir, where dirt lived in every nook and a five-minute visit left you with coal dust as a gown. No, this was pristine, gleaming, made by masters for their artists. Despite that, Tarragon seemed to be doing her level best to revert it to a more homely style. Tools were scattered about Hitch's old armour, which lay like a metal corpse on a table. Evanne didn't recognise most of the gizmos. There was a long bow to draw between, *hello, I recognise this is a hammer*, and whatever Tarragon used to repair the armour. Take the thingamabob over there. It looked like the letter C, and it glowed. When Evanne tried to touch it, it crackled a warning, so she left it alone.

The armour was being repaired. The big rent in the chest plate was fixed, all shiny and new. It still looked dead, or perhaps awaiting life. The pieces had the feel of mere metal, not purpose, rhythm without rhyme. She picked up the helmet. It was light, not like metal at all, but when she rapped a fingernail against it, it *tink'd* as if it were steel. The visor was black glass. She ran her thumb over the material, feeling its slickness.

She put it on. The world seemed cooler inside, but not black as the glass promised. Evanne could see better, as if someone had sketched an outline around everything, making the world pop. She took it off, hair a tumble, and puffed a breath. "This is hopeless."

"It's not that bad." Hitch sidled up. "It worked before."

"Tarragon doesn't think she can fix it."

"Tarragon doesn't think she can do a lot of things, but here she is, kicking ass and taking names." Hitch turned pale not-eyes to the roof. "That almost sounded like a compliment. I take it all back."

"If I put it on, she doesn't know what will happen." Evanne returned the helmet to the bench. "It killed you."

"I had a rare form of cancer. Do you know how cancer works?" At Evanne's no-doubt-blank look, he shook his head. "Neither do I, not really. But inside," he tapped his chest, "things grow. Your body is overrun, constantly making tumours. You don't know what a tumour is? Hmm." He looked at the floor. "It's something that shouldn't be there. You know how you heal when you get cut? Imagine that, but all the time, even when you're not cut. Your body keeps making new *you* and none of it dies when it should."

"So, they put you inside armour to kill you."

"To kill the tumour." He put a not-hand over the chest plate. "As long as I was sick, I was fine. The armour would eat the sickness, and I'd make some more. The cancer would put it back."

"You were cured?"

"There was nothing that would cure me." He sighed. "The Vhemin regenerate. Your father is very hard to kill. So, we didn't want to give them a weapon like this. It only works for humans."

"I'm not human. Not all the way."

"It's probably a good time to start learning how to be one, then." He leaned forward. "Only a human who is very sick, or very healthy indeed, can wear this. An impossible, wonderful human. You."

Evanne backed up a step. "I don't think—"

"You don't have to. Just put it on. It'll do the rest." He turned away. "At least, I think it did. I don't really remember anymore."

"Maybe I should find Tarragon. See what she thinks."

"Spoken like a true human. Decision by committee! See, you're getting the hang of it already."

Evanne found Tarragon on the top deck. Her wheat-pale hair streamed on the wind as she looked out over the grasslands below. *Dancing in the Storm* wasn't moving fast. It couldn't fly high, so made do by navigating around every small hill and wending through the valleys. Evanne shored up next to her by the railing. "Hello, love."

That earned her a tired smile. "Hello, yourself."

Evanne caught the twist of her lip, the cant of her eyes, and said, "I'm not staying here."

"I didn't ask you to."

"You were going to." Evanne leaned further over. "Where you go, so do I."

"I don't know if I can keep you safe."

"A group of bloodthirsty assassins found the ship and tried to murder us all. The ship is literally the largest thing for klicks. It stands out. It's the least safe place to be." Evanne flicked a speck of dust off her sleeve. "I think if we leave, and make it known we're leaving, the people who stay behind will be safer."

"Who are we leaving?" Tarragon looked back at the conning tower. "Everyone's coming with us."

"Not everyone. There's a village here now. People made it their place to live." Evanne rubbed her face. "They can keep it, I guess."

"The Raven won't agree."

"The Raven is also coming with us. She won't be in a position to argue." Evanne squinted. "Say. Isn't that a bird?"

That's about the time everyone started screaming. There were plenty of villagers on deck, squaring things away, building new structures, and trying to setup a market square, for all there was to sell.

They were the ones now running around, mostly in a circular panic, yelling things like *get weapons* and *run for your lives*.

Tarragon glanced toward the commotion, the 'bird', then sighed. "No use running from a dragon."

"No," Evanne agreed. "I want to talk to this one."

"You don't..." The once-fairy gripped Requiem's hilt. "That's not how dragons work."

"Maybe this one doesn't know that." Evanne squared her shoulders, then snapped her fingers. "Hitch?"

The spectre appeared. "There's a dragon. You should run. I'm already dead, but you're not."

"I've been dead before," Evanne breezed. "Can you find the Holomancer? I need him to get me a thing." She described the tool from Tarragon's workbench.

"That's not going to kill a dragon."

"I don't want to kill the dragon. I want to talk to it." She shooed him. "Be about it." He sank through the decking. Tarragon drew her sword, so Evanne put a hand on her arm. "No, love."

"But—"

"The sword isn't going to help. Trust me." The dragon coasted closer, then banked, doing a slow, lazy fly-by of *Dancing in the Storm*. It was massive, so large it seemed impossible for it to fly. Last time Evanne saw it, nature's fury clouded the night. She hadn't appreciated the scale of the thing. The beast roared, lightning arcing to discharge against the ship's hull. *Dancing in the Storm* trembled, but perhaps in ecstasy. Evanne knew it loved the storm's kiss.

Tarragon eyed her sword. "It would make me feel better to hold it." Then she slipped it into its sheath. "Don't cock this up."

"Got it." Evanne spoke with a confidence dredged out of pure Trickery. Her guts were water, her legs weak, her courage lost on the wind, but damned if she was going to show that to Tarragon.

A trapdoor in the deck banged wide, and the Holomancer climbed through it. He carried a wrapped bundle. He paused as he saw the dragon, then hurried over. He didn't act his apparent age, moving like a much younger man. "You could have asked for a scattergun, but you wanted this?"

She took the bundle. "Trust me."

He laughed. "Now you're getting the hang of it."

The dragon straightened up, then cruised in to land. When it hit the deck, the *SLAM* went right through Evanne's soles and into her spine. She forced a lopsided smile and sauntered to the dragon. "Hello, beastie."

The dragon pulled its head back on that long, sinuous neck and eyed her. *//YOU DON'T SEEM TO BE WORRIED ABOUT THE DRAGON ON YOUR DECK.//*

Evanne buffed her nails, then examined them. "That's because I'm an all-powerful sorcerer."

The dragon chuffed a laugh. *//OR YOU'RE CLINICALLY INSANE.//*

"My companions and I—"

//WHAT COMPANIONS?// The dragon's breath was dry, the smell of ozone hanging on the air.

Evanne glanced about. Tarragon stood in her shadow, but the Holo-mancer had taken a generous forty steps back or so, holding with Uncle Heser and the Raven. He gave an encouraging nod. "We're right behind you, kid."

"They know I don't need help." She fished out a Trick, one she'd learned from a braggart before he got knocked unconscious. It wasn't him going down she wanted, but how he stood in the face of five others without a care in the world. "I'm Evanne the Half-Made. Dead, but risen. I hold counsel with the lost and command an army of invisible tigers."

//I SEE ONE INVISIBLE TIGER.// The dragon pointed with his nose to the port railing. *//SHE'S RIGHT THERE.//*

"*Shit.*" Pakhet's voice drifted on the wind. "*The literature wasn't clear on how well they see.*"

The dragon lowered his head closer to the deck. *//LITERATURE?//*

"*There's a library you won't fit inside. Don't worry about it. It's just a collection of ignorable facts. They used them to make Manifests.*"

//I SHOULD HAVE A MANIFEST.// The dragon shorted, and Evanne tasted more ozone. *//I AM MAGNIFICENT ENOUGH TO*

DESERVE ONE.//

Tarragon leaned close to Evanne. "Love? What are we doing here?"

"Right." Evanne straightened. "Dragon, how do you feel about a job?"

The dragon offered a toothy smile. *//HOW DO YOU FEEL ABOUT LUNCH?//*

"About that." Evanne shook her head. "There'll be no eating of people, or—"

The dragon snatched her from the deck with a massive, clawed hand. It raised her to eye height, or perhaps mouth height, considering the conversation. Evanne was no expert at dragon expressions but this one looked *pissed. //WHO ARE YOU TO TELL ME WHAT TO DO, INSECT?//*

Evanne wriggled her hands while trying not to piss herself. "I thought we covered that. I'm an all-powerful sorcerer."

"Evanne!" Tarragon drew her blade and charged the dragon.

The dragon flicked its other giant, clawed hand and Tarragon *pinged* across the deck. She landed on her back, and Requiem tumbled through the air, then embedded itself point-first in the decking. Lightning crackled from where it hit.

"I wish you hadn't done that," Evanne said.

//AND YET YOU ARE POWERLESS. I COULD SIMPLY OPEN WIDE AND—//

"Nah," Evanne finally wriggled her hand enough to get it into the cloth wrapped bundle and touched the thingamabob.

Her world turned to light and fire. Energy coursed through her fingers. She arched in the dragon's grip, feeling rivulets of power run through her flesh, bones, Three's mercy even her *teeth.* Evanne made no noise, her body locked rigid.

The dragon also made no noise, because the energy passed through Evanne and into the dragon. Blue scales glimmered, and its maw filled with the crackle of power. The dragon's eyes blazed, and it overbalanced, slamming into the deck.

Evanne's heart stopped, then started. She gasped, dragging herself free of the dragon's slackened grip. She stagger-stood, spat bile, coughed, then sneezed, stalked to the dragon's head laying on the deck, and said, "Learn some fucken respect."

The dragon groaned, a low, sad grumble.

Tarragon hobbled to her side. She held her left arm to her chest like a bird with a wounded wing. "Is it dead?"

"I hope not." Evanne nudged the dragon's nose with her boot. "Dragon! Attend."

//IS THIS WHAT HANGOVERS FEEL LIKE?//

"Stop moping," Evanne said. "Only people get over hangovers."

//THEY PROBABLY DESERVE THEM.//

Evanne crouched beside the massive muzzle. "Are you ready to have a civilised conversation?"

//IF IT MEANS YOU TALK AT ME WHILE I LIE HERE IN PAIN, MY BODY IS READY.//

Evanne dusted herself off, stood, and smiled. "Dragon, we face a great evil. We could use your help. I figure you owe us, what with us bringing you to life after *Dancing in the Storm* fell all those years before."

//I ... DREAMED. OF A CITY MADE OF LIGHT THAT SOARED LIKE I DO.//

"That's the ship you're on." Evanne put a cautious hand on the dragon's muzzle, giving him a pat. "You were made as a, uh, promise. Dragons were beacons of hope for all. I would have that hope restored."

//YOU SOUND LIKE SOMEONE I MET YESTERDAY.// The dragon opened a lazy eye. *//SHE HAD EYES A SIMILAR COLOUR TO YOURS, BUT LIGHTER.//*

Evanne felt her heart, already on notice, skip a beat. "Say what?"

//SHE WORE NO ARMOUR, BUT SHE WALKED LIKE SHE WAS ENCASED IN STEEL. HER ARM WAS METAL ENOUGH FOR THE SHIELD SHE LACKED. THERE WAS A CAT. AND SOLDIERS, WHO WERE USELESS.//

Evanne leaned in. "Was her hair platinum? About so high?" She stabbed her hand at Mama's head height. "*What was her name?*"

//VERTILINE.//

Evanne fell to her knees. "You must tell me where she is."

//THIS WOMAN IS IMPORTANT TO YOU?// The dragon

wheezed, tried to rise, then flopped back. *//SHE IS IMPORTANT TO ME, TOO. SHE GAVE ME MY NAME.//*

Evanne felt a hand on her shoulder and looked up to see Meri. He had none of the fop about him, eyes stone, shoulders broad. "I see you, Myryntir the Protector. You have been given a name and a calling. You must answer."

//HOW DO YOU KNOW MY NAME?// The dragon gazed at Meri. *//I'M NOT WEARING A SIGN.//*

"It is written on the heavens. All dragon names are." Meri sighed. "Come, dragon. We have much to discuss. Armies, portents, and the evil we can stop together. But mostly, where you last saw Tilly." He glanced at Evanne. "We won't make you. We're civilised people who—"

"Hold on." Evanne brandished the thingamabob. "He's going to tell me where Mama is."

Meri took it from her, so fast she didn't have time to blink, then tossed it over the side. Evanne gaped. He ignored her, facing the dragon. "All we can ever do is what feels right. Does it feel right to persecute the weak? Or does it feel better defending them?"

Myryntir breathed in and out, a giant bellows. The dragon rose, got his feet under him, and shook like a dog. *//ARE YOU SAYING I NEED THERAPY?//*

"I'm saying it's your great honour and privilege to speak for those who can't. To stand between them and harm. To—"

//PLEASE STOP.// The dragon gazed at Evanne. *//YOU'RE NO SORCERER. BUT YOU'RE A PROTECTOR TOO, AREN'T YOU? PUTTING YOUR FEEBLE BODY BETWEEN ME AND YOURS.//* He chuffed. *//I WILL FLY WITH YOU. FOR A LITTLE WHILE, ANYWAY.//* It stamped toward the Raven and Heser, who didn't look happy about it.

Evanne swallowed the lump in her throat. *I'm afraid to speak. I'm afraid this is a Trick.* "Dragon. Where is my mother?"

//INTRODUCE ME TO YOUR FRIENDS. ONCE WE'RE SURE NONE OF THEM WILL ELECTROCUTE ME, I'LL SHOW YOU.//

Chapter Eight

Sight of Day waited for Sands Apart by an old stone mound that served as a marker for human folly. He thought it had once been a lookout tower, or perhaps a bastion for one of their mighty weapons, roaring hellfire at the sky. He turned his golden gaze on the surrounding area, imagining what it was like eight hundred years ago. Grassland, perhaps, studded with people going about their very important business, protected by this weapon and the hands that used it.

The forest took no time at all to reclaim land, once humans stopped interfering. Now it was gently wooded, with birdsong bouncing between the boughs. The air smelled sweet, a hint of pollen carried on the gentle breeze, and sunlight dappled appealing patterns against the rock.

He pressed a hand against the stone. There was very little left. It was slough-shouldered, smooth, as if something had turned a great heat upon it. About fifteen hundred degrees were needed to turn iron into the runny clay he'd made his sword from, but many minerals needed higher heats. The ancients were not known to dick about, and he suspected this wasn't 'stone' in the regular sense. His mind wandered to what would turn the foundations of the ancients' world to slurry. Was it the hot fangs of an Artifice?

No. This was dragonfire.

He glanced to the sky, then sighed. Nothing larger than a blackbird soared nearby.

I miss Ormeon.

No, that wasn't quite it, but he couldn't put his finger on the right answer. Sure, he missed the dragon. She was a wonder, and a good friend. Together, their little band had saved the world, but at a terrible, terrible price. One so great, none should have to pay it. Sight of Day imagined no birdsong rang in the skies of the demon realms. He mulled while waiting for Sands Apart. She hadn't said she'd meet him here, but he had a feeling. The humans made their slow, ponderous way north, and it gave the two Feybrind plenty of time to reflect on the choices that brought them here.

Love. Family. Duty. Forgiveness. Belonging. All were suitable words, but one kept nagging him.

Guilt.

A twig snapped and he was grateful for the courtesy. He stood, brushed imaginary dirt from his impeccably clean pants, and turned. Sands Apart stood near a tree, her lovely ochre gaze meeting his. *{Why are you here?}*

{Waiting for you.} Sight of Day offered a half-smile, the best his kind could manage.

{How did you know I would try escaping again?}

He ignored the question, because she wasn't escaping any more than he was her gaoler. It made her feel better to think she was an unwilling captive. *{Wasn't the dragon wonderful?}*

She seemed taken aback. *{He was terrifying.}*

{Yes.} He turned back to the forest, then patted the hunched rock at his side. A few heartbeats later she joined him, holding a respectful distance. *{Being terrified can be wonderful.}*

{Spoken like one with the gifts of the golden-eyed.} She touched below her ochre eyes, the self-mockery evident in the harshness of her hand movement. *{Always better, always able.}*

He felt surprise. Sight of Day turned the feeling over, looking for the underbelly of the argument. *{I see your intent. You think I'm better, and thus know no fear. That I can face a dragon, dare the odds, and escape while others perish.}*

Sands Apart seemed taken aback. *{I wouldn't have put it that way.}*

{Little sister, you are too used to speaking with humans in their slow ways, fitting between their lumbering movements, and slotting the skein of your mind to how they think.} He tapped his skull, two fingers, gently, careful to offer no mockery. *{If you think I am better than you, you must also think yourself better than them.}*

She looked sideways at him. *{We are the People.}*

{We are a People, but so are they.} He gave a gentle shrug. *{Now imagine you're a slow-witted feeble human, and an ochre-eyed wonder walks among you.}*

{Ochre is the lesser.} She looked away for a moment, before turning her attention back to his hands.

{That's not true, but even if it were, they wouldn't know that. You are a wonder, a marvel they cannot ken. They are children gazing up and you toss your disdain in their faces.} He sighed. *{It is no wonder they drive a hard bargain at the markets.}*

Sands Apart's eyes widened then crinkled at the joke. *{Why are you so patient with them?}*

{Because they share our world, just as the birds do, or the worms under our feet. All hold a place in the tapestry of creation. None of us are better or worse. We have a part to play. Did you know the world was saved by one of their kind? She had hair like fire, a lustre to it I've not seen matched by any of the People's coats. She was as slow as the rest of them but her heart was pure. She moved like a perfect-footed bison but had the strength of conviction. The Daughter of the Three threw her life into the pyre burning between two worlds to save us all. Golden-eyed or ochre, she didn't care. I think you would have liked her.}

Sands Apart looked away for a time, and they sat listening to bird-song. *{I thought there was a dragon.}*

{I think you would have liked her, too.} He rubbed his face. *{I learned a lot from the Daughter of the Three. She was there when I killed my son and mourned with me as if the loss was hers. She bled for the People, fought beside us, but also the ones we thought monsters. The Vhemin she met as equals, their ruddy, rude nature met as challenge for greatness, rather than spite. Not one*

person did she try to make like her.} He wished the People could cry. He could use it about now. *{She was very young, by their standards or ours, yet I thought her my teacher.}*

{It is peaceful here.}

He nodded. *{It is peaceful everywhere, if only we give it a chance.}*

{Why were you waiting for me?}

He sighed again. *{Because you need someone to wait for you.}*

{I don't need your pity.} Her hands tossed the words at him as if they were wasps.

{Perhaps I need yours.} Sight of Day touched his chest, just above his heart. *{I came out here for you, but also for myself. I miss my friend the dragon. I miss my friend the human. I miss the other human, too, although he was annoying sometimes. There is another dragon in the skies now, and we feel fear. And if we feel it, what do you think the humans feel?}*

{They carry their gods' Light.}

{A few do. Most do not.} He let her think for a while.

She rewarded him with slow, cautious hand movements. *{You want us to help them?}*

He thought about that. *{I don't know. I would like them to not feel guilty, when everything ends as it must.}*

She seemed to turn that over, a potter with her clay. He didn't mind her taking the time she needed. Even for the very quick People, some things took as long as they must. There was birdsong and a gentle breeze while he waited. *{I will not teach them how to fight.}*

{Would it be enough to not cast your hate upon them? Maybe start small, build up.} Sight of Day gave another half-smile, but it felt easier on the lips.

She looked down, then, *{I can do that. For you.}*

Chapter Nine

In hindsight, Morgan should have seen it coming. But no, she'd been woo'd like a doe-eyed girl by the exuberance Evanne showed at every turn. How they could *work together* or *give the magnificent ship of the ancients to the peasants*. Then things turned for the worse when the dragon landed on deck. One mythical creature too many, added atop the pile of an invisible tiger the size of a Clydesdale, a fairy turned woman, a magic sword, and a man who fell from the heavens and came back to life.

Or, the other man returned from the demon realm.

It was a lot. As ruler of the realm, she was finding it hard. As just one person aboard this ship of fools, she was simply along for the ride, whisked up in the currents, Big Events dragging her downstream to destiny. But she was queen, so that wouldn't do. Queens *made* destiny. Queens were supposed to be in charge, mindful of all. Ready. Ahead of things.

So, when someone hit her on the back of the head with a cudgel, she shouldn't have been surprised. There should have been guardsmen about, or at least Heser, but the Cheg was elsewhere. He was no doubt helping with the forge or erecting structures for habitation above decks, because he was strong. Her weak magic was not the kind to send sparks among her assailants, and so she hit the decking betwixt the showers and the dining hall in a billow of red silk and astonishment.

Morgan didn't recognise her assailants. They looked like any other peasants. Clothes better by far, courtesy of the stocked wardrobes they'd found aboard. Cheeks now filling out on a steady diet of ship's fare. But peasants nonetheless, teeth missing from a life of hardship, hair hacked not cut, neck beards all. They dragged her below. No one but the posse saw. They'd run a good game, keeping the regular Hollyhead and Wandermere folks from seeing. She could imagine the story now. *Our great ruler has deserted us. We must fend for ourselves, aboard this wonder of the lost world. Woe is us, etcetera.*

Her head hurt and she couldn't think straight.

They hauled her into a small room, gagged her, bound her hands behind her, and stacked her against a wall. She landed next to a familiar man. Lord Meriwether du Reeves, unconscious, a trickle of blood running from his temple, another leaking from his nose.

The small room was metal lined like much of the ship, and equipped with a single door leading to outside the hull. A box sat in one corner. It looked ugly, arcane runes etched across its surface glittering in the dim light. Morgan didn't know what it was, but suspected it was the kind of surprise that could kill a room full of people with nary a wasted gram of effort. She imagined what was coming next. Once they had rounded up the ruling elite, a quick knife-stab, and out the door to tumble to the green grass below. Keep them alive for leverage against each other, then tuck them all in for the long night together.

The ancients were masters at efficient death.

The dragon had flown the coop yesterday, taking Evanne's message of hope to Vertiline and Armitage. Morgan wished they were here. No one would have knocked Armitage out or come upon Vertiline unaware. Morgan groaned, head giving a nightmare stab of pain. What they could really use about this point was a giant tiger. Pakhet was the sort of threat most people noticed. The tiger was in a sulk after the dragon's arrival, and no one had seen her since.

Typical.

They dragged Heser in next, stacking his body against the opposite wall. Morgan's heart gave an unqueenly lurch at his prone form, but the rise and fall of his chest said he yet lived. She wanted to go to him and offer small comforts but her hands were bound, and that had never been her strong suit anyway.

The surprise was Tarragon. The once-fairy came trussed like a prize hog, sword still sheathed at hip, hissing and spitting like a cat. Morgan felt better at that, because Tarragon was fearsome with a blade, so if they'd managed to nab her before she drew steel, this wasn't a two-baron operation. They had skills. A shadow of guilt settled just behind her shoulder, and whispered, *You thought peasants did this, but the Vide are master infiltrators. They couldn't win head on. How better to gain local support than by selling the story of a wonton ruler leaving her flock?* It would give them the ship they craved, and a crew to boot.

Fearsome or no, Tarragon was sucker-punched by a man with an ugly scar running from temple to jaw. He had the look of one who enjoyed the work, dropping the not-fairy to the ground like a sack of rotten meal. He gave Morgan a leer, but it was perfunctory at best, the man clearly faced with other priorities. He ducked out, and Morgan wondered, *Where is Evanne?*

On cue, Hitch stepped through the wall, took quick stock of the device on the floor, then said, "That's a bomb. I'll be right back."

The Raven Queen had a moment to think in the silence following his departure. The spectre's visibility courtesy of Meri's casting was useful, but it made Hitch less potent as a spy. Then she winced, because he was a dead man, and here she was wondering what kind of *tool* he was. He'd done his service and then more, as Evanne told the tale. Gave his all, eaten by his armour and cause all in one, dying for a love and duty that couldn't be parted.

Morgan heard the tramp of hurried feet on metal decking. A moment later, Evanne poked her head through the doorway. She crouched beside Tarragon first, laying her guitar against the floor, then glared at everything, all at once. "She's hurt."

"Hmmph," Morgan agreed.

Evanne's eyebrows softened a midge, and she shuffled over,

removing Morgan's gag, then going to work on her bindings. "What news, cousin?"

"A *coup d'état*," Morgan suggested. "The Vide."

"Motherfuckers," Evanne hissed. "Where's Tarragon's sword?"

"Oi," said the scar-faced man, who now stood at the doorway.

Evanne stood in one supple, smooth motion. Morgan admired her youth, but also her enthusiasm, because her niece charged, shoulder-slamming the rough-hewn bruiser. He was not a small man, but she had her wind up, knocking him clear of the door. She kicked the door shut, spun the wheel, and looked to the other door. "Ah."

"Yes." Morgan released her feet. "That way leads to the ground, by way of a long drop."

"Hitch!" The spectre appeared before Evanne. "I need an exit."

"The, uh." The shade turned pale blue eyes on the exterior door, then to the inner. "What's wrong with punching our way out?"

"I have no problem with it." Evanne grunted. "Can you take them?"

"They're trained assassins."

"Is that a no?"

"It's a variable maybe."

"Shit." Evanne looked to the floor as if it held answers. "I need my scattergun."

The door slammed open, and the scar-faced ugly stood there, fury incarnate. Behind him, two others, purpose in every movement. Scar Face roared, swinging at Evanne.

Morgan couldn't remember actually seeing Hitch become Evanne, or she him, or whatever the spell was, but she saw it now. The ghost slipped into her, and Morgan was reminded of a great koi swimming through murky water. Hitch was one with Evanne, and the daughter of Vertiline and Armitage stiffened a moment. Took a shuddering breath and blinked. Then stepped inside the bruiser's swing.

She dropped into a low horse stance, the knife edge of her hand striking the thug's groin with truly eye-watering force. Evanne stood as the man descended, bringing her rising elbow into his jaw. Teeth flew in a bloody ivory shower. She dropped back and away, using the momentum to bounce her foot against the ground, turning momentum into torque, and landing a hellish spinning kick into the man's jaw.

One Vide in the doorway drew a scattergun. Evanne growled, "That's mine!" Then she whipped her leg about, catching the door with her heel. The scattergun fired, the noise a blow itself in the close confines of the room, but the pellets hit the door. Morgan imagined a scream from outside, but it could just have been the ringing in her ears.

The door banged back open and Evanne charged through. It slammed shut behind her. There was a scream, then more scattergun shots. Silence, then three sharp *bangs* as if a man's head was bounced against steel, but with vigour. A spray of blood showered the small window in the hallway door. Another scream, then the clatter of steel as a blade fell to the deck, and the *crrrack* of a neck breaking.

Morgan thought, *Three's Mercy. What kind of warrior was Hitch?* She'd never seen someone fight like that, not paper knights in tourneys, nor during the war. There was no brutish misconfiguration of limbs in how he commanded Evanne's body. It was precise, craft not even the Feybrind could master. The Tresward could have bested her, but they'd need more than a single gold bar's weight on the black sash, or Morgan was a turnip.

The door slammed open. Evanne stood, swaying slightly, her entire left side coating in someone else's blood. She carried her scattergun and a lazy grin. Cool, frosted mist trickled between her teeth as she said, "There are a lot of them."

Morgan noted the blue tinge on Evanne's lips. "You are pushing too hard."

"Hey, I didn't set the table here. I'm just eating at it." Evanne leaned against the doorframe, breath misting from her in a long, slow stream. She pressed her hand to her chest. "Not *now*, dammit."

"Something amiss?"

"My heart is slowing. Hitch says I'm getting something called hypothermia and wants to leave, but we've yet work to do."

"What about—"

"A moment." Evanne tossed the scattergun to the floor, rounded on an assailant who entered the room in a rush, and was taken from view as the two tussled.

Morgan fielded the fallen weapon. Empty, of course. She sighed, stood, and heaved the bomb through the door and into the corridor. *It feels good to be doing something. An explosive from ancient times may be sufficient to destroy this ship, and I'd prefer to not share air with it.* That priority squared away, she knelt by Heser's side. He was still out. She placed a hand against his face, felt the rasp of stubble on his cheek, and placed a gentle kiss against his brow. *I don't know what I am to you, but you are the most important person in the world to me. I wish I had Evanne's courage. Then I could tell you.*

The door banged open, and four people dragged a limp Evanne inside. The young woman's hands were bound behind her. They threw her to the ground. She groaned and flopped over. "Just a minute," she rasped to no one in particular. She looked vacant, disorganised, like a house with torches in the cellar, but no light in the living quarters. "I just need a minute."

"A minute you shall have." Morgan stood, pulling the ragged remnants of her authority about her as she faced the Vide. She still had the scattergun, which she levelled with a cool smile. "I have but one round in this weapon. Which of you desires it most?"

This caused a moment's reflection. The woman nearest the door said, "She's bluffing. It's empty."

"I see you want it." Morgan swivelled, pointing the gun in her general direction. "The problem we have here is a failure to communicate. We know people are on the side of good because they use their words to be understood. Villains seize power by brute force."

"Says the woman with the gun." A lean man to her right looked tense as a guy wire, so she pointed the weapon at him.

"I see you understand the irony of this situation." Morgan kept her smile in place. "It's time to talk what happens next. No, sirrah," she pointed the gun to the man edging to her left, "you will not sneak behind me."

"You kill one of us, three remain," the woman at the door said.

"I see you have your basic letters and numbers." Morgan nodded approval. "My advisers told me the peasantry had lost it all, yet pockets of brilliance remain."

"Are you taking the piss?" The Vide looked like she couldn't decide between anger and incredulity.

Morgan's smile widened. "I am using my words to communicate. We are all learning together." She gestured with the scattergun, urging the man on her left toward the door. He moved back, slow as you like. "While three remain, the one I shoot will be dead. This weapon is quite the marvel. It is not like any of the Tresward's holy weapons. They have but two rounds before reloading. This has a whole chamber of mayhem, ready to unfurl. It makes me wonder what they were fighting."

"I say we rush her," the Vide woman said.

Evanne stood, lips still blue, but eyes clear. "Okay, thanks. I got it now."

The lean man snorted. "You are bound and weaponless."

"Yes, I'm sure. Over here?" Evanne walked to the side of the room, clearly speaking with the spectre in her head. She leaned into the wall, eyes closed, while Morgan kept her weapon on the assassins. With a lurch, Evanne slammed her shoulder into the wall. She screamed, swayed, then dropped, her now dislocated shoulder allowing her pass hands under feet and get her bonds in front.

"Fuck," the Vide woman said.

"Finish the mission!" The lean man broke for the door. Evanne lurched in pursuit. The lean assassin bent over the bomb, pushing a mechanism. Morgan thought, *This is the end, is it? All our efforts, lost.*

But Evanne wasn't running for combat. She shoulder-barged the door, and Morgan heard a sick pop as her shoulder went back in. Evanne spun the door's latching wheel.

The device outside exploded, the port window into the corridor a flash of yellow-white. The entire room surged, metal shrieking, and Morgan slammed into the inner wall alongside Evanne. She bit her tongue, bashed her forehead, and then surprised herself by screaming.

Because they were falling. She could see through the exterior door, now facing the earth below, as they plummeted toward their doom.

Chapter Ten

Amir didn't like babysitting.

Vertiline and Armitage took a trip west. The hulking brute said there could be monsters that way, by which Amir thought he meant Vhemin and was trying to make a joke. It was difficult to tell with Armitage, because the man didn't smile when he delivered the punchline.

The High Justiciar had left Amir, Faust, and Larochette in charge. She had been very clear with Amir: *Stay here. If the dragon returns, send it west.*

He had no real clue how one went about sending a dragon anywhere it didn't want to go, but her cool gaze stilled his normally overactive tongue. So, Amir waited, babysitting merchants, their ponies, doing drills, and trying not to get hammered into the floor when it was his bout with Faust. The two Feybrind stayed with the camp, Sight of Day being a useful addition to their cooking rota, and Sands Apart being a useful addition to the lessons of vigilance with an enemy in your midst.

Although: *she has not tried to kill any of us*. Odd, but true. Neither were here, hunting game off in the low hills to the east. Amir was fine with that because venison would be a nice dinner to have.

The morning was chilly but heading in the right direction with gentle sunbeams that warmed his face. Breakfast was a recent memory. Amir nursed a bitter cup of coffee when he saw the dragon on the horizon. "Faust! Larochette!"

The two straightened, following the line of his arm. Faust rumbled, "Good eyes, brother."

"Heightened by fear, no doubt," Larochette said.

The dragon came straight for them, but this time landed a good hundred metres from the camp. No doubt it was learning what a hazard terrified horses were. Amir tossed the dregs of his coffee aside, adjusted his sword belt, ran a hand through his hair, and tried to stop his legs shaking. "I'll be right back."

"Do you need company?" By which Faust meant, *do you want to burn to a crisp alone or with a friend?*

"I'll be right as rain." By which Amir meant, *company would be good but two corpses won't balance the scales of our lives.*

Amir felt it important not to hurry. The dragon looked like it was very sure of himself already, and there was no need to elevate his ego further. The walk to Myryntir gave Amir some time to prepare. *Dragon, you are commanded to go west*, sounded a quick way to get crisped. *Dragon, the High Justiciar begs your attention*, sounded like something only a wanker would say.

And before he knew it, there he was at the dragon's feet. The beast was immense. His mind had allowed him to forget this small detail in the past days, but his bladder remembered well enough. He gazed up at Myryntir. "Um."

//HELLO, TINY BEING.// The dragon gazed down at him. *//WHERE'S YOUR BOSS?//*

"Ah." Amir cleared his throat. "The thing is, west."

Myryntir cocked his head. *//ARE YOU MISSING ANY WORDS IN THAT SENTENCE?//*

"Three take you, creature! You're terrifying."

//IF IT HELPS, I'M NOT HUNGRY.// Myryntir chuffed. *//RIGHT NOW, ANYWAY.//*

"That helps surprisingly little." Amir gripped his sword belt with both hands. "The High Justiciar is on a mission to the west. She has asked if you'll join her."

//NO.//

"Right you are then." Amir did a double-take. "What do you mean, 'no'?"

//THERE IS NO TIME.// The dragon knelt. *//HER SQUALLING INFANT IS IN TROUBLE.//*

Amir had never thought of Evanne as either an infant or someone who squalled, but a dragon's perspective was different. "The High Justiciar is the best person to—"

//YOUR BOSS ISN'T HERE. HER CHILD IS IN PERIL. YOU HAVE THE OPPORTUNITY TO DO SOMETHING ABOUT IT.//

Amir looked back at Faust and Larochette. They stood at the head of a gaggle comprised of merchants and ponies. None of them had moved so much as a metre from the camp. He swivelled back to the dragon. "I'm confused. You know Evanne is in trouble, but you were powerless to do anything about it?"

//THE TALE IS LONGER THAN YOU MIGHT THINK. I WILL TELL YOU AS WE FLY.//

"You what now?" Amir looked at the dragon's back. "You want me to ride on you?"

//WANT? NO. BUT YOU HAVE PUNY LEGS AND WILL TAKE DAYS TO REACH HER LOCATION.// Myryntir gave a great, dragony sigh. *//YOUR ARMS SEEM FIT ENOUGH THOUGH. YOU WILL NEED TO HOLD ON TIGHT.//*

"Can I get—"

//NO.//

"What about—"

//NOT THAT EITHER.// The dragon extended its foreleg as a mounting station. *//COME, MAN, AND LET ME TELL YOU OF THE COURAGE OF CATS.//*

Chapter Eleven

Pakhet chewed thoughtfully on a human's leg. It was a little gristly, which was to be expected of someone in such fighting fit condition.

The deck of *Dancing in the Storm* was a ruin. Or more of a ruin. It hadn't been in great shape before the dragon arrived yesterday, and dragons made a statement. She crunched, enjoyed the meaty taste of marrow, and eyed the humans standing before her. *"Do any of you have ketchup?"*

They seemed uncertain, which was to be expected. They hadn't seen much of her. The man who looked like he knew his way around a forge stepped forward. "What are we supposed to do now?"

Pakhet crunched, then picked a fragment of bone from her mouth with a razor claw. *"Why do you think I care?"*

"You ... saved us."

"Oh. That." She remembered it well. Saved them? An interesting perspective. This is what happened.

THE DECK OF *DANCING IN THE STORM* WAS WARM. THE DECKING'S black metal caught the sun's rays well. It didn't smell too bad after its eight-hundred-year internment under a lake, and the fresh air was doing further great things.

Pakhet flopped where mid-morning sun created a small nook of heat between the railing and a small structure humans probably thought was important a long time ago. She was invisible, because the humans became terrified when she yawned, and laying in the sun led to a lot of yawning.

The sun *was* a wonder. It let her mind free, her thoughts walking the lonely paths where she was sure the Manifest should have been. There were things she knew without having gone through the learning, like what the Three's Wardens were for and why you should absolutely not get in between one of them and their prize. Pakhet knew about dragons, and fairies, and magics linked to systems that healed the sick. As a guardian for the last bastion for healing the sick, Pakhet felt she was a hospitaller of sorts.

Right there in the absence of a full Manifest were instructions on how to behave or what she should do. It was why she'd run at Evanne moments after she'd been quickened, but also why she'd run away. The parts that were supposed to tell her how to be brave were all gone, and she'd never learned it the way everyone else did.

Which was, you know, *fine*. Pakhet was a cat larger than any horse she'd seen, and generally people didn't fuck her about. Except Evanne, who'd hit her in the face despite having no fangs and a tiny size. Then fed her and made sure she didn't have to be brave. That she could just be one who scratches.

Pakhet stretched, yawned, and stayed invisible, but remembered Evanne.

And remembered her some more, because come to think of it, she hadn't seen the minuscule creature the entire day. The bard was always on deck, chipping in, playing songs, or telling people all the good things inside them they somehow couldn't see. But not today. Pakhet rose, stretched again, and scritched her claws against the metal decking. It made a pleasant sound, the kind of thing that said, *If I wanted to, I could peel this metal apart.*

There was a series of scattergun shots from below deck. Pakhet cocked her head, no longer sleepy, because they didn't sound like the steady fire rate you'd get from a practice range. These were urgent, as if someone put two in someone's chest *there*, then one in their head *there*, before moving to the next person who needed it.

She eyed the sky. It was mostly clear. She eyed the deck. It was also mostly clear, which was unusual at this time of day.

Something is up.

The tiger found a door, then padded down the metal steps to the dark below. Her eyes were very good in the dark, which meant she stopped in a doorway before the twelve men and women hurrying toward the gunfire could run into her. They didn't look familiar, but there were so many humans on this ship and so little time for laying in the sun, Pakhet hadn't spent the time to get to know them.

No time like the present.

She followed them. They went down, and down some more, until they were nearing the bottom of *Dancing in the Storm*. Pakhet could smell blood, and that sharp peppery smell of someone using a scatter-gun. There were people talking further ahead. She caught the tail end of a conversation, where a woman said *Fuck* and a man shouted *Finish the mission!*

Then the corridor exploded. A man tumbled back into Pakhet, which caused her to snort in surprise and become visible for a moment. He saw her, screamed, flailed about, scrambled to his feet, and ran back the other way, eyes on Pakhet the whole time. He then fell to his death, because there was no floor, or walls, or much of anything up that way. The explosion had torn out a chunk of the *Storm's* belly. There was burnt blood and hair on the wind, and the parts of many dead people.

A few moaned. Pakhet didn't feel there was much extra value she could add here, so she curled back on herself and padded back to the sunlight above.

IT PROBABLY WON'T BE LONG BEFORE SOMEONE COMES UP HERE AND TELLS me what's going on. Pakhet watched the skyline, because she was pretty sure when random things happened in the world, a dragon was usually involved. There was but one dragon she knew of, and he'd flown off in a huff because he wasn't as magnificent as Pakhet.

We can get over that together, once he acknowledges my sleekness.

She was deliberately visible, because it was unlikely anyone would find her if she wasn't. Sure enough, a man who she was sure she'd seen beating metal with another piece of metal in a pointless and noisy fashion found her. She supposed he was of a larger size for a human, but it was difficult to tell. He sidled up, wringing his apron, and she stifled the urge to yawn.

"Hello, great cat."

"This is starting well." The tiger thought about smiling, but that would also have made the man scream. *"Out for a stroll, or is something on your mind?"*

"There has been a, uh." He looked over his shoulder, but there was no one there. "Do you know what's going on?"

Ah, shitballs. *"There was an explosion. A part of the ship fell out. People died. It is clouding over and might rain."* She felt the tip of her tail twitch, and let it. It was good to let agitation be seen by all interested parties. *"I hoped you were one of the people who might know what's going on. Where is Evanne?"*

"Missing." Pakhet gave the man a narrow stare, so he stammered on. "I, uh. There are people on the ship who weren't here before. They are saying the queen betrayed us and killed Evanne, and now it is up to us to look after ourselves. They say it is safe to the north."

"It is safe here. This is a battleship the likes of which this world has not seen for eight hundred years. Anything short of a full battalion assault will fail in fire and misery. It is also warm here."

"Uh." The man strangled his apron some more. "They look like they're in charge now."

"Where is the oracle?"

"I haven't seen him."

"Then they're not in charge. He's the only one who can tell the ship what to do." Pakhet yawned then. She couldn't help it; it had been so long

between them, and she was getting bored. The man's skin colour shifted, which was a neat trick even she couldn't do, but she didn't know if it was good or bad. *"If you want to do something useful, find the oracle and bring him to me."*

"Won't he know where you are?"

"Two things." She sniffed the air. *Definitely rain.* *"First, he is not a very good oracle. Second, he doesn't like doing what he should. If he did, we wouldn't be in this mess in the first place."*

"Will he know what to do?"

"He will have an opinion." Pakhet snorted. *"When you come back, feel free to bring snacks."*

"What's all the fuss about?"

Pakhet turned from the view of the landscape below to find the oracle standing before the aproned human. *"There are dissidents aboard your ship."*

"I know." He sounded irritable. "They're like lice."

"Perhaps you should get a delousing programme going." The tiger huffed. *"Where is the dragon?"*

"Myryntir's on his way." The oracle joined her at the railing. "We also have two Artifices incoming."

"A minor inconvenience, surely."

"The ship isn't battle ready."

Pakhet gave him a little side-eye. *"This is a warship, is it not?"*

The oracle wobbled his hand in a 50-50 gesture. "More like a one-stop shop for all your needs. It's a city. It flies. It also has, uh, *had* weapons. They don't work yet."

"How long until they work?"

"You know any fairies?"

"Not anymore."

"Long time, then." The oracle shivered. "Some systems are self-healing, but we have problems tip to stern."

I shouldn't get involved. I should mind my business. I should leave, next chance I get. Still, the man with the apron seemed nice, and Evanne liked him. Pakhet caught sight of Myryntir on the western horizon. She gazed east, and sure as rain, there were two blazing specks drawing closer. Her Manifest was incomplete, but she was sure they meant nothing good. The tiger looked to the aproned man. *"You should get belowdecks."*

"I can help."

"You can also die. I promise it would be a vexing experience."

He had an expression that she labelled as stubborn but headed toward a hatch anyway. The oracle looked toward the dragon. "You care for them?"

"They bring me food."

Myryntir made better time than the Artifices. He landed in a great gust of air right beside the tiger, all crackling energy and wide wings, and peered down at Pakhet. *//WHAT COMES?//*

"It's a long story. The short version is we have dissidents aboard. Evanne is missing. The oracle is worthless."

"Hey!"

"The ship's weapons are down. Artifices come with reinforcements. And it's up to you to save the day." She gave an encouraging nod.

//WHAT'S AN ARTIFICE?//

"We're screwed," the oracle said.

An Artifice screamed closer. Pakhet shivered into invisibility and loped sideways. The oracle ran for the hatchway. Myryntir looked surprised, then roared as twin fangs of fire raked his flanks. He blasted a hot crackle of energy after the banking Artifice but hit nothing but air. He bunched, roaring like Khiton might after stubbing a toe, and launched in pursuit, all dragony wrath. The deck shifted a micron as he took off, because dragons brought a lot of force to any problem.

The second Artifice landed on deck, but didn't shift the deck, because it was just a machine. It was larger than the Artifice that picked a fight with the dragon. It had a black glass dome at the front. A yawning side door disgorged troops. Pakhet waited until the last man was out, entered behind him, and padded her way to the flight deck. There was a human and a Vhemin there. She turned visible, and said, *"Boo."*

The human screamed, jerking in panic, and tried to free himself from his harness. The Vhemin was smoother for sure, clearing her seat and drawing a wicked-looking short blade. Pakhet backed toward the cargo door, and shimmered invisible. The human failed to free himself from his harness, shifted tactics, raised an actinic lance from his side, pointed it nowhere near Pakhet, and pulled the trigger.

He succeeded in cutting his Vhemin comrade in half in a sizzling crackle of hot death. He also cut into the control console. Pakhet picked up the pace, exiting the Artifice as it gouted flame from the rear. She turned her easy lope into a panicked run as the machine spun on the deck. It ripped up metal and people, and sprayed body parts both cooked and raw to the four winds.

The reinforcements, now roughly twenty percent of their previous number, generally panicked and screamed. A few tougher-looking individuals tried to restore order, one enterprising woman laying about her with a kosh in a valiant show of leadership before the Artifice's final death spin turned the drives on her and reduced her to free particles.

It then disappeared over the side, removing a problem from Pakhet's life.

The remaining Artifice slashed the sky overhead. Myryntir landed on the deck about fifty metres away. Pakhet turned visible. *"What are you doing?"*

//I'M NOT SURE. IT IS DIFFICULT TO CATCH ON THE WING.//

"You're a dragon!"

//I'M NEW AT THE JOB.//

A man rushed the dragon with a spear, which Pakhet knew to be a futile gesture, but there didn't seem to be an opportunity to interrupt. He ran the tip into the dragon's leg. The spear skidded off dragon hide, but Myryntir noticed him, raised the leg, and crushed him. Pakhet said, *"That's the spirit. I can see you're really getting into it now."*

//ARE YOU GOING TO HELP?//

"I am helping. I have destroyed one Artifice and am providing you moral support."

//I NEED SOMETHING MORE TANGIBLE.//

Pakhet lifted a clawed paw and slashed the air. *"You do it like this."*

The Artifice returned for another strafing run at Myryntir. The dragon raised his clawed hand like Pakhet had done, swatting the Artifice from the sky. To Pakhet it seemed an accidental win, but she'd take it. The Artifice crashed into the deck with force enough to knock men and women from their feet. The machine slid through a patch of remaining interlopers, knocking a soldier at Pakhet. Conveniently, the man tumbled into Pakhet's still raised paw, impaling himself on her claws.

She shook her paw, trying to dislodge the man, and spattered a woman running at her with gore. The woman stumbled. She wiped blood from her eyes, just as the man fell from Pakhet's claws. His blade bounced, and the sword caught the rays of that lovely sun. It bounced pommel first, and for just a split second of time the blade's tip pointed at the heavens. This provided the woman a tripping hazard, which she took, and impaled herself on the blade.

//YOU'RE SHOWING OFF.// Myryntir took a breath, and spat crackling blue-white energy in a cone. Men and women turned to charcoal in an instant.

Silence. Pakhet licked her paw. *"Now who's showing off?"*

//WHERE IS THE WOMAN THAT LOOKS LIKE A HUMAN AND VHEMIN MET IN A BAR?//

"Evanne is missing."

"She's not missing, she's just not here." The oracle joined Pakhet, pointing southward. "She's about three klicks that way."

//WILL SHE STOP THE ARTIFICES?//

"Her mission has a wide remit."

//THEN YOU GET TO HER. I WILL GET HELP.// The dragon bunched, then leaped into the sky.

Pakhet looked to the oracle. *"I'll need snacks for the trip."*

WHICH IS HOW PAKHET CAME TO BE EATING A HUMAN'S LEG ABOARD a charred deck. *"So, does anyone have anything to eat?"* She looked at the chewed leg. *"Something better cooked, I mean."*

"We're wasting time," the oracle said. He pointed to the aproned man. "You're in charge. Don't fuck it up."

"*You're coming with me?*"

"Unless you know another way to find Evanne."

"*Perfect. You can carry the snacks.*"

"No problem." The oracle beamed. "You can carry the armour."

Chapter Twelve

Evanne woke with a groan, mouth full of mud. She was face-down in the stuff. *It's better than not waking at all. Get up, Half-Made.* She got her hands beneath her, slipped, ate more mud, swore, and finally rolled over with a wet splat. *Great. Now I have mud in my mouth* and *all over my clothes.* The sky above threatened rain behind tarnished grey clouds. Evanne was cold but had only minor aches and pains. *It's better than I deserved. What the hell happened?*

They'd fallen from the sky. She remembered the explosion well; shoulder-barging the door had saved them, but she'd taken the brunt of the blast against her side. It knocked her silly and that was the last thing she remembered before *here*, wherever here was.

She lay at the edge of a lake, if you were generous. The water was surrounded by a protective huddle of tall trees and was perhaps half a klick across. Lily pads were scattered near her feet, and a frog eyed her from atop one, croaking a lament to all stupid people who fell from the sky.

In the middle of the lake were the remains of the ... room? ... they'd come down in. It looked twisted all to fuck, and that got her on her feet fast. "Tarragon? Aunt Morgan?" She looked about. "Uncle Heser? Meri?"

Nothing. She felt her heart skip when she saw a tangle of wheat-pale hair near the water's edge about fifty metres away. Evanne ran, slipping in mud, scrambling for purchase. She found Tarragon half in the water, hand in a death grip around Requiem's scabbard. Evanne rolled her over, smoothing hair from Tarragon's face. "Love?"

The once-fairy was out, but her chest rose and fell. *Alive, Three be merciful.* Evanne hauled her from the water, impressed the woman kept her grip on the sword. *She really likes that blade, but it won't keep her warm. We need clothes. A fire.* Evanne looked at the wreck in the middle of the lake, said, "Fuck it," and strode out among the lily pads. The water was cold but not dank, and she dived in, smashing her way to the wreck with powerful strokes.

The room was inserted into the water like a straw. Evanne helped herself inside, cutting her hand on bent metal. She hissed, swore again, and got inside. It was full of muck and water. And by the Three's grace, no bodies. Evanne slipped inside and dived. She found her guitar and scattergun, but everything else was trash and ruin, so she emerged, and swam back to Tarragon.

The frog continued to watch her, but silently now. *That's weird.*

She wiped water from her face, looking about. Tarragon still lay propped against a tree, but quiet had settled over the lake. A man emerged from behind the tree Tarragon lay against. He reeked of Vide, black leather and all. He had a short, curved blade, and pressed it against the once-fairy's throat. "Give us the scattergun."

"No worries." Evanne strode toward him, and tossed the weapon to him, but wide.

The assassin, slightly surprised, snatched the weapon from the air about the time Evanne made it to him. He'd overreached, knife away from Tarragon's throat, and kept his look of surprise right until Evanne's fist caught him in the side of the head.

He sliced her, cutting into her jacket, carving skin, and making her angrier. Evanne kicked him in the groin, punched him in the throat, twisted the arm with the knife, broke it, took the knife, and stabbed him in the neck. She panted, teeth bared, glaring. "Anyone else?"

No takers, apparently. She dragged the body into the trees, where she stumbled over the Vide's pack. It was slim but contained some essential supplies. Jerky. A kit with flint and tinder. And—score!—a hip flask. There was also a garrotte and backup knife, which Evanne tossed aside. She foraged, coming back to Tarragon with dry wood, some berries, and a smile. The once-fairy was still out, her lips blueing. Evanne put her jacket over Tarragon. The ancients' material felt like leather but had already dried. It was warmer than Tarragon's clothes, gladiator armour or no.

It was short work to build a fire. Evanne set her guitar near the flames to dry the strings and waited.

SHE WOKE AT A SNAP FROM THE FIRE. EVANNE HAD SLUMPED sideways as she passed out. The fire was larger than she remembered. She scrambled up, fists bunched.

"Ah, you're awake." Meri emerged from the tree line. "Did you leave a spare corpse back there?"

Evanne lowered her fists. "He threatened Tarragon."

"A fool, then." Meri sat by the fire. "I found some fruit trees. There are pears and apples. And whatever this is." He held a small fruit with an orange rind.

"Mandarin." Evanne glanced at it absently. "Is she going to be okay?"

The might-be-an-all-powerful-sorcerer-but-could-also-be-a-fake didn't glance at Tarragon. "Hard knock, that trip down." He breathed in then gave a decisive exhale. "I've got no idea."

"You what?" Evanne straightened.

"Kid, I've lived for sixteen years in a demon realm. It felt like a hundred. Time doesn't work right on that side. In all that time, I learned honesty is the best policy. Say what you mean." He shrugged. "And admit when you don't know something. She looks like she's sleeping."

"Can't you," Evanne wiggled her fingers, "fix her?"

"The Three have it out for me." Meri shrugged. "You see, I found this book."

"Is this going to be a long story?"

The wizard ignored her. "It was called the Tome of High Magic."

"Let me guess. Secrets of the universe unravelled at your feet."

He poked the fire with a stick, freeing a flurry of embers to chase each other skyward. "More or less, actually. There are rules. I can't *make* life. I can't bring something *back* to life. And I can't summon the gods." He looked wistful. "I broke one and a half of those last time I was here."

"How do you break half a rule?"

"The same way you break a cookie in half."

"This story needs to hurry up." Evanne knew she was being brittle with him, but Tarragon was *hurt*.

"Ha." He stared into the flames, his eyes capturing the orange dance and playing it back for her. "The book tells me how the world is made."

"It told you. Past tense."

Meri tapped his temple. "I remember everything I see. It's all up here." He sighed. "There are things I would prefer to forget."

"Can the book tell you how to make miracles happen?" At Meri's searching eyebrow, Evanne fetched a stick and poked the fire, perhaps too aggressively. "I started this quest because Mama and Papa were killed by a monster. I wanted revenge. Things ... got out of hand. I found a place where sick people were made well, but not anymore. I've released a giant tiger and resurrected a dragon. But all these things are ... *insufficient*. There's a bad man who's trying to kill me, but I don't think it's personal. I think he wants me out of the way so he can do," she wiggled her fingers, "all the rest of it. Mama and Papa are alive, or so the dragon said. So, now we just need to make it to the bad man and put a stop to this."

"You mean, 'kill him'."

"Yes." She didn't feel happy about it. "I don't even know Wild Sur. And I don't know why he wants to kill me." Evanne leaned forward, peering over the heat haze into Meri's eyes. "So, magic man. Can you whip up a miracle that will make that stop?"

"You mean, kill him from here?"

"I mean, make him not want to kill me. I don't want to kill anyone."

Meri was quiet for a spell, poking the fire without much vigour. "I don't think so. The hearts of people are their own. Enchanters can make people do things, but everyone hates those dickheads." Evanne snorted. "Even enchanters can't do it forever. They need to work at it. The Sway can do it, but the cost would be high. To change the nature of a person? I think it would eat the whole of the Justiciar trying it."

"Figures." Evanne brooded. "Why does he want to kill me, anyway? And how does he keep finding me?"

"The answer to the second is related to the first." Meri leaned elbows on knees. "You have an aura. It displaces the world around you, like putting your finger into water. I bet Wild Sur can use the plat-forms above," he pointed to the sky, "to see wherever you might be."

"That sucks."

"As to what this aura does, my guess is change the nature of people's hearts." He shrugged. "You speak with more than confidence, kid. You speak as if Sway is your second nature. As if you can touch the heart of someone at a level an Enchanter could only dream of. Perhaps change them forever. This Wild Sur clown? He's a zealot. A *believer*. And you're inconvenient to that."

"I just ... sing."

"Maybe." Meri sounded unconvinced. "Tarragon was reforging armour for you."

Evanne looked at her lover, still out for the count. "It belonged to Hitch."

"It's a weapon?"

"I saw a vision." Evanne shivered. "Hitch fought a demon at a gate and pushed the monster back."

"It usually takes a Knight with more than three gold bars to do that."

"He died, but he did it." She shrugged. "I think I'll need more than songs to save the world."

"You need your mother." Meri stood. "And your father, much as it pains me to admit it."

"I need more than that." Evanne gazed at him. "I need a giant ship that sails the sky. I need a dragon and a tiger. An oracle who can't see the future, and a magic man with no powers." She ignored his wince. "I need my aunt and uncle, not because they are a ritualist and warrior of significant puissance, but because they will stand with me even if they disagree. I need the strong right arm of the best woman I've ever known. All of you. I need all of you. And I don't know why."

"It's because we're family." Tarragon's voice was a husk. Evanne whirled, seeing the once-fairy sitting up, pale as a moonflower, but eyes hard as emerald. "And we'll do anything for you."

Evanne surged up and hurried to Tarragon. She stroked her face, smoothing aside her hair. "Love. You're okay."

"I hurt, everywhere at once," Tarragon confided.

"I'm sorry." Evanne pulled her close, but gently. "I'm sorry I couldn't save you."

"You saved us," the Raven said. Evanne turned to see the queen leaning on Heser's granite posture as the pair emerged from the trees. "You took the blow that would have ended us. I saw it all."

"But we fell." Evanne touched Tarragon's face again. "We fell so far."

"And scattered wide." Morgan eased away from Heser's side. "There was a ... device of some kind in the room. It enveloped the guardsman and I, and spat us out the side."

"The guardsman?" Evanne blinked.

"My, uh." The Raven Queen faltered.

"You should work out what he is to you before Tilly gets here," Meri said. "She will want to know."

"And how is the High Justiciar going to find us? We are no longer aboard the ship." Heser's gravel rumble held no resentment about being a guardsman, and Evanne wondered if that's how he thought of himself. The person best to be by the Raven's side, her shield, her support, for always.

"Easy," Meri breezed. "I turned the tops of all the trees the purple we can't see but bees can."

Evanne goggled. "You can do that?"

"Eh." He shrugged. "They'll stop being purple when I stop thinking about it. The good news is dragons can see very well indeed. I expect anyone looking down on us from above without a dragon or a tame bee won't see anything at all. But a dragonrider? One of those will find us very soon indeed."

EVANNE DIDN'T NEED TO WAIT LONG FOR MAMA TO ARRIVE. She heard it first—not the beat of dragony wings, but the intake of breath as the Raven spotted the dragon. Evanne looked up, seeing Morgan's eyes wide, mouth slightly open, face fixed on the horizon beyond the lake.

She turned, and sure enough: a dragon. The skies of Or'sen and Imshir had been free of the span of mighty wings for most of a millennium and now here was a second dragon in as many years. Even at this distance the size impressed. The creature was blue, not the lacklustre of dull paint, but the brilliant metallic hues of azure, ultramarine, and ocean. His scales caught the sun's rays and played with them.

Brushing herself off, she stood. Tarragon made to walk forward, but Evanne put a hand on her arm. "I'd best do this one solo."

"You think she's going to be mad?" Tarragon bit her lip.

"I think she's journeyed across two kingdoms to find me. She will be incandescent."

"It wasn't your fault!"

"There's fault, and there's responsibility." Evanne brushed rust locks back. "And because all the people whose fault it is aren't here, she will take it out on me." She offered a smile she didn't feel. "It's fine."

"Maybe I should come. Moral support." Tarragon worried her lip with perfect teeth.

Evanne smoothed it with a thumb. "It helps knowing you're here. Safely away from her reach."

"Nowhere in throwing range is safe," Meri offered.

"Not helping." Evanne considered her guitar, then left it where it lay. She strode from the group to the lake's edge. It was passably clear of trees, affording the dragon a place to land.

The dragon was coming in fast. He scorched the sky with the

crackle of lightning, spread his wings, and then landed right in the water. A gout of it showered Evanne, drenching her—again!—head to toe. She gritted her teeth and glared at the beast. "Motherfucker!"

//I SEE YOU REMEMBER ME.//

"Eat a bag of dicks." Evanne spat water.

"Hold on that command." Evanne's heart stuttered a moment as Mama's voice came from atop the dragon. Myryntir leaned forward, head coming level with Evanne's, and affording a view of the High Justiciar. Vertiline shone perhaps brighter than the dragon she rode, platinum hair defying the sun's brilliance, blue eyes sharper than dragonscale. She slid easily from the dragon's back as if she'd done it her whole life and stepped neatly to the shore without getting an ounce of lake on her boots. Evanne was somewhat gratified to see mud clung to Mama's shoes just like everyone else's.

Evanne wondered what one was supposed to do when your mother, who was also the High Justiciar, and angry, stepped off dragonback to stand before her. She'd rehearsed the conversation in her head a thousand times in the last fifteen minutes, and perhaps ten thousand within the hour. She straightened, and said, "Um."

Vertiline stepped forward and grabbed Evanne in a hug tight enough to crush even Vhemin bones. Evanne smelled her, that scent of flowers and home she'd missed, *yearned* for these past months. Vertiline murmured in her ear as she stroked Evanne's hair. "My love, my girl. My sweet thing. You are safe. You are safe."

And then Evanne cried. She cried for the people lost, and the people yet to die, but she cried mostly for herself, because she missed her mother. She hugged Mama back, not the High Justiciar, not the best swordswoman in the world, not the teacher of the school of Tresward, but her mother. "I'm sorry, Mama. I'm sorry, I didn't know what to do. I tried, but the people, they died, but others, um. I'm sorry."

Vertiline pulled away a little but kept both hands on Evanne's arms. Looked at her, up and down, then into her eyes. An almost imperceptible nod, one warrior to an equal of what she saw there. "There is naught to be sorry for, daughter, my dearest, my heart. There are villains, and we must end them."

"Um," Evanne said. "I had this whole speech, and you know, about how I'd have to convince you, um."

"Much has been made clear to me. One of my students rode Myryntir the Protector to your ship in the sky. He found a wasteland of destruction and no daughter mine. He found a tiger of curious stripe in the woods, then came to get me, which he should have done in the first place. I *said* to send the dragon west." This last was through gritted teeth.

//THAT WAS MY BAD. I MIGHT HAVE PRESSURED HIM A LITTLE.//

"He is my student, not yours, dragon." Vertiline didn't look at the beast. "Once the shape of things was made clear, our course was plain also. The Vide have come from the cracks in the grouting. No place is safe for you but by my side. And I will be going to beard the lion in his den."

Evanne sighed, a tension in her relaxing, a pressure released she hadn't noticed was there. "I have tried to keep them safe, Mama. The Raven Queen is stubborn. Uncle Heser refuses to die when most men would have given up the journey. An old friend of yours is here, a lordling who styles himself as the most powerful mage ever, but who can't light a candle by himself. And, uh. I've someone I'd like you to meet."

Vertiline took this news with a slow nod, not settling on any particular moment. "Meriwether du Reeves lives?"

"I didn't say his name. How did you know?"

"Because I know him well. He is my brother by choice." Vertiline looked past Evanne to the small huddle by the tree line. A small smile played at her lips as she took in the people there, her eyes turning a soft celeste. "Come, daughter. I would meet this person dear to you."

"I, um. I didn't say that, but um. She's very important. She can wield a magic sword."

"That is not why she is important." Vertiline took Evanne's hand and led her toward the group. She let go when Meri stepped forward. "Sinner. You've not aged well."

He grinned, then laughed, stepped forward, and swooped her in a hug. Evanne had only seen Papa do that to Mama; any other man would have been murdered, but here Vertiline was, not just tolerating it but laughing back. When the mage put her down, she leaned into the hug, then placed a kiss on his cheek. He seemed abashed, but said, "The years have been a kindness to you."

"I thought teaching infants would send me to an early grave, but it seems the Three have another destiny in mind." Vertiline nodded to the Raven and Heser, who stood side by side, so close to touching it was electric. "Cousin, what news?"

"My kingdom is overrun by imbeciles," Morgan offered.

"Your brother is of no moment. That problem was resolved when we visited Ravenswall. But the source of the villainy remains." She nodded to Heser. "Have you kept her safe? Have you kept her well?"

"Always, my lady." Heser gave a small bow, then a smile cracked his visage. "The Three are Merciful. Gods, it is good to see you."

One person stood back. Tarragon, a stranger amid a group of old friends. She was biting her lip again, and Evanne wanted to kiss her, to hold her. To bring her forward.

Vertiline strode past the guardsman to the once-fairy, and gave her a look up and down, eyes settling for a moment on Requiem. Tarragon looked at the sword, said, "Um. *Hic.*" Then unbelted it and offered it to her. "Here."

The High Justiciar took Requiem, her face growing sombre before turning to Meri. "What news of my sister?"

"She lived, last I saw her." The smile in his eyes died. "She is alone, Tilly. She's alone again."

"I have failed her."

"It's not your fault." Meri held up a hand. "No, I won't hear it. There will be time for settling accounts in the future. The task at hand is to open the gate and get her out. There is a functioning portal in the villain's lair, or so the oracle led us to believe."

Vertiline made no comment on 'the oracle' but gave a tight nod before turning back to Tarragon. "You have kept my daughter safe?"

"*Hic.* I tried. *Hic.* But, um. And there was, um. *Hic.*"

"Then continue to do that." Vertiline pressed Requiem back into Tarragon's hands. "You will need a good blade for the task at hand. The weapon knows you. It would brook no ill hand."

"You know the sword?"

"I know the man who forged it. He was more a wonder than this slip of skymetal." Vertiline offered a small smile to Tarragon. "Would you walk with me? I would have an accounting while others prepare refreshments and plans for our long journey."

"Um. *Hic.*" Tarragon looked past Vertiline with frightened eyes.

Evanne nodded. "Go, love. She won't bite anyone but me."

"My daughter jests. I will murder any fool on a Tuesday." Vertiline pulled Tarragon away. "Tell me what you know of *Five Skies Afire*. It is the middle set of—"

"It's my favourite pattern," Tarragon said. "It's amazing. It's got the perfect placement of feet. Um. *Hic.* Stance? Is that the right word?"

Evanne watched them go, feeling warm inside. "It's going to be okay."

Meri was at her elbow. "Things are trending positive but the war's not won yet, kid." His voice softened when he saw her expression. "But yes. It's going to be okay."

Chapter Thirteen

It took days to reach the camp. Armitage had to walk, because the fucken horses wouldn't take him. He was the sludge silting the gears of their progress. But he hurried nonetheless. Tilly said *She lives*, and so his feet knew speed.

Evanne waited for him. Of course she did. His little girl didn't miss the chance for an entrance, perched on a low boulder just around a bend in the road. She had new clothes and a lazy smile, but it didn't make her eyes. He trudged to her boulder and sat beside her. Saw those smile-free eyes, and the hope and fear in them. Thought about blood on the sands, and how much he missed her. *She'll get misty-eyed. She doesn't have time for it. Shit needs to be done.* "You managed to stay alive. Good job."

"Papa!" Evanne startled straight, all that practiced nonchalance leaving like a flock of startled starlings.

"Tilly said you managed to feed yourself, too. It's like you don't need us anymore. I don't even know why we came."

She leaned away, and gave him a long, hard stare. "I had this whole speech prepared."

"I didn't come here for your speech." He scuffed her hair, ignoring her wince and accompanying growl. "Seriously, you did good."

She laughed despite herself, then sobered. "I have missed you so much, Papa. I'm sorry. I got lost. I got so lost without you."

"You got nothing to be sorry for." He worried at his scar. "It's us, Evie. Tilly and I. We need to apologise. We weren't watching things. Didn't pay people enough mind. Imshir, you know? It felt we were far enough away from the bullshit. And then a mountain exploded."

She leaned against him. He could feel the strength in her, all that Vhemin muscle, but something else that hadn't been there before. It might have been the death she'd dodged, or the intensity of purpose he loved in Tilly. No longer shy of the world and its ways. Harder than him, maybe two in every five times. "The mountain was unexpected."

"It's hard to punch a mountain." He grunted, then looked at his hands. Strong enough for most killing business. Tough enough to get the bloody work done when needed. Scaled, like all his kind, easy enough to wash clean. "I got scared."

"Because you couldn't punch a mountain?" She pointed at the rock beneath them. "Give this one a go."

"Nah." He stood, feeling his joints creak all the way up, and offered her a hand. She took it, then scrambled in for a hug. Evanne clung to him, all that Vhemin strength and purpose put aside for a second. He smoothed her hair. "It's okay. It's going to be okay."

"You're a terrible liar." Her words were muffled against his chest. "You're saying it like you want it to be true, not because it is."

"The Three cursed me with no gift for words. They gave all that to you." He pulled her tight enough to cause a runt problems, but she didn't seem to squirm. "I want it to be true. I don't want to be that scared again. We lost you."

"I'm right here, Papa." She pulled away, staring up at him. "I'm not going anywhere."

"And who's the liar now?" He eased off the boulder, and she joined him as they continued toward the camp. "I can't even get you to promise to be safe. You're part Vhemin, and part imbecile."

"Hey!"

"I meant that in a loving way." Armitage trudged along. "Did you or did you not pick a fight with a Feybrind?"

"It was one time!"

"That's my girl." He pulled her into a hug, and she laughed. "It'll be okay." She paused, trailing behind him on the road. He turned, feeling the creak in his joints. "What?"

"You didn't lie that time."

He grinned, all teeth, and saw her answering smile. A little smaller than his, with less shark in it. But kinder, and warmer, because she *wasn't* like him. She was perfect. "Maybe I'm part imbecile, too."

Chapter Fourteen

I t took three days for everyone to join them, and Tarragon hated every waiting minute. She didn't have Evanne's attitude to *be about it then*, nor the focus of the High Justiciar to defeat the enemy. She didn't like all the new faces, or the noise they made. But mostly she hated how they looked at her. *I know I'm a Big, misshapen lump. Stop seeing me.*

There weren't enough students left to call them a handful; they clotted to the sides of the merchant's caravan like spoiled milk. They had the confidence of Tresward training, despite not having passed their Trials. The once-fairy could see three who showed the Storm's promise. A handsome, rakish fellow named Amir who thought very highly of himself, a stunning woman who seemed to hate herself in equal measure, and a shadow behind them, Faust. A man who said little, watched all, and made her nervous from his sheer size alone.

She found herself wondering if she could take him on the blade, and then wondered why she wondered such a thing of her allies.

It's the noise. They won't stop talking.

Two Feybrind came with them, a man and a woman. The cats were often close to each other, but her tail lashed where his was still. It was a curious play. Amir offered that Sands Apart was *lost, but found*, whatever that meant. The cats were elegance personified. Even their names were beautiful. Sight of Day and Sands Apart were not like buffalo. Neither gold nor ochre eyes had time for Tarragon and her Bigness.

So Tarragon snared a bow and headed for the nearby valley. Myryntir claimed deer grazed near the forest's edge, and Tarragon always liked venison.

Away from the camp she felt her shoulders unbind. She missed Evanne, but not the calamity that came with the maybe-Vhemin. *I just need some time alone.*

The bow was a good one. Unless she missed her mark, it was Feybrind made. Not a single centimetre of it was out of true, and it pulled well in her hands. She fancied some target practice more than venison, so fired shots at stray boughs that dared challenge her supremacy of the woodland.

A *crack* brought her up short. She felt her hand drop to Requiem, the blade vibrating slightly under her fingertips. "Hello?"

The Feybrind woman stepped from behind a tree. She held a stick and snapped it with another *crack. Ah. She announced herself. {I greet you, Warrior.}*

"Oh! Hello." Tarragon remembered her manners. *{I mean no disrespect by my voice. I greet you, Warrior.}*

{I am no Warrior. Not anymore.} Sands Apart slipped alongside Tarragon, and they continued through the forest. *{Your voice does me no disrespect. It is pleasant, and you use it well.}*

"You move like a warrior. Not like me. I'm so ... Big."

Sands Apart held her hands still for a moment. *{I've heard your story. One touched by Cophine and allowed to begin again. A fresh start, all past problems behind you. Many would like such a change.}*

"My problems are still with me." Tarragon scrubbed wheat-pale hair. "If anything, they're as Big as I am now."

{I misspoke. I would like such a change. I have done questionable things. Not that they were wrong at the time I did them, but I now question them in the light of a new day. There are many things in this world I do not understand, and I am over a hundred years old.}

"There are lots of things I don't understand either, and I'm closer to nine hundred years old."

{Wow. You look great.}

Tarragon laughed. "Builders do not age as others do. Old age is not how we... how *they* meet their end." She brooded a moment. "I can't even call the Storm. I know all the patterns. Every step. But something eludes me."

{Show me, then.} Sands Apart found a comfortable log and perched, tail over crossed legs. *{Humans are the one race that may call the Three's Light. I will not teach a human to fight. But you aren't human. Not all the way. Let's see if you can carry the Light, too.}*

Tarragon *hmm'd.* "I don't know if that's a good idea."

{Builder, I was a prisoner here, but now I'm lost. I don't know my purpose. It seems you don't either. Perhaps together we may find a peace that eludes us individually.} She half-smiled. *{Besides. It's not every day you get to see a magic sword.}*

Tarragon understood the Feybrind's intent. To draw her mind to the sword, not her person, to defuse the shame she might feel at her failure. *I could use the practice.* She propped the bow against Sands Apart's log, then stepped away. She drew Requiem in an easy pull, the blade casting long shadows as blue-white light hungered for foes. "Hush, now. We're just practicing." The blade shivered, then quietened down, a mere candle's worth of light puddling among the trees.

The once-fairy stepped into *Five Skies Afire.* The High Justiciar had talked to her about the pattern, and it felt right to do it here in this small glade. She stepped and turned, the sword a dance of blue-white light. Her feet found their level, her body its poise. And still, the Light didn't come. She finished the stanza after its forty steps, then stood, panting and ashamed. "There."

The Feybrind sat, mouth agape for a moment. *{That was one of the most beautiful things I have ever seen.}*

"The sword is a wonder."

{It's not the sword.} The cat looked away for a moment. *{I don't know the ways of Knights or how they can make or break the world. But I do see what your problem is.}*

"I don't believe?"

Sands Apart shook her head. *{Nothing about this is belief. It's a simple matter. You're leaning forward too much.}*

"What?"

{Leaning. Forward. Like you're used to being smaller, which you are, and are now trying to shoulder a larger weight, which you think you are, but not really. Humans are, like all things made by the Three, in perfect proportion.}

Tarragon stared, then said again, "What?"

{You'll figure it out. Do you fancy walking some more?} Sands Apart stood. *{We should get some dinner.}*

SANDS APART CARRIED THE DEER WHILE TARRAGON CUT THROUGH tangled brushwood and trees. It seemed a horrendous dishonour to a magic sword forged from metal that fell from the sky, but the sword didn't seem to mind. *It feels like it wants to be used.*

The sun was lower in the sky for their return journey. It was past mid afternoon when they paused for a snack. Tarragon felt hungry. She'd a few berries she'd scrounged, but they didn't hit the spot, and she didn't like the raw rabbit Sands Apart wolfed down. She stretched her back, heard it pop, and said, "I keep forgetting Feybrind eat only meat."

The cat dropped the carcass. *{If the Three hadn't wanted us to eat meat, they wouldn't have made animals out of it.}*

Tarragon laughed. "I mean ... it seems so unfair. All of you are gentle."

{Our nature is not to be gentle or warlike. Our nature is to be the People.}

"That sounds very wise."

The cat looked away for a moment. *{I borrowed that line from a friend. He is one of the golden eyes. They see better than most.}*

Tarragon eyed the sun-dappled canopy above. "It feels like the ancients made everything better than they were. Feybrind are smart and strong and kind. Fairies can work in irradiated wastelands. The Vhemin are pure muscle—"

Sands Apart cut her off, slicing the air with a hand. {*The monsters were made to die. Humans made them to do that better than they as well.*}

Tarragon turned that over a moment. "You don't hate the Vhemin?"

{*I did.*} A shrug. {*So many things I took as true are not. The monster's lot is to do the bleeding and the dying while dandies sit on feather pillows. Or so the golden eyes said.*}

"What's with the golden eyes?" Tarragon raised an eyebrow. "Yours hold the colour of cinnamon cast as stone." She looked at her feet. "It is wonderful."

The Feybrind leaned against a tree and rubbed her face. {*There are always those better than others. You can fence better than some, while being slower than most.*}

"Hey!"

{*It is a metaphor. I was not being specific, but if it feels close to home...*} A half-smile. {*The golden-eyed People are better in all ways.*} Her hands trembled a moment. {*It is said they are never wrong, but I wonder.*}

Tarragon sighed agreement. "Evanne is like that. She sees everything. I have lived so much longer than her, but I'm blind in comparison."

{*You are human. It is in your nature to be short-sighted.*}

"I wasn't always ... I mean, um." Tarragon kicked a fallen branch. "I have never seen well. I had no Manifest. I failed my exams. I—"

Another sharp slice of the air from a fursoft hand. {*And yet here you are, wielding a sword of unquestionable power, trusted by the soul keeper, comrade of spectres, and friend to the People. That last is more special than the others.*} She stiffened, then whirled. {*Do you hear that?*}

"I hear birds."

{*Deaf as well as blind. There is a commotion.*} The cat darted through the trees, easily clearing fallen boughs and brush. Tarragon realised Sands Apart needed none of Tarragon's help scrub cutting as she struggled to keep up. She lost sight of the Feybrind, but heard the clash of steel. She bulled on, breathing hard, cursing her giant elephantine legs, angry at her lack of wings.

She burst into a clearing. They weren't at the camp yet, but the sounds of battle were nearby, and the smell of smoke was on the wind. In the clearing were five people around Sands Apart. The cat had felled two already, and she crouched, teeth bared, hands hooked and ready to strike.

She has no weapon. Why does she have no weapon?

The question could keep. Tarragon didn't slow as she cleared Requiem from scabbard in a smooth motion that cut a man near her in half. The remaining pair turned, and she saw sooty faces, unkempt clothes, and patchy beards. The air was sour with their sweat.

The closest came at her with a pitchfork, and she whittled it down to the nub with three strikes of her blade. The tines smoked and glowed as they hit the grassy ground, the haft charred at Requiem's last cut. Tarragon took the man's arm, then his head, cutting his scream in half, leaving silence on the wind.

The remaining man lunged at her with a rusty sword. It was an antique, by the looks as old as Sands Apart, the notched edge showing no Feybrind craftsmanship. He was comically slow. She thought, *lean back. I am not a fairy trying to lift a human's body. I am me, and I am whole.* Requiem thirsted, cutting the man from groin to skull. A charred spray of ichor sprayed from his spine as the sword hissed and spat through meat. Thunder roiled above as Tarragon held her pose in high guard, looking for foes.

Sands Apart pointed toward the camp. *{Come.}* Then set off, Tarragon in pursuit. This time, the cat didn't break ahead, and they emerged behind a wagon as battle joined around the encampment.

Tarragon was about to head into the fray, sword high, fear in her heart because *Where is Evanne?* Sands Apart held her elbow, a usually gentle hand now iron. Tarragon tried to get free, but the cat was insistent. She touched her eye, then pointed across the battle. *Look.* Tarragon saw the big man, Faust. He was at the camp's other border, and one of the wretched bandits was with him. They weren't having a good time, fists raised, faces closed, but they weren't *fighting*.

"What is going on?" Tarragon looked about to see if anyone else could see, but no, Faust and the bandit were hidden from the melee by a convenient tent. She spied the braggart Amir heading their way.

Amir rounded the tent, and Faust changed in a moment from *arguing* to *murdering*. In a second, the bandit lay dead.

Amir spoke, but his words were lost against the clash of steel, and both headed back to the battle. Sands Apart pointed in their direction. *{Say nothing.}*

Tarragon bit her lip. *What's going on?*

Chapter Fifteen

Amir sat on a log. It felt good. Companionable, almost. No rough edges to sand his ass, and a non-rotted sturdiness that belied the age of its lichened exterior. It was a good place to sit, because he was outside the camp proper, and the associated chores that came with cleaning up a battleground. There were always weapons to stack, bodies to bury, and rites to be said.

Usually Amir would have chipped in, but today he wasn't feeling it. When he'd joined the Tresward, he'd been so ... *sure*. He'd travelled far to get his beating at the hands of the High Justiciar and welcomed the lesson. *I wanted to be a Knight. Hold the Storm on a leash and defeat the enemies of the world. But the more the Light touches my blade, the less certain I am.*

"Sup." Evanne sat with a grunt.

Amir stifled a small scream. "You move quietly."

"Your thoughts were loud enough to be heard a world away. It's no wonder you didn't hear my footsteps over all that noise."

"Hmm." Amir faced the thatch of trees that stood between them and the encampment. "You seem to have escaped the battle unscathed."

Evanne drew a wicked-looking machete with an air of satisfaction.

"I think I'm getting the hang of this." She brought the weapon overhead at some imagined foe, then sighted down the blade. "You beat on fools until they stop moving."

"That is the essence of it." Amir held out his hand, and after a moment she handed the blade over. He bent, elbows on knees, and examined it. *Fine craftsmanship, but with no maker's mark.* He straightened and gave the weapon a flourish. "Heavy about the blade. No cross guard. This weapon seems unsuited to one who sings so sweetly."

Evanne's eyes narrowed. "Say it plain, Knight."

"It's a brute's weapon." Amir handed it back. "All offence with no room for ... negotiation."

She slipped it back in its sheath. "It is the Vhemin way."

Amir shook his head. "You are no monster from the blasted plaguelands. You are a," he tapped his temple, "thinker first. You carry your mother's blood, too."

She gave him a sideways glance. "You're not my father—"

"No, I am not." Amir stood. "I am naught but a sellsword whose ragged past left him with many regrets. I assure you there are plenty of monsters that walk the halls of men. Vhemin have no sovereignty over power from strength at another's expense. They learned that at our feet, I think. Children brought into our world by wicked men who were tired of dying for their own causes."

She looked away, perhaps uncertain this was the right log for her anymore. "If that's true, a brute's weapon would do just as well for a human hand."

He sighed, slumping back to the log, and fished out a small metal flask. He took a pull of honey whiskey, then handed it to her. "You've the right of it, of course. All I meant is your course is yours. You *own* it. If you are born poor, change your stars and become wealthy. Ignorance can be turned to wisdom. Weakness can become strength, and power can become a gift shared among all."

He heard her swallow, then give a satisfied *ahhh* as the whiskey hit. "You speak as if your life was much different not so long ago."

Amir gave a bitter laugh. "My life was worthless before I found the Light. The man I was saw a path to the man I am. And here I sit, sharing whiskey with—"

This was where the hidden watcher at the back of his mind said, *move, asshole*, and so he stood, turning a perfect half-circle, blade coming to hand as if it was thirsty again already. A woman half-crouched behind the log, silent as whisper fog, hooded face twisted in anger and surprise. She lunged, but not for Amir. Her blade went for Evanne's back, still turned away, because bards were not known for speed or combat prowess.

Something is not right. Why is this one assassin here after a battle with bandits? The question needed an answer, and one person might have it, so rather than running the assassin through, he stepped into the path of her blade, linked arms with a surprised Evanne, and tumbled over the log, taking the bard with him. He tossed her into the mulch five metres away and rolled to his feet.

The Vide lunged past him, so he slapped the flat of his blade on her backside, and as she turned, offered her now angrier face a wide, welcoming grin. "Slept in, did you? Missed the battle and wanted blood on your steel?"

She grunted, eyes narrowing, and came at him with quick slashes of her blade. It was a curious weapon, the length more sickle than sword, but it looked as if it would let the blood out all the same. The assassin came in low then high, before passing the blade through where his stomach would have been if he'd not slipped back.

Then she turned and hungered for Evanne again. The bard had barely managed to get to her feet in the time it took for Amir and the Vide to exchange blows and was ill equipped for the flurry of hate the assassin carried within.

So, Amir tripped the Vide, slipped his sword inside the sickle curve of her steel, and flicked the weapon into the trees as the woman fell face-first into the dirt. Amir was on her like a cat with a new toy, blade against the back of her neck. "Now, let us talk."

"You will die, and all those you love."

Evanne *tsk'd*. "You're doing it all wrong, Knight."

Amir blinked. "What?"

"You've naught to offer her but the edge of a blade. There is a better way." Evanne walked a wide circle around the pair, putting herself on the other side of the log. "Bind her hands, and let's talk."

"I've nothing to say to you," the assassin spat.

Amir sighed, freed the woman's belt, and bound her hands with leather. He hefted her by brute strength and sat her on the log, blade against her neck to encourage a level of thoughtfulness that might not otherwise be present in this moment of excitement. "Then perhaps you will listen." He nodded to Evanne.

"Here's the thing." The bard sighed. "Your lot keep trying to kill me. I'm not taking it personally, but it's wearisome. So, I've an offer for you."

The woman hissed, but Amir nudged her neck with steel. "Be polite, and we'll all leave here with our heads."

"Thanks." Evanne gave a lazy smile. "Here's my proposal. Your boss wants me dead, and I want him dead. So, I propose we offer a bounty on Wild Sur's head."

"It will not stop us coming for you." The assassin sounded pleased about it.

"Of course not. You're professionals." Evanne's smile widened. "And as professionals, you hunger for the coin you deserve. We can give it to you. Even the odds, as it were."

"Wild Sur is a difficult target."

"Wild Sur is a man like any other," Evanne breezed. "All I ask is you take my offer to your boss and come back under a flag of truce to discuss terms. Then we can see who dies first. If Wild Sur dies, you get paid. If I die, you get paid. You win, either way."

Amir realised his mouth hung open. The bard was so damned *reasonable*, he would have signed up then and there. The Vide gave a grudging nod. "You will let me take this message back?"

"*I'm* certainly not taking it." Evanne flicked her fingers in a *shoo* gesture. "Now, be off with you."

Amir moved to stand before the Vide. "You heard her." The assassin offered her bound hands to be released, and he chuckled. "Don't get cute."

"Worth a shot." The Vide stood, then hurried off, very audibly crashing through the undergrowth so there could be no mistaking her intent.

Amir sheathed his sword. "You are insane."

Evanne gave a brittle laugh. "That might be the human in me. This will sow confusion among our enemies."

"Your mother is going to have kittens."

"Ah." Evanne scrubbed at rust locks. "It's probably best if she doesn't find out, no?"

Chapter Sixteen

Despite the rivers of bullshit, Vertiline was happy. She had a husband, daughter, and sword to protect both. Remnants of her school survived the death of Imshir, so her bargain with the Three held, although but one student earned the gold bar of a Knight. They had a dragon by their side, a giant tiger, and were heading north toward the enemy for a confrontation past due.

None of that was why she was happy.

I will see Geneve again. By the Three's grace, I have a chance to undo my terrible mistake.

They wound a column toward the north. Last time she'd travelled this way, it was to kill the mad lord who'd sired Meri. The sinner didn't seem to have that trip on his mind despite the terrible finale of the tale. Father, dead, and by Vertiline's will it was done. If anything, the new Lord du Reeves was buoyant.

He is happy he will see his love again, too.

"I'm worried." Armitage's gravel voice came from her right where he strode the road like he owned it. "You're too damn happy."

Vertiline laughed. "Husband, can I not be comfortable on this fine summer's day?"

He gave her a snake-eyed glare. "Of course you can. It's *why* you're comfortable that's like sand in my drawers. We march to certain doom."

"I think not." Her fingers tapped the hilt of her sword. "I have studied much since last we saved the world. I am no longer the second-best swordswoman."

"I'm not worried about you." As her eyes drifted to Evanne, he grunted. "I'm not worried about her, either. I'm ... not who I was, Tilly. I'm old. Used up. Dry, a river that no longer runs. The summers sit easy on you, held at bay by the Three's Light or some shit. They drag my heels. My people were never meant to live long."

She glared down at him. "Are we back to the fate of dying for humans?"

"We're back to the fate of being fucking old," he said. "Every morning my damn spine needs to be stretched. It doesn't ... work right. Not since ... before."

Vertiline felt a stab of guilt, or perhaps a melange made from guilt and regret. "You laid your life down so the dragon could live, and saved us all."

"There was plenty of everyone saving everyone else on the day," he grunted. "I'm not dredging for compliments. I'm just saying if it comes to swinging steel—"

"You'll hang back?"

"Fuck, no." Armitage ground out a chuckle made of gristle and excitement. "I'll still swing. But I'll die, all the same." He stamped on a few more strides as her horse provided him shade. "And I don't want to die. Everything I've ever wanted is here. Even though I won't be here, the memory of me will miss you."

Vertiline turned away. "I'll hear no more of dying on this day."

"Doesn't matter if you don't want to hear it. Still going to happen." He lapsed into an easy silence, because Armitage wasn't afraid of their bandied words. *He's fearful of the words unsaid. A poet's soul in a warrior true.* "We did good, Tilly. We did really good. Our little girl, I mean."

Vertiline sighed agreement. "She is her father's daughter."

"But with her mother's troublesome bent." He dodged her lazy kick. "Best we find somewhere to break for lunch. I could eat a bison."

IT WAS DEER, NOT BISON, BUT VERTILINE ENJOYED SIGHT OF DAY'S cooking regardless. The Feybrind worked with the foundling, Sands Apart, both in easy company. They'd set up a field kitchen in the mouth of a cave set into a cliff. The cave went back to a smooth wall, free of surprises lurking in the gloom.

Sands Apart tended bread baked against their fire while Sight of Day husbanded the coals beneath the remains of the deer. Vertiline noted the woman had secured a blade from somewhere. It was a slip sliver of metal that would bother no one from her school in the least but no doubt gave some comfort. The High Justiciar leaned against a large rock, enjoying its cool companionship as the sun hid behind it.

Evanne joined her with a hunk of steaming venison in a clump of bread. She had two, of course, and offered the second to Vertiline. "Here, Mama."

"I've eaten."

"What's your point?"

Vertiline laughed and took the offering. It was juicy, a slight saltiness to the meat giving her all the excuse she needed for seconds. "What do you think of this Feybrind?"

"Sands Apart? Tarragon likes her." Evanne chewed, then swallowed. "So, I like her."

"You trust her?"

Evanne gave her a glance. "Did you take a blow to the head?"

"Not recently." Vertiline leaned against the stone. "I feel your answer is the right one, but..."

"But she's likeable." Evanne squatted, back to the rock. "Doesn't mean I want her behind me holding steel. Her lot tried to fricassee me. A week's company with Sight of Day doesn't rob someone of their cause."

"Maybe," Vertiline said. "Have you considered how she only ever tried to get away, not murder us, once the clouds parted? As if her heart knew."

"Pretty hard to murder Tresward. You keep saying so."

"Not impossible, though." Vertiline swallowed, the bread suddenly stale. "There are almost none of us left."

Evanne slowed her chewing, and Vertiline was reminded how much she'd grown in the past weeks. *Depravation and constant fear of death will do that.* She felt a pang, because this wasn't the life she'd wanted for her daughter. *I made a Three-damned deal. The school, and they'd leave her alone, because they couldn't set foot here.* Gods or no, harm had come for her wonderful child, this blessing against everything people said was possible. "Mama, you know we may not make it, right?"

Vertiline looked away. "You will make it. While I draw breath—"

"Oh, aye, yes," Evanne waved her away with the deer sandwich. "While I draw breath, too. I'm not saying it as some noble gesture. I *tell* tragic stories. I don't want to be in one. But I'm worried about Papa."

"Armitage?" Vertiline glanced around as if her husband were near, but no, he was over by the horses, trying for the thousandth time to get the creatures to settle when he drew near. *His heart wants to be gentle, but everyone sees the monster. As I did, before.* She tried the lie. "He is unkillable."

Her daughter snorted. "He wouldn't say so. No, don't get all icy eyed at me. He would say," her voice dropped into the gravel, *"Daughter, I'm but a man, rah, grunt,* and then do something wonderful like hug me. And then when the *real* monsters came, he would stand before them, a lone candle against the hurricane, and he'd fight, and fight, and keep fighting, even though his injury hurt and pulled his arm to the left, and then he'd die. And I know he doesn't make anything of the scar, just shrugs it off like he's made of stone and spite, daring anyone to tell him he should take it easy. But I see how it drags his steps."

Vertiline wanted to storm off, and she felt her right hand tremble, itching to hold a blade, not against her daughter, or even her words, but the vision she conjured, the hordes behind the tale waiting with sharp steel and hate. She hissed, "I will not allow it."

Evanne shrugged. "I know you won't. But it might happen anyway."

"What do you want me to say?"

"Nothing, Mama. You don't need words for a shield against the truth." She finished her sandwich. "I am going to play. I need the practice." She stood, moving into the camp, wending her way with an easy smile and an offered hand as she worked toward the cooking fire. *She is so good with people. How did I never see it?*

"What are you going to do?" Tarragon slipped into the place where Evanne had been moments earlier.

"You heard?" At the tiniest nod, wheat-pale hair swaying with it, Vertiline sighed. "I must keep them both safe. It is my task."

"But not yours alone." Tarragon leaned in beside her as Evanne sat by the fire, guitar across her legs, and teased early notes from the strings. A ripple spread through their company as people turned to see, to hear, to *feel*. "There are two here of passable skill with a blade."

"A magic sword doesn't—"

"I speak of the braggart," Tarragon said. "An A-word. I'm sure of it."

"Amir?"

"The same." She huffed. "He walks with two others as all Tresward do, but they are not his equals. Larochette is too busy hiding what she was to become what she needs to be. Faust studies like a man told if he frowns enough at lead it will become gold. But Amir? A poet with steel. Not that you should tell him that."

"He does think well of himself, it's true." She mulled it over. "He too has a past of smoke and flame."

"As do we all." Tarragon smiled as Evanne hit a sweet melody. "It doesn't mean we have a future of blood and tears."

"Does it not, then? I have known much of blood and a little of tears, too." Vertiline flexed her metal fingers.

"And of smiles and music." Tarragon shifted, making a face as her back scraped rock. "Being Big is hard. It's hard *all* the time. Gravity pulls you like an anchor. You've no wings to reach the stars. And yet you manage."

Vertiline grunted. "You would have me set Amir as guard on Armitage?"

"Amir is already guarding Armitage." Tarragon pointed with her chin as the Adept joined Armitage at the pens, hand on a horse's neck, a soft word calming wide horse eyes. Her husband gave the man a filthy look, but stayed and talked nonetheless. "Amir is like you, because—"

"I'm a braggart?"

A small smile, at that. "Truth, few would claim to be the best swordswoman in the world with a straight face. But no, I mean you both found yourself where you were needed, not where you wanted to be. Just let it happen." Tarragon eased away from the rock. "I'm going to get a drink. Want to come with?"

"Not yet. You go on." Vertiline watched Tarragon head toward Evanne, iron to a magnet. She thought, *Tarragon asked for no one to watch Evanne.*

Then she smiled despite herself. *Because she has taken that job for herself.* And she smiled wider, right until the dragon bellowed in rage.

Chapter Seventeen

Evanne was on her feet and running before her brain caught up. She held the guitar in one hand as she raced toward the dragon's bellow. Her machete slapped against her leg as she ran, and she thought about tossing it. *Don't be stupid. I'll need a blade soon enough.* Her legs whipped through tall grass, the honey-sweet air urging her on.

It wasn't hard to locate Myryntir, because he hadn't stopped roaring fit to break the heavens. He was around the curve of the mountain they'd camped beside, no doubt chasing butterflies or whatever nonsense dragons did when bored. Lightning lashed the sky, the dragon's breath discharging again, and again, as he tracked something she couldn't see because of the damn hill.

Holy fuck. I'm at the front of a charge toward a dragon in trouble.

It was true she'd been first on her feet, not weighed down by the burden of Tresward armour, but she was a little surprised she was ahead of Sight of Day. The cats were the fastest thing she knew of, except Pakhet, and Pakhet only ran *away* from danger.

She rounded an elbow of rock jutting from a cool green drapery of hanging vines to see exactly what happened when a dragon was pissed off. There: Myryntir, up on his back legs, wings wide for balance, maw wide as he blasted lightning. The lightning: it tracked a curious set of orbs made of metal. Three hovered and darted above the earth. They were ringed about with blue runes. The runes: these blazed with starlight, each reaching out a curling tendril of raw energy to rake the dragon's hide. The energy: with the dragon's lightning and the orb's whatever-the-fuck-it-was, the ground five hundred metres around the dragon was charred, the air heavy with ozone. A trench perhaps two hundred metres wide lay north of the dragon, and it took little imagination to consider it the source of the orbs.

Evanne let out a battle cry, completely worthless next to the dragon's roaring, but it made her feel better. Her machete was in hand, and after a moment spent staring at the orbs high above her head, then the weapon, she cocked back her arm and threw it. The weapon spun in a grey-silver whirl, and for once her aim was true. It clocked the side of an orb, which rang like a gong, and then completely ignored her. The machete fell to earth, landing blade-first into the rude and rocky ground.

And there goes the weapon I needed.

"Hitch!" The spectre popped out of the rock to her left and snapped to her side. "What are those things?"

"Curators," he said. "Odd there are only three."

"Are they good or bad?" At his blue-eyed stare, she amended, "I mean, are they going to be a problem for Tresward?" Because her mind was already thinking of what the High Justiciar would do, no doubt but moments away.

"Just three? Unlikely." He crossed his arms, then added, "Uh."

"What? Oh, *fuck*." Out of the trench spewed an excitement of Curators. She stopped counting at ten. "Okay. Come on, we need to get in there."

He goggled at her, holding comment for a moment as Myryntir spat blue-white death in a line across the sky. The dragon tracked one of the new Curators, marking a hit against its runed side. The orb wobbled, perhaps now the equivalent of a drunk Curator, then arced a stately fall to *crump* into the ground five metres from Evanne. The runes in its side flickered, then died. He pointed at it. "There. If the dragon can't take them out, what do you think we can do?"

"The dragon took it out just fine!"

The orb's runes flickered, blue changing to green. A man's voice, smooth and round like a river stone, emanated from the fallen device. *"REFECTIONE. PATET EXCUBIAS."*

Hitch said, "Better do what it says."

"Which is? I don't speak Ancient Asshole."

"Roughly? 'Get back, I'm fixing my shit'." He shuffled away as if making a point.

Vertiline pounded around the hill's shoulder, blade clear of its sheath. She didn't have the good grace to take stock, just sprinted past Evanne, blade in high guard. Evanne heard thunder's threat. The Curator lifted from the ground as she reached it, blade a yellow-white arc.

By the Three, but she is amazing. Evanne had seen her mother fight at the school, but never like *this*. Outnumbered, fifteen or twenty airborne enemies, an enraged dragon, and still her steps were as perfect as a summer sunrise. Energy arced from the orb, and Vertiline wasn't there, pattern taking her past, blade going from high to low by way of the orb's hide. It left a glowing vermillion tear in the Curator's side, the runes flaring red in sympathy. Vertiline stepped backward, blade rising from low to high, in time to catch an arc of energy on the edge of her steel.

Thunder stopped threatening, and lightning struck. The heavens opened with the Three's rage, a pillar of power striking Vertiline's blade, and she took it from high to low once more, discharging all that power through the Curator.

It gave a low, musical tone, then cracked like a dropped egg, white light glaring from within. Vertiline took three steps back toward Evanne, who in all this time had managed to make zero moves, snatched her guitar, spun it about like a shield on a stick, golden light limning the instrument, and braced just as the Curator exploded. Fire roared past them, a dome of gentle yellow holding the flame at bay, then Vertiline turned and offered the instrument back to Evanne. "Get back!"

Then Vertiline ran into the fray. Evanne looked at her guitar, the Curators, the dragon, and the guitar again, then said, "Fuck that." She plucked the strings, feeling the instrument want to call out encouragement, and let it. Brazen chords challenged the Curators. The high string trembled as it reached for the heart and tugged it to faster action. Evanne stamped in time to the song, reaching out to anyone who could hear. The Tresward, not what was left of them, but what they were meant to be. She called to the Feybrind, and their link to this world. And the dragon, of *course* the dragon, all mighty wings.

In a world of ancient steel, the Curators soar,
   Blue runes of power, a threat we can't ignore.
   Tresward knights, Feybrind's might, Myryntir by our side,
   In this battle we unite, with courage as our guide.

Tresward, Feybrind, and Myryntir, we stand tall,
   Together we will rise, and the curators will fall.
   In this epic quest,
   Ancient machines will be put to rest.

Myryntir roared in delight as the sun kissed Vertiline's sword. In accompaniment to Evanne's beat, the Tresward Amir raced past her and into the fray, too few students in his wake. The two cats were there, one with bow and one with steel. Armitage too, her father roaring like he was young and angry again, the fence picket in his hands looking as comfortable as any halberd.

The Curators turned about, diving to meet new threats, and the battle was joined.

Evanne scanned the crowd, not for Mama and Papa, because they'd be fine, but for one with wheat-pale hair and a magic sword. She didn't see Tarragon, and her fingers trembled against the strings for but a moment. The song stumbled, tried to find its footing, missed the beat.

She was going to *lose* it, dammit, and people would fucking *die*, so get it together Evanne, just sort it out, you've got this one fucking job—

"What news?" Tarragon was at her side, Requiem a slash of blue-white fire. "The song was nice. You should keep it up."

"I couldn't see you." Evanne wanted to sob in relief, but it wasn't the time, because the battle needed winning, and of course Tarragon would be putting herself in more danger in seconds. She wanted to hold this slice of time, stretch it out, and make it never end.

Tarragon gave a lopsided, half-crazed smile, and Evanne noticed she had a small nick above one eyebrow. "They're attacking from the rear. Or were. Faust and Larochette hold the line."

"More of these?"

Tarragon gave a jaundiced stare at the Curators as one dove for Armitage. Evanne's father swung his fence paling like a bat, knocking the giant machine in a wobbling arc away. "Yes. Flying spheres that attack all. They burst from the cliff side."

"Have you seen these before?"

"No." Tarragon shook her head. "These are new. A special surprise from one side or another. They do not look Vehement, and they do not seem Itikari." She leaned in, stole a kiss from Evanne's numb lips, and charged into the fray.

The guitar trembled in her hands, and Evanne laughed with it, raised her hand, and brought it down against the strings. The music flowed from her instrument in a torrent, a song that made them mighty, that promised the halls of kings awaited the victors and the fallen alike. Evanne closed her eyes, stance wide, feeling the words of the song about to come, then fell on her side, *hard*, all the air going from her in an *ungh* sound. Her eyes snapped open, meeting the ochre gaze of Sands Apart. The woman's eyes seemed feral, the colour of blood and anger, her fangs bared.

Evanne was on her back, the Feybrind on her. Her machete was lost amid the field of battle. *Three's mercy, but this is how I die.*

The cat pressed a finger to Evanne's lips, then pointed the blade of her hand at a Curator hovering but five metres away. *{They see sound.}*

Evanne wanted to say, *are you cracked*, but that would emit sound. She watched the Curator turn a slow circle above where she'd stood moments before the Feybrind knocked her over. It made a harsh, flat tone, then sped away. Evanne let herself be helped up, and said, *{How did you know?}*

Sands Apart pointed to Sight of Day, his arrows hitting Curators over and over with no apparent effect. He moved about the field of battle, feet cat quiet, not a mark on him. *{They go to where Sight of Day was because of his bow's song, not where he is.}*

Evanne wanted to scream. *{I've got one stupid Trick and I can't use it!}*

{It's not stupid,} the cat said. *{It's inconvenient.}*

Evanne almost laughed but held it in by biting her lip. *{Let me get my sword.}*

{Did I knock you onto your head?} Sands Apart made a great show of looking at the back of her skull. *{I was so careful.}*

Evanne looked past her at the battle. The pace had faltered since her song fell. The Tresward were not doing well; those who'd not yet passed their Trials placing inadequate blade against ancient might. Vertiline was doing well enough for all, Armitage at her back, the pair fighting as one. Curiously, Uncle Heser was husbanding the Raven around the mountainside, which didn't bode well for Faust and Larochette's rearguard.

At least the dragon looked to be having fun. He had a Curator in one clawed hand, the machine spitting lances of blue energy, which the dragon directed at its allies to great effect, a sphere bursting into flame and tumbling into the ground.

Which cracked. The sphere rolled toward Vertiline and Armitage. Evanne screamed, "No!" She was running, legs pumping, no thought for how she'd gone from standstill to full sprint. Her hand reached out, fingers stretched as the fallen Curator rolled toward her parents. "Mama! Papa!"

The sphere exploded. The earth sank as rock spewed skyward, then heaved. Men and women screamed. Evanne was knocked from her feet and added her own scream to the mix. The ground caved away and she fell, rock around her. There, Tarragon's glitter-bright blade. Around her hips, Sands Apart's arms. Against all reason, her machete fell past her face.

She hit the ground with a *crump*. Myryntir fell like a slow-moving bolt of lightning, rocks hammering his wings, starving his flight, binding him to gravity along with the rest of them.

Evanne hit, and spared a glance at the falling dragon, rocks, and then curled her Vhemin-strong body about Sands Apart. *I was wrong. This is how I die.*

Chapter Eighteen

Vertiline fell, and for half a second she was an Adept again, no clue of what pattern to lean on. The world was full of rock and dust, her lungs locked up, the golden glow dying from her blade. She slammed against an outcropping of rude stone, jarring her shoulder, the pain something that would come knocking in a moment if she lived that long.

Evanne passed her, her daughter falling straight as a shot arrow, somehow balled around a Feybrind, good fortune sparing them from smashing against the wall. She heard a roar, and Armitage was there, her wonderful husband, his body about Vertiline's, for all *she* was the protector. They hit another spur, and she felt it through his body, but he didn't let her go for all the long, long ride to the bottom. The trip felt like hours but was seconds at best.

They landed, and Vertiline remembered who she was. Not an Adept at all, but the High Justiciar, the head of an ancient order, protector of the world. *And I'm on my side in the dust, my husband keeping me safe, my daughter Three knows where.* She surged to her feet, feeling the weight of falling stone above her, the presence that would crush them all. The dragon was a blazing meteor as he plummeted. Vertiline sprinted toward a sliver of steel, a cracked shield sticking from between two stones, tore it free, and held it up.

Stance planted. Legs just so. Perfection in her movement, timed exquisitely as the dragon landed not five paces from her, a nimbus of gold arced above them. Vertiline knew, *felt*, this was the shield pattern Knight Champion Mireille used when the ancients' weapons smote the earth with enough force to destroy the world. *I am not Mireille. I'm not strong enough.*

She thought of Evanne and Armitage and tightened up her right heel by half a millimetre. The shield above her flared, and then the rocks hit, a cascade of rubble that felt endless. Here they were, a tiny bubble of souls as the earth tried to eat them for the sins of all who came before.

Vertiline screamed but kept her form. Held it, as if it were a stallion bucking to be free of the reins. Heard Israel's voice, of all the damnable people, his whisper against her neck. *"Your shoulder must be forward. Yes, like that."* The shield held. The golden glow flared brighter, and rock above smoked and hissed, turning red and molten as it broke like waves against the Three's Storm. Israel's hand was on her arm, finger a moth on her elbow, correcting her, gentle as he always had been, firm as he always must be. Her muscles wanted to tremble, but he soothed them as if she were a wild horse. *"The Storm will work for you. Be its equal."*

"How am I supposed to equal a god?" she hissed.

He was gone, of course. He'd never been there. He was dead, like all the rest she'd loved. But the shield held, the faux ceiling above cooling, and she lowered her arm. She stood in a domed room, unbearably hot from the rock, but also safe because the weight above was held by a perfect arch.

"Fuck me," Armitage said.

Someone teased forth a little light. Amir, of course. He was always faster than Faust and Larochette, the other two not yet holding the Storm, and here he was using the Sway. Vertiline saw the faces about her. Armitage, by her side, and—*Three's mercy*—Evanne getting to her feet. Tarragon was nearby; Vertiline's daughter helped the once-fairy up.

The dragon was hard to miss. He tried to rise, knocked his scaled head against the low ceiling, and said, *//COULD YOU NOT HAVE MADE THE ROOM BIGGER?//*

Vertiline swore there was nothing beside Myryntir two eye blinks past, but no, there was Pakhet, the tiger looking dusty, all flat ears and lashing tail. She turned to see the sinner crouched beside the merchant Amber and his sister Jade. Sight of Day and Sands Apart examined the wall of the dome, hands moving fast as they spoke at a speed no human could keep up with. Heser was a boulder next to a stunned Raven Queen. The guardsman's armour was beat about and dusty, but Morgan looked unharmed. Her protector still did his job well. *Good.*

The spectre, Hitch, completed the group as he stepped through the wall and headed toward Evanne. Ghostly blue footprints faded in his wake. "Well, this is cosy."

THERE WAS, OF COURSE, NO WAY OUT. THE WALLS WERE A PERFECT dome of cooled rock. The only person—if he could be called such—who could get in and out was Hitch.

The spectre hung about Evanne like a gloomy cloud. "There's a lot of rock, like, everywhere."

Vertiline's hand twitched above her sword hilt. "I'm not certain I can murder a man already dead, but I'd be willing to give it a try."

He *tsk'd*. "The good news is, soon you'll all be dead, and we can have a proper ghost party. No need to sleep or eat. No getting tired! We'll all hang about this domed room forever, waiting for a future archaeologist to unearth us, or the world to crack again and spit us out."

"I'm thirsty," Meriwether said. "I think I speak for all of us when I say, I'd like a drink before I die."

Vertiline glared at the sinner. "What would you propose? Can you conjure water?"

"Well, yes."

"Can you conjure water without the Three taking your soul?"

"Probably not," he conceded. "You have the Sway, though. Can you not," he wobbled his hand like a bird with a broken wing, "magic some up?"

"I could," she allowed. "I would age and die if I kept it up, and then you'd die of thirst anyway. I'd prefer a more permanent solution to our situation. If it comes to it, I will—"

//I'M GETTING CRAMP.//

"What the lizard's trying to get across is, it's tight in here." Armitage stretched, then put a companionable hand on the dragon's leg. "Isn't that right?"

Myryntir stared at Armitage's hand like a person who's had a bee land on their nose. *//YOU'RE TOUCHING ME.//*

"You're warm."

"*The whole room is warm.*" Pakhet uncurled from near the wall. "*It's rather nice.*"

"Hitch." Evanne stood. "Can you wander about and see what's out there?"

"Rock," the ghost said.

"Further on."

"More rock."

Vertiline's daughter growled. "And past that?"

"What about up?" Meriwether glanced at the domed roof. "Have you tried up?"

Hitch gave the sinner a blue-eyed stare. "Well, of course not. That's where the sky is."

"We'll never dig that far. Just a little way up." He sighed. "Those things that attacked us—"

"Curators," Hitch said. "A late-stage invention during the war designed to—"

"Yes, sure," Meriwether said. "I'm sure they're very fancy. The thing is, Myryntir might be big and fat—"

//HEY.//

"But he's not *that* chunky—"

//THANKS.//

"He's not big enough to crater the earth down five hundred metres, which is about where we are. Which means the Curators were close to the surface. We blew one up—"

"Technically it blew itself up."

The holomancer closed his eyes, pressing his fingers into his temples, and took a deep breath. "What I'm getting at is there's got to be a middle laneway. A place they all hung about for Curator parties, waiting for a stupid dragon to—"

//WATCH IT.//

"My apologies. A clumsy dragon," Meriwether ignored Myryntir's glare, "to break the crust off the pie and get to the meaty centre. We need but travel the small distance to that place and find the doorway out. It'll be a cinch. Why, Tilly and I have done this hundreds of times."

Vertiline could feel the frost in her stare. "Hundreds?"

"It's more than zero and less than a hundred, perhaps. I'm hazy on the details. The only thing we need worry about is avoiding Personates, because they're nasty pieces of work."

"Personates won't be down here." Hitch crossed not-arms. "They are Vehement creations. The Curators are not. The Curators were made as a kind of antitoxin to the wiles of Vehement and Itikari."

"Who is their master?" Vertiline watched Hitch's body language. *He is concerned, not afraid. He fought them before and won, but lost comrades perhaps.*

"No one, now." Hitch sighed blue. "They should not have attacked, because there are no treasures for them to guard."

"Treasures?" Amber perked up. "Perhaps this caravan is not a complete loss."

"I'll go check... up," Hitch offered. "I'll let you know if there are treasures or Curators."

"I just care about a nice, soothing corridor," Meriwether said. "We can remove the vermin at our leisure."

PIECE BY PIECE IT BECAME CLEAR. HITCH DESCRIBED A CAUSEWAY collection a few metres above their head. He said it was connected to other tunnels higher up by way of a vertical shaft. This was sadly caved in by the explosion-meets-dragon incident. The spectre said digging up ten metres would bring them into an open space.

//AND HOW ARE YOU GOING TO DIG A HOLE BIG ENOUGH FOR ME?//

The spectre gave the dragon a withering stare. "You great clod, *I'm* not digging. I'm dead! I don't have hands, and if I did, they wouldn't be real. The rest of me isn't real either. *You're* digging."

//I'M NOT A DOG.//

"No, you're a bloody great dragon with clawed feet. Get cracking." The ghost crossed his arms.

//THEY'RE HANDS.//

"Three's mercy," Vertiline breathed. "It is no great surprise to me why dragons became extinct."

//WE'RE NOT EXTINCT. I'M RIGHT HERE.// The dragon gave a cerulean, toothy smile. *//SEE?//*

"You were a corpse when I found you," Evanne reminded him.

//A TRIFLING TECHNICALITY. WE DRAGONS ARE VERY RESISTANT TO DEATH.//

"He's not wrong," Meriwether said. "Ormeon is tougher than a bag of stones. She also has a higher work ethic. I guess the reds are just better than the blues, hey?"

Myryntir rounded on the sinner. *//BLUES ARE THE BEST.//*

"Then blues best get digging."

The dragon growled, then turned on the wall of the dome and smashed into it. He clawed great furrows in the rock, mighty muscles bunching under scale as the creature turned rock into sand. Meriwether watched with a smile on his face. Vertiline sidled up to him. "I see what you did there."

"The best part is, Myryntir saw what I did too, yet he must dig or prove me right."

"You're entirely too pleased with yourself."

His smile dimmed. "There is carrot and stick, but I find neither fits my hand right. I am sick with worry for Geneve, and I will use any trick I can to get to her."

"Could you open a gate by yourself? You are a Holomancer." Vertiline ducked as a chunk of rock spun free of Myryntir's excavation.

"Perhaps." Meriwether looked at his feet. "The book had nothing to say on the matter, but I will try if we have no other course. No, don't say it. I know Geneve would kill me if I opened the portal and died in the attempt." His lips twisted in a wry smile. "She would bring me back to kill me again."

"She has brought you back once before. I can see her doing it again, it's true." Vertiline tried for levity but failed. "I miss my sister of the blade. What is she like?"

"Marvellous." He shrugged. "You know Geneve."

"Sixteen years, though—"

"If you are wondering if she hates you Tilly, be at peace. She yearns to be here, not only because she misses this world, but the people in it. You did naught amiss. The portal opened, it closed, and that was on me."

"On you?" She felt vaguely sick. "I was set to guard it."

"By all accounts, guard it you did, but after it closed it was just a rocky floor. The magic ... left. We fell a long way. Time and distance are different there." His fingers clutched the air, struggling to catch an explanation just out of reach. "We couldn't find our way back. Oh, we looked. We looked a *lot*. And when you opened this latest portal, we saw it as if it were a beacon just over the horizon. Geneve ran toward it, Ormeon overhead. It wouldn't have been the first trick the demons tried on us, and she always broke their line while I held the rear. I turned, and she was gone, the portal open, and I, I..." His face had a glassy, fixed stare, a man trying to explain a great sin. "I stepped through."

"Because you thought she was here."

"Obviously she wasn't. I should have *felt* it, Tilly. She is my heart. She is in my blood. And I missed her, let something so precious slip through my fingers." He straightened. "So, if coaxing willing from a belligerent dragon is what I must do to see her again, it is what I will do."

Vertiline chewed on that, the sickness still with her, but fading. "You say you held the rear. You've learned some skills since you were here."

"Ha! Geneve is a good teacher."

"She's a *terrible* teacher." Vertiline held up a hand because it looked like the sinner wanted to start something. "We must all try teaching those who come to Tresward keeps. It is not a task reserved for those who carry the black. Teaching is how we learn best." She smiled at a memory, bright and clear even after all these years. "There was one time Geneve stood before a class of children, barely more than a child herself. Iz and I, we'd taken her out a few times, me lovestruck and him a liar."

"Easy, Tilly." He wasn't admonishing her, hand on her arm a gentle touch. "He loved his daughter more than he loved life."

"It is in the past." She straightened. "She showed aptitude with steel, but the Light evaded her. She had perfect form, though. Geneve stood before this class, demonstrating how to hold the blade, how to stand, but also how to *be*. Geneve was *pure*, Meri. She brooked no error, because it was against the Three's purpose. She made a bad teacher because she could see no room for mistakes in serving the Three."

"Ha! The good news is, she's changed."

"You what?"

"I think if she meets the Three, she will have words. About how humans are not pawns, about how being mysterious and godly is a dick move, that kind of thing."

She snorted a laugh. "And you?"

He glanced sideways at her. "I've always thought they were dicks."

Vertiline's snort turned into a bray. "I've missed you, sinner."

Meriwether grabbed her arm, his grip firm, insistent, so unlike him. "You were ever in our hearts, Tilly. You, and the cat, and Armitage." He let her go. "It looks like the dragon's broken through. Let's go see what's out there."

Chapter Nineteen

Evanne scrabbled through the hole Myryntir made. It was big enough for a dragon; thus her size was no problem at all, but the dragon's claws weren't shovels. The floor was rough, the craggy visage of an ancient man, each wrinkle threatening to grab her foot and twist an ankle.

Mama, up until two seconds ago thick as thieves with the lordling, appeared to notice the dragon had finished, and her wayward daughter was once again about to leap into danger. "Evanne! Let me go first."

Evanne waited, because while being wilful had its own rewards, her machete wasn't a match for foes in quite the same way as a Knight with the Storm as her ally. Her mother made it beside her, not having the good grace to breathe hard. "The floor is treacherous."

"And the sky is blue."

Vertiline gave her a little side eye. "You have the bit between your teeth."

Evanne showed her not-quite-shark-teeth in a feral smile. "A bit implies a bridle."

Vertiline laughed. "Truth." She turned her face upward, to where the tunnel broke into another room. Evanne could hear Myryntir's bellows breath from up ahead. No sound of violence. "Trap?"

"I don't think so." Evanne closed her eyes, listening. "There is something there, though. A lost soul."

"You have learned much since we parted."

"I don't know." Evanne looked at her feet. "I think you taught me a bunch of stuff I ignored, and I had to stop ignoring it."

Her mother held silence for a spell. "You have grown into a strong woman, daughter."

"But not a warrior?" Evanne heard a slight tone of bitterness in her voice and tried to iron it out. "I am no Tresward. My blood is ... *dirty*."

Vertiline looked up the tunnel, then back down. "Armitage!"

"What?"

"Hold the troops a moment."

Her father looked up the tunnel. "There are no 'troops', Tilly. There's me, the runt, and—"

"Hold them. Perhaps set the guardsman to keep a rear picket against further incursion. The Raven Queen should not be placed in danger."

Papa pursed his lips, looked at Evanne, back to Vertiline, then turned around and bawled, "Take five! You. Yeah, you! Pretty boy."

"My name is Amir—"

"I don't give a shit. You're with me. Let's count our supplies."

Evanne watched her father stride out of view, then turned to Mama. "We should—"

"Your blood is full of starlight, Evanne." Vertiline cupped her cheek. "All know it. There is naught but the brilliance of the heavens within you."

Evanne bit her lip. "But..." She growled. *Words are my thing. Why do they vex me now?* "I've never been able to ... *be* with you at the school. That's your most important thing. You've dedicated your life to it." Her mother looked to be about to boil over, so she pressed on. "I can't be Tresward. And I know you hold me far from the front line. You, um. You are a warrior, Mama. And I'm not."

The space between them seemed to stretch as Vertiline's hand fell from Evanne's face. "You are right. You are no warrior."

"I'm ... what?" Evanne felt the hot stab of envy, a little anger in there. *I fucken knew it.*

"But you are not right about the rest. You are no warrior because I kept you from being one. I carry steel so you don't have to. It is my wish you are never in harm's way. I know it's not possible, so I built a city around you to keep you safe. I trained warriors to guard it, and brokered a deal with the Three to never set foot upon our land while I built their new Tresward. They promised to keep you safe in return. You've become what I can't be, and your father could only dream of. You are a leader true. You command because people love you."

"I ... command?"

Vertiline straightened. "A woman with the gift of swords put down her wings to walk in your footsteps. A tiger of impossible strength journeys by your side. A dragon listens when you speak."

//ONLY BECAUSE SHE IS SO LOUD.//

"But I'm ... Half-Made." She scrubbed at the human skin of her forearm. "I'm not human enough to live in their world. I'm not Vhemin enough to be welcome in theirs."

"Perhaps you are welcome in none. Perhaps you are welcome in all." A shrug. "Is the glass half-empty?"

"You're saying I should stop moping."

"I'm saying we should go up here to see what the dragon's uncovered. A lost soul, you called it."

//IT'S NOT LOST. I FOUND IT.//

"Come." Vertiline's hand fell to the hilt of her sword. "Let me show you why I'm so proud of you."

It was a ghoul. Evanne walked a circle around the hunched creature. Human once, no doubt about it. Thick, ropey muscle promised a world of hurt if it ever got over what looked to be just fear of a dragon busting into its home. The room Myryntir furrowed into was smooth-walled, made of a cream-coloured material that offered a pale luminance. It was huge, big enough to hold a handful of dragons and their riders. A giant structure of metal bars rose against one wall, and a single Curator lay there.

This room is a holding place for the Curators. Where they ... sleep? Evanne glanced at a massive door, which looked the obvious exit. She could imagine—once they broke it down—Myryntir would be able to stride through with wings outstretched.

Hitch pointed at the ghoul. "We've seen these things before."

"I don't think so." Evanne crouched at a safe distance. "The ones at the hospital had their souls taken away and encased in stone. Metal sat in their skulls whispering dreams of death. This one is just ... *here.*"

Tarragon appeared at the tunnel's mouth. "You found a ghoul."

"I was just saying that." Evanne frowned. "Why is there just one in here? How long's it been here?"

Pakhet popped into visibility beside her. *"Perhaps it is a guardian like I was. Left to hold the fort, and no one told it the war was over."*

"The war isn't over," Evanne said. "The war just ... slept."

"My, you're cheery today."

"She's right." Vertiline examined the struts holding the one dead Curator. Evanne saw the Tricks she told herself to be the High Justiciar. How her mother hugged herself, but made the posture look like the crossed arms of defiance. And how her body was deliberately relaxed, despite the razor wire of fear for Papa and her daughter running through her spine. "The war never ended. The only thing that changed was who did the bleeding." Vertiline dropped her arms, her metal hand flexing, grasping at an old memory.

"Everyone is cheery."

"People die." Tarragon strode up to the ghoul, halting at a lunge's distance. "And others live forever with the burden of it."

Evanne sidled up to her, reaching a cautious hand toward her arm. She felt the heat there, the very humanness of her, yet still not as warm as when she'd been a fairy. "New people join them, too."

"Aye." The once-fairy nodded. "It is a treasure to travel this road with you."

"YoU wIll alL diE." The ghoul straightened as much as it was able. The words coming from its rotted lips were soft, a verbal slurry mixed into gruel by too little meal and too much time.

Myryntir turned his long neck, leaning his head toward the creature. *//AND YOU'RE GOING TO MAKE US DIE WITH WHICH ARMY, EXACTLY?//*

"iT is wRitTeN." The ghoul raised a crooked arm to the ceiling. "CaN you NOt seE it In thE StaRS?"

"I'm going to end this horror's misery." Tarragon drew Requiem in a swift motion, blue-white radiance spilling across the floor.

"Hold." Evanne's mouth was—once again—running off ahead of her brain. "Something's amiss. This man doesn't bring us a threat, but a warning."

The ghoul nodded, pale decayed eyes seeing everything, or perhaps nothing. "We aRe chaInEd."

"Curators," Meri murmured. "Curators of what?"

"You move really quietly for an old man." Evanne glared at him. "Where did you come from? And what do you mean?"

"You put a curator in charge of a library, or—"

"Sinner, not everyone uses libraries." Vertiline was still facing the struts. "They must have had hundreds in here."

"Fair. You put curators in charge of something needing curation. Right there in the name, see?" The Lord du Reeves circled the ghoul. "You need a curator to look after artefacts and treasures." The ghoul nodded. "And here we are, right in the nest. I suspect our friend here is giving us a friendly warning."

Evanne tapped her fingers on the hilt of her machete, drumming out a little ditty to lift her spirits. The beat circled her feet, walked across to Tarragon, and relaxed her lover. The once-fairy lowered her sword. Evanne let her fingers fall. "That's not what we need to know."

"It's not?" Meriwether blinked.

"It's not," she agreed. "What we need to know is why he's here. This ghoul has been in this place for hundreds of years. We've seen the Itikari chain souls to their purpose before. At the hospital, the dead were wardens, an undying army to protect those still living. On *Dancing in the Storm* spirits were chained into furniture to act as tireless guardians. And here," she gestured at the room, "we have a place full of curious devices and another undying creature."

"This is not Itikari." Tarragon's voice carried an edge as sharp as Requiem.

Ah, I see. Evanne touched Tarragon's arm again, gentle like a sea breeze. "Not all the Itikari made was wrought wrong. No, I can hear the words before you say them. You didn't pass your exams. You are the only one still living who carries the burden of that. We know Vehement Systems tried to make better Feybrind and turned out the Vhemin. They forged Artifices to fight the dragons. Personates to defeat the Tresward, all in an effort to make a better sword than the other had. Is it so odd to consider here we find a ghoul crimped in the image of Itikari's guardians by another smith?"

Tarragon's shoulders slumped, her voice small. "We were the good ones. The best ones."

Evanne wanted to spend more time with her in this moment, but there was an everliving monster prophesying annihilation to her right. She turned. "Creature, what awaits us here?"

"DoOm—"

"Yes, of course." Evanne waved her hand. "Specifics. Try being precise."

"Or, *they* could tell us." Meri's tone was artificially bright. Evanne followed his pointed arm toward the big doors. There was a small doorway set into it she'd not spotted earlier, and the nagging concern of *where is Sight of Day* was answered as the golden-eyed cat came pacing through, followed by Sands Apart.

Sands Apart slammed the small door shut while Sight of Day sprinted toward them. He appeared to be entirely unfazed, bar the lashing of his tail. *{While you were making new friends, we found a silver pool.}*

Evanne narrowed her eyes. "I don't like pools. The last one I found at the hospital had an ancient scapegrace that tried to eat me. Is this the same?"

Sight of Day wavered his hand in a *maybe so* gesture. *{Similar. Metal warriors come from the pool. They are agitated.}*

"Time to get to work." Vertiline broke off her exacting examination of the struts.

"KiLl me, pLeaSe." The ghoul reached out with a sloppy gesture.

"Hmm." Meri frowned. "He could have useful intelligence. We should—"

He stopped talking as the ghoul's head bounced to his feet. All eyes turned to Tarragon, her perfect slice held at neck height a moment longer before she sheathed her blade. "I have lived in service to masters without the ability to say no."

Meri looked at the head, then her, seemed about to say something, checked himself, opened his mouth, checked himself again, then said, "You know what? Fair enough."

She has done the right thing. The only thing, and yet we feel there must have been another way. Evanne kept her voice low, no Trick in it. "Mercy isn't always easy." *The undead horror seemed ... healthier than what we've seen before. More of a person. And perhaps more aware of what his unlife became.* "It could be the hardest thing." She turned to the door. "Let's see what's—"

The small door exploded inward, showering the room with fragments of metal and that strange, alabaster material. Myryntir was between them and the door and took the worst of it. The big lizard was tossed over Evanne's head like a dog's chew toy. He rolled, wings tearing rents in the ceiling and floor.

Dust billowed into the room. Stalking into it were silver figures. They flared, living energy shaped as people. Evanne counted five as she drew her machete. Vertiline ran at them, each perfect step cracking the floor, sending rivulets of golden light across the ground. Tarragon screamed, Requiem high, sprinting past Evanne.

She looked at her machete and thought, *what am I even doing?* Everyone was faster than her and had magic swords or godly powers. Then she saw Papa, just a man, but with a big rock in hand, because his family were on the field. He shouldered it, then launched it into the pack of glimmering enemies. The rock was the size of a human head, and when it hit the lead figure, Evanne expected the glimmering form to fall.

The rock superheated to white and sloughed into spattering, molten material in an eye blink.

Evanne looked at her machete again. *We are so boned.*

Sight of Day tapped her on the shoulder. She would have screamed if she hadn't been numbed by the explosion, and she briefly wondered how he'd got there. *{You should get to cover.}*

"You're not!"

{I am getting you, then getting to cover.} He gave a half-smile as Vertiline clashed with the first figure, her golden blade spraying yellow and white as her enemy's shimmering weapon darted with the speed of dawn. *{This is not a fight one can win with simple courage.}*

Evanne sheathed her machete, angry, and if she was honest, frightened. "Get Sands Apart. Keep them," she stabbed an arm at the startled Amber and Jade newly emerged from the tunnel, "safe."

{When you say safe, do you mean—}

Evanne lost what the cat said as she spun to Myryntir. The dragon lay on his back, dazed, tongue lolling like a giant dog knocked into a coma. She ran to him. *Courage might not win the day, but that's why we brought a dragon.* "Myryntir!"

The dragon said nothing, eyes a glassy blue. His chest rose and fell like a bellows, his body silted in debris. She heard Vertiline's war-cry, the clash of Light and energy showering the room with flickering illumination that clouded her vision. It was bright, and hot, and both her human and Vhemin eyes could make little sense of it. Tarragon's yell joined Mama's and she heard the arcing sizzle of Requiem. *The sword brings justice*, she realised. *But it is but one blade.*

She put a hand on the dragon's snout. Tapped the hilt of her machete as she'd done before. Leaned close to Myryntir's skull and hummed to him. She knew no dragony songs, or if they could dance, but she knew his heart. *You are brave. Proud to a fault, but never have you left us alone. We need your strength.*

We need your love.

The dragon snorted, sneezed, and surged upright. Evanne backpedalled, almost lost the beat with her feet, but kept her tapping going, her balance upright. *//HAVOC?//* He sounded uncertain.

"Myryntir. Dragon!" His head swivelled to her, and she saw his eyes mark her fingers on her machete. And watched as a slow, iceglare grin spread as his jaws widened, the crackle of energy arcing between his teeth. "We need you."

The dragon turned to the melee. Vertiline and Tarragon were joined by Amir, the three fighting as one. It might have been backwash from Mama's Light, but it seemed as if Requiem's blue-white glow was joined by a haze of gold as the once-fairy patterned alongside the Knights.

The creatures they fought were pure energy. She saw Tarragon run one through with her blade, spatters of liquid metal hitting the ground, electricity flurries dancing away like sprites. The quicksilver creature didn't slow, rounding on her with an overhead slash. Tarragon swayed like the wind, tearing the blade through the side of the creature in a manoeuvre that would have ended any other opponent, then blocking with high guard. *//THEY ARE MADE OF LIGHTNING AND METAL. I'M NOT SURE I CAN HURT THEM.//*

Evanne made a big show of her surprise, offering a Trick alongside her drumming fingers. "And you call yourself a dragon?" She snorted for effect; the dragon wouldn't have heard it over the noise, but he saw the cant of her head. "*Quitter.*"

He roared, rounding on their foes. He breathed in, a gods' forge bellows, then spat energy in a crackling thunderstorm at their foes. Lightning leaped from creature to creature, the room incandescent. Evanne's vision whitened out, and she lost her rhythm for a moment.

When her sight cleared, Tarragon, Vertiline, and Amir stood amid a smoking battlefield. Five pools of liquid silver bubbled and hissed on the ground. Evanne patted Myryntir's hide. "Good dragon."

//I AM NOT A DOG.//

She started running to Tarragon, then stopped. The room felt colder, her breath steaming white. The pools continued bubbling, then shimmered. One crowned, a head rising from the morass, silver white eyes full of fury.

Meriwether touched her arm. "Attend. They are—"

"I see it," she snapped. "They are dead, as the ghoul was."

"I was going to say, 'getting back up', but your version works." He pointed to the door. "We must run."

{There is a pool out there made from this stuff. I don't feel like running that way.} Sands Apart was joined by Sight of Day. She looked angry, tail lashing. *{We need a better option.}*

"Three's mercy," Evanne strode forward.

Vertiline's eyes widened as she saw her daughter approaching danger, metal hand up. "Back! It isn't safe. We must—"

"I don't want to hear it." Evanne closed her eyes, reached down, and felt for that place she'd entered at the hospital, when the unliving masters tried to take her Tarragon. Saw the chains about her, white and hot rather than green and vile, but chains all the same. Touched them, grabbed, and snapped.

She opened her eyes in time to see a warrior slump back into a puddle, no energy remaining. The pool was no longer living metal, cooling to a mirror's surface.

Myryntir leaned forward, nose to the pool, then faced her. *//MAYBE LEAD WITH THAT NEXT TIME.//*

Chapter Twenty

The cavernous passage was chilly. Tarragon rubbed her arms. *In the world above it is spring. Here, everything sleeps but the dead. I don't even have my glimmer anymore.* She eyed Evanne. Her lover walked with a straight back, head on a swivel, but also hugged herself with the cold. *Her Vhemin blood is no good here.*

By agreement, they had left Heser the Cheg and Morgan at the cave-in site. They needed a rear-guard almost not at all, but it gave the guardsman something to do other than fretting his queen was in danger. They would go back for him later.

The source of the silver men was clear. The passage was five klicks long, easy as you please, and a good five hundred metres wide. All along one wall were human-sized capsules, spaced about a metre apart, and stacked ten to the ceiling. Tarragon checked her math. *Say three hundred pods a klick gives us fifteen hundred columns. By ten rows, that's an army of fifteen thousand souls.*

And souls were what they were. She'd checked a capsule as they entered. Within was a shimmering humanoid form, eyes closed in somnolent repose, but the once-fairy could *feel* the energy within. A whole bank of the things had been crushed in some long-ago cave-in, allowing a silvery fluid to pool on the floor. The living metal the souls inhabited created a long, shallow millpond Tarragon imagined must have shimmered before Evanne's magic released the dead to their deserved rest.

Myryntir placed a clawed hand in the pool, then lifted it and took a sniff. *//IT SMELLS OF NOTHING AT ALL.//* He shook the fluid off, then continued their weary trudge south.

Tarragon sidled up to Amir. He brightened at her approach. "Ho, shieldmaiden."

"Ho, dickhead."

He laughed. "I meant no disrespect, lady. Where I come from the term is given with respect."

"I meant no disrespect either. Where I come from, dickhead is often given as a moniker of warmth and love."

The smile didn't leave his face as he turned eyes front. "We come from very different worlds."

Tarragon nodded her agreement. "It makes you wonder, though." At his quizzical glance, she gestured to herself in a *see?* motion. "You hail from Imshir—"

"I hail from the lands beyond the sea. I do not call Imshir home."

Curious, but whatever. "My makers gave me this," she tugged wheat-pale hair, "and this," she tapped her bare, honey-brown forearm. "Your hair is dark as night, but your skin and mine are a match. The people who made me were trying to say something."

He walked on in silence for a spell, mulling over what she said. *I like this man from not-Imshir. I like his brazenness. I like how he holds the line. I like how he tries to listen to what I mean, not what I say.* "I have no special knowledge of what being a fairy is like. I envy the experience of being a bright spark in a dark world." His eyes hooded for a moment, some memory clouding his mind. "I imagine the Itikari thought to make a marvel, and they succeeded. No, don't interrupt. I see it in the set of your shoulders. You think your magic sword is what makes the difference in each fight. I saw many battles before I took the black sash, and there is nothing in the weapon. It's all in the man." He brightened. "It is not your skill with steel that makes you a marvel. It is how you are made from all the pieces of beauty put together."

"You're saying your skin is beautiful?"

"Of course," he said, and she laughed. "The Itikari made things pleasing to our eyes, although we've learned their purpose wasn't pure. It pains me to admit I have always felt lesser to the Feybrind and their wondrous ways." He ignored Sands Apart's glance. "Dragons are amazing, and with all I have done, it is a blessing to have lived to see one grace the skies."

//FINALLY. SOME RESPECT.//

Tarragon teased that through the fingers of her mind for a moment. "What do you mean, all you have done?"

He took off his cloak. "Give this to Evanne. She is cold."

"You're dodging the question."

"I'm buying time to answer."

Tarragon took the cloak, marvelling at how dust-free it was. *Amir is prideful, but that has charm too.* She sidled up to Evanne, draping the cloak about her shoulders. "Here, love."

Evanne drew it closer, then leaned into Tarragon for a moment. Her voice sounded thin as if strained through cheesecloth. "Thank you."

"It's more than the cold, isn't it?"

"I released a clutch of souls from an ancient prison. I felt them go, Tarragon. I felt them all go." She looked away. "Some of them wanted to stay."

"Mercy isn't always easy," Tarragon quoted.

She was rewarded with a wan smile. "As you say." Evanne nodded to Amir. "You are breaking his shell to get at the sweet secrets within?"

"You should do it. You're better at these things."

Evanne snorted. "Amir is scared of me. He's more scared of Mama. He will tell you things he won't say to me." She tugged the cloak tighter. "Besides. I'm in no mood for Tricks. I wouldn't mind a rest." The maybe-Vhemin glanced at the rank of glimmering cylinders. "There may be a time and place for peace, once we're clear of here." She made a shooing motion. "Go. I'll be fine. Give my thanks to Amir for the cloak."

Tarragon hurried to catch up with Amir. "You were saying?"

He pointed to the ceiling. "Faust. Now there's a man with a past. Have you noticed how he moves ever so quietly for such a large man?

We locked blades with the Vide, and much of how they spar reminds me of Faust before he learned the Three's patterns."

"Why are we speaking of Faust?"

"Larochette, now there's a marvel. The woman fights with ferocity, but do you know where it comes from? I do."

Tarragon blinked. "You're speaking of your fellow students? Why—"

"I mean to tell you a story, lady, and it is hard for me to speak it. There is much blood behind me, and I wager more ahead. I tell you of Faust because his past is his own, but his calling to the Three is pure. Larochette found herself in a poor situation because of those she wronged but serves the Light now. As do I."

Tarragon pursed her lips. "I don't understand."

"Then let me tell you."

Chapter Twenty-One

The smell was never something Amir got used to. It wasn't anything like sewage, nor the musky reek of an unclean animal pen. He'd been in a lot of places. Did a stint in the army, because he wanted to leave a horrible place, without understanding you can find new horror just over the next hill. He'd spent time throwing drunks out of taverns. Even kept a special pair of boots for the work, as drunks contained more bile, gram for gram, than anyone else in the world. He'd even sold his sword that one time. He'd slipped a blade into the grossly fat back of a wannabe sultan who hadn't bathed in five years because an 'oracle' said it would wash away his power.

None of those smells, not the sewage, pens, barracks, vomit, or the sultan of slime were like the cages.

The bars weren't the exciting, Smith-forged constructs made to hold a sinner and their power on the inside. He'd seen those; well-made, fashioned by people who cared about who was on justice's docket, but also sure to see those on the outside safe, too. No, *these* cages were all rust and spite, the bars—if you were brave enough to touch them—a riot of bumpy edges cast in rust relief and shit-stained divots.

Within, souls. More people than should be in one place, and then they added more atop. Calling them souls was a kindness, because those on the inside were the worst kind of fuckwit. Murderers, they had plenty of those in stock. Shake that cage at the front and a whole sweaty armpit of rapists would fall out. He glanced to his left, because that's where the torturers were. Torture, apparently, was a thing you could get paid well for, but only in the service of a lordling. This lot were *entrepreneurs*. They'd taken it on themselves to put neighbours, dogs, or whatever poor mange-ridden creature passed their gaze into a chair or table, and then worked on them until someone went to find out what all the screaming was about.

They had a few terrorists, too. Amir didn't know what made a terrorist different from a soldier, but maybe it was the same as the torturers. If you had a writ from the just and high saying what you were doing was fine, it was all well and good. These people hadn't taken the time to get the right paperwork.

The one type of criminal they didn't have were slavers, because that's what Amir was. By the Three's watchful gaze, they had writs, seals, promises, and gold saying their work was sanctioned. Slavery was still a crime unless you marched under a ruler's banner. He didn't much mind, because it paid well, and murderers and torturers weren't the kinds of people who should be on the same streets as someone's children.

Still, no one here had a sense of humour, and that was worrisome. It left evenings boring, but fights were worse because Amir held no truck with a man who couldn't laugh. One of those at your back, well, perhaps you'd be better off standing alone.

Except for the big man. That one they'd picked up a few stops back. Amir was surprised such a person would want to hire on with the caravan, what with his expensive clothes and fine weapons, but such a monster would be good in a fight. He nudged his horse closer to the giant. "Roust, was it?"

"Faust." Even the man's voice was giant-sized, deep like a cavern, solid like a mountain.

"Not a name from around here." Amir played the line out.

"It is not." No bites, clearly.

"A name like that could be from wealth." Amir raised a suggestive eyebrow. "If you need a hand writing your will, I'm good with my letters."

The giant snorted, then returned to his sombre repose. The horse beneath him was also a monster, yet managed to look put upon as it eyed Amir's nimble mare. "You would only take a portion, I imagine?"

"No, I'd fleece you for the lot." Amir turned his eyes front. "I figure I'd spend some of it on soap."

"For these poor souls?" The way Faust said 'poor souls' made it sound like he was reading lines for a play.

"Murderers deserve little from us, and they'll return some meagre value to the world before we wear them down to the nub. No, I need a good camomile lather to get this smell out of my gear. This," he tugged his leather jerkin, "used to smell of a horse's ass. Now it smells of general ass, and something worse."

"Effluent?"

"If it was mere shit, good Faust, I could do something with that. It's like the unhappy marriage of shit and despair, I guess."

"You've been married?"

"Never had the luck."

"I have." Faust sighed. "It was good, until it wasn't."

"She must have been a mighty woman."

"Aye. Good of soul, good of heart."

"No, I meant, you know." Amir tugged an invisible woman onto his seated lap. "Because you'd crush the air from a lesser person."

Faust gave him a long, hard stare. "I have killed men for less."

"As have I, but then you'd have no one to talk to while trying not to think of the smell."

That earned a tight smile. "And your story, Amir?"

The monster knows my name. What a day. "Running from something, or to something. I can never work out which."

"And which would you prefer?"

"I don't know." Amir turned the idea over. "I guess I'd like to stop running."

"Ah." Faust turned his eyes front. "There is a way. But it's long, and not many know the road."

"You're an odd one. You're not old Khiton in disguise?"

"Khiton?" Faust spat. "The gods have earned none of my love, but least of all that one."

Amir felt a pit was opening before him and skirted it. "Have you named them?"

Faust gave him the best side-eye of the trip. "The gods already have names."

"No, this lot." Amir pointed to the torturer's cage. "That one without all the fingers of his left hand looks like a Three-Fingered Romullo."

"Remarkably specific."

"It passes the time." Amir looked to the front, where the murderers were. They, for the most part, ignored him. All but the woman, who'd watched him from the moment she'd entered the cage. "What's her story?"

Faust sighed. "Regret. Remorse. Woe."

"I'm glad woe's in there. You were running out of R words."

The giant stared at him for a moment. "You jest, Amir, but mark: no one in that cage is there because they made the best choice they could."

Amir sighed. "You're missing one thing. They're also all there because they made a mistake."

"Killing someone? That's hardly an error." Faust's tone said he was used to that kind of work, perhaps on all days of the week barring Wednesdays.

"No." Amir scrubbed road dust from his hair. "They got caught."

SHE KEEPS LOOKING AT ME. IT WAS THE MOST DAMNABLE THING. NO matter where he was, her eyes followed him. Mess tent? He'd look up from a bowl of gruel and there she was. That made sense, because even gruel was better than what they got. Then he left the row of tents providing faux modesty for the latrine and, right there, right *fucking there* her eyes were on him again.

It got eerie, then it got funny. He chipped in shoeing the horses. Looking up, sweat dripping from his brow, he saw her. Hands on bars, eyes intent.

So, he made a game of it. Tried to sidle past rows of tents, the side of a wagon, even mingled in with other guards. No dice, of course. Eyes everywhere.

There was nothing for it. *I have to talk to her.*

Speaking to the merchandise wasn't forbidden. The usual advice was given by the caravaner. *Don't believe them* was front of mind. *Don't give them anything. Saw a man kill a guard with a piece of stale bread that one time.* Amir had trouble believing it, but he'd been in enough places to know death found a man whether he wanted it or not. The only thing uncanny about death was its persistence, much like the woman's eyes.

"Don't do it," Faust said.

Amir jumped. The giant found him as if by accident, uncannily quiet on those big feet. "You know what they say about men with big feet, hey?"

"Big di—"

"Big shoes," Amir said. "Yours are very quiet. How do you do that?"

"Stop changing the subject." Faust leaned against a stack of crates. "You were going to talk to her."

"Of course. She has some kind of devil's eye."

"Have you ever had a dog?"

Amir blinked. "You what?"

"A dog. Usually about so high," he placed a hand level with his knees, "but they come smaller and larger depending on your fancy."

"No. I've never had a dog. Wouldn't mind one, but—"

"Dogs have an ability to know the soft touch in a group. The one most likely to give a treat or a pat when it's wanted. They'll follow such a man most anywhere. The privy, for example."

"She's not followed me there. She's in a cage."

"She's watched you enter and leave. I'll bet she knows more about you than your own mother." Faust wasn't smiling. "And she's learned that just by being patient. Imagine what she'll do if she gets to trade words."

"Words are more or less my thing."

"You jest, friend Amir, but you are good with a blade."

"You've never seen me with a blade." Amir frowned. He was *sure* he'd remember drawing steel around someone so full of promised menace. And were they friends? Sometimes it felt like it, but others...

"Two nights back there was a scuffle in the torturer's cage."

"Aye. I remember." Amir nodded. "Some fool left a spoon in a mongrel's bowl, and—"

"And you walked into the middle of it. Unbolted the cage, knocked out three men, disarmed the imbecile with the spoon, and kicked him in the groin. Good blow. Made me wince."

"I didn't use a blade."

"You *had* a blade. It's the same one you wear there." Faust pointed at Amir's hip. "No one took it from you. The way you moved said you knew how it would feel in your hand. Like you were lovers but not talking because of a tiff. And you walked into a cage of violent men intent on harm and you never drew it. You left without a scratch."

"Luck," Amir lied. "You also know the weight of steel unless I miss my guess. You're silent. We've covered this before. But you're silent all while wearing ringmail and carrying whatever you call *that* thing."

"It's a mattock, and we've spoken on the matter of changing the subject. I said before: there's another way. Do you want to hear it?"

"Not particularly." Amir straightened his sword belt, turned away from Faust, and set off toward the murderer's cage. It wasn't far, but he took his time, avoiding getting his wind up, because he didn't want to breathe too deep. The smell was still everywhere and sipping a shallow breath was the path to not throwing up.

He arrived at the cage, and sure enough, her eyes were right where he expected. On him. Unblinking. There were four other men in the cage, and unless he missed his guess, they were as far from her as they could get within a cage but three metres long. He watched her for a while, hands on hips, matching stare for stare. It wasn't a staring contest; they both blinked, but Amir felt they spent the time in useful contemplation. After a while, he sighed. "Faust says you want to kill me."

"He said no such thing." Her voice was rich, lush like long grass. He was sure if she wasn't covered in filth, she'd be a beauty, but you'd need dragonfire to burn off the grime to know for sure.

"He most certainly did. He wasn't direct about it, because that's not his way." Amir waited her out.

"All right. He said I want to kill you." She lifted her chin. "Do you believe him?"

"About half-way." Amir tipped his hand in a so-so gesture. "I think you want out of the cage, and you want me to do it. Then, when free, you'll kill me."

"It sounds like you've experience with the world."

"More than my share. Less than you, I'll vouch."

"Sir," a man behind her said, "can I get another cage? I'll be ever so good."

The woman's attention shifted from Amir for a moment. It was just a fraction of time, nothing more than anyone else when distracted, but it left him with the understanding of just how focused on him she was. "Shut it, Gribbs."

Gribbs shut it. Amir couldn't help but smile. "I see you've created a fiefdom in the tiny island of your cell."

"I've done no such thing."

"Yes, you have. You've convinced Grubbs that—"

"Gribbs," the man offered.

"Whatever," Amir breezed. "The men in the cell are convinced that you're a demon, and that you'll kill any of them as surely as the victim of the crime that landed you here. No mean feat, since you're all here for the same reason."

"Not the same," Gribbs said. "We did it honest, like."

Amir pursed his lips, then faced the woman again. "Honest?"

"I'll talk to him later. Etiquette is important." Her voice had a damnable accent, like she was from Or'sen, but hadn't been there for a long, long time. It was fetching enough, and he could imagine liking the lilt of it if he were ever in a situation where he could relax around her. Which was, obviously, never.

"Well, it's nice to see you're making friends. We'll be at the slave markets in a week and a half. It could be a shade longer if the rains come. You can teach Gribbs table manners in that time, surely."

The woman's eyes hardened. "Etiquette is more than how one sits at table."

"I'm sure it is." Amir doffed an imaginary cap. "Well, good day to you." He turned and made sure his walk had just enough saunter in it to be highly annoying to anyone, but especially to someone in a cage.

"My name's Larochette," she called, her voice completely the opposite of annoyed.

"I don't care," he called back, not turning, but slightly annoyed himself.

Fuck it. Maybe I do care.

He found himself watching Larochette as she watched him right back. Or, maybe she'd watched him first. It was difficult to remember. He'd wake, scratch his balls, take a piss at the latrines, and look up to find her right there. It didn't seem to matter where the murderer's cage was; she found him just fine.

Maybe I found her. Maybe that's why I'm in this shitty place, doing this shitty job.

It didn't sound right, not even inside Amir's head. Least ways because he knew he should be in the cage right alongside her. The natural order of justice was perverted, and here they were, murderer on the outside, and something else on the inside.

He stamped up to the cage. "Who'd you kill?"

She gave him a long, appraising look, like the last thirty minutes of staring hadn't been enough to answer the question. "Does it matter?"

"Always matters." Amir kept his tone light. "Why, you're in a cage destined for a market, a hog trussed for slaughter, and I'm out here, enjoying the sunlight."

"It's raining."

"I live in eternal hope."

"Do you believe in justice?"

"Not even a little bit." Amir's tone still *sounded* light, but he felt the weight of it right in his chest. "If there was justice, I'd pay for crimes you couldn't imagine."

"I can imagine a lot." She gave him steady regard. "The woman you took on your blade three years back?"

"Not her. Her children." He didn't even ask how she knew. "They came at me, you see. She'd found some damnable holy weapon—"

"A scattergun?"

"I took the shot against my shield. Never really liked shields before that day. Still got pellets in my hip but didn't notice them until after. What they don't tell peasants about holy weapons is the reload speed. I figure it's because a Knight can take you on the edge of steel just as easily as they please. Reloading's not something they worry about."

"No." She leaned away from the bars.

Curious. "You know the ways of Knights? Odd, for someone in a cell."

"The children?" she prompted.

"Oh." Amir scratched under his jaw. *Missed a spot shaving this morning. Always thinking about eyes, never about the job.* "There were two of them. Brats, I suppose. Didn't like seeing their mother's head a distance from her body." He thought about adding a laugh here, but it wouldn't come. "I didn't take them seriously until I got a knife in the gut."

"And then there were two dead children?"

"And then I knew there was no justice." He shrugged. "It was war."

"Except, it wasn't."

He narrowed his eyes. "You know a lot. Some might call that suspicious."

"Some might," she allowed. "It doesn't come the way it used to. Not anymore. They stripped me of my power, you see. Took my name and took my honour."

"Called you a sinner?"

"No longer. Can't sin without power."

"You seem to have enough, still."

"Fragments," Larochette said. "I was a diviner."

"I don't care." *But I do. I really do. I should just walk away, but I want to know.*

"Then leave," she tossed at him, as if knowing what was in his head. "Diviner, not enchanter?"

"Enchanters use a person as a tool. I see... *saw* what's writ in the stars. There's only so much seeing what's coming before you need to do something about it."

"I've never had that problem."

"Not many can read the stars."

"Still fewer care about doing something about it." He jerked a thumb at his chest. "I look after myself. Why I'm here, and you're there, I expect."

"You could be better at hiding it." Faust's rumble took them both by surprise.

Amir spun. "You really must tell me how you walk so quietly."

"The path of revenge is often silent," the giant said, perhaps a shade too cryptically for Amir's liking.

"It is never silent," spat Larochette. "It ends in screaming, no matter the whiteness of your robes or the silver bars you wear."

Amir blinked. "You killed a *Justiciar?*"

"And what of it? They'd done the same to mine and were about to do the same to me."

Faust took a step closer. "You have hidden talents, little sister."

"I'm not your sister, freak." Larochette looked up at his full height. "Was there Vhemin in your family tree?"

He chuckled, but Amir didn't think it was a tone full of amusement. "There is naught left in my history but ash and broken promises."

"And bad poetic turns of phrase." Amir looked at his feet. *Faust, the dead dogging his heels. Larochette, a killer of power. And me, a murderer of children.* "A fine trio we make. All servants to revenge."

"There is another way."

"You said that before." Amir studied Faust. "What should we do? Become monks atop a mountain, eating our meagre bowl of rice per day?"

"I don't much like rice," Faust said. "There is a school."

"Oh, and teachers we should be?" Larochette's mockery landed like the lash she knew too well.

"Students," Faust said. "They take killers and make them better killers."

Amir hooked his thumbs into his belt. "And what do you need to learn of killing? You make less noise than a dead man. You carry weapons like one born to them. And you?" He eyed Larochette. "I'll wager you've skill with a blade."

"Give me one and I'll show you."

"Revenge," Faust said. "The school will make us unstoppable."

"There are no unstoppable warriors but Knights of the Three, and they're fresh out of Tresward hereabouts." Amir tried for a confident smile, but he let it drop after seeing Faust's expression. "Wait, what? You want us to be Tresward?"

"Oh, aye, a fine trio," Larochette said. "The braggart. The anchorite. The damsel."

Faust turned a steady gaze on her. "You are no damsel."

"Did you just call me a braggart?" Amir said.

"It is fitting," Faust mused.

"I'm done with Tresward," Larochette said. "I wouldn't be here except for them."

"Hang about," Amir said. "We are talking as if this is a solid plan. As if one of us isn't in a cage, but a day from market. As if the school would take us in."

"The school will take us in." Faust's shoulders rose and fell in a heavy sigh. "The headmistress is a fallen star. She forges the impure into starlight."

"You sound like you've met her."

"I went there. They would not teach me." His voice was dead, the stillness before the storm. "They said a man without friends is a man without purpose."

"And are we friends?" Amir gave him a once-over. *Could be handy in a fight, I suppose.*

"No. But we are liars." Faust glanced at Larochette. "Could you lie well enough to convince a Justiciar to take you in?"

"I lied well enough to get close enough for bloody knife work," she said. "But I've killed the Justiciar who needed it. I've no purpose with this new lot."

"There is always purpose. A vengeance against those who take power and deny it to others."

"Ah, shit," Amir said. "This night will end in blood, won't it?"

I don't really want to do this.

Amir stared at the ceiling of his tent. Around him, snores. No privacy in a group like this, not unless you went close to the cages where the smell was worst. And there? Criminals. Not really that private at all.

I really want to do it, though.

It was an odd sensation, as if being pulled in two by a team of equally strong, and strong-willed, oxen on each side. Ropes bound to the arms of his soul, strain thrumming through the knotted cords, and him in the middle.

I don't want to do this because these slavers have done nothing wrong, except being slavers, of which part I am equally guilty.

That was true, and he felt that team of oxen give a triumphant shuffle, a half step that way, offsetting his balance. He felt sick, no joke on his lips to barter with the prosecutor for a smile.

I want to do this because Larochette is more innocent than I, yet lives a criminal by the whims of fate. The Three have not watched over us, and if they don't, who will?

Also true, and unfortunately, the oxen on the other side gave a heroic grunt, pulling him back into tension. If there was a handy wagoner to scold the oxen, *But no, it's not Amir's job to right the wrongs of the Three, nor is it his job to feel guilty for men justly charged with crimes*, that would be useful. His lips moved soundlessly. "This isn't my fault."

The hour would soon be upon him. Where he would need to be at the murderer's cart, blade in hand, ready for violence. Meet Faust and break the woman free. Run, hopefully fast enough to escape justice, or its close cousin revenge.

I know it's not my fault, but that's not what the wagoner would say. Amir chased imaginary oxen into line for a spell longer, worrying at the problematic cords around his soul. He'd left where he was to be free and took up steel in another woman's war when she sat a throne besieged. Killed the innocent and became a slaver to take a different kind of guilt as burial mound for the old.

Lying to himself was easy. He'd done it for a while. It was easier than getting to the school teaching other lost vagrants how to wield the Light in the Three's name. Amir was not made to shoulder the cares of the gods while they were on vacation. It wasn't for him to take on the cares of the world.

Right then, it clicked. A tumbler in his mind, and a sawblade to the binding guilt around him.

It's not my fault, but it's my responsibility. It's all our responsibility. This world is broken because we keep kicking it in the teeth, and if no one reaches out a hand, who will help it back into the fight?

It felt a bit shitty, deciding he was arbiter. Did it mean that others were up for Khiton's dark end if they crossed him? If they hadn't reached this same milestone in their life's redemption journey quite soon enough, did that mark them for the burial cart?

All this accountability is making me sick. It felt better when I didn't care.

Was this the curse Larochette put on him with her constant accusing glances? *No, that's witch hunter's thinking. Peasant superstition. If she were an enchantress, I'd have no doubts. Bound to a cause greater than the holy Knights' crusade. My doubt means she is true.*

My doubt means she didn't lie.

Which was troublesome, as they'd need to lie soon enough. *That's Tomorrow Amir's problem.*

He slipped free of his blanket, fingers finding boots beneath his bunk in the dark through a soldier's hard-won habit. He slid his feet into them, lacing them tight through feel alone. His blade was wrapped in a cloth to keep the steel's whisper silent, the only possession he cared about aside from his cloak, which he snared on the way from the tent.

Outside, the night sky was cloudless. No moons, because they'd fucked off sometime ago. The stars shone prettily enough, which was unfortunate as it gave enough light for a skilled marksman to shoot them if they didn't have cover.

So he padded to the quartermaster's tent. A rude rack of bows and crossbows awaited a ready hand, which wouldn't do at all. He slipped his blade free of its shawl and, *snick snick snick*, cut the bowstrings. It would buy them some time. Almost absently, and not quite sure why he did it, he freed a pair of shortswords, barely more than daggers, but with an edge keen enough to leave a bloody smile.

Next, he padded to the commissar's tent, liberating a collection of coin. The wages chest wasn't well secured because someone cheapened out on the purchase. It acquiesced to the gentle touch of a bent wire. The loss of a pouch of barons and solars would teach someone a valuable life lesson.

He almost felt like whistling as he sauntered to the murderer's pen. No Faust, not yet, but Larochette was ready. Wide-eyed, watching him as always. "You're late."

"I'm early," he countered. "Your nervousness sped up the clock."

"The stars shifted—"

"Let's not, love," he said. "Soon enough we'll banter about my habits often enough we'll both be sick of it. Until then." He bent to the lock and went to work with his wire again.

Faust appeared as if by sorcery. "What news?"

Amir eyed him. "I saw you coming. Not so quiet this time, no?"

"I didn't want to get knifed in the dark. It was intentional."

Amir growled, bending to his task. In moments, the lock sprang open, the cage creaking wide. Larochette made ready to bound free, but Amir held up a hand. "Do you hear that?"

"I hear nothing." She froze, eyes everywhere.

"My point exactly." He offered her the daggers, now knowing their purpose. She took them. He pointed at the prisoners asleep in her cage. "Those clowns should have woken with the ruckus."

"Fuck," she said.

"We must run," Faust urged.

"Allo," called a man from the cage. "Where you fancy cunts off to, then?"

THIS WAS WHEN THE PRISONERS SHARING LAROCHETTE'S PRISON sprang into life. They were miserable creatures but motivated by a gaoler's promise. Freedom, or a half extra ration of food, it didn't matter.

'Sprang' is a tall word, Amir. This is like watching a rickety table right itself.

Faust offered his hand to Larochette, who ignored him as she left the cage under her own impressive speed. She landed, cat-light, next to Amir, and pointed behind him. Amir still hadn't looked at the guards no doubt coming to murder them, his eyes on the murderers in the cage. He shook his head. "Not yet."

"The guard will kill us," Faust rumbled.

Amir felt an explanation would only weigh them down, so he stepped into the cell, and ran a prisoner through. The man was unarmed, full of spite and anger, and all that left him, his body deflating like a wineskin suckled by a thirsty man. Larochette hissed, perhaps alarmed at Amir's casual approach to murder. It took but a moment to kill the rest, Amir's blade black with hate and blood without Cophine's pale face to guide him.

Then he was out, the unpleasant business done, and on cue, there were the guards.

"We should have run," Faust said.

"Murder so casual, aye?" Larochette asked.

"If we had fought guards with evil behind, we'd have fallen." Amir didn't understand why they couldn't see it. "Now we have a chance."

"A chance?" Faust barked a laugh, hefting his mattock. A guard surged forward, then learned what a mattock wielded by a large man felt like. Faust's blow knocked the guard clear from his feet, as it knocked the teeth from his skull, and the skull from his neck.

There was no time for congratulations on a job well done. Amir's blade thirsted, and who was he to deny it? He stepped two paces ahead of Faust, ducked low, and cut a man's shin in half. He rose, blade coming in a black, eager line, and took another man's arm off at the shoulder. Out of the corner of his eye he saw Larochette, dirty, matted hair wild, daggers plunging in and out of a man's chest who was, by that point, well past caring.

Faust's hand on his arm, and a yank, pulling him from the path of a broadsword. Amir shoulded-checked the giant, pushing him from the path of an arrow. Larochette, throwing a knife at the bowman. Amir, kicking a fallen sword into her waiting hand. Faust, throwing a man into the villain looking to run Larochette through.

Larochette, her blade at the commander's throat.

Quiet.

Then the *thud* as the commander's head hit the ground, and the easing sigh of his body joining it a moment later. The trickle and spurt of blood. Panting.

Then, again, quiet.

"What have we done?" Amir looked at the fallen.

"We should run." Faust looked more grim than usual, but it could have been the play of blood on his face that lent him a rougher air.

Amir turned and pointed past Larochette's old quarters. The cage was full of the lifeless. "That way."

"The same way we were going?" Larochette's eyes were wide and bright.

"Trust me."

"Not fucking likely, you—"

"Later." Faust started in that direction, and they followed.

Amir took the lead. He didn't want it, because in his view being on point was the job most likely to get you killed by arrow, trap, or bear, but he was also the one who knew where they were going. Oh, sure, Faust *thought* he did, and Larochette knew *of* the place. Both were almost as good as a firm destination.

But I have a plan.

They scampered along the rutted road until Amir saw a boulder taller than Faust. "This way."

"What's here?" Larochette's suspicion hung in the air.

Amir weighed the cost of a delay versus the cost of not delaying now and having this every three steps. *No contest.* He turned on her. "What's here is a giant rock. And—"

"I can see that—"

"And what's beyond that are trees filled with guards waiting to kill you. They've been sharpening blades all night."

He watched as the words made it past her filter. "What?"

"Of course, it could also be a clearing, with three horses, supplies, and clean clothes for you." Amir glanced at the sky. "Could go either way at this point. You've got to ask yourself why I'd let you out of the cage, mark myself as a wanted man by killing my fellow soldiers, abscond into the night with a fugitive from justice, all without a plan."

"I'm not a fugitive. I was wrongly imprisoned."

"I meant him." Amir jerked a thumb at Faust without looking. "He is no simple guard, and you're no simple slave." Amir tried not to tense, because now was when Faust could strike him down easy as you please. Amir's back, Faust's mattock, and an unhappy end to 'friend Amir' out here in the wilds.

"I am not a fugitive. I hunt," Faust offered.

"Whatever." Amir's shoulder blades were still tense, because the way Faust said *hunt* made it sound a more purposeful affair than simple maiming, murder, or vengeance. "The point? We three all have secrets. I am not the man to ask after them. We are now three friends, seeking the new school in Imshir. Or, we are vigilantes who don't trust one another. Which is it?

A shout came up from the camp behind them, and Amir wished he'd had the kind of stomach it took to murder men in their beds. But he waited, watching Larochette.

She nodded, slow and steady. "We are now three friends."

"Seeking the new school in Imshir," Faust finished.

"Then let's be about it." Amir slipped off the trail, his friends behind him, and the night close.

Chapter Twenty-Two

"Umm," Tarragon said.

"Quite." Amir's gaze was hooded.

He wants me to say something. To give him something. Tarragon flailed around the vaults of her mind. She wasn't good at fixing reactors, and no Manifest said *anything* about what went on in people's heads. "So... you killed a caravan of slavers, and are fugitives from justice?" Tarragon heard the words come out one after the other but couldn't stop them.

Vertiline, ghost pale, stepped toward them. "Knight Adept, you should not have said this."

"I apologise." Amir bowed. "I meant—"

"You should not have said this, because we all have a past. We have a future, too." The Justiciar's eyes found Evanne for a moment, before sliding back to her Knight. "But I wager the story's not done."

"I, uh," Amir said. "I didn't leave anything out. I even told you the parts where I murdered my comrades."

"The story's not done, because you left out the why." Vertiline turned from Amir, gazing at the wall capsules as if they fascinated her. "Many who seek the Three's Light do so because they think it will make them pure. As if the radiance of the divine will wash their souls clean." She turned back to Amir. "I will give you a free lesson: more wrong has been done in the Three's name than anything else I know of. Many who carried the Light were righteous, and yet we almost ruined our best salvation." Her eyes found the lordling this time. "All of us are drenched in blood. All that remains is the time left to you, and what you do with it."

"Tilly." Meri raised his hand as if objecting the point. "What's done is past and buried."

"What the sinner means is that I near killed him."

Said sinner tried for levity. "Couple times, sure, but you didn't mean it."

"Is that true?" Tarragon blurted. And then everyone was looking at her, with her magic sword and giant Big body, and she just wanted the world to swallow her up. "I mean, about the past. That it doesn't matter."

"The past matters," Hitch said. "The past reminds us of all the things we shouldn't do again."

"It reminds us of what we should do twice as much of," Evanne countered. "Sure, there are those moments you cringe from a memory, wishing it wasn't you who'd said that stupid thing. But there are many others where you've but to take the recollection out, shine it up, and see it for the marvel it is. That you were *there* and made wonders."

"I didn't make wonders," Tarragon said. "I got captured. I got my commander killed. I can't fix a plasma torch. I've got some rude skill with a sword, and—"

"She was talking about me," Hitch said. "I made the wonders."

"Don't be a dick," Evanne chided. "Now's not the time."

"It's true. What Tilly said." Meri toyed with a small stone, then tossed it to the ground. "Also true what Evanne said. We have time ahead of us. There are great works behind. But there's a secret to it all."

"Three's mercy, here we go." The Justiciar rolled her eyes.

"You're only being like this because you don't know the secret." Meriwether nodded to Evanne. "I think she gets it."

"It doesn't matter if you are good with a sword," Evanne said. "It matters if you are good enough to stand by the people you're with."

"But the sword thing helps," Hitch said.

"Hitch."

"What? All I'm saying is, it's useful. If you had someone to stand with, would you want them to be good with a—"

"What I mean to say is, not all of us are sorcerers of the high arts, Justiciars, great warriors, or even warriors trying to be great." Evanne shrugged. "Some of us are making it up as we go along. Doing our best. But we're doing *something*."

Tarragon hunched. "Let's just keep moving."

THE CORRIDOR WAS COOL, BUT NOT UNPLEASANTLY SO. MERIWETHER walked beside her, examining another small stone. "Odd."

Tarragon eyed him. "That we're in a dangerous ancient ruin filled with horrors that will eat us?"

"I don't think they want to eat us. Not all of them, anyway." Meri handed her the stone. "What do you make of that?"

"It's a river stone."

"Exactly."

Tarragon gave him her full attention. "Are you trying to get punched?"

"Not really." He tossed the stone aside, then picked up another. "Here."

"Another river stone. What of it?"

"Do you, and this is an important question, see any rivers here?"

"Are you saying this is a causeway that will flood and drown us?" Tarragon gritted her teeth. "I don't think it's a causeway."

"I'm saying there are river stones here, and in my experience the ancients were impeccably clean. Not a stray pebble."

Tarragon coughed. "I'm one of your ancients."

"It's nothing personal. You don't look haggard or anything."

"Haggard?" Tarragon heard her voice go up an octave mid word.

"I mean—"

"It's not a causeway," Tarragon said. "I'm from around this time, remember? This is a standard-issue corridor. It just connects parts of the base."

"You'd think they'd build those parts closer together."

She gave him a hard stare. "What if there was a research wing that needed to be near a geothermal power plant, and another area that needed to be clear of fumes, but they needed to still be connected?"

"What?"

"Exactly." She *hmm'd*. "Still. There should be ... *more*. There are the sarcophagi holding horrible liquid metal guardians, that feels standard, but—"

"Standard?" Meri's voice also went up an octave. "What *were* you people? How is it standard to have murder metal in your hallway?"

"Hallway, that's it!" She slapped fist into palm. "This is a big hall-way, and there should be more rooms. They're probably hidden, like with Pakhet."

"Was invisibility a casual thing back in your day?"

She raised an eyebrow. "Careful. You're getting back into the same lost lands of misery words like 'haggard' took you to."

"Fair." He sucked air through his teeth. "Okay. So there should be rooms, or at least doors, but there aren't any." He held up a hasty hand. "That we can see."

"Right."

"I can fix that." He smiled, then frowned. "It would be helpful if I knew where a door was."

"Over there." Hitch pointed at a patch of wall laden with glowing sarcophagi. "It's plain as day once you see it from the other side."

Meri walked to the wall and peered up at the glowing cylinders. "How can you tell?"

"If you're going to call me a liar, at least have the decency to walk through the wall and do it from the other side."

"A good rejoinder. I'm regretting making you visible to everyone."

Tarragon joined him, placing a hand against a cylinder. The illusion was perfect. The cylinder was slightly warm, a small hum vibrating through her hand. "It's this one."

"How can you tell?"

"If this was made by Builders, it wouldn't have had any transformer inefficiency leading to wasted noise or heat."

Meri just stared at her. "What was in these exams you missed out on?"

"The secrets of the universe."

"I never studied either," he admitted. "Behold."

They stared at the wall. Evanne joined them. "Is something happening? Because if Hitch made you all stare at a blank wall, that would be fun."

The lordling cleared his throat. "Apologies." He threw his hands wide. "I said, *behold!*"

The illusion of the cylinder-covered wall flickered like a struggling candle flame then vanished. It was replaced with a plain if serviceable wall, with a wide door set into it. At the base of the door was a scattering of pebbles. Tarragon bent, picking one up. It was cool and smooth, just how a river stone would be. Tossing it aside, she said, "I don't think we should open it."

"What if it's a path to the surface?"

"My people would never have built a system that let stray stones fall about." She pointed at them. "If there are stones, either we didn't do it and it's a lowest-bidder venture, or something behind the door is badly broken."

//LIKE THE HOLE IN THE GROUND THAT OPENED UP AND LET THE CURATORS OUT?// The dragon took an interest from a safe enough distance.

"Exactly. Wait! No." Tarragon shook her head. "You're thinking that if one thing broke, and created an opening to the surface back there," she pointed back the way they'd come, "it stands to reason something breaking here will do the same thing. What if behind here is a river, full of angry piranhas?"

"What's a piranha?" Armitage had his arms crossed.

"It's an omnivorous fish, but it's the part of them that likes meat that's the problem. A school can strip a cow carcass to the bone like that." She snapped her fingers.

"I'm not afraid of fish," Armitage said. "They should be afraid of me."

"There's no river behind there," Hitch said. "There's a small lake. Might once have been fed by a river. Not really my area. I was more of a fighting man. I think."

"Can we open it?" Vertiline joined what Tarragon charitably thought of as the circus outside the door.

"Is no one listening to me about the danger?" Tarragon felt her face flush. "I used to, *hic*, I used to live in this time!" Evanne put a hand on her arm, but she shrugged it off. "*Hic*. There are things we made. Horrible things. *Hic*. Then we killed the world."

Silence gathered for a moment. Vertiline pushed through it, her voice strangely gentle. "I do not discount your counsel. It is because of it I would like to open this door. Hear me out," she raised a hand as Tarragon started to boil over. "In battle, the thing worse than the foe you face is the one at your back. The one you can't see. I would rather flush out an enemy now than have it join against us later. I see in your face the fear you have for us, because the people of your time made marvels we can only dream of. But they were just people. They were just us."

Tarragon sighed. "You're right. They were just people. But people are dumb."

"Can you open it?"

"It's easy." Tarragon pushed past Meri and placed her palm against a blank piece of wall. "Here."

"Nothing's happening," the lordling said.

"Give it a minute. It's been a thousand years." As Tarragon spoke, the door cracked open, then shuddered wide. Cool air flowed out, laden with the smell of the grave.

REQUIEM WAS IN TARRAGON'S HAND. THE BLADE SHONE, A crackling length of blue-white fire that pushed the darkness back. Details in the new room came as her eyes adjusted.

The room looked to have been a fabrication facility before some forgotten cataclysm cracked it down the middle. To the north and south, vertical rents split the walls floor to ceiling, and dripped with melancholy rivulets. The northern one had a spew of stones about it, and Tarragon pieced it together: the room broke, an underground river bifurcating it, and stopped the fabrication. The machines in here were lost, all hunched and rusted metal. The room and its sombre, broken machinery stretched on for a couple klicks to the west.

Something hissed. Tarragon pivoted on the balls of her feet, blade hissing right back. A bank of old devices she imagined as terminals waited in the gloom, and a shape scuttled behind them. She raised her sword in cross guard. "I don't think we're alone. I think—"

A rat the size of a pony launched from behind the terminals. She breathed out, stepping sideways into *Courtier's Rise*, Requiem moving from cross guard to high cut. The sword hummed, and she felt how it was just slightly wrong. What had Sands Apart said to her? She cast about for the Feybrind woman and saw her battling another giant rat with Sight of Day.

Nothing about this is belief.

If bringing the Storm wasn't belief, what was it? Requiem sliced through the giant rat, the beast thrashing as burning metal cut it in half, cauterising the innards and leaving it to land in two places. The top half, complete with claws and giant rat fangs, dragged itself toward her. She moved into *Courtier's Rise's* second and third steps, slipping backward into a low stance that mocked a half-bow. A second rat, destined for her face, sailed over the top of her.

It's a simple matter.

Simple or no, she conjured no Storm. And yet she felt *something*, the lightness of her sword belying its true weight, the smoothness of the floor at odds with its crumbled, crusted surface. She should have been hot and wild, the blood surging in her veins, but she was calm. An eye at the heart of nothing, no Storm to hold her. Tarragon brought Requiem left to right, taking off a giant rope of tail from the latest rat, then stabbing down, skewering the original half beast as it reached her ankles. The air here was foetid, carrying a foulness beyond age, but she only felt it as a passing breeze. And she remembered Sands Apart's last words.

You're leaning forward too much.

Tarragon straightened no more than a finger's width. A third rat joined the second, bounding from the gloom, red eyes gleaming in Requiem's luminance. She brought her shoulder blades closer together, pushing the barrel of her chest out just so. *I'm not Big. Everything else is small.*

The chime of a bell tolled, and snow gusted past her. The edge of Requiem glimmered gold amid the blue-white. She raised her sword and stepped to meet her foes.

Lightning arced from the doorway behind her as Myryntir blasted the room. Energy leaped from wet surfaces, surging between rat bodies in the dark. It connected hundreds of them, a brilliant, glimmering net of charring as the lightning coursed through ranks of foes.

Tarragon lowered her blade, the rats before her now ashy forms frozen in mid-strike. *Was that the Storm? Did I call it? Did I really see Light on the edge of my blade?* She poked a rat, and it crumbled into ruin. She glanced to the doorway where a smug dragon peered inside. "Maybe you should go first next time."

Evanne walked from the dragon's side, coughing as she stepped through a stray haze of ash. "What is this place?"

"It's a fabrication facility." At literally everyone's blank stare, Tarragon said, "They make things. Machines," she pointed to the slumped, corroded devices, "worked tirelessly to make stuff. Like Curators, but that doesn't feel right. These aren't big enough."

"There are a lot of them," Vertiline said. "Did they make the rats?"

"The rats are new," Tarragon said. "Just ordinary rats, but big. Maybe came in when the wall broke." She eyed the northern fissure.

"What did they eat?" Armitage kicked a rat into a pile of silted ash.

"Wrong question," Tarragon said. "What were they fabricating?"

Chapter Twenty-Three

Evanne picked her way through the ashy remains of the rat horde. Mama and Papa had stayed in front of her, iron and stone before an army of paper, but the dragon had made it all moot. She wondered if anyone would have died if Myryntir hadn't been there. *I bet the ancients liked having a dragon on their team.*

She gave Tarragon a small, shy smile, feeling awe at her lover's poise and courage. Evanne knew Tarragon was good with a sword, but skill and bravery weren't the same thing, and Tarragon had just charged right in. Unless Evanne was going blind, Tarragon was close to commanding a sliver of the Storm, the icy gust of snow accompanying her pattern a dead giveaway to anyone who'd spent time slumming about Mama's school.

The room they were in had seen better days. Evanne turned over a fallen hunk of metal, trying to work out what it was. Chair? Table? It looked more chair than table, but the frame was too long, the arms too stunted. She kicked it aside, covering her mouth as ash drifted.

"You should be careful." The too-sure-of-himself Amir was by her side.

She gave him a single raised eyebrow. "This place is proper fucked. The dragon barbecued everything. We're fine."

"Flying orbs that shoot lightning. Quicksilver warriors that won't die. Giant rats." The warrior pointed to the fissure in the north wall. "A cave-in. This place is a far cry from 'fine'."

"Mostly fine? Fine for now?"

He gave her an easy smile, all white gleam in the gloom, before pocketing it away. "Fine for now, I'll allow. What do you think this place was?"

"Tarragon said it made things, but it doesn't look like any smithy's forge I've seen." Evanne tugged her leather jacket back into line. "There are no tools. No fires or saws. Nothing to bend stubborn wood or melt metal with a hot kiss."

Hitch drifted through a collapsed chair-table-thing. "What if you were making ideas?"

Evanne stared at him. *Playing wholesale with another's mind seems fanciful, but...* "Sure, why not?"

"You took that onboard surprisingly fast."

"It's been a day of revelation." Evanne raked at rust locks. "Do you *actually* know something?"

"I don't even remember my name. Just ... a tug from the past." He shrugged, all ghostly uncertainty. "I don't think we should be here."

"It's fine," Evanne insisted. "Besides, we either go forward, or back to a dead end under a pile of rubble. Forward's got to be safer."

"How do you figure the odds? Our track record shows every pace takes us farther from safe, and closer to worser."

"Worser isn't a word." Evanne peered into the gloom. Her Vhemin eyes saw no heat, her human vision giving back nothing but gloom. All cold blues and dark blacks. "What do you suppose the rats were eating, before they came for us?"

Hitch and Amir shared a glance before the warrior said, "Why would you bring up such an unwholesome question?"

Evanne kicked aside a rack of twisted metal, revealing a small passage. "Here."

"You first." Amir crossed his arms.

"Oh, but you're so strong and brave," she said.

"Fuck it, I'll go." Hitch drifted through the wreckage and into the wall before emerging a moment later. "It's a rat warren. Goes about twenty metres that way," he pointed westerly, "before opening into a room of pipes and such. Some of the pipes have burst. Whatever magic powers this place is still pushing some kind of sludge through the pipes."

"Right." Evanne slicked back her hair, hunkered down, and crawled into the passage. She ignored Mama's *Wait!* because someone had to go, and Evanne could see in the dark better than humans, and Papa was too big to fit in. Made sense.

After a few grunts and curses, she made it into the chamber Hitch spoke of. The spectre waited for her. "Took you long enough."

"Does it bother you that everyone can see you now?"

He turned luminous blue eyes at her. "It spoils my surprise potential at children's birthday parties." When she didn't laugh, he sighed. "I miss our thing, too."

"Thing?"

"Whatever it was. Privacy. Closeness. Call it whatever—"

"Intimacy. Friendship."

"Those words work too." He sighed again. "I'm still here. I'm still me. Just, all the time."

"We could ask the sorcerer to undo it."

"Best leave it. He looked so proud."

"Yeah." Evanne poked about the room, finding no living rats, but much rat shit. The ghost hadn't been wrong about the pipes. They were large, easily big enough to stand up in if she were inclined, which she wasn't because of what was in them. A sluggish, oozing paste leaked from the cracked side of one. "I wonder if this is the same stuff Vehement Systems kept Tarragon alive with all those years."

"You what?"

"When we found Tarragon she said she'd been a prisoner in an old place. Kept in a cage, with food coming in through a tube."

"Smaller tube, probably."

"Likely." Evanne frowned. "Or, these pipes go to smaller pipes, which in turn go to the kinds of tubes you might feed a fairy with."

Hitch glanced at the cracked pipe. "That's a lot of feeding."

"For a long, long time." Evanne took a step away from the cracked pipe as if it were a hibernating bear and spring neared. "The rats were eating it. But not all of it. Look how many pipes there are."

"There's a path through, over there." The spectre pointed at a wall, where masonry sagged like an old man's paunch over the belly button of a hole at its base.

They made it to the wall. Evanne bent and picked up a cracked piece of stone. "Odd."

"Not so strange a wall would break after eight hundred years."

"Strange it's made of simple fired clay and mortar, when everything else here is wrought in metal and the magic mineral the ancients used." She tossed the brick aside. "What if someone else moved in? Found a nice, warm place with no peskersome ancients left alive, and a handy crew of guardians to zap interlopers."

"And they shored up the odd wall breach to stop carnivorous rats from—"

"Aren't all rats carnivorous?"

"They fixed a hole to stop rats of any dietary preference from getting to them. But not recently. Because their maintenance programme is sloppy."

"Let's keep on." Evanne bent to get through the hole in the wall, finding a passage on the other side. It was constructed much like the tunnel with the silver warriors, all smooth flooring and fine materials, but much narrower. *No dragons will fit in here.* Perhaps four Evannes abreast could walk its length.

She walked on, Hitch drifting at her side. They followed the passage around a left-hand turn, then back to the right. The route ended in a door. It was cracked down the middle, but otherwise unmarked—just a useless broken door she could squeeze through if she wasn't afraid to lose a little skin. Her human eyes were useless in the midnight surrounding her, but her Vhemin blood heat vision saw a glimmer of warmth beyond. "Look, there. A door."

"Your powers of observation astound me." Hitch drifted through the door, then came back. "It's not a good news story in there."

"There is heat."

"It's not a good kind of heat." The spectre hunched. "There are corpses lining the walls. They are connected to machines, and I'd guess they're what you're seeing. If I had to guess, this is some kind of eternity chamber, a place for the wealthy to live past the reckoning. But it failed. They're all dead."

"Wait." Evanne frowned. "There are bodies?"

"On the walls." Hitch gave an encouraging nod.

"And the door's broken?"

"Exactly as you see it, yes."

"And this passage was full of giant rats?"

"I'm following along. It's an exciting path, seeing how your mind works!"

"Are there rats in there?"

"Not a sausage."

"So," Evanne spoke slowly, as if to a child, "why didn't the rats go in there and eat all the bodies?"

Hitch's mouth worked for a moment, then he glanced to the door and back to her. "No clue."

"The heat means more than sleeping machines, surely." Evanne approached the door and peered inside. Her Vhemin eyes weren't much good for fine details, but she spied the bodies Hitch mentioned. Each was mounted on the wall, hung by their armpits as if they were tools aligned on a shelf. There were many machines inside, all giving off the delightful heat she'd seen.

The door was stuck. It had cracked wide at the top, the bottom seized firmly shut, providing her a triangle of opportunity. She grunted her way through, skinning most parts of her not protected by leather, and flopped on the other side.

"Truly graceful," Hitch murmured. "Now what?"

Evanne found her feet, dusted herself off, and sneezed. "It's dusty."

"Eight hundred years will do that."

The edges of the floor glimmered a soft tangerine orange before waxing to a steady yellow white. It provided easy illumination for her human eyes. No lights in the ceiling flickered on, leaving Evanne slightly disappointed in the ancients' lack of consistency. *Everywhere else had lights in the ceiling. Why not here?* The room was of significant size and would allow Myryntir in if he was wanting to stop by for a pint.

There were three ways out of the room. The southern door she'd already used. There was a large door to the east, which her mental map said led to the rat room. The western door was similar to the eastern one, also still intact and providing a passage large enough for dragons. The northern wall was a giant pane of glass, beyond which were various mouldering chairs, one of which supported a corpse. The corpse wasn't getting in Evanne's face about anything, just being a dead person reclining in a chair. It was like the ones she'd found on the bridge of *Dancing in the Storm*, all skin and tissue missing, leaving hair, clothes, and bone. She turned back to the wall-ornament corpses. "Weird."

"What is?" Hitch peered at one of the bodies racked to the wall. "There are like twenty of these guys."

"That is odd." Evanne joined him and pointed at the head. "You can still make out the face, the suggestion of eyes under the lids. Lips, the works."

"It's mummified."

"I'd argue it's still juicy." She stabbed a finger at the glass wall. "The loser in there doesn't have their skin anymore. These ones do."

Hitch glanced at the door they'd entered by. "If the room had been sealed, we could have argued for hermetic containment, but—"

"Hermawhat?"

"But as it is, that theory holds no water. I wish Tarragon was here."

Evanne felt her eyes widen. "You what?"

"Don't tell her I said that." The spectre added, "It's just, she's handy with machines and such."

"Were you?" Evanne let her voice soften. "Before you lost your memories. I mean, I know you can't remember what you can't remember, but—"

"I don't think so. I think I was a man of action. Hah." Hitch drifted to the east door. "We should try getting this open."

"And *such* action." Evanne followed him. The door was smooth, unmarked by time, not even a cobweb. She spun as something *clicked* behind her. It wasn't the sound of metal machines or an ancients' device, more like the pop of an unused joint. Nothing. She eyed the bodies on the racks, but none of them eyed her back. "Did you hear that?"

"Yes. We really should get this door open."

Evanne felt around the sides of the door but found no convenient panels that lit to the touch of her fingers. Another *pop-click* behind her. She turned. Had that body on the western wall moved? She could have sworn its head was at a different angle to before. "Hitch?"

"I'm here. I'm not going anywhere."

"Yes, you are. Get Mama."

"She won't make it in time."

"I need her, Hitch. I think I really need her." Evanne put a palm against the door. "And she's just back there."

The spectre eyed the room, then gave a tight nod and slipped through the door. Evanne drew her machete, feeling her stomach clench. *I just have to hold a few minutes. Then Mama will be here and these fuckers will be really sorry.*

The fuckers didn't move though. Evanne felt sick with fear but also a little foolish, her machete brandished against twenty unmoving corpses.

Then, one of them twitched. It was in the corner between the western door and the window to the north. The twitch was violent, a spasm pulling its body rigid, the sound of joints popping in rapid fire, before it stilled, only to spasm again a moment later. Evanne faced the corpse, machete held in both hands, teeth bared.

I'm sure that wasn't the body that moved before. It wasn't a helpful thought to have.

The door at her back *clanged* as if some massive force hit it. It shook in its frame but didn't cave. Was Myryntir trying to get in while Vertiline came through the passage?

Another series of pops drew her attention. A corpse near her, by the cracked door, twitched three times before spasming right off the wall and landing on the floor. It lay like a landed fish for a moment before dragging a shuddering breath.

Hang about. Corpses don't breathe. Three's mercy, are these living souls awaiting the reawakening of the world as Hitch thought?

The 'corpse's' eyes opened, banishing the idea. There was hunger there, and need, but no patience or mercy. Evanne held her machete in a passable cross-guard. "Why don't you just stay there and rest, and we'll not have any problems."

The corpse got one hand under it as the one on the far wall shimmied off its rack. *Great, two of them.* She eyed the cracked door, wondering if she could get through, but the corpse nearest it surged upright, chest out. It bawled a challenge, its desiccated throat not quite up for the task but the rest of it spoiling for a fight.

Fuck it. Everyone's trying for a piece of me? A piece they'll have. Evanne charged it, swinging her machete like a bat. She struck the monster in the arm, wound back, and hit it again, and then again. The arm came free, but what came out wasn't blood. A sticky, viscous, sap-like fluid spattered to the old stone, her blade mottled with the same lime-green fluid. The smell wasn't heady, rich, and bloody, but sharp, like pickle brine.

The creature used her moment of inattention to rake her with the claws of its remaining hand. Evanne shied away from the strike on pure reflex but took a glancing blow, claws scoring her face and down her chest. She stumbled back, swinging the machete in a graceless one-handed arc and was rewarded with a hit to the monster's head.

Her blade stuck and there she was: connected to it by way of her steel. She dropped her shoulder and barged it, lifting the thing off its feet. *It's light, as if all the dreams have left it.* Its fall threatened to tear her machete from her, but she was having none of that, wrenching the weapon from her enemy's skull. It hit the ground, more of the green sap spattering to the stone.

Unlike a living foe that would have taken a moment to wonder why a sword had entered its skull, or perhaps where its arm had gone, this thing started clambering upright straight away. *It's all purpose, like an old machine made of meat.* She kicked it in the head, hitting it square in the jaw, and was rewarded with the popping clatter of freed teeth. After the monster realigned its jaw, it just kept trying to get up. It was fouled by having just one arm but seemed game for the challenge.

Evanne swung the machete again, hitting it in the neck, and wrenched her blade free. As it tried to get back up *again*, she rewarded its efforts by a second strike that freed its head from the body. The head bounced away, the body slumping, and her blade clanged to the floor.

She goggled at the machete's handle, still in her hand. The ancients' weapon, steel no doubt forged in the very heart of a star, had broken off at the hilt. She ignored the creature's head, which was still animate, eyes tracking her, jaws working, because it wasn't going anywhere. She saw that where the sap stuff hit the ground it smoked, pitting the stone and burning into the very heart of the bedrock. Evanne held her machete up for a closer look, seeing the blade's nub equally ruined by whatever was in the monster's blood.

The one by the western door freed itself and ran for her just as the door to her back *boomed* again. Evanne snarled, lowered her head, and bullrushed the monster, hitting it square in the torso and taking it to the ground, where she buried the stub of her machete in its forehead, right into the brain.

It didn't appear to care, snapping and clawing at her. She punched it in the head over and over, its skull hitting the stone floor, rebounding up, and letting her do it all over again. It clawed her, careless of the ruin she was making of its head, and Evanne took slashes against her face, and through her jacket. She let the pain spur her on, right until something knocked her sideways.

Another of the creatures was on her, and behind it she saw two more. She bucked her hips, tossing this one off, scrabbled on all fours, and lurched toward the broken doorway. She made it three steps before five of them piled on her and she was borne to the ground beneath a mass of dead, hungry things.

Chapter Twenty-Four

They'd been trying to forge a light source, but nothing down here was burnable. Vertiline knew you couldn't just set fire to a rat limb and use it as a torch, and besides, they were fresh out of rat limbs after Myryntir destroyed their enemies. The rest of the ancients' materials were made of metal and stone, not handy wood. Or, the wood had long since perished in the passage of time's march.

She gritted her teeth, because she kept forgetting the Sway. *Is it really forgetfulness, or do I resent it? Do I hate the power because it ties me to the Three, who have forsaken this world?*

It didn't matter. The Sway was a tool, and her child might be in danger. She breathed in and spread the fingers of her metal hand over the ground before the tunnel. *//LIGHT.//*

The floor glowed, the rat warren's very walls illuminating. She crouched and was greeted by Hitch's legs as they emerged from the wall. She surged upright, a hard word on her lips, but he beat her to it, a rare feat in itself. "Evanne fights an army of the dead."

Vertiline's hand dropped to her sword. "Where?"

"There." He pointed at the western sealed door. "I can lead you through the tunnels to her, and—"

"No." Vertiline walked past the spectre and his wide-eyed goggle and faced the door.

The ghost hovered at her elbow. "There is little time."

"Then stop wasting it." She drew sword, reminded of a time when her sister of the blade went into a tower after a certain luckless sinner while Vertiline faced the keep's gates alone with nothing but glass and steel.

She set her stance, picking the very same pattern as she'd used to assault the barred port of Calterburry's castle. Her blade glowed a fierce yellow, and she struck with the Three's Storm. The blade hit the ancient's metal door and it shook the very frame. The metal glowed a sullen red but didn't shatter or bend.

Armitage arrived at her side. "Wife."

"Now is not the time, husband."

"What if she's right *there*," he pointed to the imagined base of the door on the other side, "and you bring this down on her?"

Vertiline felt her lips press into a line. "She is not some snivelling fool. She is *ours*, love, and knows the way of things. She will step aside."

"Can you ... break it a little easier, though?"

Break it 'easier'? Whatever is he on about? She gritted her teeth, and changed the angle of her blade, selecting a different stance in a different pattern. He stepped back as she swung Light, the door shuddering again, molten flakes coming free. Vertiline stepped along the line of the door as if it were a set of foes, swinging high to take their heads and low to their feet. She was Tresward, or once was, and her steps were fast and sure, the whole business taking three breaths.

She stepped back as the door groaned, then collapsed.

Beyond, a horror. What were surely corpses filled a large room. They were focused around a point, a seething mass of conflict, and Vertiline picked out urgent details. There, the end of Evanne's blade. Over there, a spatter of red. And then a hand, cast out from the body pile. Her daughter's fingers, bent, ragged, but still fighting as she clawed for freedom.

Myryntir couldn't kill all these, not with Evanne in there.

Vertiline groped for a pattern, something that would deal with the horde. *Something that will keep my baby girl alive.* She felt her metal fingers tremble, the coolness of her mind melt under the onslaught of panic, a fog burned away by the sun. Armitage roared past her, hulking into the melee, careless of his own skin, taking slashes by the score.

All while she froze, not a single pattern to conjure against the fear inside her.

She heard Myryntir inhale, readying his weapon, perhaps unseeing of Armitage or uncaring, perhaps unaware of her daughter in the ruckus, or again perhaps uncaring. She spun and saw no, the creature wasn't killing Vhemin for sport, his eyes intent, locked on Vertiline. She held her useless sword in weak fleshy fingers and threw her metal hand up as the dragon gouted lightning. Her metal fingers tangled about the burning cascade, and she rounded on the brawl, electricity on the leash. *I don't need the Storm. I just need to get in there.*

She charged, a scream breaking free, noise to get the enemy's attention, and it worked. A clutch of creatures came for her and she wondered if there were too many for her alone without the Storm as her ally.

Again, she missed the heart within her companions, because the sinner had started running before she'd caught the dragon's twist of power. He was slower than her, body older, but his head start meant they clashed with the enemy at the same time. Vertiline struck with whipping energy, tendrils of power cascading into a foe, sending the monster across the heads of her enemies and into the western wall where it impacted with bone-crushing force.

The sorcerer slipped between two, catching an arm in a curious hold she had no time to wonder at, before he kicked the legs from beneath his foe. It let her bring the dragon's justice down in her hand, smashing the fallen monster. It convulsed as her fist clove skull, skin ash in an instant, bone fragmenting and scattering beneath her feet. He nudged his second enemy to her, and she drove her metal fist between its ribs, the body exploding into burning fragments. They turned as one and powered toward the main melee.

Her husband, her love, her life, was on his knees. His body was a ruin, cuts everywhere, and terrible burns across his scales where his foes' blood spattered him. The old injury dragged his back and shoulder, but his hand was around Evanne's, holding their girl, trying to drag her free.

Vertiline could tell he wasn't strong enough, just as she could tell what the response must be. She needed no pattern, just the fear within her to guide her path. She pulled her fist back, then charged above Evanne, year upon year of footwork from the Three's patterns keeping her steady. Vertiline swung a roundhouse, a ridiculous punch for the unschooled, but she had dragon rage in her fist, and she powered through five bodies in a single whirl.

It bought time. Armitage dragged Evanne back. *Don't look. Don't see. Not yet.* Evanne might be dead. Past saving. Part Vhemin, but only part, and her father was beat beyond reason. Burning smoke from acid blood caused her eyes to water, but she didn't need her eyes, not to blindly flail with her fear and panic and anger all bound together in the clutch of her metal fingers.

Agony speared her, one of her foes striking with those vile talons into her back. Vertiline arched and took another strike in her gut. She turned, fingers trembling. *I can't let my fist open. I can't. I will destroy everyone. I will kill those most beloved to me.*

A strike took her at the joint between collarbone and throat, and she went down, coughing, choking, tasting blood, fingers loosening, but *no, dammit, a little more time, just a little more life.*

She looked up, a moment of calm, or perhaps time stretched because her life was ending. The sorcerer, Meriwether du Reeves, the man she'd originally condemned to die, stood above her. Old, and kind, and with her despite all she had done.

He reached to her, fingers stretched, but she couldn't reach back. The lightning in her fist raged for freedom. He said, "Let it go."

"You'll die."

"Wouldn't be the first time." He said something in the ancient's tongue, just one word, but the world held its breath. She heard the rumble of the Three's anger, his doom waiting for his mistake. And she wanted to scream at him, *not for me*, but she couldn't talk, the blood bubbling in her throat. He spoke a second word, and the lightning in her fist yearned for him.

Meri said a third word as her fingers relaxed. The power of the dragon, amplified by the ancients, flowed to him. Energy coiled about him, blinding, brilliant, roaring louder than Myryntir. He grabbed it with both hands and laid about him as if with a mighty whip, and turned their enemies to char, ash, and a greasy residue.

But she didn't see how it ended. She didn't see anything else at all.

Chapter Twenty-Five

Everyone had been working so hard to save Evanne they hadn't noticed what happened to Tarragon. She'd leaped in just as the High Justiciar had, sword a living brand of white fire, battle cry on her lips, and been mobbed by a swarm of undead monsters.

She got it, she really did. Evanne was in trouble, and Evanne was also a kind of lodestone for the mind. If anyone else felt about the maybe-Vhemin even a little like the way Tarragon did, they wouldn't be able to stop thinking about her.

It all went bad about the time Vertiline sent one of the monsters flying into the western wall. Tarragon saw a clutch of creatures over there, all coming off the racks they'd been stored on like tools in a well-kept workshop. She'd done the math, seen just how many would come if the once-fairy didn't do something, and so she'd charged there.

What with all the whips of lightning and furious cries behind her, no one remarked on her, or her sword. She was in the thick of it, a press of bodies all about her, and it seemed no matter how many limbs or heads she lopped off, there were more right behind them. She'd felt the whimper in her chest, the rake of claws on the side of her face, the burning heat of Requiem as the blade came too close to her now-human skin that couldn't take the heat of a starforge anymore.

Then, the dandy fop she'd discounted as a waste of calories used the old language, borrowed the power in Vertiline's hand, and laid about him like justice itself. The whip of energy cleared the room, all standing corpses cut in half about waist-height. Tarragon would have been one of their number except she held Requiem in a desperate mid guard.

The whip of energy parted against the blade's edge with the sound of glowing steel quenched in water, the force of the impact picking Tarragon off her feet and throwing her right into the very same spot the High Justiciar had tossed an enemy a minute earlier. It was lucky, in a way, as the wall was weak from that blow, only dislocating Tarragon's shoulder as she crashed through it in a shower of rubble. She landed in a dark room on the other side, Requiem tumbling from her nerveless fingers, blade glimmering out in sympathy. Tarragon slid across the floor, knocked her head, and slid the rest of the way in a daze, right until she sailed over a pit and fell, knocking elbows, knees, and skull on the way down to blessed darkness.

WATER ON HER FACE. SOMETHING DAMP AGAINST HER LIPS. SHE couldn't breathe.

Tarragon screamed, convulsed upright, blade of her left hand lashing out, her right pulling back for a follow-up, and at that point she almost passed out from the pain. She thrashed, because there was someone there, right fucking *there*, in her grill and with hands on her, but he was saying things like *it's okay* and *calm down* and *hush*, which she probably wouldn't have listened to except for the pain in her sword-arm's shoulder holding her back.

She subsided, then scrabbled back. Tarragon was on a cot, old and threadbare blankets atop it, which she wanted to spend more time thinking about because they were made from her time, and things in her time didn't *wear out* or *become threadbare*, not unless they'd seen eight hundred years of use, but no one down here could still be alive from that long ago, so there was clearly another explanation.

The room was cosy, a warm glow coming from a portable heat lamp. She wanted to touch it, to see if it was real, because things that used electricity seemed to be in short supply, but there was another thing from her time just doing its job like it always did. A door lay beyond a man, and the man crouched at the side of the cot. The door was easier to focus on because there was something wrong with the man, so she started there. The door was open, and it was just an ordinary-ass door. Beyond was a corridor, leading no doubt to a den of horrors.

Look at the man.

She did. He was one of the living dead from above, but unlike them, he wasn't trying to eat her face. Same basic mummified appearance, like all the water had been sucked out a long time ago, but without the ravening hunger. He held a damp cloth in one hand, and a spilled bowl of water was beside him on the floor.

Her eyes slid to the bowl. "Did I do that?"

"You've had a rough morning." He picked it up, fussing with the cloth before putting it in the bowl and placing both aside. He sank on his haunches. "You fell quite a long way."

"Where's Evanne? Where am I? Where's Requiem?" Tarragon pushed herself away from the wall she'd hunkered against, then slumped back because, like a moron, she'd used her right arm for the trick. "Where is ... everyone?"

The dead man regarded her with surprisingly alive eyes and counted on his fingers. "Evanne is coming. You're in my bedroom, which is at the back of my shop. My shop is the premier supply of anything you might need down here, although that hasn't been tested for some years now due to a lack of customers. Requiem is wrapped in a towel in the kitchen, because it tried to kill me when I picked it up." He frowned at the three fingers, then beamed as he extended a fourth. "Everyone else is with Evanne."

She looked at his fingers, then back to him. "Who *are* you?"

"Would you like breakfast?"

"Is it food or the flesh of your victims?"

"Flesh from my victims would still be food, but I get your drift." He stood, arching his back, and she heard what sounded like every bone in his body pop and click. "It's eggs on toast. You have to use a kind of existential belief you're eating eggs on toast, because the eggs are powdered and the toast is freeze-dried, but I'm sure you've had worse."

Tarragon felt herself unclench a little bit. "You're dead."

"Yes." He gave a sad nod.

"And you're not trying to kill me."

"Not yet. Your meat is juiciest when you're relaxed and sated, at which point I'll creep up behind you and," he ran a finger across his throat, "before hanging you to drain in the larder." He laughed, then sobered at the horror on her face. "That was a joke. Do people still make jokes in the world above?"

"Only ones that are funny."

"It was pretty funny."

"Only if you're not punching down." Tarragon unclenched her jaw. "It's like this. My whole life I've been small. Getting under people's feet, in their way, and doing nothing useful. So people make jokes, calling me a Sandwich, or, or," *hic*, "now I'm Big, they'll drain my blood and hang me in a smoker."

"I didn't say it was a smoker. I said it was a larder." His dead eyes twinkled.

"I'm not afraid."

"That's right."

Hic. "I'm angry."

"You got it."

"I'm angry at *you*."

"Not quite but keep going." The dead man crouched on his haunches again, perhaps to make himself a less formidable presence.

"I'm angry at everyone?" She felt the curiosity in her voice and tried to hold onto the anger. "Because life's unfair."

"Yes, but sometimes it's unfair in your favour." He shrugged. "Not many would get the chance to wield a sword of power, or hold the heart of the first, and I daresay last, Soulkeeper. They probably wouldn't learn of the Three's Wardens' patterns or have a mentor like

Helio who taught them how to be kind, even when it was hard. Because you *are* kind, Tarragon. You're the gentlest person I know. Uh, who's still alive, that is."

Hic. "I'm not gentle. I've killed, like, lots of people."

"Gentle doesn't mean avoiding the necessary when dawn comes. Kind doesn't mean laying down when night falls. Neither mean not standing tall in the tricky, messy middle."

She surged from the cot, fists clenched. "Who the everliving fuck are you?" *Hic.*

"Not very bright, though." He stood, unfazed by her fists. "Come. I promised breakfast, and I always keep my promises. Even though I'm dead."

THE EGGS WERE GOOD. TARRAGON WOULDN'T HAVE KNOWN THEY were powdered. The toast was rich and buttery, with a crunchy crust. *I don't know where Evanne is, but this is good.* She stuffed her face.

They were in a small kitchenette. An ancient glass cooking surface glowered black along one wall, and she knew without feeling it the obsidian surface would be cool to the touch despite having just toasted bread and made eggs. It looked in perfect condition despite the eight hundred years since it was new. She and the dead man were along the opposite wall, facing each other across a faux wooden table.

He'd led her here through a narrow hallway. A door at the end had led 'to the shop' he'd said, and another held 'where people who sweat go to get clean', which she figured for being a shower, and she was seriously uncertain whether food or hot water had been more important, but the smell of the eggs had drawn her nose like a hunting dog's, and here they were. He eyed her, those dead eyes still glinting with gentle humour. "It's good, then?"

"Hmmph." She stuffed another mouthful in atop the one she was still working on.

"Do you know why we gave you the sword?"

Tarragon swallowed. "You didn't give it to me. It came through a demon gate."

"Tomato, tomahto." He waved a hand. "Almost nine hundred years ago, we made a promise to protect this world. But all of us were tricked. Deceived, by the best deceivers in the world. Three of us gave our souls to the world, with a promise to be returned with the power of gods."

Tarragon felt the colour drain from her face. "You what?"

"Demons," he clarified. "They were here, and we knew it. What we didn't know is how deeply they dwelled in the hearts of humans. For all our craft, all our vision, all our raw power, the starlight we captured, and the watchers we became, we were trapped in our new bodies. Not the dawn, not the night, and no freedom to become the in-between."

"Err," Tarragon said, realisation dawning perhaps a mite late. The eggs sat in her stomach like lead.

"We were still strong, though. That part was true. Gods, immortal, all powerful. My sister, the dawn warden, warrior of the first light. My brother, strong as the long dark, as faithful as night. And me. Broken, oddly-formed, little me."

"Gah," she offered. "Uh. Erk."

"You're taking this well."

"My lord Ikmae." She scrambled up, knocked her head on a shelf, staggered back, and knelt on one knee. "Forgive me."

"Get up," he said. "There is nothing to forgive, or if there is, it's our fault anyway. We touched the butterfly's wings a thousand years ago, and here is the hurricane we made."

She didn't look up. "I, uh, *hic*, was angry, uh, at you."

"Yes, but that's to be expected. I get it a lot. Not one thing or the other. My curse, you understand, for wanting to be there for all the people the start and the end forgot or found inconvenient. A prism of people, trapped in one body." He pursued his lips. "Ask your question. I can see it bubbling away, a cauldron simmering without end."

Tarragon risked a glance at him. The dead man sat, eyes still glittering, arms crossed, and he looked nothing like a creature that wanted to eat her face. "How'd you get into a corpse?"

"The bargain."

"You'll need to try harder." Tarragon winced. *Hic.*

He offered a gentle smile. "At the end of the last, great war, the Three's Wardens were scattered. A shell of the host they once were. No one wanted to serve, you see. People saw the cost, how it wasn't just parades and glamour, but toil and death. And how no one thanked you for it. You could march into the breach a thousand times, and if you were really lucky, a single someone might clap you on the back with a 'nice work' and that was that."

"People are dicks."

"People are people." Ikmae shrugged. "I've never asked them to be anything else."

"Work with what you've got?"

"Celebrate what you're given. You should sit. Finish your breakfast."

Tarragon got off her knee and shuffled back to her seat. The eggs tasted just the same as before, but this time, her heart wasn't in it. "You didn't answer the question."

"The body?" He seemed surprised, glancing at himself. "When we asked Vertiline to set up a new school, she had a condition. She wanted a child, one precious thing with the man she loved. An impossible creation, like welding copper to water. And we said," he wobbled his hand in a fifty-fifty gesture, "that was tricky."

"Evanne."

The corpse ignored her. "We asked if we would get the school if we did this for her and she said, only if we never drew breath atop soil, and protected her child. She made us promise."

"You're standing on the ground right now."

"Under," he corrected, but gently. "I'm *under* ground."

"You, you," she spluttered, "*lawyered* your way around it?"

"We were true to the bargain. When you saw Cophine and her brilliant wings, did she land on the ground? No? Did Khiton leave his ship? No. And did Ikmae, one who is all, face the sun these last, lonely years?"

"No?" Tarragon hazarded.

"Correct." He beamed, a horror grimace with kind eyes. "We gave her a child, a thing that could never be."

"She's not a thing."

"I'm talking science, not people." He shrugged. "And yet she exists. Draws breath. And we got something we never bargained for at all."

"Wait." Tarragon pushed egg about with a fork. "I thought you knew the future?"

"We know what is possible. How the tap of your tines there," he pointed at her fork, "will mean a sword misses tomorrow."

"Whose sword?"

"You're missing the point." He hunched for a moment, then straightened. "We got a Soulkeeper. Someone who speaks for everyone, although she doesn't know it."

"Evanne?" Tarragon blinked. "She doesn't speak *for* people."

"Of course not. It's what lets her do it."

"My head hurts."

"The people you want in charge are the ones who don't want the job." Ikmae stood. "Coffee?"

"You have coffee?"

"I have everything." He sighed. "Except the sun on my face."

"Because of your bargain?"

"No. This body." He bustled to the ancients' stove. "They made these as hell warriors to scour the earth, but they had ... deployment problems. They get iffy under my sister dawn's radiance."

"Did you think of sunscreen?"

"Cophine can't be denied. She doesn't like them very much." He tapped grounds into a small device, which he slotted into a larger device, and then pressed a button. After a moment, the rich aroma of roasted arabica filled the small kitchen. "Evanne can speak for everyone, but she can also speak *to* them. A language of the heart."

"Music."

"It's a bit more than that, but you're on the right track."

"And the dead?"

"She can speak to *everyone*. That's the point. The first and last of her kind. An impossibility, because we welded copper and water together." He poured.

Tarragon took the offered cup. "Why are you telling me this?"

"In a few short moments, she will bust through that wall," he pointed toward the door, but implying something farther afield, "and try to kill me. There will be raised voices. An argument. Terrible portents. The end of the world."

"We have a dragon."

"Exactly." He leaned against the stove. "And I would like you to calm her down."

Tarragon considered the coffee, which was delicious, but a little hot. "You did something, didn't you?"

"Me? No. But a bunch of dead things that looked like me? Sure. And I'd very much like to speak with Evanne before she gets too excited."

"And you think I can stop her?"

"And I *know* you can stop her." His mouth quirked into a small smile, and he pointed to her plate. "I saw it in the eggs."

Chapter Twenty-Six

It was all coming apart. Evanne rubbed tears from her face. "Mama?"

Vertiline leaked a horrible amount of blood. Red seemed to be everywhere. Evanne's stomach churned with the conflict between the delicious copperyness of it against knowing who it came from. Papa cradled her. Amber crouched beside them, pressing a red cloth to her throat. It had been a white scarf but was dark burgundy now.

Vertiline's mouth worked, but only blood came forth. *She can't use the Sway. She can't talk. Can't bend the world.* Evanne glanced at the broken wall. Tarragon had gone that way and not come back. Was the once-fairy dead as well? Evanne felt like she was on cracking ice, the lake beneath her eager for something warm and hot to drown.

Amir touched her elbow. "Sing."

"I... can't." Her voice was a croak. "There is no joy."

"Then she will die." His voice was soft but held an urgency that turned her head. "I can't use the Sway. Not for this. You can bind the world. I have felt it. Your works are not just for inspiration and war. Try now, or all is lost."

"I need a guitar."

"You need nothing." He pointed to Vertiline, and all that red. "Nothing but purpose. Find it here."

Evanne sank to her knees. "Hitch."

"I'm here."

"I need you."

"I know." He slipped into her and found his place under her skin. The chill of the grave held them both. "It will be all right."

"She's dying."

"Then sing."

"I don't know the words."

"Yes, you do." He gave her a small mental shove, as if he pushed her to a door she couldn't see. "Over there. Behind your fears. Hidden beneath the anger. Do you see it?"

"I'm afraid."

"I said that."

"If she dies, I'll kill them all."

"I said that too. What else?"

"Why are you so wise?"

"Because I've lost everything." She imagined him right behind her, leaning forward, hand out, but hesitant to touch her. "*Remember*."

And she understood. Closed her eyes. Wet her lips, took a breath. Let it out. Thought about Mama, sun behind her, hair flowing, smile on her face, that one she kept just for Evanne. Mama, at the Imshir docks, scolding a labourer, then showing the *other* smile when she saw Papa. Armitage, bounding to her.

Dinner, hearth, the old stone keep the devil used to live in, but home now, the dark pushed back by Vertiline. Dawn, light coming in, Evanne a child and sick with fever, and Mama there, a cool washcloth to her daughter's brow. The cold of being half-Vhemin, and the warmth of Vertiline's embrace despite her daughter's pointed teeth and scaled shoulders.

The bargain the High Justiciar made, a deal with the gods for more warriors of Light, and Evanne saw the reason now: to build a wall against the dark that would come for her child.

It is so much. It is too much.

Hitch, within her, nodded. *It is everything. Can you lose it?*

Never.

He stepped back, leaving her space. *Then show her.*

Evanne took another breath, then sang. Her mother, always there, letting go the patterns to pull Evanne to safety. She felt the tears, the hot wet saltiness of them, her mended heart beating within her chest.

IN THE SILENCE, WHERE SHADOWS LOOM,
I stand in this darkened room.
Memories flow like a gentle stream,
Your smile is in my dream.

YOUR BARGAIN WAS A PACT WITH THE DIVINE,
More warriors of Light, a wall to define.
Against the darkness, a shield so strong,
For me, beside you, where I belong.

TOO MUCH TO BEAR, A WEIGHT SO GRAND,
Yet within you, a power to withstand.
I step back, leaving space to show,
The strength within you for the healing flow.

I BREATHE, AND MY VOICE TAKES FLIGHT,
A melody born from the depth of night.
Your heart, a dance in harmony,
Against all odds, we're rewriting destiny.

TEARS FALL, HOT AND SALTY, YET SWEET,
Heart mended, a rhythm complete.
Your eyes mirror love and surprise,
At Papa's embrace, for a love that never dies.

. . .

EVANNE FELT VERTILINE'S HEART JOIN HERS, SYNERGY AND harmony. Blood halting its flow, reversing, the tide pushed back against all odds. Evanne sang, the words falling to the ancient stone floor where monsters made other monsters.

She ran out of words and opened her eyes. Saw Vertiline, blue eyes soft, and wide with awe. And so alive. Neck no longer slashed, a thin white line across Mama's throat instead. Papa sobbed and hugged her like a vice. "You're okay."

"Enough, husband." She pushed him away, mock struggling under the weight of so many eyes. Amber's astonishment. Amir's raised eyebrows. Myryntir frozen like ice, mouth slightly agape. Even Pakhet making an appearance, one paw raised in mid clean, tongue out, astonished. Mama rose a little unsteadily, then moved to crouch by Evanne. "I—"

"Mama, I'm sorry. I shouldn't have—"

"Hush." Vertiline pulled her close, stoking the back of her head. "It's all right."

"But it almost wasn't."

She felt Vertiline breathe in, then let it out. The calmness of it steadied Evanne's breathing. "It almost wasn't," she agreed. "I have been in many battles I almost lost. I do not spend time imagining a different future. It is a waste of time."

"I shouldn't have—"

"A waste of time."

"But there was—"

"Still a waste of time." Vertiline held Evanne at arm's length, then stroked a lock of hair from her daughter's forehead. "There is a lesson here. That is worth spending time on."

"I thought you didn't like being a teacher."

"I don't." Vertiline stood, then helped Evanne up. "I hate it. But I love being your mother." She turned away, examining the carnage, suddenly businesslike. "What were those things?"

"A scourge of the ancients, perhaps." Amber looked doubtful. "We heard no legends of them. An enemy saved until it was too late?"

"Nah." Armitage scratched under his chin. "You don't save a weapon. You run the other guy through with it." He nudged an again-corpse with his foot. "I figure this lot weren't ready. No control, no organisation. They just rushed us."

"They almost did us in," Amir said.

"You need a hug?"

"No."

"Then deal with it." Armitage rolled a body over. "If I hadn't seen these guys up and about, I'd say they've been dead a long, long time. They're ... mostly dry. But you know what's really bothering me?"

Evanne watched Amir process that, the Knight Adept's eyes widening a micron in surprise, then his lips pressing into a line as if to say, *There's something bothering you more than unholy risen fiends?* "I'll bite."

"Where are the cats?" Armitage arched his back, and Evanne heard a *pop*. "Sight of Day. About this high," his hand went out to the Feybrind's head height, "with a companion, Sandy Vagina."

"Sands Apart," Amir murmured.

"That one." Armitage squinted at the dragon. "Did you eat them?"

//I'M OFFENDED YOU WOULD EVEN SUGGEST SUCH A THING. BESIDES, I PREFER VHEMIN STEAKS.//

"*They went through the hole in the wall. They followed the little one who became big.*" Pakhet pointed with her nose. "*It smells bad in there.*"

Chapter Twenty-Seven

Tarragon quested through the shop. The shelves were lined with all manner of marvels. She found freeze-dried food packets of all kinds, like coq au vin, beef stew, and even the marvellous eggs Ikmae made for her. There were everlight lanterns that would never run out of power, rope spun from spiders raised in orbital habitats, a wishing stone with a single charge, and there, beyond all reason, a broom that appeared to do nothing. She hefted it, admired how the wood was unchanged by the charge of eight hundred years, and put it back. "Will we ever make things like these again?"

"Hmm?" The god looked up from behind the register. It was an antique even by ancient standards, made of brass, with big keys and a mechanical display totalling some long-forgotten purchase of four dollars and thirty cents. "No, I don't think so."

"Because there are no more fairies?"

"There are plenty of fairies if you know where to look." He ignored the widening of her eyes. "It's because you'll make better, different things. All this," he gestured to the stocked shelves, "came from a time when everyone wanted theirs, and when they got it, they said, 'Fuck you, now I've got mine'." He rubbed his nose with a long finger, the nail on the end a weapon itself. "You're different, now. I hope."

"I used to be a fairy."

"You still are."

"How did you get to become the shopkeeper? Did they," Tarragon wiggled her fingers, "make a special sales assistant from a corpse?"

"No. This corpse was like the others upstairs. It made its way down here and killed the shopkeeper some time ago." Ikmae's devil eyes turned sad for a moment. "He was a short man. A little round. Loved to laugh. Discounted often, even when he shouldn't. I buried him when I ... took over."

"Took over?"

"After we signed our covenant with the High Justiciar, I needed to get my feet off soil, and this looked a good, quiet place to weather the squall. Then you turned up." He glanced at the sealed, vault-like door to the south. "And them."

"Is it Evanne? Is she here to kill you?"

"No, she's coming through there," he pointed to the western wall. "She'll be bringing the dragon, once they work out how to get something that big through the eye of a needle."

"Then who?" Tarragon hefted the broom and marched to the door. *I've had just about enough of surprises.* She palmed the ancient lock, waiting as lights grudgingly flickering into pale luminance. It gave what she supposed to be a trilling noise, but which time wore the end off, making it more of a dying warble. The big, round lock set in the middle *clanked*, dust silting from the mechanism, then it churned, bars sliding back, the door rising in a smooth *hush* of escaping air. Tarragon raised the broom, swinging it like a *bo* staff. "Ha!"

She froze mid-swing. Kneeling on the other side was Sight of Day, frozen in the act of trying to pick an electronic lock. Sands Apart bared her fangs, preparing to leap at Tarragon, before relaxing in relief. *{We thought to rescue you from evil.}*

Sight of Day stood. *{It seems you need little rescuing. Although that man looks evil. Shall we dispatch him?}*

"That's Ikmae." Tarragon lowered the broom.

{He seems less glamorous than when we last met.}

"You've met Ikmae?" Tarragon goggled. "Twice, now?"

{He gets around.} Sight of Day walked past her into the store.

Sands Apart followed. *{This place has a lot of stuff. It's all junk, of course.}*

"Junk?" Tarragon felt like the conversation had already departed on a ship bound for nowhere.

{It's made by human hands. Feybrind craftsmanship is better.}

"Some of it's made by fairies." Ikmae shrugged. "You make do with what you've got."

Tarragon bristled. "Hey!"

Sands Apart clicked her fingers, drawing everyone's eye. Sight of Day padded to her, Tarragon drifting in his wake. *{What did you find?}*

Sands Apart tossed him a small cardboard box. The ink on it had faded almost to illegibility. Tarragon tried to peer closer, but Sight of Day gave her a raised eyebrow and raised shoulder to hide his prize, secreting it about his person. *{We'll need something else. The Justiciar is tenacious.}*

"What are you doing to Vertiline? And..." Tarragon gathered her thoughts. "And, what do you think you *can* do? She's Tresward. The best of the best. Immune to pranks and sword thrusts both."

"She's not as immune to everything as you might think." Ikmae handed a roll of delicate, orbital-spun twine to Sight of Day. "Will this do?"

The cat took it with a nod of thanks, then paused in great delight at a collection of small metal cylinders. To Tarragon's eye they looked like emergency extinguishers, the kind you'd use if you were fresh out of fairies willing to walk into a fire to put out its cause. Sands Apart's tail swished, and the woman steepled her fingers before speaking. *{I think so.}*

"What do you mean, not immune?" Tarragon turned to Ikmae as the cats loped off through the aisles. "What happened to Vertiline? Is Evanne okay?"

"Evanne and her mother will be here in a few moments. They will come through," he pointed at the western wall again, but harder this time, "that. They will not be subtle. They will have swords and Light and command the Sway. Her mother is very angry because she almost died."

"She what?"

"It is of no moment."

"It's a big moment! Is Evanne okay?"

"The Soulkeeper survives to keep more souls, yes. She is also angry, because she feels guilty and afraid. You can see it written on the stars."

Tarragon looked at the ceiling, seeing no stars. "We're not outside."

"The stars are exactly where they are supposed to be. They swing in their celestial rhythm and we know where they'll be because we know where they were and where they're going. We don't need to see them to see them."

Tarragon closed her eyes, pressing fingertips to temples. "My head hurts again."

She felt a soft touch under her chin. Her eyes snapped open. The god was right before her, hand tilting her chin toward him. His fingers weren't sharp or scaly like she expected. They were infinitely careful, moved by a mind that woke the universe before time's clock started. "All will be well, Tarragon. You have gathered all the friends you need. They are good friends, too. They will do what's required, before it's too late."

"Too late for what?"

In answer, the wall exploded in a shower of rubble and Light. The High Justiciar led the charge, summerglow blade held in high guard, feet cracking the floor where the patterns placed them. At her side was Armitage, the Vhemin ferocious, angry, and not looking like his old injury pained him at all. The sorcerer strode with them, his skin pale and stretched but his eyes hard.

Pakhet flickered into visibility then snapped out. Amir strode with his blade bare, its length dripping molten Light on the ancient stone. Behind them all, Amber and Jade, siblings, merchants, and now warriors, both holding lengths of steel that would serve to sever soul from body well enough.

And, of course, the dragon. Azure electricity crackled around Myryntir's jaws, his eyes fever-bright, inhaling to roar or blast foes.

Tarragon's gaze fell on Evanne, her lover a step behind Vertiline, broken machete in hand, a song on her lips, and Tarragon *felt* it, really, right in the middle of her chest. It was a song that said *you are absolutely fucking with the wrong person.*

The extinguisher canister tumbled toward the group from where Sight of Day hid behind a shelf. The Feybrind rose, loosed an arrow, and crouched behind cover again in one smooth motion. He was all flair, his cloak flapping, golden eyes fierce. Vertiline, nobody's fool, sliced the arrow from the air, but her turning away allowed Sands Apart to slip from behind another shelf, throwing a blade underhand. The steel was lampblack, difficult to spot amid the dust and debris, and hit the canister dead centre.

It exploded.

It was packed with white motes, and these filled the room almost instantly, making Tarragon feel like they were standing inside a cloud. Sight of Day tossed the ancient cardboard box next, and this time his loosed arrow wasn't cut by Vertiline, who was merely human, and currently blinded. The box also exploded, colouring the cloud red, and bringing a harsh spicy rasp to Tarragon's throat, even at this distance. *Cayenne. They've tossed pepper at a dragon. Are they mad?*

Evanne coughed, and her song died. Armitage sneezed, then so did the dragon, lightning crackling through the cloud. Amir caught a blast on the edge of his steel. The bolt arced to the floor and blasted him from his feet. A conduit of energy danced from the floor to a previously-invisible Pakhet, who suddenly became both visible and unconscious.

Sight of Day and Sands Apart stood at the same time, and Tarragon caught the spider's silk gleam of the orbital-spun cord stretched between them. They ran forward, and neatly clotheslined Vertiline, Armitage, Evanne, Amber, Meri, and Jade. The Feybrind, cat-quick, spun through their fallen friends, liberating an arsenal's worth of weapons, pacing clear of the miasma choking everyone, and stood before Ikmae, who as near as Tarragon could tell hadn't moved a muscle.

"Now's your moment," the god murmured.

Vertiline staggered upright, a snarl on her lips, and she tried to speak, but the Sway died in a coughing fit. Tarragon hurried forward, hands outstretched, realising she was making herself a target, and also a Big subject of everyone's attention, including a pissed-off dragon, but excepting the unconscious giant grey tiger. "Hold!"

"I'm gonna kill a motherfucker." Armitage surged upright, his snake eyes wild. "And that motherfucker looks like a cat."

"I'll help," Meriwether offered.

"Hold! Three's mercy, hold!" Tarragon rattled around in her head, mental fingers landing on a possible solution. "This is not what it seems."

"It seems like someone wants a beating," the Vhemin insisted.

"They disarmed you to stop you killing a god," Tarragon blurted.

Everyone took a moment then. Evanne dusted white chalk from her black clothes, then scrubbed some from rust locks. "I have sand inside my sand."

Vertiline's normally cool voice held a hint of cayenne-induced rasp. "Which god? There should be no gods here. I made a *bargain*."

"Them." Tarragon stepped aside, revealing Ikmae behind her. "Ikmae. Lord of the—"

"I know who they are." The air turned icy around Vertiline's words. "We've met."

"Um." *Hic.* "So, they need to talk to Evanne, and they look like a monster, and we know you were trying to save us, but *hic* we just need to calm down."

"I made a bargain. A compact, signed upon the heavens."

"I know, the stars." Tarragon waved a hand upward. "They're still where they were, last time we looked, and going where they're needed, because we know where they started and where they want to be."

"Very good," the god said, *sotto voce*.

Evanne pushed past her mother, scrubbing more extinguisher dust from her hair. "Why does Ikmae want to talk to me?"

Chapter Twenty-Eight

"You're not much to look at." Evanne kicked a stone, her boot scraping on the old stone floor. The pebbled rattled off into the gloom, the ancients' lights flickering and stuttering after it.

"For a god?" Ikmae walked beside her, the corpse's midnight eyes tracking the gloom. The body they wore was male, dead, slightly hunched, and gave the impression of being more solid than granite.

"For anyone. You're a dead guy. And you don't smell amazing."

"I don't smell of anything. I'm a reanimated corpse designed for deep insurgency strikes on enemies. Odour would defeat the purpose."

"Well, your clothes don't smell amazing."

"Fair. Now, ask me."

"Ask you what?" Evanne gave Ikmae a little side eye.

"What it's all about. Why you're here. What you need to do."

"I know all that stuff." Evanne ignored the widening of the god's dead eyes. "I'm here because there's no one else. There's a thing I've got to do, over there," she waved a hand at a wall, unsure if it was the right direction, "because Wild Sur is trying to break the world again. He's been dredging up old hates with a new shovel, grabbing ancienttimey weapons to kill those who aren't like him. I know the music. I hear it when I try to sleep."

"Do you know what you need to do?"

"Kill Wild Sur."

"Consider delegation," the god advised. "Wild Sur is an old Feybrind, wily, and good with a blade. He can't be Commanded—"

"He what?" Evanne halted, the god coasting to a stop just a few paces forward. "I mean, I wouldn't, because it's wrong. But if he can't be Commanded..." She *hmm'd*. "Could we use that Trick for other Feybrind? Set them free?"

"I knew we chose the right one." Ikmae gave her a little devil smile, those sharp teeth a rival for the shark-toothed grin her father had. They sobered. "Sadly, no. His ... route to that solution isn't typical. Other Feybrind would be unhappy with adopting his method."

"So, his logic is to erase the non-Feybrind to solve the problem?"

"That's a part of it." The god bent, retrieving the stone she'd kicked earlier. "Do you know what's important about this?"

"It's a stone."

"It's a stone that was waiting down the hall we came from. It was made in the heart of a star millennia ago. Or lots of stars, over time, growing bigger, and collapsing on themselves. The forges of the heavens pushed out stronger, denser materials at each fall."

"You sound like Tarragon."

"Tarragon is wise."

"Tarragon was an innocent." Evanne bristled. "You took that from her. You made her like *us*."

"My sister did, yes. And a little bit more. But we didn't take her innocence away. She's still got that. What we did for Tarragon started over eight hundred years ago. We made her empty, so she could be full. We made her of material you can't find inside any star."

Evanne growled. "The stone?"

"The youth have no eye for poetry." The god rolled their shoulders, as if loosening up for a fight. "The stone formed when this planet did. Some of its materials were caught in a deep ocean lava floe. The seas surged, spitting chunks of black rock to the shore. A sick camel ate it by mistake. Its teeth cracked the stone, making it smaller. It fell through the fissures of the world, waiting inside this mountain. Thousands of years, the busy bees of industry rising and falling, until Susan Mercantile made—"

"Susan who?"

"She's not the important part of the story. Susan designed this facility. All the nooks and crannies, how it should huddle under the earth, and how it should be strong. But she didn't design for the war that came, or the long wait in the dark after. The ceiling broke. The crack became a lesion. The stone escaped, falling down here, until you found it."

"So I could kick it?"

"So you could kick it *here*, for me to pick it up, and this conversation could happen. So, in turn, I can do this." They turned, whippet-quick, tossing the stone down the corridor. As he turned, the lights flared to brightness, showing three dead warriors on approach. The stone hit the skull of the first, cracking it like a dropped gourd. It careened off the creature's spine, bounced into the eye socket of the second, rattled inside its skull a moment, popped out the top, ricochetted off the ceiling, and burrowed through the top of the third monster's skull.

All three dropped.

"Show off," Evanne said.

"Conversations are important," Ikmae countered. "Are you listening to this one?"

"Things in motion, blah blah, important stuff, blah blah, end of the world."

The god rolled their black eyes. "You need to hurry up. You've got everyone you need. So does Wild Sur. His army amasses. He is trying to get control of the orbital weapons. When he does…"

Evanne waited for them to finish, and when the god just stood there like a coat rack, she sighed. "When he does, doom."

"Doom." Ikmae nodded.

"If he's got an army, what do we have?" She counted on her fingers. "A dragon, and not a very good one. He's a bit enthusiastic with the friendly fire. A cat, terrified of shadows. A sorcerer who can't magic, because of some mistake he made. Mama and Papa, who are so scared of what will happen to me they'll get themselves killed. And Tarragon, who so badly wants to stand in front of me she'll get killed too." She felt her throat clench and took a couple deep breaths. "Two merchants. An Adept who's so confident he's just the kind of person who'll fall into a hole by accident. And me. Just me, who can sing, but nothing else. I mean, I get too cold in the winter and too hot in the summer. I can't fight a war."

The god gave her an appraising eye, then counted on their fingers. "The dragon is a blue. They think they're the best, and they might be. The dragon is the best thing to have when you meet another dragon. Pakhet—"

"What other dragon?"

"The tiger has a good heart. You just need to stop expecting her to be someone she's not."

"I don't expect that. She does. It's why she's so scared all the time."

The god sighed. "Have you told her that?" At Evanne's blank stare, they continued counting. "The sorcerer made no mistake. He only thinks he did. He will help you if you help him."

"By rescuing Geneve? I keep hearing about her, but what if she's dead?"

"If you think Geneve needs rescuing, you've missed the point." They shook their head. "Your mother, father, and lover will fight for you, so you can fight for the world."

"I can't fight for the world. I've got a, a," she pulled her broken machete free, "whatever this is."

They swayed back from her erratic waving of a broken blade. "You've got a suit of armour built for just you."

"Eric's suit? It's broken."

"Eric. Eric." Ikmae turned the name over. "I'd almost forgotten that name."

"So has he, and he asked me not to mention it to him. What about the merchants?"

"You need balance in all things. Real people, to remind you not everyone is a hero."

"And the Adept?"

"You're right. He will fall in a hole." Ikmae gave a tight smile. "But it's a hole he dug, some time ago."

"Nice pep talk."

"I'm not here to cheer you up. Sit by a fire, have a cup of cocoa, and harden the fuck up." They stepped closer. "I'm here to tell you there's work to be done, and you're taking far too long to get to it."

Evanne thought about that, feeling the anger at his words turn to a roiling sickness in her gut. "I—"

"Yes, *you*. And *only* you. We don't ask for the world we're given. But we're given it anyway. What are you going to do about it?"

She thought about that. Looked at the fallen warriors, and wondered about how gods thought, planning for things people couldn't see across the span of a hundred lifetimes. "If you know how this is going to turn out—"

"We don't know. We *try*. We got it wrong before, and badly. Which is why we agreed to your mother's bargain. Too many cooks in the kitchen. Everyone died. Time to try something different."

"I could fail?"

"Sure."

"That's not helpful."

"What would be helpful?" They tipped their head to the side.

"Breakfast."

Ikmae blinked. "Breakfast?"

"For a start. Then you can fix the armour. And show us the way out."

Chapter Twenty-Nine

"**Y**ou lied to me." Vertiline stalked the corridors, not caring if the god kept up. "I'm done with you. The school? It's gone."

The corpse that held the soul of Ikmae bustled by her side. If it weren't for the horror eyes, the sabre teeth, and the claws, she'd be fooled into thinking it was just a man. *Another lie*. "The school lives. It's ... troubled."

"I mean, *I'm* done with it."

"That's why it's troubled. You were done with it before it started."

She whirled on Ikmae, hand on the hilt of her sword. "I did my part. I taught them everything I knew."

"Not everything." The god didn't seem to notice her hand or sword, or perhaps they didn't care. "You taught them your hate and anger. You didn't teach them to love."

"Love?" Her laugh was flat, hard like iron. "There is no love in war."

"There is only war if you don't love." Ikmae shrugged. "It's not that hard."

Vertiline realised her jaw was clenched tight enough to crack teeth. She breathed, relaxing her shoulders. "And I should have given them flowers?"

Ikmae put their hands in their pockets, then continued walking in the direction Vertiline travelled. "You should have given them a family. If you'd done that, who knows how many would still be alive."

"Is this a test?"

"There are no more tests for the High Justiciar. You've passed them all. Your sash is heavy with ten gold bars of the Storm, married to the ten silver of the Sway." Ikmae turned a corner into a room lined with dark stone. The glower of a forge hunkered against a wall. An ordinary anvil hunkered, and smithy's tools lay alongside devices whose purpose Vertiline could only guess at. *Ancients' sorceries. Sinners by another name.* She tasted the bitterness in her mouth. The god didn't seem to notice her expression, in the same way they'd ignored her hand-on-sword of a moment ago. "But the teaching must still be done."

Vertiline tore her attention from the irritating fuckwit and took another look at the room. She smelled something besides the heat of cooked metal. It was like the air after lightning struck. On a work-bench was a disassembled suit of armour. She knew it well; they'd carried the worthless, broken thing half-way around the world. A door against the far wall opened, and through it came Tarragon, followed by Sight of Day, Sands Apart, and last of all, Evanne. Tarragon and Evanne were still recovering from some hilarity in the prior room, the cats half-smiling in benevolent tolerance. Tarragon carried a shaped sheet of golden metal, and the foursome gathered about the bench as the once-fairy fitted it against the breastplate of the broken armour.

"They can't see us?" Vertiline looked between her daughter, friends, and the god.

"Or hear us."

"I don't like this trickery. I should not be spying on them."

Ikmae gave her a small, sad smile. "Mother of the Three, you are not spying on them. You're here for something completely different."

"Don't call me Mother of the Three." She settled some. "It reminds me too much of her."

"Geneve? She was always our daughter." Ikmae gestured to the four before them. "Watch. Listen."

I've got nothing better to do except be angry. Vertiline crossed her arms, and tried to think what Iz would have done. He'd no doubt say something like *there is a lesson in everything*, and she'd have wanted to punch him for it, but he'd not have been wrong. The only things he'd ever been wrong about was the value of the Chevalier at his side, and believing he could love his daughter from a distance.

The group continued working on the armour. Sight of Day flipped the torso section over; it was clearly heavy even for the Feybrind. Vertiline caught the words stencilled on the device's back. *Itikari Stardrive.* The cat fussed with something, and a hatch opened, revealing a nightmare of devices and wires. Golden eyes widening, he pressed his fingers together. *{I wonder what all these things do.}*

Sands Apart pointed at a silver tube. *{That appears to be a cylinder. We're making progress.}*

Tarragon laughed. "It's a synergy buffer. It's for catching dreams."

Evanne hunkered close to the once-fairy. "Why would you catch dreams in armour?"

"When people die, they release all their dreams. Everything they were is given back."

"So, the armour collects dreams?"

"I think the armour gives them to the pilot." Tarragon bit her lip. "This is as much protection as weapon. It needs power to soar. Dreams might be a part of that."

{Magnificent. Another device of horror. What wonderful people you were.} Sight of Day put his hand on Evanne's arm. *{You do not need to wear this.}*

"There is no one else. We know it killed Hitch. Or *ate* bits of him. He died because of the last demon he fought. Maybe he died because he hadn't killed enough people for the synergy buffer, so it snacked on his body." The others fell still, and Vertiline wanted to step forward, to take Evanne in her arms and say this wasn't her fight. That Vertiline, not Evanne, should wear the armour. The god's hand settled on her arm, stilling her. Evanne looked at her three friends. "I am half-Vhemin. And half-human. This will kill a Vhemin outright, and a human will be consumed. I'm the only one who can be tolerated within, and whose body will heal the hurt."

Sands Apart gazed at the bard. *{Just because you're capable doesn't mean you're obliged.}*

"You guys don't get it." Evanne scrubbed rust-red hair. "If I don't go inside, then you all die."

"A CHIP OFF THE OLD BLOCK," VERTILINE GROUSED. "JUST LIKE HER mother."

Ikmae eyed her as they walked. "What do you mean?"

"I was always the last to volunteer. I was only there because..." She trailed off. *Because of a man, at first.* "There was no one else."

"You are the only one who didn't give up. That's why we picked you." Ikmae stopped before another doorway. This one worked well enough, not too much stiction in the jamb, and it hissed open with only the faintest stuttering nodding to its age. Somehow, the inhabitants of the room failed to notice. "You started a school by a demon gate because your sister of the blade asked you to wait."

"But I didn't go in. I didn't go after her."

"Perhaps you're just looking for reasons to feel sorry for yourself." As Vertiline rounded on the god, they held up a hand. "Listen. It's starting now."

The room held two men: her student Amir, and her husband, who had been her teacher these many long years. She yearned for his embrace, a single moment for them to sit beneath a shady tree and share ice wine. Listen to him talk to her about how it would be all right. Him, a Vhemin from the blasted plaguelands, giving her, the High Justiciar, advice. And so heavy with wisdom it was, all simple matters that came back to blood on the sands. Whose it would be, and whose you'd protect from spilling alongside.

She let her eyes drift to Amir. "He is my most promising student."

"And yet he thinks he is the least of you." Ikmae shrugged. "I wonder where he learned that?"

"He leads with his heart too much but uses wit as a feint against his cares."

"Hmm."

"What's that supposed to mean?"

Amir, oblivious to his audience, bent over the table between them. Armitage had broached an ancient cask of wine; she could tell her husband's work by how the rim was ragged, torn, yet retained enough roundness to avoid spilling a drop. The Knight Adept held up a finger, eyes owlish with drink, perhaps unaware of a Vhemin's ability to metabolise hard liquor. *Or, he is aware, and sets himself the challenge anyway. It is what a Tresward would do.* "You shee, I mean, see: behold, there is a bottom to this cask."

"I didn't say there wasn't." Armitage scooped another fill from the cask, drank, then wiped his lips with the back of his arm. "I said the wine wouldn't run out."

The Knight Adept considered his almost empty cup, then filled it. Sipped. Thought. "How does the wine not run out if the cask is empty?"

"You think in straight lines, baby Knight."

"I think there is an empty cask."

"Yes, your eyes work well enough, but it's your brain I'm worried about." Armitage nudged the cask. "This has friends."

"There are other cashksh? I mean, casks?" Amir's eyes widened in delight. "How have you kept them hidden?"

"The only one I need to hide them from is Evanne." Armitage looked about, conspiratorial. "She stole four bottles of summer wine we'd laid in for the winter. Drank the lot in one afternoon."

"The lying bastard," Vertiline mused. "He told me he drank them."

"She has a tolerance, then?" Amir retrieved the cask, pouring some into Armitage's cup, then his own. "Like her father, no doubt."

"Like Vhemin, I guess." Armitage shrugged, those massive shoulders rolling like the ocean. "But she's wily, like her mother. A Vhemin would have taken the wine and challenged any who denied their right to drink. Evanne waited until we were before hearth, then broached the topic like a child might. Her eyes, so wide. A babe in arms, asking why there were six bottles less in the cellar."

"Six? But you said four."

"I drank two," the Vhemin admitted. "It was her doorway in, see?"

"And you didn't call her on it?" Amir frowned. "I'm going to need more wine to understand this."

"I was already in trouble."

"He was," Vertiline said. "He didn't share."

"See, I'd just wanted a taste, then that led to the bottle, and then two, and then the afternoon was gone. I knew I was cooked, and Evanne knew it too. And she wanted to see if I would take the fall."

"And whether you'd take her with you," Amir offered.

"Nah," Armitage said. "She already knew the answer to that. Can read people, my girl. Can read 'em like one of Tilly's books."

"Then why'd she do it?" Amir and Vertiline spoke at the same time.

Armitage leaned back, then pushed himself upright. "I'll get more wine."

Amir's hand shot out, fast as a cobra. *No, fast as a Knight of the Tresward*. His eyes were no longer dull, his speech firm. "Why did she do it, friend Armitage?"

The big man laughed. "She had a girl she was sweet on. Needed the wine for a good cause."

"She had no such girl," Vertiline hissed. "I'd know."

"'Course, her mother never knew. But the sands did, and they'll tell you if you know how to listen."

VERTILINE HUNCHED. SHE STRAIGHTENED WITH EFFORT, BECAUSE the pose was unbecoming of the High Justiciar, let alone anyone north of fifteen years old. "I don't like this."

"The universe doesn't much care what you like." Ikmae hunched right along beside her. "Imagine being a god and seeing it all before it happens. And it still blindsides you."

"Hope for the best, but plan for the worst?"

"Hope is for fools. Planning is for gods." Ikmae hunched further. "I still hope, though. Even though I shouldn't." He brightened. "Ah. Here we are."

They'd arrived back at their shop. Or the shop of someone who died a long time ago, leaving a god to take over the corpse of a monster and play grocer. Some shelves were still in disarray, but change had come like the coming of spring after a hard winter. Some of the knocked over stands were upright. The mess on the floor had been tidied. It was so clean you couldn't even tell dust and debris had been here. There was no fixing the giant hole in the wall where they'd made their entrance, but the giant chunks of rock and metal had been stacked. Vertiline blinked. "Someone tidied this up? To what purpose?"

Amber made his entrance from the doorway leading to Ikmae's bedroom, kitchen, and washhouse. He carried a bucket made of a matte material, water slopping over the edge. "Come, sister. There is still much to do."

Jade joined him, a mop in hand, hair swept back beneath a kerchief. Where Amber was enthusiastic, she was grudging. "We are leaving tomorrow. Why are we cleaning up?"

"I asked that," Vertiline offered, but of course the siblings couldn't hear her.

"Someone else might come. They will want to see wood stocked for a fire and water drawn from the well. These are the tricks we caravaners have used since the dawn of—"

"You're a caravaner. I'm a caravaner's sister."

He put the bucket down. "You're a caravaner true, mop in hand, with a fierce will to share the road as you found it. It burns within your heart."

"I've got something burning in my heart." She brandished the mop. "Why aren't *you* doing the scullery work?"

"It's not a scullery. That would imply a kitchen and dishes. This, wise sister, is janitorial."

"I should have drowned you in the bath when we were younger."

"And forego this learning experience?" Amber beamed. "While you're mopping, I will be packing."

"I could pack."

"Yes, but then we'd starve." The brother continued smiling like a star. "You'd stow too many herbs and not enough oats."

"You're not wrong about that." Jade sniffed. "I don't even know what an oat is. In its natural habitat, I mean. I'm familiar with gruel."

"Not familiar enough! We shall remedy that on the road."

As Jade mopped, perhaps overacting the sulking in Vertiline's eye, Amber made a show of going through shelves and selecting supplies. She noted how his eyes were always moving between his sister and the hole in the wall. How his brightness was a sheen, not even skin deep. She turned to Ikmae. "Why do they come? They will surely die."

"They live in this world, too."

"There are others better suited to fighting."

"There are none better able to show you what you fight for, though. Oh, I know about hearth and home, the child you cherish, and the husband you stand beside. This," they gestured at the siblings, "is a smaller thing. But greater for it."

"You don't make any sense."

"Perhaps you should start thinking for yourself rather than asking for answers all the time."

"You're the one dragging me through this warren."

"Hmm." Ikmae turned from her to observe Amber and Jade. "You're not my favourite, you know."

"Thanks." Vertiline snorted. "I don't like any of you Three, so I guess we're even."

"Your daughter is my chosen. She is made of oil and water, earth and light. Things others might see as uncomfortable so close together, but they miss the mark. Being made of two things gives power."

"Like you?"

"You're thinking of the wrong sort of power." They stepped back as Amber walked through where they'd stood. "Evanne chooses for who she fights."

"Her family." Vertiline nodded. "She is stubborn and wilful and I love her for it."

"She fights for everyone's family. Even these people here, because she can *see* them, Justiciar. She *knows* them. She lived as the odd one out, not comfortable in her skin, seeking clarity through the lives of others, and so knew them. Your daughter calls herself the Half-Made. Tarragon calls her Well-Made."

"I call her perfect." Vertiline bristled, unsure why. The god wasn't casting stones at Evanne. "What's your point?"

"We're just talking," the god offered. "The point is for you to learn."

"I thought you said there were no tests left for the High Justiciar."

"Learning doesn't mean there is a test."

"You're the annoying middle child, aren't you?"

That got a small smile. Ikmae nodded. "Come. We have one more stop to make."

The dragon was in the large cavern, because Myryntir couldn't fit into the corridors below. He was curled, nose to tail, but not asleep. There were no bodies left about, and Vertiline didn't have to think too hard to guess what had become of the nightmare monster corpses. The dragon's blue eyes tracked her. *//SHHH. SHE SLEEPS.//*

Atop the dragon's back was Pakhet. The grey-striped super-sized tiger was stretched out, much longer than Vertiline would have guessed even such a large cat could be. She lay with her belly facing the cavern's ceiling, eyes closed, the dragon her pillow.

"You can see us?"

"Dragons do not miss much," Ikmae said. "Some find it charming."

//I AM MADE OF CHARM.//

Vertiline closed the distance to the dragon's nose, and put a hand on Myryntir's muzzle. The heady heat of his bellows breath teased her hair back. "Hullo, dragon."

//HELLO, VERTILINE, SHIELD OF THE WORLD, INCARNA-TION OF THE DAWN MAIDEN, AND MOTHER OF OUR SAVIOUR.//

Vertiline let her hand fall. "The what?"

//SHHH,// the dragon said again. *//THE CAT NEEDS HER SLEEP.//*

"The cat is either feigning sleep or dead, as they can hear your voice in Imshir." Vertiline sighed. "Evanne is not your saviour. She's my little girl."

//SHE CAN BE MANY THINGS AT ONCE.// The dragon eyed the god. *//WHAT HAVE YOU BEEN DOING, SLEEPING? I EXPECTED YOU TO HAVE COVERED THIS GROUND ALREADY.//*

"She's a difficult student," Ikmae murmured.

Vertiline did the mental calculus on how long they'd been here. "Have you been laying here for two days?"

//YOU DO NOT DISTURB A SLEEPING CAT ON YOUR LAP.//

Vertiline kicked a small piece of granite, and watched it hop into the gloom. "We are going to fight Wild Sur. He is, by renown, a Feybrind."

//SOME CATS USE THEIR CLAWS MORE OFTEN.// The dragon yawned, but Vertiline noticed he didn't arch his neck, perhaps to allow Pakhet undisturbed rest. *//NOT ALL OF THEM ARE GOOD.//*

"And dragons are benevolent?"

//DRAGONS ARE DRAGONS.// Myryntir rolled an eye in her direction. *//MUCH LIKE YOU FRAIL THINGS, WE CAN BE GOOD AND BAD. I THINK WE'RE MADE WANTING TO BE GOOD, AND THE WORLD MAKES THAT HARD. I DIED BEFORE I WAS BORN. I WAS SAVED BY THE SOULKEEPER. THESE ARE FACTS, NOT MORAL OUTCOMES. WHAT I DID WITH THEM BECAME A CHOICE THAT CHANGED THE WORLD.//* The dragon looked away for a moment. *//THAT SOUNDED CONCEITED. I DON'T MEAN I AM MAGNIFICENT BECAUSE I CHANGED THE WORLD. I MEAN THE SAVIOUR CHOSE TO SAVE ME, AND I EXIST. I AM MAGNIFICENT FOR OTHER REASONS.//*

Vertiline dropped a hand to her sword. It made her feel centred to have the blade so close at hand. *There are not many problems that can't be solved with steel or glass.* "You are but a stone cast into the lake of the universe?"

//LET'S NOT BE DICKS ABOUT THIS. I'M BETTER THAN A STONE.// The dragon gave a toothy smile. *//BUT NOT EVEN DRAGONS CAN DO ALL THE MAGNIFICENCE. THERE IS MUCH POTENTIAL SPARKLE TO GO AROUND.//*

"Do you mean fighting?" Vertiline clenched her sword's pommel. "I can do that."

//YOU DON'T GET TO CHOOSE YOUR FIGHTS. THEY CHOOSE YOU.//

Vertiline glared at Ikmae. "Did you coach him on being obtuse?"

"He means there will be fighting, but there will also be dying. I will, of

course, be elsewhere." Pakhet stretched, forepaws trembling, yawned, then rolled over onto her feet. *"You know this. You are stalling."*

"And you?" The High Justiciar glared at the cat. "You're always running away. What will happen if Evanne needs you?"

"Evanne would not need a frightened, mewling creature like me." Vertiline detected a tone of self-loathing in the cat's voice. *"I am a stone skipped across the lake of creation, but I'm not smooth. I won't fly true. I'll splash and be lost forever. They made me wrong."*

//IT'S OKAY. THEY MADE ALL OF US WRONG. IT DOESN'T MEAN WE CAN'T TOUCH THE SUN.//

"You've got wings."

Vertiline snorted, then at Pakhet's glare, sobered. "Sorry. It's just ... you're a giant tiger. You frighten everyone by walking into the room, and you're ... scared?"

"You have changed the shape of the universe. Stars moved aside to let you be born. You command Light and Sway. And you constantly doubt yourself. Why am I not permitted the same courtesy?" Pakhet leaped from the dragon's back, graceful, so full of muscle and power, and bunted Vertiline to show she meant no spite.

Vertiline took a stumbling step back at the cat's strength, then leaned into her, hugging the creature about the neck. "Stay with me, cat. I will keep you safe."

"I know you will try. But all I want is a lap by the fire." She gave Vertiline a final bunt, then headed through the breached wall, perhaps in search of a lap, a fire, or a cauldron of cream.

//DO YOU KNOW WHAT YOU MUST DO?//

"The universe waits," Ikmae added.

"I must be the shield," Vertiline said. "It's what the Tresward do."

"The Tresward do nothing, by themselves." Ikmae frowned. "I'm surprised you don't understand this. The people who want to carry the weight of all those gold bars? They are *called*. They can't *not* answer."

//TO BE FAIR, WE DON'T NEED A SHIELD. JUST A BIG STICK.//

Vertiline smiled, straightened her shoulders, and adjusted her scabbard. "Don't worry, dragon. I'll keep you safe, too."

Chapter Thirty

Morgan stared into the fire. Of course, it wasn't a fire, any more than the food she ate was food. The 'fire' was an ancient simulacrum, a glowing orange plate with flames that danced within its surface. It radiated heat but consumed no wood or coal. The food was meat skewers. Heser the Cheg had found them in a slim box that seemed made from card stock. It was no larger than something that would hold a fine quill. When he added water, moments later a savoury aroma arrived as the sticks puffed and grew, meat arriving as if by magic.

The meal was hot, too. No cooking was needed. Just water. Powerful magic indeed, and the ancients carried stock of this on shelves next to commonplace items like axes and brooms.

"Why do you brood?" Heser's voice drew her away from her half-eaten meal, and the flames that weren't fire.

"They left us behind."

"They did that because you are the queen. After all was safe, they retrieved us." He nibbled at some meat. "Tell me of your real fear."

"Nothing is real."

"Here?" He sucked in air, his big chest inflating. There was true power there despite his advancing years, and she wanted to be near him, somewhere quiet, where they would not be disturbed. They'd had quiet at the cave-in, but it hadn't seemed the right time. Or place, perhaps. Morgan would like to be with Heser above ground, in a field, with wine. Which was, of course, madness.

"Maybe anywhere, Guardsman. It could be reality is just what one is used to. And I am unused to this." She held up a skewer of eight-hundred-year-old meat.

He seemed to chew that over at the same time as stealing another of her meat skewers and removing a portion with his teeth. "You are real. I am real."

"But are *we* real?"

"We may need to get used to ... being *we*." He looked away.

"Will there be time enough for the world to grow accustomed to the idea?" She wanted to turn the conversation aside because the idea remained preposterous. "Anyway, I wasn't brooding. I was contemplating with intent."

"Sounds like brooding," the sorcerer said from the doorway. "You have brooding to a fine art."

Heser winced, no doubt at her expression, and Morgan turned to face Meriwether. "May we not have a private moment?"

"Down here? Unlikely." He invited himself into the room Morgan had claimed. It wasn't fancy, but also wasn't close to anyone else's. She'd picked it for those reasons, hoping to get some time with Heser, before there was no time left. "We're about to go to war against a large force with great power, and you're our ace card."

"You are mistaken." Morgan gazed at him, hoping she had the angle right to be aloof despite being seated.

He glanced behind him, as if checking if there was someone else to whom she spoke, then did a double-take. "Mistaken? I don't think so. There's a god free ranging these corridors, dragging Tilly along for the ride. The dragon seems more cocky than capable. I *can't* help because my doom waits for just that kind of fuck-up. There are a lot of people on the field against us. Whether this Wild Sur has an army or just the Vide makes no difference. We are out manned."

"You are mistaken," Morgan rose to her feet, "in saying we are about to go to war. We have been at war for years. The war took the life of my father and bent yours to corruption and misery."

He pursed his lips, then gave a tight nod. "Although I'd say dear old dad was pretty far bent already."

"You are also mistaken in that I am the ace card. I am the least useful person here. Queen of no kingdom. I command no one."

"You command me, my queen," rumbled Heser.

She closed her eyes, immediately sorry at her clumsy use of words, then turned to him. Morgan took his hand in hers. "You are the person I least want to command in all the world. But I acknowledge your gift. I am grateful."

"You are," Meriwether injected himself into the moment once again, "a Ritualist. Your magic isn't fire and lightning. It isn't the Sway or the Storm. It is careful. Calculated. Rich, and ripe with promise if nursed in the sun of planning."

She let Heser's hand go and regarded the sorcerer. "Are you saying I'm slow?"

He laughed. "Morgan, you are the least slow person I know. You have the wit of a master statesperson. The calculated genius of a general. But also the confidence of the small child her father didn't believe in."

"Sirrah, mind your—"

"Hold up," Meri said. "I know you want to yell at me, and I'm fine with that, but let me say my piece so you can yell at me for the whole lot at once." He waited for her nod, which she gave with great effort, before continuing. "The thing is, there are plenty of people here, *now*, who believe in the Raven Queen. The woman who sat on her throne, facing the miserable lot against her. Heser, a finer man I'm unlikely to meet. Tilly, who gives you stick when you need it, but also the carrot, because you deserve it. Evanne, who argues with *everyone*. It's nothing personal, but what's unique with you is ... she trusts what you do. And then there's me. A sometime sorcerer, who sees your great purpose." He shrugged. "We are all here, together, in this moment. And we need you."

She pressed her lips together for a long time, then bowed her head.

A weaker person would shout at him. A stronger would wonder what must be done. "You have a point in all this?"

"I don't have a point. I need you to do something. The one thing you can do, which might save us all."

"Back when I served under a hard but fair man, he told me that pressure could unnerve any soldier." Heser put his cleaned skewer aside, a kind of magic in itself as Morgan had not seen him eat the rest of it. "That sounds like a lot of pressure."

"It is," Meri agreed. "But no more than she wants. Because, right at the heart of it, Morgan was born to rule. She's better at it than anyone else. And a ruler knows one thing."

Morgan eyed him. "Strength."

"Sure, but also service." The sorcerer crossed his arms. "You've not gathered riches or flags to your standard, my queen. You have served your people. And now I need you to serve just a little more."

She breathed, wondering, *What does he want?* "What if I can't do it?"

"Then we'll find another way." She heard the lie in his voice. "But I think you can."

"What must I do?"

"It's simple." He smiled. "You must summon a demon army into this realm to destroy us all."

Chapter Thirty-One

Tarragon thought Evanne looked amazing. She couldn't take her eyes off the maybe-Vhemin. Strong, her shoulders back. Violet eyes, a hint of a snake's focus in them. Rust-coloured hair, tarnished and glorious. And the armour fit. *Oh yes. It definitely fits*.

They were in a train. It was a novelty creation, the type that tourists or executives might use when on a tour of a facility. It had folksy old-style maglev locomotion, still smooth after eight hundred years. And it smelled clean! Not like dust or mould. The once-fairy wondered if anything would ever smell good again since getting above ground. Other than Evanne, of course. She always smelled good.

Tarragon looked toward the back of the car. The merchants fussed with supplies. Nearby, Amir, watchful. Beside him, Sands Apart, never far from Sight of Day, who looked out the train's window at the passing tunnel's darkness. *Perhaps his Feybrind eyes can see something out there*. Next was Armitage, the giant Vhemin brooding, perhaps about the day ahead, but in Tarragon's experience, Vhemin didn't worry overmuch about slaughter.

Then there was Tarragon herself, trying not to simper over Evanne, who stood in the ancient armour, right beside her mother. Somewhere in the car, and really, who knew where, was Pakhet, but the tiger was invisible. Near the front of the car stood Ikmae, the dead man's body they inhabited restful and ready. The sorcerer stood near the god, head bent in quiet conversation, and Tarragon caught *but will you tear me from this world*, to which the god merely shrugged. Beside them, Morgan and Heser, watching, listening. He planned, perhaps, to do important Holomancer things. They were all concerned he was still bound by his doom.

The dragon was on the caboose. They'd torn the roof and sides off so the beast could hunker down. She could see his blue-white eyes as excited as the lightning as the train raced along at close to three hundred klicks per. Tarragon wasn't sure if she could take that speed even when she was a fairy, but Myryntir seemed to be having the time of his life, gripping the flatbed of his rail car, grinning like a dingo.

"Hey." Evanne's voice, husky as evening, brought her back to here and now. "You okay?"

"I'm terrified," Tarragon admitted. "Ikmae said at the end of the line there is a fortress filled with spears of light, machines of war, and an army. We are few, and they are many." She wrinkled her nose. "In the old world, we'd say we're hopelessly outgunned."

"Cheery."

Tarragon forced a spark of levity. "We'd also say it's better to think about it as having a wider selection of targets."

That got a laugh. Evanne sobered. "How do I look?"

"Glorious. Um." Tarragon bit her lip. "Um."

"I mean, does the armour fit?"

"The armour is the least of your problems." Hitch stepped through the wall of the train. "The god did not lie. We are outmanned and outgunned. And this," he flicked a not-hand toward Evanne's armour, "hasn't been field-tested for eight hundred years. The welds might not hold. The capacitance might not be at tolerance. So many things."

"Spectre." Tarragon turned to the ghost. "Hear me. You carried the purpose of this weapon for eight hundred years, preparing it for the one person who could finally use it. You taught us how to fix it. Your work is good. Be at peace."

Hitch gazed at her for a moment. "Was that a compliment?"

"Don't ruin the moment." Tarragon turned back to Evanne, fussing with the bandoleer running across the armour's breastplate. The metal orbs Hitch described as weapon and shield both were held to it as if by magnetism, but they weren't made of a ferrous metal. More ancient technology, or perhaps plain old sorcery. "Are you ready?"

"Sure." Tarragon could tell Evanne lied. "How long until we fire this up?"

"Not in here," Hitch warned. "Not a good idea. And you don't know how to fly yet."

"How hard can it be?" Evanne raised an eyebrow.

"It's pretty hard," Tarragon said. "You're not a fairy, born knowing wing and gust."

"Eh." Evanne waved it off. "Ikmae! Attend."

The god raised an eyebrow in return, facing her. "Did you just command me?"

"Yes. Now, listen. Are you sure you must keep your promise?"

Vertiline eyed her daughter, then the god. "What does Evanne know of the promise?"

The god frowned. "Soon we will exit this tunnel. I'll be above ground, and will have broken my word. There would be ... complications if that happened."

"I understand." Evanne eased a finger under her gorget. "How must it be done?"

"Kill this body," Ikmae said. "I could walk out that door and suicide against the tunnel wall, but the vacuum effect of our speed would no doubt suck a few of you out along with it. Best done quickly, and with a blade."

Vertiline pursed her lips. "You want us to cut off your head to end this body's life?"

Ikmae frowned. "I wouldn't go straight to the nuclear option, but—"

Whatever Ikmae was about to say ended as Vertiline's sword whipped from sheath, a flash of golden light living on the edge of the steel, and severed the god's head. There was little blood, perhaps on account of the body being already dead, and the corpse toppled to the floor, the head bouncing right beside. The High Justiciar looked on the body, then sheathed her blade. "One less annoyance for the end of the road."

"Mama!"

"Hah. I didn't see that coming." Meriwether didn't look too surprised. *He has known the Justiciar for half a lifetime.* "And not a moment too soon. We are here."

The tunnel's walls lightened, then they burst from the darkness into the outside. Rolling, barren plains beckoned them. Tarragon craned to look out the forward window. There, the seat of Wild Sur's power. A castle fit for the clouds but mortared to the earth. The old stone facade showed few marks of time, still gleaming a coconut white. It was massive, the maglev line leading right to the door.

Between the train and the castle was an army. Men and women, both human and Vhemin, stood cheek by jowl in a rolling cascade of field fortifications and entrenchments. There were hundreds of thousands of them. Tarragon counted twenty Artifices striding along the plains, their weapons of light and heat ready. She breathed. "Oh."

An Artifice took flight from the castle, a blaze of flame behind it as it made toward them with all speed. The train rocked as Myryntir nosed into the slipstream, air resistance fighting dragony strength. The beast roared, then leaped to the sky, lightning crackling a challenge.

"It's go time," Evanne said. "How do I turn this on?"

Hitch leaned forward. "Like this—"

"No, I've got it. Wait. I don't have it. Here it is, I think." Evanne slapped her helmet on, the visor dead and lifeless. "Shit. It's broken."

The visor burst into luminance. There was a stuttering, clanking sound as if a mighty chain was dragged through gears of rusted steel, then a flat, male voice said, "Vehement Systems detected." A pause. "Human detected." Another pause. "Vehement Systems detected."

"Just fucking work," Evanne said, her voice louder as the armour amplified it for them.

"Human approach acknowledged." The armour trembled, then blasted through the roof of the train, debris shredding in their wake. Tarragon watched as Evanne flared into the sky, an arrow of starfire, her scream of panic reedy with distance almost immediately.

Vertiline watched through the hole, a smile of satisfaction on her face. "One other problem solved."

"What do you mean?" Tarragon felt panic inside her. *Evanne is on the wind.*

"My daughter is now out of the fight. She is safest away up there," the Justiciar waved her hand behind and above them, "rather than here."

"What about them?" Tarragon pointed to the quickly approaching army. The train was not fucking around as it whisked them toward conflict.

Vertiline readied steel, and favoured Tarragon with a lopsided smile. "I'm not worried about them. They are just flesh and metal."

A bolt of fire raked the side of the train and Tarragon screamed as it tore their car from the tracks. She knocked her teeth together, and tasted blood as the cabin rolled. Earth and sky changed positions in rapid succession. They trammelled across the ground, the screaming of metal accompanying the car as it tore a mighty furrow in the earth. The train shed speed. A final lazy roll of the cabin as the train set its useless maglev feet on broken ground.

She hit her head. Broken glass and blood.

They were here.

Chapter Thirty-Two

This day is not getting better. Amir scrubbed dirt from his hair, then pulled his shirt by its collar, freeing more dirt. The dirt, no stranger to gravity, descended. Rather than making its way to the ground where its friends lived, some made its way into his pants.

He rolled his shoulder. He'd come down on it, hard, but the training had kicked in, and he'd rolled. After a lot of earth-sky-earth-sky, which a man could get tired of very quickly, he'd hit the welcoming side of an embankment. Wreckage fell about him. It was strange inner machinery from the ancients' track carriage, and all of it was burning. It peppered the ground around him, casually tearing a Vhemin soldier in half in the process and dumping hot dirt into Amir's shirt.

Also, he was surrounded by fire.

Amir drew steel, checked the blade for balance, and gave it a flourish to remind himself of the balance. It sang as it cut air, the blade sharp as metal could be. His backup blade was lost, so he checked about for a shield, and found one on the arm of a soldier come to reinforce the first. Amir stepped forward into a power stance, the ground trembling beneath him, his blade shining with Light, and dismembered the soldier in four quick strokes, saving the shield arm for last. He caught it as gravity took hold, shook out the spare arm from the cinches, and strapped it on.

I remember my teacher of the platinum hair. I remember another woman with skin like honey. He oriented himself on where he thought the High Justiciar and the once-fairy had travelled and set off through the enemy fortifications. They were well done, good workmanship all around, and would have created a barrier to entry if he hadn't been tossed over the top of all that hard work.

Blood dripped from his forehead and into his eye. *I didn't even know I'd been cut.* He dabbed it with a finger, the digit coming away grimy red. Sound came to him, a lot of yelling of orders and the firing of cannons at Three knew what, and it was then he realised his hearing hadn't been with him over the last spell. With sound's return came ringing, and he winced. Shook his head, got a little dirt out of his right ear. A woman, Feybrind and angry, rounded a trench corner, leaped to the ground five metres away, and raised a spear.

He held up his sword arm, fingers out, in a *hold up* gesture. Amir spat grit, then said, "Who are you with?"

The woman threw her spear, which Amir swayed to avoid, giving it a gentle bat with the shield, then impaled her at the follow-up jump, her outstretched arms going slack just as they found his throat. He shook the Feybrind from his blade, looking away from staring emerald eyes.

Cannon fired again, and he saw lances of light flying overhead. He gazed in that direction but saw nothing but cloud and smoke. Was it Myryntir? Or Evanne? He'd have to square the cannons away if the dragon were to be much use. *I think the bard is out for the fight, though. She had no control of that armour.*

He found Tarragon first. The once-fairy was atop a small rise and surrounded by dead troops. She held the burning blue-white brand of Requiem before her in a two-handed grip, her hair streaming in the smoke- and char-laden wind. Her eyes moved to Amir, then away—a flash of recognition, then back to guard. He saw in her something foreign to himself. It was how her face set. *She would make a good Tresward. Better than I; she feels the calling, not for the sake of power, but of service.*

"What news?" he called.

"Everything's shit," she said. "The train blew up. There are a lot of soldiers trying to kill me."

"Me, too." He frowned at the collection of ten or so bodies between them. "Well, not a lot if we're comparing tallies. I had two at least, though."

"Do you know of the others?"

"The High Justiciar went that way," he pointed north, toward the castle wall. "She was tossed quite high and may be injured."

Tarragon gave him a little side eye. "She is the High Justiciar. She's not going to be injured by a little fall."

Amir gazed at the sky, as if measuring the distance. "She seemed small to my eyes. Perhaps two or three hundred metres up."

"Piece of cake," the once-fairy assured him. "Have you seen Evanne?"

"Not since she blew through the roof. I thought she went south."

"Aye." A cautious nod, Tarragon's elfin features showing a hint of worry. "If the Three are merciful, she'll keep going south. This is not a fight for her."

"She is handy with the machete."

"She is the woman I love, and knows the way of people's hearts, and seems a warrior true. But her own heart is gentle, Knight Adept. She is not made for killing." Tarragon pointed with her chin to behind Amir.

"I have no argument to offer." Amir turned, decapitating a man who'd snuck up on him, then shook blood from his blade. "Thanks."

"No trouble. There's a lot of noise. Head on a swivel." She bounded down from her hillock.

Amir waited for her. "You've done this before."

"I was a spy."

"You were no spy. You are a warrior born. Although by all accounts, in the wrong body to start with."

"I liked my body." She looked away for a moment, and he wondered what she thought of. Loss? Regret? Or satisfaction she was now on an even footing? "I like my body still. It's Big, but I can kiss Evanne, and that's enough."

Amir unstrapped his shield. "How sweet." He wound up, then tossed it, a disc of burning yellow-white Light. It impacted against the chest of a massive Vhemin woman leading the charge of a small cohort of five. The shield went through her, and the two men behind her, showering the remaining two in smoking gore. They slowed their run, looked at each other, then ran away.

"We should get after them."

"They'll come to us soon enough."

"That's what I'm afraid of."

"If we run after them, we'll just get tired. This way, they'll spend all their effort closing the distance." Amir pressed his lips into a line, considering. "I don't want to die tired."

"Do you think today is the day you die?"

"Hmm." He thought about it. "I think so."

"You don't seem sad." She looked at him from beneath her hair.

"Regrets are for the living, and I have plenty enough to want to set them aside for a while." Amir headed toward his smoking shield. "Let us find the Justiciar."

They found Vertiline in classic low guard, her blade held two-handed, a mirror of how he'd found Tarragon. Vertiline's stance was perfect, her shoulders just-so, her arms held at the right angle, feet not so much *in a stance* as *owning the ground*. Amir felt the power radiating from her. Golden Light glinted on her steel and haloed the air about her. Every so often Light dripped like molten metal to smoke and hiss against the ground.

She was at the bottom of a small crater, the sides steaming and hissing. There were many, many dead soldiers about her. They were a carpet leading to a clear centre: where she stood, ready for more. The High Justiciar glanced at Amir and Tarragon as they reached the top of the crater. "I thought about finding you, but knew you'd spend the effort to get to me. Why die tired?"

Amir gave Tarragon a glance. "See?"

The once-fairy ignored him. "Evanne?"

"Not here." Vertiline shook her head once, curt, but Amir detected relief in the gesture. "I can't see what the cannons are firing at through the smoke and cloud. I hope it's not her."

The cannons fired another volley on cue. They were now closer to the main battery. It was perhaps two hundred metres north. The noise was immense. It was a force that pressed on Amir's skin, not helping his hearing recover at all. "The dragon is up there."

"Seems a lot of fuss to go through for one little dragon." Vertiline glanced north. "But we should clear them out so Myryntir can land."

Amir faced Tarragon, feeling an explanation was in order. "It's okay to move to the guns, because they can't run to us."

"I get it," the once-fairy assured him. "Running is for fools."

"Except if we *must* run," Amir said. "But here, we shall walk."

"Of course." Tarragon turned away, a slight growl of exasperation escaping her. "We must make it safe for Evanne."

"And the dragon," Vertiline said. "Because the dragon is more likely to arrive than my wayward child."

Amir squinted at his commander. "Did you do something, High Justiciar?"

"No." Vertiline tossed a small cylinder to the ground, then crushed it underfoot. "I did nothing at all."

Tarragon's mouth worked for a moment, no noise coming out, then she said, "You took the synergy buffer? So her armour wouldn't work?"

"If that was a synergy buffer, and it was in her armour, and I wanted to keep my child safe from harm, I might have taken it. But only because a mother wants to keep her child from a war zone." Vertiline looked away from Tarragon's stupefied goggle and met Amir's eyes. "Shall we astonish our foes by reminding them of the Three's justice?"

Chapter Thirty-Three

Meriwether groaned as weight lifted from his chest. The load was heavy, made of metal and dirt. As it let his lungs take in more than a teaspoonful of air he gasped, then coughed as what felt like a mountain of shale went down his throat.

"He's alive." Amber stood on one side of the metal sheet he'd helped lift from Meriwether's chest.

On the other side stood Jade. "He doesn't look it."

The siblings tossed the metal aside, and Amber offered Meriwether a hand. Taking it, and feeling all his years at once, the Holomancer let himself be helped up. "I'm not really sixty. I just look it."

Jade gave him a once-over. "You look more than sixty."

"Jade!" Amber brushed down the front of Meriwether's shirt, then leaned close. "Perhaps sixty-five, but not a day older."

Meriwether looked from one to the other. "I'm, uh, about thirty-five. I guess, anyway. Time doesn't … *feel* the same on the other side. Sometimes I have trouble when I realise I gave years of my life paying the Three's price to solve a problem I didn't make, so people could stand about telling me how hard living has cost me my looks."

"It's cost you more than looks," Jade assured him.

"She's just scared, because we're armed with provisions, not swords, and all the people who know how to fight are not here." Amber peered at him. "Do you know how to fight?"

"Me? Hah!" Meriwether stepped past him and toward a Vhemin soldier. The man had emerged from behind the ruined back half of the caboose. Meriwether swayed sideways to avoid the highly predictable spear thrust, then slipped in nice and close. The Vhemin used a short spear, none of that pike nonsense. It was perfect for a close dance. The Vhemin smelled of old sweat and new wine. The sorcerer reached a hand inside the Vhemin's guard and placed it atop the haft, and his other hand outside and below. He grunted, gave a twisting heave, and used torque to disarm the Vhemin.

Stepping back, he continued the momentum and let the spear haft connect with his enemy's jaw. He felt the *crack* run through the wooden haft, kept a grip, and tossed the weapon. It spun, thrumming, and connected with the nose of a Vhemin woman arriving to support her comrade.

The Vhemin man hit the ground, joined a heartbeat later by the woman. Meriwether brushed his hands off. "I'm *terrible* at fighting."

"If that's terrible, what are you like at things you're good at?" Amber nudged the nearest Vhemin with a toe. "They're out cold."

"You have to go for the head. They shake just about anything else off." Meriwether tugged his ear, then winced. *I've pulled something in my shoulder with that last stunt. Being old sucks.* He parked the regret almost savagely, because the years had paid for something priceless. "Where is everyone else?"

"Not sure." Amber pointed toward the castle, an impressive off-white edifice that chose that moment to spit light and fire at the cloudy sky. Thunder rolled toward them. "I think that way."

"That way looks shit," Meriwether said. "It looks like there are soldiers and cannons."

"I don't make the rules," Amber said. "I don't even know why I'm here."

"Fair enough." Meriwether retrieved his borrowed spear and examined it with a critical eye. The head was poorly made, blunt, and looked sure to give a savage infection to anyone who took a hit and tried to walk it off. He put the head against the ground, then kicked the haft, snapping it off. "Perfect."

"You just broke our only weapon." Jade looked at him like he was an imbecile.

"Two things." Meriwether leaned on the spear. "First, I needed a walking stick. This spear is too poorly made to be a good weapon."

She eyed him, then gave a cautious nod. "The second thing?"

"Another weapon will be along soon."

"Shall we be off?" Amber hefted a pack onto his shoulders.

Meriwether gave the castle a critical glance. "Any horses around?"

"Are you afraid of walking?"

"I'm sixty-five, remember?"

"I thought you were a sorcerer," Jade said. "Can't you sorcerer something up?"

"I'm not that kind of sorcerer." Meriwether rolled his aching shoulder. "I'm the broken-down, used up kind. Let's go."

Chapter Thirty-Four

The slender blade of grass survived despite the odds. Sight of Day watched it from a mere hands' breadth distance, the left side of his face against the churned earth, the right side open to the sounds of violence and slaughter.

The stem was slender, pale-green in colour, and twisted to the north as a gust of wind tickled it. He let his golden eyes roam that way. He saw Armitage, the Vhemin enraged, bloody gore down front and back where a spar had gone clean through him. His body was laced with what looked like a hundred cuts, but Sight of Day expected that was merely his concussion talking. The monster collected a slender man hiding behind a shield, stomped the hapless fellow to the ground, hooked fingers under his chin, and tore his head from his shoulders.

Sight of Day didn't want to look at that, so he let his eyes wander further still. Yes, his feet were still there: pointed to the castle, as if they were trying to set him on the right path. *I don't want to go that way. There will be more dying, possibly involving me.* He also saw the piece of steel going through his abdomen, and tried not to think about it, because it hurt quite a lot, and there was blood leaving him in a steady flow to soak the ground. *Perhaps it will water another blade of grass, and more things will grow here because I'm gone.*

The Vhemin shouted something that sounded like *get that fucking cat up*, but that couldn't be right. Armitage knew Sight of Day was mortally wounded, dying, and unable to move, let alone fight. Dead weight, and Sight of Day knew that out on the crucible of the sands that forged his mighty friend, there was no room for sentiment. *He knows he can't take me. I have little time left, and nothing to give. But if I stay here, I will water the earth, and a new blade of grass will grow. That is something. It is better than nothing.*

Who was Armitage shouting at? *Oh, yes. Sands Apart*. The woman of the People who'd been taken by a warped man and twisted to a hateful purpose. *I am good at making things. I hope I remade her the way she wanted to be. I wish her to be happy. She must grow, like this grass. And like the grass, she can only do that with my passing.*

Ochre eyes came into his field of view. The woman was coated in blood, and some of it might even have been hers. But the People were *strong*, forged by a hateful race in a detestable time. Their gemstone eyes were able to see the long years behind them, the cost the first Feybrind paid to exist, and the narrow path ahead. *A step to the left or right and we fall, lost to time and memory.* The world would turn on without the People, their gemstone eyes, and their wonderful creations.

Will anyone miss us?

Sands Apart shook his shoulders, and Sight of Day felt himself flop in response. There was no strength left in his long, lean limbs. *Oh, dear. Not long now.* He put a hand on hers, an effort that felt harder than lifting his first blade in war. {*Dear heart, you must go. There are others who need your strength, courage, and wisdom. They are lost on me.*}

She shook her head. Her teeth bared, not in anger, but fear and confusion. Her fingers trembled for a moment. Behind her the giant Armitage beat three men back using what looked to be the leg of a Vhemin, blood spraying from the stump with each swing. {*You are the only one who understands their worth. You are the only one who understands the worth of anyone.*}

Sight of Day thought about that for a few weak beats of his limping heart. {*I think you see it too.*}

Her teeth clenched, ochre eyes going hard like sheet metal

burnished by the forge. *{I didn't want to. How will I see what must be obvious to the golden eyes when they aren't there anymore?}*

{Golden eyes are just eyes.} He reached a trembling hand to touch her chest just above her heart. *{This is all that matters.}*

Sands Apart shook her heard a violent *no*. *{You matter. You matter to all of us.}*

{This grass will not grow if I live. Who am I to say whether I am more important than it?}

She opened her mouth in a soundless cry, then grabbed the steel running through his middle, and tore it free. The pain was bright, so very bright, like looking into forgefire just after the bellows had brightened it enough to bend and shape the hardest metal. He gasped. The pain of her binding him with cloth was almost a relief. She grabbed the front of his jerkin, hauled him upright, and slapped his face. In Sight of Day's view, she hit him unnecessarily hard. *{I say.}* She pointed to the spot he'd touched, right above her heart. *{I say you are more important.}*

She got a shoulder under his arm and staggered toward the castle. Toward the guns, and the violence, and away from the grass. Sight of Day looked back to Armitage. The monster held an armoured soldier above his head and was bringing the unlucky fellow down on another over and over. The Vhemin's rage was frightening, and Sight of Day wondered who he was angry for. His daughter was safe in the skies and his wife was safer than houses in any weather.

He let his gaze slide to the grass one last time. They were far enough away the green stem would have been hard to place for human eyes. But the fallen Itikari had made the People with their gemstone eyes. The People were able to see almost anything, at great distance, in almost any light. All the better to watch the hurts of the world, and weep.

And he wondered, if this was the battle where the People finally fell from their narrow path: *Will there be anyone left to miss us?*

Chapter Thirty-Five

Evanne's head shook like Papa had grabbed her by the ears and was wrangling her about. Not that Papa would ever do that, but he had the same strength of the skies. There was a subtle roaring that went along with the shaking. It came from somewhere below.

I'm flying. I'm fucking flying.

She looked down and the shaking of her head got worse but she still managed to catch a glimpse of the ground. Soldiers, lots of them. There to the north, the castle-slash-keep thing, lots of Artifices walking about like they owned the place. *They probably do. We're so boned.*

Below her ascent was a pillar of fire. It was a long, curved tongue that reached through her wake, tapering to nothingness. Her instincts said that was the source of the roar, but it didn't explain the buffeting her head was getting.

"Please state clearance codes or be ejected." The voice was calm, from everywhere at once, just the kind of soothing motherfucker who could deliver bad news regularly without people wanting to throw him out a window.

"Who's that?" She flailed with her arms, which was harder than she expected, and upset her trajectory. Instead of going straight up, she started going south, which was all wrong, because it was away from the castle, Tarragon, Mama, Papa, Sight of Day, and everyone else.

"This construct has no name. Please state clearance—"

"I get you," Evanne said. "Hitch?"

"That's not a clearance code."

"Hitch! Where are you?"

"Please repeat clearance code."

The blue spectre appeared before her. As per usual he seemed at ease with an uncomfortable situation. He stood on the open air as if there was a moving piece of ground following her up. "Hello? What have you done this time?"

"Hitch, I'm in your stupid armour, and this idiotic thing wants a clearance code or it'll do something to me."

"Eject," the voice supplied helpfully. "I will eject you."

"That would be bad," Hitch said. "You shouldn't have taken off without a code."

"Not as helpful as you might think," Evanne said. "How did you do it?"

"I can't remem—"

"If you say you can't remember, by the Three I will punch you the fuck back into the grave." Evanne hit a cloud bank, the shaking increasing. "Why am I being rattled around?"

"Air," Hitch said. "You are moving at close to Mach one."

"Mach?" Evanne frowned. "You what?"

"You're going really fast," he said. "Super fast. The air at this speed is like..." He pursed his not-lips.

"Like a hurricane?"

"Not even close. A hurricane is strong but relatively slow. A super big one's air moves at about two hundred and fifty klicks an hour. You're moving at..." He frowned. "What's the number in the lower left say?"

Evanne looked down. There was a set of green letters glowing in her vision down there, some kind of arcane bullshit sorcery she didn't have time for. "It says twelve hundred."

"There we go. Not even close."

"Hitch!" she screamed. "What the fuck is the fucking mother-fucking code?"

"Oh, right," he said. "I keep forgetting you're not dead." He paced through the air, a feat of engineering she could only marvel at because she was now flying horizontally, and he was therefore walking with his torso parallel to the ground, defying gravity and physics on a truly epic scale. "Try whiskey tango foxtrot."

"Whiskey tango foxtrot?" Evanne said. "What the hell?"

"What the fuck, actually," Hitch said. "It sounds like something I'd have used."

"Clearance code accepted," the voice said. "Welcome aboard."

"Thanks," Evanne said. "How do I stop flying?"

"Beginning tutorial sequence," the voice said. "Fuel reserves are low. Are you sure you want to continue?"

"Hitch? What does it mean?"

"Ah." Hitch looked down to his not-hands. "It ... feeds. On the pilot, or those around."

"It's going to feed on me, or other people?"

"Synergy buffer missing," the voice said.

"Then it's all on you," Hitch said. "It needs a lot of power. My cancer ... helped. You're a bit Vhemin—"

"A bit?"

"Half," he corrected. "By volume. I think I died because it ate too much of me, and there was no one else around to power the shields, and then the demon did the rest."

"You remember that?"

"Bits and pieces." He looked away, his blue-white not-eyes scanning the ground.

There was a shuddering of the armour, a real jolt, then smoothness. "What was that?"

"Sound barrier," the spectre said. "You're now moving faster than sound."

"Is that good?"

"It's *fast*," he said. "It's *good* in a way because you're going away from the danger."

"I don't want to do that," Evanne said. "Everyone is back there, trying not to die, and I've got the super weapon."

"Which you don't know how to use."

"Which I don't know how to use," she agreed. "How do I use it?"

"Training commencing," the voice said. Evanne felt pain lance into her forearms and calves. She screamed, flailing, and the armour pinwheeled briefly before going into a spin. Her shoulder wrenched but the pain was trifling compared to the burning, *hungry* feeling in her limbs.

"What are you doing?" She bit her lips, feeling sick, as the sky churned and turned around her.

"Training," the voice soothed. "This is your first lesson."

Chapter Thirty-Six

Morgan stood, a fell wind trying to wrestle with her hair. Raven locks withstood the onslaught as she surveyed the battlefield. "This looks bad."

"My queen." Heser the Cheg stood slightly below her. They were both on a half-mud, half-rock mound that allowed some vantage of the battlefield. It was a distance from the melee, nestled under the shade of a stubborn oak that somehow kept root amid the turmoil.

It would be nice to stay here and not go where all the swords are for a change. "We should help them."

"My queen," Heser said again, but as if he meant to say something else.

"Out with it."

"Here is relatively safe." His hands didn't move from their position, leaving thumbs hooked into his sword belt. "Over there is not."

"We do not win by staying safe."

"Delegation," he suggested.

"To whom?"

"I will—"

"Three's mercy." Morgan glared while Heser bided his silence. She softened. "Who will protect me if you leave?"

He glared at the ground. "If I had but another Queensguard... but no. You have the right of it." He gazed at the keep. "Where is it?"

"There." She stretched a slender arm toward a central hump warting the castle's top amid other crenellations. "That dome."

"I expected it to be bigger. Perhaps that one." Heser gestured toward a slender needle stretching to the heavens.

"That does look impressive, but no." Morgan shivered, rubbing her arms. "I can ... *hear* it, Heser. It calls to me."

"What does it say?"

She closed her eyes, listening for a moment. Heard the sound of guns in the distance, and the clamour of battle. Closer, a starling daring song, before startling to silence. Beneath it all, a hum, almost a call. *Morgan*, she heard, *come to me*. It had her father's voice, something of command about it. The Raven Queen shook her head, rubbed her eyes, and glared at the dome in the distance. "Nothing important."

"Hmm."

"Why would he give this task to me?" Morgan bit down on an unqueenly wail. "Why, of all our troupe, does it fall on my shoulders?"

"You have the skills."

"Vertiline could open the gate with a word. She holds Sway over all."

"I don't think so." Heser looked at her for a moment, head tilted, considering. "I think the High Justiciar has many abilities, but if opening demon gates was a thing in the Tresward's power, they'd have done it before and taken the war into their enemy's kingdom."

"Is it what you would do?"

"Beyond doubt." He heaved a breath in and out. "But the point is moot. They cannot, and you can. The task is yours."

"You're saying the Holomancer wants me to break open the seal between worlds because I can?"

"The Lord du Reeves is no fool. He might play the part, but ... no." Heser shook his head. "Put him in motley and he would still be wise. He has asked you to open the gate for three reasons. The first is that the task must be done."

"But it will break open—"

"And yet still must be done. The second is because you can do it, and no one else."

"Because I'm a Ritualist. A faded charlatan in a tattered gown, holding a tarnished crown."

He looked away for a moment, but not in chagrin, his face relaxed, the set of his shoulders easy. "The gown is not tattered. The crown gleams on your brow like no other's."

She grunted, acknowledging the point. "I do wear a good crown. And self pity is not becoming."

"Quite."

"The third reason?"

"Hold a moment." Heser held up a hand as a man jogged past their position. He was an enemy grunt, a farmer play acting at war, narrow shoulders scarce up to the task of supporting his chainmail. The soldier slowed to a halt, then took a few steps back, before turning to look at them. Heser the Cheg offered a nod. "Fine morning to you."

"You are not of our army." The soldier looked about, saw no friends, gathered his courage, and drew a rusty sword. "Come with me. The captain will want to speak with you."

"Best be on your way, lad." Heser the Cheg's tone was calm. *I'm not sure the farmer is a 'lad;' he wears at least thirty summers.* "There's nothing good that will come of your captain and I having words."

"Be as that may, I—"

"I'm not used to repeating myself," Heser rumbled. "Be back about your business, and we'll be about ours. We're scarce a harm to you, naught but two travellers on the road, caught unawares by the battle. Screams drew our attention, and we thought to help, but see the problem is of a scale two pairs of hands can do little for."

"Are you a healer?" This directed to Morgan, who stood beneath the oak, trying to be invisible.

"I have little to offer in the way of healing arts. My talents ... maintain a different course."

The farmer clearly heard *little* and failed to parse it as *none*. He gripped his blade all the harder. "You'll come with me. Now."

"I think it unlikely anyone will win if that happens." Pakhet materialised

behind the farmer, who turned, saw the giant tiger, screamed like a child, turned around, and ran.

The hapless fellow's charge took him directly toward Heser, and by association, Morgan. His eyes were locked on the grey and black striped tiger, not on the captain of Morgan's Queensguard, and so he didn't see Heser move from *we're having a conversation* to *we're having a different conversation.*

The captain stepped aside smartly, stuck out his arm, and straight-armed the farmer. The luckless soldier rotated about Heser's arm like a fence plank tugged by a gale, landing with his full length stretched upon the ground, all air leaving him in a rush.

Heser followed him down with a fist, connecting with the man's face, bouncing skull against the ground, and ending the conversation. The captain stood, examined his knuckles, then sighed. "Best we be off."

"The hill's not safe at all, is it?" Morgan eyed the keep. *We must be about our task, then.*

"Nowhere is safe. But here is marginally safer than anywhere else."

"Come, cat." Heser strode toward the tiger. We'll need your strength before the day is done."

The tiger looked over her shoulder, then back at Heser. *"You know I'm terrible in a fight, right?"*

"It often comes down to the size of the dog in the fight, no matter what anyone tells you." Heser turned. "My queen?"

She straightened and stepped gingerly around the fallen farmer. "A moment, Captain. What was the third thing?"

"Third... Oh." Heser absently rubbed the side of Pakhet's neck, the tiger leaning into his strong fingers. "My Lord du Reeves gave this task to you because you are the only one who will not break under the load."

Chapter Thirty-Seven

The first piece of good news was spotting Faust. The second was seeing Larochette beside him. The giant waited for them, hands resting atop the head of a giant hammer that came up to his chest. Larochette leaned against a broken fortification looking like it was a chair for ladies who lunch. Amir raised his sword in greeting. "Faust. What news?"

"Blood and fire," the giant said. "There are plenty of things going wrong today."

"And precious few right," Larochette said.

"But I'm here," Amir said. "That counts for something."

Larochette's eyes slid sideways to Amir's companions. The High Justiciar, who stood like an angry storm to his left, and the once-fairy to his right. "There are things that count higher."

"Adepts." Vertiline sheathed her sword. "Status?"

"There are guns," Faust offered. "Many soldiers guard them."

Vertiline looked back the way they'd come. "I've seen naught but enemy troops."

Larochette glanced at the sky. "There seems to be a war going on."

A grim smile from the Justiciar. "I'd like to know where this Wild Sur got the soldiers."

"The dispossessed," Faust said. "The world has been shaken. The oil and water do not mix." He glanced back the same way Vertiline had. "Where is the queen?"

"We have not seen the Raven," Vertiline said. "Others are missing."

"Your daughter?" Larochette straightened.

"Accounted for," Amir said. "It's been an odd day."

"Hmm." Faust leaned his hammer away from his body, like a boy might when playing with a stick. "We must save the kingdom."

The High Justiciar gave him a narrow look. "And what do you think we're doing, Adept?" She leaned on the last word perhaps overmuch.

"Talking," Larochette said. "Standing around."

"And look at you doing it so well." Amir kept a frown from his face, voice light. *Something isn't right here. Perhaps it's the war.* "Do you have a plan of attack for the guns?"

"We were ... waiting," Faust said. "There is a bigger prize."

Vertiline straightened. "What do you mean?"

"The guns fire at the clouds. Perhaps they bother the dragon, but I don't think so. They have fired a long time and have yet to hit anything. If anything, the dragon distracts the enemy's mind. If we attack the cannons, we will be similarly distracted. We must go inside, to fight the battle that must be won." Faust looked down, and Amir wondered if his friend had simply run out of words.

"What he said." Larochette glanced over her shoulder at the castle. "There will be fighting aplenty inside and out. Outside, the fighting saps our forces, but inside, it serves a purpose."

"Well said, Adept." Vertiline glanced at Amir. "Your thoughts?"

He raised an eyebrow. "You're not going to admonish me for not thinking of it first?"

"You are already doing that for me. Consider admonishment delegated."

"It seems right." Amir looked at the sky. "I wish I knew what they were firing at. It seems a lot of fuss for one little dragon."

"Come." Vertiline faced the castle. "Let's go knock."

THE GATES OF THE CASTLE WERE MONSTROUSLY TALL. TWIN DOORS rose skyward, twenty storeys if not further, each side wide enough to sail a ship through. Amir huddled with his companions behind a ruined wagon, the charred wreckage on its side. It gave them an opportunistic vantage a mere three hundred metres from the doors. Smoke curled through broken wagon wheels. *I will smell of coal until the day I die.* Vertiline was at his elbow, peering at the defences. Tarragon squatted a few paces back, eyes on the sky, her face a picture of thoughtful mien.

Faust and Larochette stood at the opposite end of the ruined wagon, Faust surveying the defences, and Larochette watching Tarragon. Amir wondered what the almost-Knight thought of the once-fairy. *She wonders if she can rely on her skill. If the sword she carries is magical or cursed. Whether Larochette will have to carry Tarragon in the battle ahead or learn from her example.* They were thoughts Amir had too, although his heart told him Tarragon was capable. As unbreakable as any Knight Chevalier, despite completing no Trial to earn an Adept's black.

Still, it is disconcerting to see her distracted by clouds.

He was pulled by his reverie by Vertiline's voice, calm, ready, and assessing. "There are many foes."

"This is why she is the High Justiciar," Larochette said. "She sees past the sight of mortals."

Vertiline's mouth quirked, perhaps daring itself to smile, and she pressed it flat. "I count a battalion's strength before us. No weak and simple conscripts, these soldiers have well-maintained armour. The ballistae behind them could give us pause for thought."

Faust rumbled in agreement. "Five hundred souls against our five. While there are only three ballistae, I'm concerned by the Artifice. The ancient's machines have ever been tricksy."

Amir sighed, coughed smoke, and smoothed back his hair. "You are concerned for a mere Artifice? I will remind you the High Justiciar's child, a brat of mean years, managed to defeat one with Tarragon in the bowels of an ancient ship." He checked himself. "I mean brat in the nicest way."

"She *is* a brat." Vertiline seemed distracted. "But Faust is right. The

Artifices are difficult to take on the edge of your blade. Leave that one to me."

"I don't think we'll need to." Tarragon stood, still staring skyward, visoring her eyes with a hand.

Amir felt like sighing again, but the movement was overdone. "You see something?"

"Seeing's the wrong word." She looked at him, her eyes the luminous green of deep, still water. "In this world there are forces we aren't meant to understand. My people, who you call the ancients, tapped deep. They mined the forbidden magics, married it to technology, and made marvels. Devices to tame starlight and fly, or weapons to raze cities. Even whole peoples were cast from rude clay to stand next to us. The very gods trembled, and were afraid."

Amir let his gaze slide sideways to Faust, mouthing *what the fuck*. The big man shrugged. Amir pointed behind him at the gates. "What does it have to do with that?"

"There are ways of thinking at a..." Tarragon clenched her fingers in frustration. "The right words aren't known to you. The best way to put it is your thoughts aren't at the right scale. Always it is sword on sword, person against person. My people thought across ages and at the distance of the sun. They would not walk to the door and fight an Artifice. Oh, they could. The Three's Wardens were put here to fight the impossible when we couldn't. But always at the end of the rest of our tricks, when hope failed and darkness called."

"Mireille," Vertiline breathed. "Geneve spoke of the last Knight Champion who stood against weapons thrown from the heavens. Her dragon, Rulbenen, kneeling at fate's feet. Dying, so we could live."

"But are we living?" Tarragon's voice was sad. "Or are we just dying, but slower? More miserable, sadder, and smaller?"

"Umm." Amir pursed his lips, thinking hard. "Is your heart not in this fight?"

"It matters not," a strange voice growled, which afforded Amir the opportunity to look away from the loss in Tarragon's eyes. A man had rounded the wagon, fit-looking, perhaps thirty-five summers, a stout halberd held in a manner that suggested he knew how to use it and intended to.

Behind him, adding some weight to a potential argument, was a group of twenty men and women, all with the same battle-ready look. Amir's fingers touched his sheathed blade, reminding him of the weapon's weight, how it would feel, and what the Light would need to do to take so many at once.

"Hey now," the man said, seeing his fingers. "Let us not get ahead of ourselves."

An *urk* came from behind Amir, and he turned to see another troop on the other side of the wagon. Less in number, but two massive Vhemin had Faust, one on each arm, and a woman stood behind him with a blade at his throat. Larochette was frozen, blade half drawn.

Vertiline's eyes blazed. "Strike him down, and you will all die."

"Maybe," the man mused. "But he'll still be dead. Come along, now." He frowned. "What's with her?"

Amir followed the man's gaze to Tarragon, who once again stared at the sky. Requiem was still safely in scabbard, the once-fairy seemingly unconcerned with the arrival of forty soldiers meaning harm. "Tarragon?"

"They called me Tarragon Greyflight," she whispered, words almost lost on the wind. "Grey, because I was mismade, malformed, not one thing or the other. I was supposed to be an engineer making devices that lifted us to the stars, not a spy or warrior." She turned back to Amir. "He's right, you know."

"What?" Amir glanced back at the enemy captain. The other man was clearly equally confused, readying his halberd and voice both.

But Tarragon wasn't done. "Then the gods took my wings, so I could no longer fly. I'm just Tarragon now. But they didn't take my sight, and I can still see what they made. Have you not wondered *why* the cannons fire? There are no people left in this world who can make them work. Not like this, an endless fusillade of fire aimed at the clouds. This is a Vehement Systems fortress. And there is but one thing the ancient machines remember."

"Itikari," Amir breathed.

"He was right when he said it doesn't matter. There are things coming that still think at the right scale."

The clouds tinted a dull red, then orange, moving to a brilliant yellow almost all at once. A lance of pure heavenly fire speared from the heavens, the clouds roiling aside in the wake of immense heat. The fire in the sky touched the doors of the keep, and they exploded in kindling and sand, melted iron, and screaming soldiers. Another lance fell, hammering the cannons, but a shimmer of blue-white bubbled about their position. *Some kind of shield*, Amir marvelled, and realised he was flat on his ass, knocked to the ground by the force of the god's flame.

The sky continued to spit fire, the cannons firing back, beams of fire and light tossed by the souls of giants long dead, their corpses continuing a lonely war. Amir screamed and wept, then was knocked flat, a man's torso—no head, no arms, no legs, just the middle piece—landing atop him.

He crawled, deaf, mute, trying to reach the Justiciar, or his fellow Knights, but there was no sign. The wagon's shelter was no more, mere ash blown on fell wind, the gates ahead a ruin, the keep open, waiting.

He felt a hand on his, and panicked, pulling away. Above, green eyes beneath wheat-pale hair. An arm stretched out to help. Tarragon, her lips moving, but he couldn't hear. She pulled him upright, pointing toward the fortress. Blue-white shields bloomed over parts, keeping the interior safe. Her meaning was clear. *We must get inside, or we die.*

He nodded, and she helped him, the pair shuffle-running toward the gate. Amir risked a glance back over his shoulder.

There, shouldering the sky aside, was *Dancing in the Storm*, the last Itikari warship, coming to finish her fight. The sky fortress was ablaze, cannons raining fire, smoke billowing from her decks where the Vehement Systems weapons had found their mark. But she fought on, a warship eight hundred years dead, now crewed by the damned.

Chapter Thirty-Eight

When Meriwether poked his head over the mound of rubble, he saw efficiency in action. Row upon row of men and women, loading what looked like cannons with what didn't look like shot. The cannons were long, elegant affairs, machined from pure crystal, eldritch inner mechanisms glowing with a lambent, heavy light. They pooled yellow luminosity like rain pooled water, a syrupy illumination that clung to the boots of the soldiers loading them.

The soldiers were methodical, well-disciplined, and a mixture of human and Vhemin. They were intent on the task of schlepping perfect cylinders of what seemed like limestone or chalk from an orderly pile of munitions. The magazine stores were legion, enough fire power—assuming each chalky block was one shot—to blast ordnance at the heavens for weeks.

He waited, watching as one crew opened a cannon's side, the inner workings making the air shimmer with heat. They sealed it, then turned away, the cannon roaring at the sky. Meriwether glanced at *Dancing in the Storm*, which took the shot and kept on coming. When the ship shouldered through the clouds he'd been surprised, but only long enough to realise everyone else would be surprised too, and thus making it the perfect time to sabotage the cannons.

The noise of the cannons wasn't as loud as he expected, and the sound was ... odd. Scatterguns were all might and muscle in one big bang. These cannons carried more build-up, similar to Ormeon's wrath as she banked her fire in preparation for barbecue. The lance of fire at the sky pulled wind in its wake, tugging his hair and cloak.

"How do we take on those?" Jade was at his left elbow.

"Forget the guns. What about the people?" Amber was at his right, eyes wide, mouth doing a good gape.

"Easy," Meriwether lied. "See the magazine?"

"The what?" Jade squinted.

"The pile of cylinders." At her nod, he turned away, hunkering down. "We get in there and set fire to the magazine. It'll cause an explosion, destroy the cannons, and let *Dancing on the Storm* dock here."

"You say that like we don't have to deal with the troops stationed there. I counted fifty men." Amber rubbed his forehead.

"It was closer to seventy, but the numbers aren't the important thing."

"They're not?"

"No." Meriwether glanced at the ship approaching steadily albeit slowly in the sky. "We need a distraction." He frowned, then picked up a stone before turning back to the cannons, winding up, and tossing the pebble. It soared through the air and hit the shield, bounced, and fell to the ground. "We also need a way through that shield. That's a more pressing problem."

"Shift change?" Jade scrubbed at her hair, silting dust and dirt. "They must need relief at some point. We wait until the troops arrive then steal in with them."

"Brilliant," Amber said. "Only one small problem. Where do we get uniforms?"

"We could go in as their prisoners," she hazarded.

"Now there are two more problems," Amber said. "The first is that we would then be their prisoners, which will make setting the magazine alight difficult. The second is that is not a stockade. If we are prisoners—"

"I get it," Jade said. "It's a stupid idea."

"It has merit," Meriwether said. "Not the prisoner part, but the bones are there. Entering alongside an expected cavalry would be the ticket."

"Hold," said a woman, causing Meriwether to look up. Standing before him was a soldier, a sergeant by her bearing and Vhemin by her breeding. Behind the sergeant, five other Vhemin, all wearing armour, carrying spears, and looking angry.

"Oh, shit," Amber said.

"Perfect." Meriwether stood. "Captain, I wonder—"

"Sergeant," the Vhemin corrected. "I work for a living."

"By your bearing I'd assumed... no matter." Meriwether tied on a brilliant smile. "You couldn't have arrived at a more perfect time."

"To arrest you?" the sergeant hazarded.

"No, to get us into the magazine." Meriwether beamed. "We are on special deployment from Wild Sur, looking to get an update on ammunition levels. The castle is concerned about the amount of ordnance expended at the enemy."

"Really." The woman didn't phrase it like a question.

"Really," he nodded. "The only real problem we're faced with is a lack of—"

"The problem you're faced with is that *we* were sent to check the ammunition levels."

"How extraordinary," Meriwether said. "Imagine two teams being sent to do the same job. Well, that's the military for you."

"Imagine," she said, looking completely devoid of anything resembling a theatre of the mind.

"Well, nothing for it but to progress together," Meriwether said.

"I tell you what," the sergeant offered. "Let's go back to command, get you thrown in the stockade, and then be about the business of interrogating you."

Meriwether held up a hand. "I'm not sure—"

A shape of silver-gold hurtled in front of him, the wind tugging his hair again, and the sergeant was gone. He wondered if he'd got turned about, or if the cannons misfired on his position, but there was no heat. One moment he was having a very reasonable conversation with the enemy, the next she was simply missing in action, leaving her spear to topple to the ground.

Meriwether looked at it, as did the five soldiers behind where the sergeant was. He glanced at them. "Did you see that?"

"'Ere," one said, hefting his spear. "Let's—"

And then he was gone too, but in the other direction. He took his spear with him though, leaving nothing but the memory of his bad diction. Meriwether looked after him, catching a glimpse of metal buoyed by an eddy of dust. "Merciful Three." He glanced at the remaining soldiers. "Is this you?"

"It's not us," said a large brute with a broken nose. "I thought it was you guys." And then he was gone, a single boot left in the mud. It still had a leg in it.

A woman said, "Fuck this," turned, sighted, and threw her spear. There was a *clang* and then she vanished with a yell carried off into the distance.

Amber sidled up to Meriwether. "What's going on?"

"I honestly don't know." Meriwether felt the wonder in his tone. "I've been in a demon realm for sixteen years. Saw a lot there. Nothing like metal wind that steals soldiers from the ground, leaving naught but a memory though."

"I don't want to go," one of the remaining two said, but he didn't get his wish. This time, the ground was dappled with his blood.

The last woman broke and ran. She made it about thirty metres, arms and legs pumping, head down, full sprint, armour clattering, the works. This time, Meriwether saw the approach of their saviour, a metal saint flying above the ground. It slammed into the running soldier, carrying her in its arms, and streaking past Meriwether. He spun, watching as both impacted the shield in a haze of blue-white fire.

The soldier exploded into component parts that showered gore like a rapid and amateur vivisection, but the metal saint skidded across the top of the shield dome, metal scraping, sparks showering.

"Hang about," Jade said. "That's Evanne's armour. Isn't she off somewhere else?"

Meriwether realised his mouth was open, so he closed it. Evanne was atop the shield. Below her, troops rushed about, gathering weapons and forming a huddle beneath her. It all looked inexpert to Meriwether's eye, but he supposed not many soldiers had to learn defence against a metal flying saint that stood atop a dome above them.

The armour: now that was a marvel. Goldfire eyes above all, the metal fluid, almost a liquid as Evanne paced the dome. He could mark no seam in the suit, nothing at all like it appeared on the repair table. The Itikari stardrive on the back gave off waves of heat. Gold lines ran down its length. The shield continued to spark and glow at every step. Meriwether called out, "Stop moving. You're just making it worse!"

Evanne stared at him, or at least he hoped it was Evanne, but she had the same set of her shoulders, and he would wager a platinum solar the same jut of chin. But she stopped pacing, hands on hips. "Satisfied?"

"Perfect," he said, and she slipped through the dome, arms pinwheeling, to land in a melee circus below.

"How surprisingly simple," Meriwether breathed. "It appears all you must do is move very slowly to get through."

Inside the dome, soldiers piled atop Evanne. Spears were thrust. Shouting.

Amber looked at Meriwether. "And why would we want to go in there?"

Chapter Thirty-Nine

The castle interior was cool. And it was quiet, as if a blanket had dropped over the ruckus outside. Some magic was at work inside too; Amir's footsteps made little noise and the squeak of leather and rattle of buckle were muted, as if the sounds came from the bottom of a deep well. The ceiling was high, with no visible pillars or bracing. That giant weight of stone above seemed to be suspended on the very air. Along the walls were many doors, the number difficult to count as the hall was perhaps a klick long.

Amir and Tarragon walked side by side. There were no tracks hinting at where Vertiline might have gone. Amir feared the High Justiciar might be dead, but it wasn't a great fear. His teacher had a deeply annoying habit of surviving things that should have killed her.

This place gives me the shits. Amir looked to Tarragon, the warrior at his side alert, her eyes everywhere at once. "What is this place?"

She gave him a glance, then slowed. "This is the chief operating offices of Vehement Systems." At his blink, she offered, "It's where all the bad people are."

"There is no one here." Because, indeed, there was no memory of another person in the hall. Distance blurred detail at the far end, but Amir was certain no one stood ready to fight or welcome them.

"They're here," she assured him. "This is the reception foyer. It's not where the boss is."

"The reception what? Some kind of location to receive the guilty and judge innocence?"

She scrubbed wheat-pale hair, then huffed a sigh. "Things from my time are not like your time."

"This I know."

"We had ... rules about how we killed people. An iron fist in a silken glove, hard men working from the shadows, grim women who taught fear through doubt." She frowned at herself. "I don't mean to imply those were their actual jobs. Like, no one interviewed to be a silken glove."

Amir blinked again, but slower this time. "What?"

"The point is, you'd welcome people into your office, then take them out back and off them. This isn't the back. This is the front."

"Why is it so quiet?"

"No one likes a crying baby," she said, perhaps more mysteriously than Amir felt the situation demanded. Light bloomed as a great ring set in the far wall glowed a sickly green, then climbed in colour to a steady, soft purple. Tarragon put a hand on Amir's arm. "Hold."

"The problem is some distance away." Amir checked his sword and tightened the strap on his shield. "We will never get to it if we stand about."

"Hold," she repeated. "There should be no great gate in the foyer."

Amir rubbed his brow, his fingers coming away sweaty and dirty. "Speak plain. Gate?"

"That thing," she stabbed a finger at the purple ring, "is a great gate. It is like a doorway that connects two points. One point is here, the other," she glared at the ceiling, "could be anywhere. We know Wild Sur wants Morgan to open a gate, but this one is already open. Why? To where? And there should be no gate here. This is the *welcoming foyer*." She said these last two words as if explaining why water was wet to a supreme imbecile.

"Right," Amir said. "But what if the thing you wanted to bring into the welcoming foyer was larger than anything from those little doors? What if it was a really big welcome?"

She glanced between him and the walls, then did it once more. "What could they want to bring through that's so large?"

"What *can* they bring through?" Amir frowned. "I don't know what these are. Where I'm from, we use doors like normal fucking people."

She counted on her fingers. "You can make a portal go anywhere there's another portal. Which means," another finger, "you can put them on the other side of the world, or in the ocean."

"Why would you put them in the ocean?"

"It's the fastest way to the bottom," she said. "Once you've been there once, you don't need to swim down again."

"Can you swim to the bottom of the ocean?"

"I think you're losing track," she chided. "You can also put a gate in space. Or..." She drifted to silence.

"Or?" Amir looked at the purple ring. "Were you thinking of a good place?"

"What do you think?"

"Just tell me," he said. "It's better if I take the shock up front."

"There is one place you don't need another gate." She looked at the portal. "We don't know why. I always thought it was because it was a kind of ... *not*-place, a realm where all things end up." She looked at the floor. "Where the demons are."

"Are demons big?" At her glance, he said, "You thought I was losing track, but the size of the portal is important, right? Can demons be as big as that thing is?"

"Yes."

"Are they easy to kill?"

"No."

"Have you killed one?"

"Yes."

"Of that size?"

"No."

"Help me out here," Amir said. "The one-word responses are precise but they don't give me much to work with."

Tarragon fingered the hilt of Requiem. "No one would open a gate to a demon realm. Not anymore."

"Because they killed your world?"

"Yes." At his glare, she elaborated, "My world ended because the demons got here and drove everyone at each other. People who should have worked together were at war. I didn't see how the war ended because I was locked in a cage, but I saw what came after." She looked miserable and lifted her arms in an *all this* gesture. "Mud and misery. Blood from a juicer. I heard Knight Champion Mireille gave her life at the final battle when the orbital strikes came. Everyone died. *Everyone*. But the demons were still here. Still hunting our starlight. And each time we died, they got a little hit. They grew stronger and opened another gate. And the High Justiciar's best friend, who was apparently the spitting image of Mireille, in deed if not looks, gave her life to close the gate. Shut it for good. The gods came. The world stopped, and time went backward, and night became day. And we were saved."

"That was more than one word. Thank you."

"Any time." She looked away. "No one would open a gate there. Not again."

"A couple of things." Amir took a few more steps toward the gate, then thought better of it. "People are stupid. They don't learn fire's hot if they've never been burned, and the people here now have never even laid a hearth. Second, someone opened the demon gates in the first place. They had reasons. Maybe those reasons came back."

"Doesn't matter. You'd need a … oh. Three's mercy." Tarragon looked at the door, then to Amir. "You'd need a Ritualist. Or a Holomancer."

"It's a good thing Morgan's not here. Nor the fellow who walks like he remembers a younger man's steps."

"Meriwether?" Tarragon eyed the door again. "But they're both so close."

"So, we must keep them away."

"Amir," came a booming voice.

Amir turned, eyes widening in surprise. His giant friend Faust had stepped through one of the many doors along the west wall. "Faust?" He glanced back at the entranceway. "How did you get here?"

"We are both here." Larochette entered from a door on the east wall. "We came to see the enemy's forces."

"There is no one else," Faust said, too cryptically for Amir's liking.

"Do you know about the gate?" Amir pointed to the far wall, picking up his feet to join his Tresward siblings. He felt an absence behind him, and faced Tarragon, who was still mired in indecision on the pavers behind him. "Tarragon?"

"Something is not right here," she hissed. "There is a gate. There are no soldiers. There are two previously missing Tresward, who happened to know how to get through the foyer and into the rooms beyond."

Faust closed the distance, pace by pace. "The doors were not locked."

"Yes, they were," Tarragon said. "They can't *not* be locked. This is *Vehement Systems*."

"Many things from the old world broke," Amir offered.

She looked at him like he was a simpleton. "They're *doors*."

"Do you call me a liar?" Larochette was very close now.

"Hey, now," Amir said. "Perhaps you could tell us what you found."

"For certain," Faust said.

The room was bathed in blue-white light as Tarragon drew Requiem. Her eyes were hard green stone, her face chiselled granite. "Stop walking."

Larochette looked like she might have something to say about that, but Faust raised his hands. "Peace. Allow me to explain." He nodded as if agreeing with himself. It was a typical Faust-like expression the large man got away with because no one else tended to disagree with him on general principle. "We don't speak of our past. Not to each other."

"No," Amir agreed. "No need."

"Except there is now." Faust held a hand out, palm up, toward Larochette. "Our sister in battle was a slave when we found her."

"With you so far. I believe I was pivotal in springing her from the clink." Amir wished Tarragon would sheathe Requiem, but the once-fairy was cast iron, immobile, eyes moving between Faust and Larochette.

"I was a slave because I killed a Justiciar," Larochette said. "My fellow mages stripped me of my power—"

"You're no mage," Tarragon said.

"If I'd been allowed to finish my sentence, I'd have explained that nothing drives incompetence in quite the same way as bureaucracy," Larochette said. "I drew the wrong sort of attention. The coven was at risk, so I was denounced, readied for trial, the Tresward summoned." She barked a harsh laugh. "Then some imbecile put me in a slaver's cage, and when the Tresward arrived they ended my brothers and sisters." She looked at her hands. "If you can't beat someone, learn their tricks. I became what hunted me, so I didn't need to fear again. And if I find the head of the slavers, well, so much the sweeter."

"Hmm," Amir allowed. "What's this got to do with the doors in here?"

"Ah," Faust breathed. "You always were the clever one."

"I try." Amir spread his hands.

"His past is worse," Larochette said. "His life before was ... sweet."

"I was married." Faust's eyes gazed over Amir's shoulder, seeing something in the amber of memory, the man's eyes soft as he remembered great sadness. "Your precious queen began a hunt for the Vide. Cut the head from the assassins. But she cut the head from my wife."

Amir took a cautious step back, the ground no longer seeming so safe and firm. "The Raven Queen had it in for your wife?"

"IQs definitely dropped over the last eight hundred years," Tarragon hissed. "The Raven has not been the best ruler this world has seen, but she is far from the worst. Most I've seen touched by her grace are better for it. She is no tyrant. No crusades. No meaningless purges. This was—"

"This was because my wife knew someone high up in the Vide," Faust rumbled. "I have learned the tricks of the best sword masters in the world to make my way to her and cut out her heart."

"But, why?" Amir blinked, confused. "She ... Morgan only hunted Vide."

"Do you not see it, friend Amir?" Tarragon pointed with her glowing blade. "Faust killed his wife."

The large man's eyes blazed, two coals under the bellows. "I did no such thing."

Tarragon spat, "He killed his wife because he was the head of the Vide."

The words dropped on the stone floor, the silence following

profound, a deep lake of knowledge that could not be unlearned. Amir opened his mouth, closed it, and tried again. "Faust? Is this true?"

"It is true." Faust straightened. "And I will have her head. We have allies now, Amir. We have a leader who doesn't hide his gifts. Wild Sur has been as harmed by the world as we three. We are trusted by him and can bring you with us." A slight hint of appeal entered Faust's tone. "Please, Amir. Join us."

"Or die, am I right?" Tarragon's tone was mocking. "That's some starter villain shit right there."

Faust glanced at her. "There is no third path."

Amir took another step back. He looked to Tarragon, and suggested, "Run."

"I will not leave you."

"These are *Tresward*."

"They are hacks," she pronounced. "Let's dance."

Another door opened down the hall. Amir realised his sword was half-drawn, and he wasn't sure who he was fighting, or why. *This is fucked. These are the two who made me whole. There must be another way.* "Don't do this."

The door widened, and an elderly Feybrind entered. 'Elderly' was like saying lightning was bright; the cat's fur was grey beyond any Amir had seen, but he walked without stoop. He wore human-like clothes. It was ancient's attire if Amir was any judge of style, of which he believed himself to be one of the world's foremost experts. The clothes were cut well to fit the Feybrind's frame. There was no hint they were destined for a different species in how they hung.

The cat was disfigured. Both ears were gone, leaving ruined holes in his skull, but his golden eyes were forge-bright. About his throat was a collar and at his waist a sword hung, but Amir's eyes were drawn to the other weapon he carried. It had the look of one of the ancient's beam weapons, all fire and spite, a heavy thing for dirty work. "We are here to set the world right."

Amir blinked. *Did that fucking cat just talk?* The Feybrind's mouth had opened every so slightly, throat working, but not much else going on. The voice was smooth, soft, inoffensive. "A talking cat?" The words had the hollow ring of vapidity, but they were out there now, nothing to be done about them.

"Your kind stole the voices from mine," the Feybrind said. "I forgive you." He touched the collar at his throat. "Our Handspeak was too difficult for some of the ancient world to master. A weary burden on the master over the slave, so they set to work making these. It is hard to use but gives me speech. So many things about this place," he turned, taking one hand from his weapon to gesture at the room, "require a voice to use. I will take my enemy's devices and make them regret their forging."

Larochette stepped to Amir's right, positioning herself. Amir supposed he should be flattered they thought tactics were necessary, but then he caught the glimmer of Tarragon's blade in his peripheral vision on the same side and he understood. *She is wise to mind Requiem. And I carry the Storm. I've not seen those two command it with any honesty.* "Am I your enemy?"

"Her," the Feybrind gestured with his weapon at Tarragon, "and those like her. Ancient, ideas so old they rust in the skull. Those who would call others servant, or slave. Those who crave power. All the corrupt queens lording majesty over others who barely have enough to eat. People who crowd others to the edges."

Amir tried to keep track. "You're saying humans, or any lucky enough to have survived these long years?"

"Not all humans. But most."

"But I might not be the enemy?"

Faust, a stone to this moment, shifted. "Friend Amir, Wild Sur has—"

"*This* is Wild Sur?"

The giant nodded, nice and slow. "He—"

"I expected an evil overlord to hide in the shadows."

Faust rubbed a weary hand against his forehead. "Can I finish?"

"No problem. Get to the good parts first, though. Larochette is trying to get the drop on Tarragon, and I admit I'm unsure how that fight will end."

"It will end with Larochette dead," Faust said.

"Hey," Larochette said. "I'm good with a blade."

Wild Sur stalked closer, his weapon ready. "She holds a magic blade forged from a fallen star, and she knows the patterns of the Tresward well enough to summon the Storm. She once was a fairy. Her heart burns with the fires of shattered atoms."

"Three on one, though," Larochette said. "Four, if we're lucky."

"Shouldn't it be three on two?" Amir felt unstable, his heart drifting to his friends before him, to his friend beside him, and back again.

"We're hoping you might be convinced to join us," Faust rumbled. "Failing that, we hope you will stand aside." He frowned. "This is the way of it. The people of this world are broken, and we have a remedy."

Amir tossed a glance at Tarragon. "Have you any idea what they're talking about?"

She didn't blink, eyes locked on Larochette, her feet easy in classic mid guard. "There is an orbital weapons platform above. It has many weapons capable of destroying this world, or large parts of it."

"Seems bad," Amir suggested.

"It is how the world ended once before."

"We will cleanse the unworthy," Wild Sur said. "The barbarians will fall, leaving us to inherit a cleaner palace. We will destroy all the ancients' works at the same time. *This* time it will be a blow that removes all taint from the world."

"Sounds final."

"It will be." The Feybrind tapped one horrible scar on the side of his head. "This was a gift, you know."

"I'm lost," Amir admitted. His sword was still half out of its sheath, and he wondered if now was the right time to draw steel.

"I can't hear." Wild sur half-smiled. "A group of your kind found me after the weapon broke the world. They thought—"

"You're eight hundred years old?" Amir's eyes boggled. "You look great for your age."

"I'm older than all that. I've had time to learn many things, like the shape your lips make when producing certain sounds. I also learned Feybrind must hear to be Commanded."

"A truly free soul," Tarragon whispered.

"I prefer 'liberated'. But 'prepared' works well, too." He opened his ancient's shirt one-handed, weapon ever ready, still levelled at

Tarragon. Beneath he revealed a scarred coat, and a shiny medallion hanging from a thick chain about his neck. Wild Sur's golden eyes were heavy on the once-fairy. "You know what this is?"

Amir turned to her. "I don't. What the fuck is that?"

"A ... weapon of hubris," she said.

"The fairies made these."

"We *had* to."

"Were you Commanded?" The cat's eyes were harder now. "Did you *really* have to?"

"It's complicated, because—"

"If I may." Amir cleared his throat. "What is it?"

Tarragon's eyes darted to Amir's, and he saw hopelessness there, alongside guilt and fear. "A weapon of last resort."

"It's the weapon you never have to use, until you don't care if you have to." Wild Sur's half-smile got a millimetre wider. "It is bound to my life. My soul, perhaps. I don't know how it works. But if I die, then I explode."

Tarragon snorted. "That's not right."

Amir looked between them. "What. Is. It?"

"It is linked to a personalised weapons platform in the heavens above. There is a single large yield device that will strike the location where its wearer died."

Amir's hand trembled a fraction on the hilt of his half-drawn sword. "What does 'large yield' mean?"

"It will end the world again," Faust said. "But our preferred way is cleaner. You join us. We kill the ... whatever she is," he waved a hand at Tarragon, "and then open this gate to the platform above."

"You need a Ritualist," Tarragon said.

"That is the only reason the Raven Queen yet lives," the large man said.

"Also, that gate doesn't go to the platform above."

"We can remedy that," Wild Sur said. "I have studied its magics."

"Faust," Amir said, then ground to a stop. *He has spent his life hunting the person who he believes killed his wife. He has the Vide behind him, and the Storm is millimetres from his grasp. What can I say?* "Faust, please."

"Stand with us or stand aside." Faust moved, oil back in his machine, and hefted his hammer. "All is as it should be."

Tarragon took a step back, her eyes hard, and she glanced at Amir again. "Don't listen to them. *Please*."

Amir slipped his blade back in its sheath. He straightened, closed his eyes, and bowed his head. *Think, man. Think.* He remembered Faust and Larochette at the slaver's camp. Their long road of toil to learn the Treswards' patterns. Their companionship, and their friendship. Then he thought of the once-fairy, who failed her exams, and was one of the ancients who broke the world. About how she loved one of the corrupted, broken people who ... *meddled.* Then he opened his eyes and drew his sword clean and swift, then turned to face Tarragon. "You are one of the ancients."

"Please, Amir."

He took a step forward. "Your death could pave the way for a cleaner world."

She backed up. "Amir, it's ... complicated."

He took a final step, their blades almost touching. He could feel the white heat of Requiem on his face. "The thing is, I don't like clean. I *like* complicated. And the only person in here not calling me *friend* is the one who is." He pivoted, facing Faust, Larochette, and Wild Sur. "I swear, you will not harm this woman. She is good where I am not. If a trade of life is to be made, I will pay it."

Tarragon's voice cracked. "Wild Sur has a—"

"I see it. Get behind me."

Faust rolled his shoulders, then charged.

Chapter Forty

That's a lot of assholes. Evanne was swarmed by a collection of soldiers. They piled on her and down she went. *I made a mistake*, she realised. *The armour is strong. It can fly. But in here, I'm a wasp in a jar.* She stood, uppercutting a man to the top of the magical dome, where he bounced right off and smashed into her.

"Error in judgement," the armour said, as she went down again.

Some enterprising fool was beating on Evanne with a mallet as she struggled upright. *Clang, clang*, each hit against her breastplate, shoulders, helmet, and leg, before she kicked him, lost her balance, and down she went *again*, just in time for a third fool to take a good run-up and stick her with a glaive.

"Structural integrity holding." The armour sounded smug.

It didn't pierce her shell, but it annoyed her enough to roar, raging upright, and right then was where it went quite bad indeed. A trio of soldiers rushed her, collecting her in a kind of meat clothesline tackle and tossing her into the barrier.

Her world went blue-white, the armour ringing like a clock tower bell, and she felt a burning heat run through her, tasted lightning against her teeth, and felt her muscles convulsing. The good news was the armour had nothing smug to say. The bad news was everything went dark, her vision losing those lovely floating symbols the ancients loved so much, her world restricted to a narrow window through her visor.

The armour's full weight came down on her, whatever magic assistance that made it strong and light failing. Evanne collapsed with a *whuff*, going face first into the dirt.

Clang against her back as someone hit her. "Hitch!"

"It'll be right," the spectre's voice said from above her. "Give it a moment."

Clang, clang, clang...creak. "I'm not sure I've got a moment."

"Get that armour off her," a man shouted. She was manhandled, flopping to face the sky. Evanne saw a circle of angry faces, and above them, *Dancing in the Storm* floating in the clouds.

"*Artifice engine restarting. Starlight drive engaging.*" The armour didn't sound smug any more so much as like the young lad back home with a head injury. *What was his name? Claret? Clarion? Something red, to call the warriors to war. Then a horse kicked him.* Odd memory to have now, with the creaking from her left side where an enterprising soul wedged a pry bar in. They were trying to shuck her out. "*Magnetic arbalest online.*"

A fucking what arbalest? Evanne clawed ineffectually at the pry bar in her side. This armour was so damn heavy it was stupid. "Hitch? What's a mag... a mag. Um."

"Magnetic arbalest," he said, with that same tone he used when he thought he was being helpful, but almost never was. "An arbalest is a—"

"I know what an arbalest is!"

"Right. Well, this one uses magnets."

"What are those?"

"*Starlight drive restored.*" The little symbols in her visor bloomed, all hurrying into the lower part of her vision like a curious clutch of puppets on a stage show. The armour *thrummed*, then surged upright, no help from her required at all. It tossed the soldiers off her. It no doubt looked comedic right up until one hit the dome opposite her with a *crunch-splat*, the back of his head hitting with such force he'd be joining Casper or whatever the kid's name had been.

"Get her!" shouted a woman, just as a *rattle-clank* sounded from around Evanne's torso. The spheres anchored there spat free, then orbited her waist in a circling ring. They span faster until they were a blur of silver-gold metal. The woman, nobody's fool, took a step back as her friend, a large man the size of a well-fatted ox, surged forward.

He was turned into bloody chum by the spheres, the metal passing through his body like a very quick series of axe cuts. His legs slopped against Evanne's, his torso impacting hers then getting mouli'd rapidly as it slid into the orbiting hail of spheres. Red sprayed against her attackers as centrifugal force flung her foe's remains at them. The spheres turned red, then buzzed themselves back to a shiny silver-gold halo.

"*Magnetic arbalest fully operational.*" The armour was back to being smug.

"That's not how an arbalest works," Evanne said. "It's like a cross-bow." She pointed, sure the armour would take her meaning. "You aim it, and it shoots an arrow—"

"*Bolt.*"

"It shoots a bolt, and that's that."

"*Magnetic operation changes engagement parameters,*" the armour assured her.

"Magnets do stuff," Hitch supplied, less helpfully than he might have intended.

"I get you," Evanne said. "But here we are, in a dome of imperme-able force, unless we step very slowly through it, trapped with a dozen maniacs with sharps sticks and an attitude, and—"

"*Remedying,*" the armour said, and a sphere shot from the orbit at her waist. It went straight through the head of a man to her right, hit the barrier wall, followed the curve around, and returned to the ring spinning about her.

Another sphere shot out, another soldier down, and the rest panicked and ran, all impacting the shield dome with the predicted result of it flaring bright, but not letting them through. The armour fired another arbalest shot into the curve of the wall, where it followed the line of the barrier, going through a clutch of soldiers without any sign of slowing down, before rejoining its friends in her defensive halo.

The armour's fangs dipped into her arms, feeding, and Evanne whimpered. The pain was bright, but it hadn't killed her yet, and would be worth it if she could save Mama, and Papa, and even stupid Morgan. Her head bowed, breath hissing through her teeth. Then it let her alone, and when she looked up, the last living soldier had eased through the barrier, hotfooting it into the distance.

Standing on the other side of the barrier was the lordling, next to the two merchants Amber and Jade. He put a hand against the barrier, then gave a small laugh of delight. "What a marvellous thing." He slowly stepped through, his hair standing on end as it passed the barrier.

"Meriwether?" Evanne's step hitched as the spheres clattered back into place on the bandolier, the spinning circle of death quiet for the moment. "I took care of the guards so you'd run!"

"Yes, I see that now, but I'm not the kind of monster that leaves a child to face a fortress alone." He held a hand up as if sensing her fire building about the *child* comment. "Would your mother kill me, or not?"

Evanne bridled, but gritted out, "She would probably kill you. If she knew."

"She knows. Vertiline knows everything! I tried to shake her back when she captured me, and that woman is *tenacious*." He stalked to the device with all the pipes and energy, then walked a circle about it. "Did she ever tell you how we met?"

"You didn't come up."

"How odd." He brightened, reached into a tangle of machinery Evanne could make nothing of, yanked, and all the lights died. The guns firing above quietened. He tossed a cube at her, golden filaments streaming as it flew.

She caught it, turning it about. It was plain metal, no markings bar the holes the filaments emerged from. "How'd you know to yank this piece?"

"Simple. It was the only piece that looked *ordinary*." He dusted his hands against each other. "Now we've solved that problem, let's clear the way for Morgan."

"No," Evanne said. "The evil warlord of this place wants a Ritualist to re-open a demon gate."

"Yes." Meriwether nodded encouragingly.

"And that would be bad."

"No." He sucked air, shaking his head in disapproval. "It is the only good thing we can do today."

"I'm not sure Morgan would agree!"

"Morgan signed up for it when I told her what the plan was."

"The plan?" Evanne's voice rose an octave. "I've been ... *flying*, Meriwether, and this armour's been drinking my blood, and I came here to save you, and you, you what, you had a *plan* all along?"

"Uh." He took stock of her posture, then offered what was supposed to be a disarming smile but just made Evanne want to punch him. "I had the skeleton of a plan. Look, you get up to that city above. I'll break into the castle—"

"Break in?"

"I used to be a very good thief."

"The door is *right there*."

"Yes, but people expect us to use the door. Come now. Time is pressing. Use your wings, or," he waved a hand in the general direction of her torso, "whatever you've got in there. Morgan is out there with Heser the Cheg, and about now she will be breaking the bad news to him."

Chapter Forty-One

"My queen, perhaps we should decamp." Heser's low voice was calm.

He is always calm. Morgan surveyed the fortifications leading to the castle, the ground weapons having quietened their heavenly assault, the flying city above having eased up its response. She caught a flash of bright blue scale as Myryntir made a beeline for the castle gates. "No, I think now is a good time for us to rejoin the fight."

"*Are you cracked?*" Pakhet put her head under Morgan's palm, nosing it up. "*Scritches while you think of a good answer.*"

She gave a small smile, feeling the large cat's flat nose, the coarse fur, and the sensitive spot behind her ears. Morgan slipped her fingers through the tiger's pelt, the creature almost knocking her over as she leaned into the pat. "The thing is, my Lord du Reeves asked me before we got here how I'd feel about opening a gate ... to the *demon realm*."

"Uh." Heser's eyes were straight ahead, marking the battlefield, that tiny noise his only show of emotion. "I admit to not being the best general, but opening a doorway for enemy reinforcements when you're already outnumbered seems unwise."

"As he explained it to me, there are two ways opening the portal can go. The first," and with her free hand she pointed to the sky, "there are supplies and weapons above."

"That sounds like something the enemy would find useful. That is their *whole purpose*."

"The other small item of benefit would be pointing the gate into a demon realm."

"*Still good for the enemy... yes, right there. That's a good spot.*"

Morgan leaned harder on the scritches. "What they don't know, none of them, is how to open the gate. Or, what opening a gate to the sky versus the demon realm looks like."

"Which is why we don't want you with them?" Heser's voice had a questioning tone.

"Knowing how to open the gate gives me value," Morgan said. "Knowing where to open it gives the world value. And a queen must always know her worth."

"To the enemy? Or the world?" The question didn't fade from Heser's tone.

"The thing to consider is what else comes with the supplies above, or the demons below," Morgan said. "My Lord du Reeves has put some thought into this."

"He has been on the other side of a demon gate for sixteen years." Heser's tone was mild. "His judgement may be impaired."

"I fear his judgement is sound." Morgan's stomach felt unsettled, a fluttering uncertainty there. "His faith in me may be misplaced, however."

"My queen—"

"So, Guardsman." Morgan straightened, and a shade regretfully stopped patting Pakhet. "I need you to escort the tiger away."

"My queen?"

"This is a battlefield. It is no place for a beast of peace. It is a place for warmongers and their ilk. The wretched and the maligned. It is, in short, a place I will be quite at home." She stepped off the small hillock, striding toward the castle.

"My queen!"

"That is an order, Guardsman." *Don't look back. Don't let him see you.*

You will be undone. This is your last chance to save him, and you will keep your spine straight and your eyes forward.

Morgan stepped through the battlefield, and if a tear passed down her cheek, no one would think it anything but irritation at the ash on the wind.

Chapter Forty-Two

This place is a warren crossed with a maze. Vertiline hunted sinners, but she now knew what the term meant. She was—finally—on the right side of that fight. *I put the innocent to the torch, but evil's timely arrival allows redemption.*

She stalked the pale, cool hallways of the ancient castle. She'd been thrown far by the explosion. Her poise had stood her in good stead, her glimmering gold-lit body ploughing through the wall of the castle, landing her where she stood, surrounded by broken stone and angry stares. Her shield cracked under the force of smashing through castle walls despite the Light infusing it. *Perhaps it was as poorly forged as I.* Beyond the angry stares was a long, narrow room, lined with benches and wardrobes. A dressing room, perhaps an annex to a barracks that promised reinforcements at the merest cry.

Her eyes drifted back to the staring people. Eyes visible through slits in black headwear. Leather armour was the clothing *du jour* of her opponents, stylish and black, and grimly reminiscent of those Evanne described attacking *Dancing in the Storm*. She offered a thin-lipped smile. "Vide lice. I should have known you were at the heart of this."

A man rushed her from the left. He was fast and true, his hook blade seeking the join between cuirass and rerebrace. The tender armpit promised much arterial blood if the edge found a way in. Israel might have said, *Look, Tilly. Observe how* fast *he moves but note the lack of* speed.

Speed and excellence were factors born of repetition, prized much higher than hurried rushing. Form grooving the body into a slick pattern that could ease its way into any of twenty-one hundred patterns at a moment's notice. Vertiline took as much time as needed, no more, no less, stepping through his strike into *Eternal Conflict*, a classic opening move she favoured in Cophine's stanzas. Her sword rose as her body turned, Light licking blade, caressing her gauntlet, and casting long shadows as she stepped in the middle of her opponents.

The man who'd rushed her fell in two, hooked blade clattering into a corner. Vertiline continued the *Conflict*, taking a bolt from a hand crossbow on her steel as she hoisted the blade into high guard. She turned the edge behind her, a cavalier strike unless you were in the pattern. She hit the woman trying to knife her in the spine, cutting her arms off and leaving her with the hint of a scream as shock registered and breath drew in.

When Vertiline was learning, she'd asked Iz why the Tresward put themselves in the middle of their opponents as often as forming a defensive line. He'd offered her a frown as if it was obvious. *Adept, it is because it is where there are most enemies.*

The woman's scream hit as Vertiline struck three broad strikes against new enemies. She went top left to bottom right, bottom right to top right, and top right to bottom left, then took steel to low guard as three Vide fell burning from a touch of the Light. A large man rushed her, but the *Eternal Conflict* was ready, her shoulder braced, Light flowing from sabaton to pauldron. She shoulder-checked him, the man's chest caving in with the Three's power, his lifeless body smashing into the wall behind him.

"Wait!" said a man frantic with fear, before her steel took his head, surprise in his eyes fading in death as his head bounced along the stone floor.

A woman took her comrade's place. "We have—"

Vertiline sheared her through the middle, forever oblivious as to what they had. Her foe slumped in two places. *It is done.* There was little to recommend staying in the room with its small collection of smoking bodies. Two doors out, no doubt evil behind each, so she picked the southern exit. It was a barracks, with cots laid out in four rows. It promised a heady number of sinners yet to meet her blade. No one was in residence aside from an old man shuffling about with a broom. She gave him a raised eyebrow, to which he replied, "Even evil overlords need help."

"You know your leader is an evil overlord?"

"Hard to miss, what with the castle, the oppression, and the fanaticism." He raised his left arm which ended in a stump. "Not a lot of work in these parts. Those that hire pay less than a copper baron a day for most jobs that suit such as me."

"He pays more than a baron for cleaning floors?"

"He does. You'll be wanting to head that way," he pointed to the west door, "and count your way past three doors on your right. The fourth will take you to what you seek."

Vertiline turned the raised eyebrow into a frown. "Which is?"

"I don't want to spoil the surprise."

VERTILINE STALKED THE FINAL PACES TO DOOR NUMBER FOUR. TO get from one end of this corridor to here, she'd had to cut her way through another three guards, all of whom seemed fuelled by hope rather than brains. She left a collection of smoking body parts behind her, armoured heels clicking on stone as she paced forward.

The door was the same as the others barring a bloody handprint. She raised her own hand, sizing up the difference. *Larger than mine, but only a shade. A slight man or larger woman.* Vertiline kicked the door open, all brute force, and stood in the entranceway as part of it hung off its hinges, a torso-sized fragment clattering to the stone before her.

Inside: two Feybrind, and five Vhemin. The Feybrind were known to her. Sight of Day and Sands Apart were lashed to tables by leather straps. Various tools of torture were set about. Vertiline's vision went red with rage as she saw Sight of Day's wound. The grievous gash in his middle bled fiercly. Sands Apart was untouched.

The Vhemin were surprised, even the one she knew, who looked like he'd been worked over. The others: three strange men, two of whom held the one she knew, the third fingering a nasty-looking awl, and a larger, thuggish woman. She ignored them, looking at the man they held between them. "Husband. What news?"

"You've caught me at a bad time," Armitage admitted, briefly struggling against his two ox-sized Vhemin captors.

The thuggish woman looked down at Armitage, then to Vertiline. "You ... lay with this one?"

"She's tougher than she looks," Armitage growled. "A bit scrawny, but you get used to it."

Thuggish backhanded him with ease born of hours of practice. Armitage rocked with the blow. Vertiline raised her blade, the motion drawing all eyes, even Sight of Day's hazed, golden glance. "If you move to touch him again, I will end you."

"You mean, if I touch him. You said move." Thuggish frowned, speedy thoughts clearly not why she held her position as chief torturer.

"If you move to touch him, you'll die before your hand reaches its mark."

"She's not fooling around," Armitage said. "She's being really honest right now."

"You're by the door. I'm here. There's no way you get to me between when I raise my arm," Thuggish raised her fist, "and me doing *this*."

Between the words *me* and *doing*, golden light flashed, and by the time *this* made it from her lips, her arm was already following gravity's insistence to the ground. Vertiline's sword burned with Light, embedded in the wall behind Thuggish, the stone glowing about the blade. Thuggish howled, clutching her cauterised stump.

The fool with the blade made an idiot move toward Armitage, clearly meaning to be the second imbecile to try Vertiline's patience alongside her speed, but she'd been ready for it, shoulder descending as she'd tossed her steel, gathering the door fragment at her feet. It was unwieldy for a kite shield, but her fingers found the willing edges all the same, and she tossed it like a glowing frisbee. It hit the man rushing Armitage, but Vertiline knew her work was sloppy, not having had the weight or balance before grabbing it. Light flickered out, but it was enough to knock the Vhemin back a pace, his knife clattering free.

Vertiline followed her 'shield' throw by drawing the sword from the sheath of the closest man holding Armitage and running through the clown who dropped his knife. She took the head off the closest man, kicked the legs of his body aside, stepped in the gap, and thrust steel through the gut of the remaining Vhemin.

He wheezed a cry before she took his head, pushed Armitage clear —*gods, he's a unit*—and followed up on knife-dropper by splitting his skull. She tossed the borrowed steel aside and liberated her sword from the wall.

Armitage blinked. "You seem angry."

"I'm not angry." Vertiline's steel licked the binds holding Sands Apart, then she moved to Sight of Day's side. Her blade freed him before finding home in its sheath. She held her friend's hand. "What happened? How did they hurt you?"

Soft finger-snapping drew her eye. Sands Apart said, *{It was the crash. He was thrown clear. These lot didn't know why Vhemin and Feybrind would be together outside their special club, but that one,}* she pointed to knife-dropper, *{knew me. They sought information.}*

"Did they get it?" Vertiline placed her other hand over Sight of Day's, holding him gently.

"They didn't get shit."

Vertiline gave Armitage a tight nod. "Good. Now, to amends. I've taken steps to put Evanne out of harm's way—"

"She's never going to stay out of harm's way."

"Too much of her father in her?"

{Mother, more like.} Sands Apart lowered her hands, perhaps realising this wasn't a conversation she should be part of.

"Be as may." Vertiline faced Sight of Day. "Friend, I will heal you."

Sight of Day's hands trembled. *{The Sway costs each time you use it. This injury is deep. It will remove many years of your life.}*

Vertiline sighed, feeling her face soften. "Years are worthless with no one of quality to spend them with."

{That's funny.} His half-smile was weak. *{Not too long ago, I wondered if anyone would miss the People after we're gone.}*

"This world would be immeasurably diminished without you." Vertiline stood. "I have never done this for a Feybrind. I wonder why not?"

{We're not as clumsy as you.}

"Or, we have been blind to your hurts." Vertiline rubbed her throat. *This will be painful, but pain is just weakness leaving the body.* "I don't know if this will work."

"Stop stalling, wench," Armitage said. "If the cat dies, it'll be bad, but we've still got all his stuff back home. It won't be a total waste."

Sands Apart's eyes were wide, trying to check if Armitage were joking.

Stop stalling, indeed. Vertiline threw her hands wide, eyes up. "Cophine, hear me. Khiton, listen. Ikmae, I beg your ear." She looked to Sight of Day. *Please work. Please work. Please work. //BE HEALED.//*

Chapter Forty-Three

I *never sweated as a fairy*. Rivulets of perspiration ran down Tarragon's scalp, her back, got in her eyes, and fouled her vision. Amir stood with his back to her, eyes front, facing his friends.

He fights for me.

Faust was an impressive piece of machinery, all lean muscle, stacked what looked like six metres tall, but Tarragon knew that was the rush, the rage in his face, and the glowing hammer he held. Light, in all its power, wielded by an enemy of the Tresward, against one they used to call brother. Their deepest secrets were held by those against them.

It was this kind of daydreaming that almost got her killed. Larochette slipped up beside her, and offered her a blade, point first, right at her ribs. Tarragon's parry was wild, a hack rather than step, Larochette's Light-rimmed weapon sparking and hissing against Requiem's actinic brilliance. *Both Faust and Larochette have the Storm, now. Weak, more of a squall, but their weapons will bite with more than main strength.*

She saw from her left Amir and Faust clash. The room shook as the hammer hit the sword, Amir underneath the mighty swing, but unbowed. Amir's form was good. Tarragon could see it was better than Faust's, but both men were horses, reins held in the savage grip of emotional masters. Amir used speed, Faust brutality, keeping the match even.

Tarragon stepped away from Larochette. *I have my own problems.* She took steel on skymetal once, twice, then aimed a savage riposte flurry, finding her own footing on the offensive. There was a *hmmmm-MMM-crack*, and she tossed herself to the right, a beam of fury from Wild Sur's weapon discharging through where she'd been. *It must be faulty after so many years. The auto-targeting should have had me.* A weapon like that was sure to hit soon enough if held by Feybrind hands. *Only an imbecile brings a knife to a gunfight.*

Larochette's counterattack was savage, blade coming under and up, another coming over and down. It was a classic teaching of Khiton's. *In mid-battle, use your weapons' strength where the opponent is weakest.* The long blade in Tarragon's hand could only be in one place at once.

She felt a wrench of fear. *I'm not ready. I'm just a fairy. I'm not a real Big.*

Wild Sur's weapon fired again, but Amir was there, the fancy man dancing from Faust's strike to catch the beam on the edge of his sword. Light hissed and roared, the blast ricocheting to the ceiling. Ancient stonework cracked and fell. Rubble and smoke, silt and sand.

Tarragon rubbed her eyes, sliding right foot back, left to follow, vision clouded, enemy's location uncertain. She weaved Requiem in a figure eight, the weapon humming as it tasted air.

A *huff* from Amir as something meaty smacked home. A clatter of a dropped weapon, then a hiss and curse from Faust as steel tasted flesh. Tarragon's vision cleared. She overbalanced as Larochette came for her head, then caught her heel on stone. Larochette, hungry for the victory, surged in. *I'm not a Big. That's good. I don't think like a Big.*

The feint worked, and Tarragon screamed fury as she brought her body around in a perfect pivot, Larochette's face the picture of *what the shit* as Requiem took a bite out of one of Larochette's blades, making it shorter. She straightened, Amir stepping back behind her as Faust swung, and she stepped in the gap, blue-white sword coming to face yellow-bright hammer.

The room rang like a bell, the impact pushing both back, Faust's breathing ragged. Tarragon stood, a pool of radiance about her, Amir at her back. "Swordsman. Can you stand?"

"I feel like this could be going better." Amir moved to her side, his blade ready. An eye was bloody, nose leaking red, but he seemed calm. "Swap opponents?"

"I'm good, thanks." With that, they stepped off, she back to Larochette, him to Faust.

The giant roared *you were supposed to join us* and Amir hollered back *is that because you thought I was as stupid as you*, but Larochette was all silence, a slight mocking smile, one short blade, one shorter, the Adept finding balance as all Tresward did.

Tarragon held Requiem in mid guard. "You shouldn't do this. It's wrong."

"Some pretty speech about good and evil, and here's me on the wrong side?"

Tarragon shook her head. "It's not about right and wrong. You use the god's power against the chosen. The Storm is a gift meant for service, not subjugation."

"So sad. Never mind." Larochette hungered forward, so Tarragon stepped into Khiton's *Perfect Melody*, a pattern designed for the uncertain outcome of too-certain foes. The Adept was good. The once-fairy felt her steps too slow, a hint out of alignment, not good enough to call the Storm and its Light, her saving grace a magic sword only hers through chance. The mocking smile widened. "We're almost at the end now, you and I."

A beam from Wild Sur's weapon went for her, and Amir was there again, the man lightning quick. Faust swung the hammer into Amir's guard, and Tarragon's friend skidded back. She stepped into the breach again, not seeing the gap for the trap it was. Faust stepped back, Tarragon overbalancing, a rookie mistake no Adept would make. But of course she wasn't an Adept. *I've only watched them.*

She felt Larochette's sword enter her side, and she screamed, the white-hot pain lancing through her, something liquid freeing inside, and she coughed blood. Amir was there, shouldering Larochette aside, the smaller woman falling to the floor.

That's when Amir took a hit from the hammer, full-force, and his body hit the stone like a dropped anvil. Tarragon raised her blade to guard him, but Faust knocked her back contemptuously, raised his hammer in the same motion, and hit Amir, Light blurring the weapon. The strike was true, Tarragon's scream drowned out by the crack of stone as the floor beneath Amir's corpse spiderwebbed into fault lines. She wanted to take back time, or raise the dead, but the Storm was only the barest friend to her. The Sway was beyond her reach.

The Storm is the only friend I've got left, because I was too slow.

Larochette was on her, hungry to stick another blade after the first.

I need to be Big. Just this once. Strong, like Evanne. Even if it cost pain, because what was pain but life, seen through a different lens?

Tarragon sagged forward, Larochette's blade entering her stomach, but Requiem was ready, the skymetal blade sizzling from its useless low guard to high, right through Larochette's body. The woman's innards spat, mere roasted meat. Faust turned with a bellow, just in time for high guard to become mid, separating the man from his legs by way of a long cut from shoulder to hip.

She swayed, blade trembling. No golden Light was to be seen in the blue-white sheen of magic skymetal. Wild Sur's half-smile was all victory as he raised his weapon.

The eastern wall exploded in rubble. Not Storm, but something ancient and angry. Wild Sur ducked, his shot going wide.

Vide spilled into the room by the bushel. Tarragon felt despair but stood by Amir's body. *They will not have him. Not while I live.* But that wouldn't be long. She raised her sword, standing strong despite the blood leaving her body as the end came for her.

Chapter Forty-Four

Morgan watched Evanne, her shiny armour all sunlight and rainbows, fly—*actually fucking fly*—to the castle. There seemed low resistance below her. Morgan suspected it was because armies were out of practice dealing with flying infantry. Whenever enemies showed initiative, like firing an arrow at the bard, a flash of silvered bronze would spit from the armour to hit whoever shot at her, and that sorted the problem.

A small gaggle of people hurried in her wake. *That looks like my Lord du Reeves, with the merchants. What an odd retinue.* Evanne was going up, ignoring the main entrance. *Dancing in the Storm's* approach had slowed, the ancient battle city silent, trailing smoke. It was too high up to see if anyone still lived on its decks. Myryntir soared, a condor against Evanne's starling, the two combating forces that would try to innervate the keep's weapons against the sky fortress.

She wasn't fussed about the bard, dragon, Holomancer, or the Lord du Reeves' gaggle of advisers, because she and he had already had this out. He'd started like this:

You must summon a demon army into this realm to destroy us all.

And she had said:

Are you cracked?

He wasn't cracked, as it turned out, but he was gambling the world. The convincer had been his final line:

Geneve hunts them with all her purpose.

Morgan could get behind that. The Saviour of Ravenswall had good instincts. She strolled across the battlefield, feeling sanguine because the fighting was elsewhere. At one point an enemy soldier, perhaps eighteen by the looks of her, had come over a rise and shouted, "Stop!"

Morgan sneered. "Don't be ridiculous."

And that was that. She made it to the castle, the main entranceway unguarded, the general scattering of bodies and their components reminding the queen of the last battle at Ravenswall. She was on the besieger's side this time, but the effect was the same. *Dead, some innocent, but all ended before justice was seen.*

Light flickered from within. She squared her shoulders and stepped into the keep. *This is surprising, but somehow not, because the High Justiciar is here.* Her statesperson's eye could see how the enormous room was designed to be a cool welcoming balm from the heat outside. Unfortunately, someone had set to destruction with great excitement inside. The damage looked like what a supervolcano might do, the walls slagged, and the floor wracked by fissures. The very ceiling was charred and blistered. Gaps let the daylight in.

Morgan took in a battlefield worse than anything outside. Black-armoured troops, all stylish leather—*perhaps I should talk to the quartermaster of the opposition, they have a good eye for flair*—fought against a warrior bathed in purest Light. *Vertiline.* The High Justiciar was glimmering with all the power of her tiresome gods, and Morgan saw Armitage by her side, two Feybrind in tow. *Sight of Day and the renegade Sands Apart.* She wondered if she should keep an eye on the once-enemy cat, then discarded the idea. There was a bigger problem to solve: the gate, and its very closed nature.

The trick is not to run. Morgan strolled up the long distance of the room, avoiding eye contact as all parties converged on the High Justiciar. An ancient-yet-sprightly Feybrind used some form of ancient crossbow, firing at Vertiline, who seemed not at all concerned. *She is beautiful to behold. This is why they say she is the best swordswoman in the world. It makes you wonder what things would be like with the Saviour of Ravenswall by her side.*

She made the gate in good time, surprised by her own success. It was mighty, standing as tall as the room. It made an impression. Morgan put a hand on it, feeling its coolness, but also its deadness. Something was missing inside, a pulse absent from the body all these long years. *Do you want to open?*

The runes about the gate glimmered purple in answer.

She felt a hard object press the back of her skull. Morgan froze, then very slowly turned about. The should-be-decrepit Feybrind was right there, weapon at her head, half-smile on his face. "*You've arrived just in time.*"

Morgan goggled in surprise at a speaking cat, then iron control asserted itself. "I arrived when I meant to, sirrah."

The half-smile didn't dim. "*I need you to open this.*"

"Did they make the People stupider back when you were born? It should be perfectly obvious that is what I'm about to do."

"*I need you to open it to the platform above.*"

"In this, we are agreed."

The half-smile wavered a notch. "*We are?*"

I see—his voice comes from that clever collar he wears. "We are. The real question you should answer is whether you think you can access what's up there without me."

"*I speak as your kind do.*"

Morgan offered him a withering smile, all the condescension she could stack on it, and she could stack pretty high. "Well, if that's all it takes, perhaps you should open this gate too. Or did you think *my* kind were stupid enough to leave pretty baubles about so their slaves could steal the kingdom?" She eyed the melee behind them. The Vide forces were thinning against the implacable force that was Vertiline, but Morgan was sure she'd seen far more enemy troops outside than were accounted for. *I wonder where they are?*

The Feybrind's face showed a shadow of doubt, quickly hidden. "*I have read their texts. Deciphered their works. I know how to unlock their power.*"

"Good-o." She turned back to the gate. "Now let me work."

The trick, Meriwether had explained, *is it must be believable*. Morgan pressed her palm against the gate again, feeling the trickle of *want* that powered the device. It needed to be used, to be connected to a far place. She left her hand on it and breathed. Closed her eyes and leaned her head against its surface. It felt chilled, like metal left in water. It was smooth as glass but smelled of stone. The Raven Queen reached inside herself, to that well of power she'd always had, and said, "Open."

She heard Vertiline's shout of *No!* as the Justiciar finally took notice of what was going on. Felt the gate *click* and *crack*, the runes on the outside rim rotating, the grind of ancient rock deep and insistent. Dust silted, and the gate shimmered. Beyond: the stars. A platform stretched, a strip of white material within a glass tube heading toward a tower. Farther still, the orb of this world. Morgan saw clouds and the blue-green wonder of it, the real jewel of the Three, and wanted to reach out and touch it.

A blaze of Light reflected against the gate's stone drew Morgan about. Vertiline was carving a path to her position. The Feybrind at her side once again placed that odd-looking weapon at the Raven Queen's head. That by itself was concerning, but more worrisome was that each and every door in the room opened.

In flowed troops by the battalion. Morgan's math said Vertiline might be good, but those were terrible odds. The weapon at her skull pressed harder.

Chapter Forty-Five

Everything hurts. *This is why I try and keep away from sharp objects.* Sight of Day turned his golden gaze to Vertiline. The platinum-haired warrior fought with efficient ferocity, the signature of her type, trained by the human's Three to murder their foes. Every move just so, every foot placement a work of art.

The People could fight well, but the Tresward were the great barometer. They were also great healers, but Vertiline's Sway hadn't ... *fixed* him. Something on the inside tugged and pulled at every movement. *The good news is I'm no longer leaking. Leaking is bad.* He didn't blame Vertiline for this. *She is best with a blade in hand. The Sway is something few master, and the People are ... different to humans. The Three's gaze does not fall so evenly on our needs.*

His eyes turned to the Vide, rank upon rank of assassin storming the room. *The Tresward are arbiters, but there is only one of them here.* He took a weary sidestep as a human tried to skewer him, then helped himself to his opponent's weapon by using his clever fingers to pinch *there* and *there*, the blade popping free like a seed from a squeezed lemon. Sight of Day caught it, kicked the assassin in the groin, and sidled up beside Armitage.

His friend was wholly motivated on trying to keep his body count up to his wife's level. Sight of Day admitted there was a large number of ambient bodies to show proof of his endeavours. The Vhemin made a tremendous amount of noise and it hurt Sight of Day's ears, so he slipped on by, heading toward the Raven Queen. The gate behind her showed a starry void with a spire overlooking a world that Sight of Day expected he stood on. He resisted the temptation to look up and wave, if only because the roof was in the way. No one seemed to have noticed Morgan except for the fossil who accosted her.

Oh, and Sands Apart, who padded at his side. Her ochre eyes were wide, everywhere at once, and focused on all the wrong things. He gently slid behind her and ran a woman through who was aiming for his friend's back. Sands Apart whirled at the clatter of dropped weapon, Feybrind hearing picking out the slightest noises through the howl of the melee.

{*I didn't see.*}

He offered his sword to her, then retrieved the fallen blade. {*Your first epic battle?*}

{*It doesn't feel epic!*} Her fingers were angry, her tail a-lash. {*It feels terrifying!*}

{*Just wait until you hear the bards sing of it. There will be at least a thousand Vide against our four.*}

{*There are a thousand Vide!*}

{*See how stories come to life?*} He offered her a half smile, then parried a spear thrust, letting the weapon slide along the edge of his steel. The borrowed blade was surprisingly good, and he looked for a People's maker's mark on the pommel while his assailant recovered his balance. *Nothing there. Maybe humans are learning our tricks after all.*

The spear man had another go, and Sands Apart cut him down with irritation. {*Are we going to help the queen?*}

{*It's she who may help us.*} Sight of Day padded through the melee, taking care to not move so quickly as to draw undue attention. There were a lot of humans in this room, and all headed toward the Light blaze of Vertiline.

The fossil noticed their approach, as did the Raven Queen. Sight of Day had a soft spot for her. Troubled by her past, but more troubled by her present, because of the people in her care. She thought longer-term than most humans, and tried to look after others, and like the People, was diminished for it, her kingdom in another's hands, and with a cruel gun to her head as a reward.

"*That's far enough,*" the fossil said.

Sight of Day half-smiled. *{You have one of the slaver's speech collars. Don't you think the world is noisy enough already?}*

The fossil's weapon didn't move from Morgan's skull. "*The world will be rung like a bell, and all will hear Wild Sur's thunder.*" He paused a moment. "*Yes, that is my true name. This gift,*" he touched the horrible scars on his skull where his ears had been mutilated, "*took my hearing. No one Commands me, so I walk free. But this,*" he touched the collar at his neck, "*lets me use their devices, including one of these.*"

The fossil extracted one of those annoying boxes from his belt. Sight of Day had seen their like before. They could harvest one's true name and allow the holder to use one of the People as their slave. It could push a person beyond all limit to perform atrocities.

The fossil pointed the box at Sands Apart, so Sight of Day took a quick step toward her, then decked her. She went down like a dropped rock, ochre eyes closing, about as much use to Wild Sur as a sock puppet. The fossil's golden eyes blazed with anger. "*You wish your own slavery to come so quickly?*" He pivoted the box to Sight of Day. "*Well, then—*"

Morgan dropped her shoulder, putting her elbow into Wild Sur's solar plexus. The fossil's weapon discharged. Sight of Day dropping below the burning path of heat and rage. He kicked Morgan's feet out from under her. It was the fastest way to get her below the line of fire. He ignored the surprise beginning to bloom in her eyes, sucker-punched the fossil as his weapon started coming back to Sight of Day, grabbed the box from mid-air, and tossed it into the beam.

It vanished in a haze of particles. Wild Sur stumbled back, golden eyes agog. "*Those are rarer than unicorn blood.*"

{Unicorn blood is quite common, if you know the right unicorns, and are very polite.}

The weapon swung about to face Sight of Day. He saw the glowing barrel, heat hazing the air, and wondered if this was how he'd die. It seemed fair, and he was fine with it. He'd stopped Sands Apart from being Commanded. No one should have to face that. And he'd stopped Morgan from being turned into a haze of particles like the ancient's Command device.

The Raven Queen was slowly pulling herself toward the gate. *I can still be useful as a distraction.* He half-smiled. *{Brother, you have fallen far. Your age has mired your wits as much as your body. Their trinkets are not the People's way.}*

"*You see a fall, but I have flown. Our way has gotten the People killed, whittled away, shavings from a stick no one cares about. Who will stand and protect us, if not I?*"

{And yet.} Sight of Day folded his hands together for a moment, stilling his tail. *{I live, despite the weapon you point at me. Do you still see the way back?}*

"*I see one who I would have join me. The golden eyes are the rarest of all Feybrind. We are the best ones. They made us that way. Let us use it. Let us fix the world.*"

Sight of Day felt his side tug. It was a reminder of Vertiline's healing word, and of his friends who didn't have golden eyes but were very good people despite it. *{You say 'fix' but I think you meant 'rule'.}*

Morgan had made it to the gate. She pressed her hand against it, huddled, small, a pool of potential. Sight of Day continued ignoring her as Wild Sur thrust his weapon at him for emphasis. "*It is the same thing. You can't fix what you don't own.*"

{I have fixed many swords and suits of armour. I have put wheels on broken carriages and mended garments. I owned none of those things.}

"*You split the argument into meaningless pieces. You are filled with cowardice.*"

{There is meaning on both sides of any argument. Bravery doesn't have to roar.} The gate above Morgan surged, the starscape vanishing, and Sight of Day took a step back. *Oh, my. What has she done?* The gate turned an inky black.

Wild Sur spun, weapon rising to face the black. He looked set to parrot more words, so Sight of Day felt it a small mercy that demons broke through at that moment, a cloud of hate and villainy flowing into the world again.

Chapter Forty-Six

The tide of demons leaped over Morgan. One tried on a leer, but the expression was stillborn as it was trampled by its brethren.

I hope my Lord du Reeves knows what he is doing, or I have damned us all.

As a curiosity, the demon horde swept right on by the three Feybrind before her, wings, claws, and gangly legs all diverting past them like a stream around stones. The monsters surged toward the humans in the vaulted room. The mass of Vide were a beautiful target for things that feasted on the corrupted, warped things in a human soul.

She saw men and women taken mid-stride, their smooth motions turning jerky for a few paces before they straightened. Newly gleaming, silvered eyes looked over the room, their mouths widening in smiles that hungered for more than food.

Sight of Day stood stock still, his mouth hanging wide, golden eyes wider, as the demon horde thinned, their ranks surging into human hosts. The flap of leathery wings subsided to a trickle of slower horrors. Wild Sur was similarly carved from basalt, the two People viewing the world totally differently, yet united in their horror. The ancient Feybrind turned to her, his weapon held in slack hands. *"What have you done?"*

"What was necessary. It has ever been my lot to finish what others left undone through lack of wit or motivation."

"You think me ... unmotivated?" The synthetic voice was cultured, but Morgan was sure the Feybrind's tone would have risen octaves at a gallop if it were able.

"I think you lack vision." Morgan stood, dusting off her raven black robe and straightening her collar. "Here, I have given you what you always wanted. An army of monsters."

"I don't control demons. No one can."

"You also lack education." She plucked a mote from her sleeve. "One who can destroy a thing controls it."

"You think you can destroy them? You are a back parlour Ritualist."

"And it seems you lack wisdom. A single person must not hold all the cards. A good ruler must play a varied hand." Morgan's eyes hunted the throng before her. Vertiline hunkered behind the weight of her shield, a Light-rimmed guard protecting her husband. Tarragon stood in her shadow, her blazing sword held in mid guard. Armitage was frozen in astonishment, an unconscious Vide held slackly in one hand. The Vhemin let the woman drop. It was the only movement in the room. "I admit, I expected my Lord du Reeves about now."

Sight of Day turned to her, his gaze unreadable. *{He has not traditionally been overly reliable.}*

"He has but one task."

Wild Sur looked at the heavens. *"Perhaps this type of incompetence is why the ancients destroyed the world. How marvellous."* He swung his weapon to bear on Sight of Day, then looked to Morgan. *"Put them back where they came from, or I will destroy all you love."*

Morgan offered Sight of Day an apologetic smile. "You were going to destroy all I loved before things turned poorly for you. Your hand is lacking aces."

"Your hand is lacking any cards at all!"

Morgan turned her smile sad, and directed it toward Wild Sur. "For all your long years among us, you understand us not at all. The world functions as a marvellous clockwork. All things happen for a reason.

For example, did you not wonder why so many demons were waiting right at this portal? It seems convenient for them to huddle at a disused entrance to our realm."

Wild Sur's golden eyes narrowed. *"They are always eager to run to our lands."*

Morgan's back was to the gate and the blackness within. She hoped it remained midnight, because the damnable Holomancer was still nowhere to be seen. Her eyes settled on Tarragon, because the once-fairy struggled with her blade, as if Requiem were an unruly goat unwilling to take the collar. The sword stuttered and flared, skymetal brilliance and lightning fury in flashes, before it tore free from the warrior's hand, tumbling end over end and into the gate behind Morgan. Her smile, still regal, still ready, turned wintry. "Run to? Not quite. They are running *from*, sirrah."

Wild Sur took a sudden step back as Sight of Day's expression turned to the intersection of Surprise Road and Terror Street. Morgan felt hot breath on her back for a moment before a black-clawed stumpy leg smashed the stone beside her. She recoiled, stumbling left, just in time to avoid being squashed as a companion leg joined the first.

She looked up, up, and *up* to the massive demon forcing its way through the gate. Horns, wings, fangs, and a terrifying visage atop all. It clambered through the gate like a burglar through a window, huffed a great bellows breath, then stamped toward the melee.

And then *across* it, slamming Vide aside as it made for the exit. Morgan froze as another giant demon came through, a third, and then a fourth, each a mistake the Three would not countenance. *What have I done? What have I done?*

The first demon made the great doors and slammed them aside, great lumbering strides taking it to the battlefield outside, the other three in pursuit. Morgan was about to get up when a massive, red-scaled, taloned forearm slammed into the ground beside her. She looked up into a redfire dragony grin.

//NOW IT'S A PARTY,// Ormeon the Redeemer said.

Chapter Forty-Seven

The calm of the sky belied the carnage below. Evanne perched on the side of *Dancing in the Storm*. She saw four massive creatures burst from the castle. They looked like they were *super* pissed off, and in a hurry to boot. They lumbered away from the action.

Hitch glimmered blue at her side. "Elder demons."

"Does that mean they're old, or in charge?"

"Both."

"I think I saw you fight one of them."

"I think you saw me get my ass kicked by one of them." He tapped the shiny new metal over her breastplate. "Not even this is impervious to them. Don't get in a punching fight. In fact, leave them to someone else, like your mother. She's just about angry enough to do for four, I reckon."

"You're looking at the wrong thing," the Oracle said.

Evanne stifled a scream, but still jumped in alarm. "Where have you been?"

"I've ... travelled. Now, attend." He pointed, directing her attention to the roof of the castle. "See there?"

Evanne's visor helped her weak human sight. Her vision swam with detail as her viewpoint raced across the distance. She swung her arms wildly, trying to get her balance as she adjusted to the new perspective. *Breathe. You're a bard. Look like you meant to do that.* She stilled, then cleared her throat with the Trick of confidence. "Looks like the lordling and those two merchants."

"I think you should go get them."

"Why's that?" She looked at him, the visor seamlessly switching back to the here and now. "You planning something?"

"No. We're crashing." He shrugged apologetically. "The ship's taken a lot of damage. We'll go down somewhere. It's probably going to be on top of them."

Evanne frowned. "No, you're doing this all wrong."

"I'm ... I'm an *oracle*. I know the future! I see truth in the stars. I am physically incapable of doing anything wrong."

"Except that time you fell to your death."

"I got better."

"Leave this one to me," Evanne said. "Best settle down before you hurt yourself again." She cocked a glance at Hitch. "Can I carry people on this?"

"You can carry one or two at a time. Depends on whether they've eaten recently."

"Got it." Evanne stepped off the side of the flying city, her armour flaring, the fangs in her wrists drinking deep as she powered toward the castle. She bit her lip, pushing past the pain. The demons had made good time, and she spied Myryntir dogging their steps, the great blue dragon showering them with lightning, which appeared to bother them not at all.

She almost flew into the side of the castle in astonishment as a red dragon burst from the gates, bounding on all fours before springing into flight. The dragon's hide was pitted and scarred, not all shiny magenta. Some scales scorched or cracked, but none of that looked like it slowed her down. "Hitch, is that dragon wearing a *saddle?*"

"Where there's a dragon, there should always be a dragonrider."

"Where's the dragonrider, then?"

"Stick the landing, then we'll talk."

She took a turn around a crenelated tower and came in for a shaky landing right in front of the lordling, who had the good grace to look surprised. He'd been peering through a hole in the castle roof, Amber and Jade shoulder to shoulder beside him. He gave her a once-over. "Evanne, why are you here?"

"The sky city is going to crash on you."

"That's bad," he admitted.

"I can get you up there."

"Why would I want to be on something that's going to crash?"

"I've got a plan," she said.

"I'm quite nervous."

"Okay. How's *your* plan working out?"

He frowned, then glanced at the sky behind them where the red dragon and Myryntir swooped, lightning and fire blasting the demons below. The demons answered with bolts of purest black. "Not great. I was hoping for something better than a dragon."

"Something ... better?" Evanne squinted. "Are they turning around? It looks like those Elder demons are coming back here."

"That'll be Ormeon. She's great and all, but—"

"*That's* Ormeon? The one all the stories are about?"

He looked hurt. "The stories are only about the dragon?"

"Dragons are cool."

"She'd love to meet you at a better time." He turned back to her. "What's your plan?"

"Style."

"I'm on board," he said. "Let's go."

"THIS ISN'T STYLE," JADE SAID. "THIS IS TERRIFYING."

"Hush," her brother said. "How often do you get to ride a crashing sky city into an ancient building full of demon terrors?"

"That's the whole 'terrifying' part."

The lordling ignored them, turning from the vista of a rapidly approaching castle to face the throng of people on *Dancing in the Storm's* deck. It was the remains of the people they'd 'rescued' from Hollyhead and Wandermere. They all looked as terrified as Jade. He raised his arms as if to speak, so Evanne clapped him on the shoulder. "I've got this."

"Speeches are my thing."

"Step aside, old man." She stood by Meriwether's side, back to the castle. "Friends, in mere moments this city will crash into that building." She pointed behind her without looking. "Within, a demon-possessed horde of monsters fights the last Tresward in the world. She's doing *great*," she slipped in as a few concerned glances were shared. "The thing to focus on is *you*."

"Us?" It was the blacksmith, Turner.

"You," she nodded. "We're going to ride this ship right down the throat of the enemy castle. I'm going to make a lot of noise. Meriwether will hustle you down the breach and outside to where it's safe."

"I'm waiting for the style part," Meriwether murmured.

"You'll know it when you see it," she promised.

"I don't want to die a needless death," Turner said. It was a simple statement, heavy with honesty.

"Do you want to live a coward?" Amber strode forward. "My sister and I have come right to the heart of the devil's keep to see the world saved. We stand with you, and against tyranny."

"We do?" Jade's voice was a whisper.

"You miss my point," the blacksmith said. "I'm not running. We've got an ancient's living city. It may crash—"

"It's definitely going to crash," Evanne said.

"But we can get it flying again. Other people did it, and so can we. I don't want to flee. You just die tired. I want to *fight*." He clenched his strong fists. "You can get the others out, but I'm swinging."

"Ah," Meriwether said. "I see the style, now."

I NEED TO GET DOWN THERE. EVANNE JUMPED FROM THE SIDE OF THE city. The massive structure was perilously close to impacting the castle. The demon lords shouldered their way back in through the double doors. The gate was now proper fucked but created a wonderful aperture. She sailed through, and into madness.

She saw Mama first, Vertiline's Light a blazing inferno. *And there's Papa.* Armitage waited on her right. On the opposite side—*praise the Three*—was Tarragon, the once-fairy standing with fists held in a boxer's stance. By her feet was the still form of Amir.

Oh, no.

Evanne could see all his starlight was gone.

She soared past the grasping claws of an Elder demon lord, its maw wide and angry, and sent a couple spheres to pester it. They bounced off but gave it something to fret over other than snaring her. She soared above the throng, a horde of black-armoured troops facing Vertiline and her two honour guards.

Looks like I arrived just in time.

At the far end of the room was an ancient Feybrind, with Sight of Day facing him and standing ready. Her friend's tail gave a single lash, but otherwise he was still. By their feet, the fallen Sands Apart, and Evanne feared her dead, but the armour didn't think so. While she'd been gawking, it put a map of the room in her mind and catalogued a thousand different bodies for her. It wasn't a picture; she just *knew* where everyone was, the living, the dead, and the big presences of the Elder demons. The armour thought Sands Apart was alive in the same way it told her Amir was dead. A big-ass gate was at the far end, swirling with pitch, purple runes about the edge.

By the gate, the Raven Queen stood, pale, alone, back to the portal. *She must have cracked it open.* Evanne didn't spare a thought for why, just headed right for the ancient Feybrind, who was pointing a weapon at Sight of Day. *That won't do.* She landed right between the Feybrind as the ancient one fired. Her armour spun metal spheres in a blur. They caught the beam from the enemy's weapon, spitting molten flame about her like flung motes of lava.

The ancient Feybrind looked at her, his weapon, then back to her. "*I must have that armour.*"

"You can have it when I'm dead." Evanne raised her fists in a mirror of Tarragon's stance, because she was going to beat this fool bloody. "Let's dance."

"You should know the enemy wears a device that will kill us all if he dies," Morgan said.

"Useful to know." Evanne lowered her arms. "How?"

"A terrible weapon from above."

"Got it," Evanne said.

The ancient Feybrind took a step forward. "*I will kill your friends while you watch.*"

"I don't think so."

"*Why not?*"

The entire side of the room exploded inward as *Dancing in the Storm* impacted the keep. The room shook like the inside of a baby's rattle. Evanne took flight to avoid falling. She hovered while everyone about her dropped like skittles. Even Sight of Day fell. *I never thought I'd see a Feybrind lose their footing. This truly is the end of days.* "Because of that."

Her voice was drowned out in the tremendous noise of the rock walls falling inward. Everything from fist-sized stones to boulders the size of a person tumbled inside. Some of the enemies facing Mama, Papa, and Tarragon were crushed by rocks, but most were still alive.

The belly of *Dancing in the Storm* hung above them, the ancient city having enough go-juice to remain airborne, if only just. She picked out the figure of the Oracle giving her a cheeky wave, then the blacksmith Turner jumped over the side, scrambling down the rubble slope, hammer in hand.

A moment later, what looked like the rest of the city's people surged over the side, yelling various war cries, some holding proper steel, but most with makeshift weapons. Evanne saw a woman with a chair leg, and beside her, a man with a broom handle. The enemy in the room drew blades. *That doesn't seem fair.*

The Elder demons seemed torn between heading for Evanne by the gate, and the plumpness of the fallen city. Their eyes were greedy and bright. Then they did exactly what Evanne would have done, and split up. One went for Vertiline, another for the city, and two for Evanne. *I should be honoured.* The ancient Feybrind was up and about again, so she plucked his weapon from him, the armour's speed and strength making it trivial. She pointed it at the leading demon and fired. The ember lance hit the gargantuan creature, carving a glowing line across its hide, but spilling no blood. She looked at the weapon in astonishment. "What a piece of junk!"

"If it were that simple, we wouldn't have had a problem with them." Hitch bloomed before her. "Evanne, you must run."

"You didn't!"

"I died," he said flatly. "This is *how* I died."

"There must be another way." The demons gathered speed, as their strides shook the ground.

"There is no other way. Please, Evanne." His not-eyes were wide, and desperate. "I can't lose you."

The roof above them crunched open, a slab of rock the size of a building falling in and hitting the lead demon lord. It staggered, slowing its roll, but didn't fall. The one behind it slowed too, both looking up. Evanne followed their gaze, right into an emberfire grin. *//GENEVE SAYS I SHOULDN'T PLAY WITH MY FOOD, YET HERE WE ARE.//*

Ormeon's voice was immense, the sound of birthing mountains and dying stars. Myryntir sounded magnificent, but this one sounded ... *real.* Like she displaced the world by being in it. The big red dragon scraped through the hole she'd made, her wings wide to slow her descent, and crunched between Evanne and the demon lords. Hitch goggled. "Okay, maybe there is another way."

"Can she beat them?"

"Rulbenen couldn't."

"Can *she* beat them?"

Hitch's not-eyes narrowed. "She looks pretty angry."

Lightning slammed into the leading demon lord. Evanne's visor went midnight black for a hot second before clearing. Myryntir slithered through the gap in the roof, settling beside Ormeon. *//IS THIS LUNCH?//*

Ormeon gave the blue dragon a little side-eye. *//YOU'RE TOO DAMN PRETTY FOR THIS FIGHT.//*

He looked startled, slender neck snaking up and back into a question mark. *//YOU THINK I'M PRETTY?//*

The leading demon lord recovered its poise, then grated a laugh like thunder dying. "YOUR MAKERS MADE YOU WEAK, TINY WORM."

Myryntir's eyes narrowed. *//ARE THEY INVINCIBLE?//*

Ormeon grinned hot smoky ash, slipping left, muscles rippling under dragonscale armour. *//THEY LIKE TO THINK SO, RIGHT UP TO THE END.//* Her eyes glowed like tiny apertures into the forge of the sun. *//THEY WOULDN'T BE RUNNING IF IT WERE TRUE. THIS LARDASS IS ATERREGIS, THE BLACK KING.//* Here, a dragony chuckle. *//IT'S A NAME MEANT TO INSPIRE FEAR. I THINK IT SOUNDS CLICHÉ, A DOLLAR STORE HAND-ME-DOWN WORN THIN THROUGH OVERUSE.//*

"Now's the time to run," Hitch said. "Flee, while the dragons are tanking the demon lords."

"If I go, then Mama will start some shit, and I don't think she's up to four demon lords." Evanne shifted her shoulders, the armour heavier than she expected. *It feels like duty.*

Aterregis' gaze swivelled to the spectre, then locked on Evanne. "YOU ARE THE ONE."

"Of course," Evanne said. "But you need to ask yourself, the one of what?"

The demon lord blinked. "WHAT?"

"That's what I said." Evanne pushed past Hitch, ignoring the pleading in his not-eyes. "See, your whole thing," she waved the what-ever-it-was away dismissively, "is world domination. Enslavement. Ruin for the sake of it."

Aterregis took a step forward, the room shaking. Ormeon's jaws widened, a warning hiss the demon lord ignored. "AND YOU ARE THE KEY THAT UNLOCKS THE PORTAL FOR ALL."

"No, that's her." Evanne pointed to Morgan.

Morgan's eyes widened. "Don't bring me into this."

"Doesn't matter." Evanne's feet took her closer to the dragons, and by association, the demon lords. The people from the fallen sky city were scrambling down the slope of fallen rock, some already making a loose ragged line at the base. Possessed Vide were shifting foot to foot, weapons ready. "See, this is all about to go to shit. Those assholes," she pointed to the Vide, "are going to rush them," her arm moved to the villagers from Hollyhead, "which means she," here she pointed to Vertiline, "will rush in like a murder hobo, and everything fails."

Another demon lord crept closer. "SHE MAKES A GOOD POINT. FEWER SOULS FOR THE REAPING."

"EVER THE PESSIMIST, VENENARUM." Aterregis ignored the demon lord Venenarum, eyes still on Evanne. "THE UNDYING QUEEN THINKS THIS IS ALL YOUR WORLD HOLDS."

"Undying Queen? Really?" Evanne cast a glance at Ormeon. "Clichéd *and* trite."

///I TOLD YOU.///

"Evanne!" Vertiline straightened from her guard position. "What are you doing?"

"Poking the bear," Evanne called back. "You protect the living, and I will see to those not yet born."

A third demon lord sidled next to Venenarum. "YOU WEAR ARMOUR THAT PROTECTS NEITHER LIVING NOR DEAD. IT IS PAPER TO OUR WRATH."

"Let me guess: you're Fuckface, the Keeper of Badness," Evanne said.

"You can't leave, Evanne." Vertiline's voice was hoarse. Evanne imagined Mama trying to work out how to save Evanne if she flew away with a demon on her tail. "Please."

Evanne took a final step past Ormeon's warding bulk and ran a hand down Myryntir's foreleg. *Ormeon's right. He's too damn pretty. Not like me. Half-made, and poorly so. Not one thing or the other. But made just right for this fucking armour. Made just right for one more song.* She eyed Armitage, her Papa's hands clenched around a hammer, his shoulders rigid. *They can't fight with me here. They can't protect those who need it most.* Evanne turned her visor to Tarragon. "For the living."

Tarragon mouthed, *Evanne, no.* Her hands were empty of magic swords. Her eyes were full of fear.

Evanne turned away from Tarragon, striding toward Aterregis. Staring the motherfucker right in his twisted face. "Gods, but you're ugly."

"AND I SEE YOU. BROKEN. FEEBLE. A WEAK HEART.

HAVE YOU COME TO BE THE FIRST SACRIFICE?" He raised a fist, ready to strike.

Bring the rain. She told the armour that *now*, right *NOW* was the time, and the magnetic arbalest whined into gear, spitting a hail of metal spheres at Aterregis. The demon roared, bringing that house-sized fist down on her, but the stardrive at her back blazed with light, and she was airborne, already moving faster than the swiftest hawk.

Aterregis roared, black tendrils snaking after her, but Evanne was on the wind. The magnetic arbalest split its fire between Aterregis and the wall ahead of her. It slammed spheres into the keep's stone wall. She hurtled toward the rock barrier, the armour telling her useless things like *structural integrity holding* and *impact imminent* before she hushed it. Evanne thought, *trust me.*

The armour let her know it did not, but it redoubled its efforts on the exterior wall. She hit, blasting through into the sunlight outside, the demon lords Aterregis and Venenarum on her tail.

For the living.

Chapter Forty-Eight

My *baby is going to die*. The gut feel punched Vertiline harder than anything in her life. Her sword point dipped, shield lowering as the one joyful thing she'd been able to do for the world flew out through the wall, demon lords in tow. Vertiline tried to remember anything she'd heard about Aterregis or Venenarum. *Black King*. *Undying Queen*. Just names for *death*, and she could do nothing about it.

A hand gripped her arm. Despite the metal of her armour, she felt strength there, the kind that could pulverise rock. "Tilly. We've got work to do."

Armitage. *My love*. She turned to him. "Our little girl."

"Yeah, she's fucked right off through the wall. I saw it. Blood on the sands, maybe." He jiggled her arm for emphasis, a move that from another man would have seen a hand severed, but from him it was *look here, this shit's important*. Not a lack of respect, but the deepest kind. He pointed her to the villagers massing across the chamber. "Those people are all going to die."

"And our girl?"

"Through the wall. Or did you miss that? *Tilly*." He got right in her grill. "We can't help her. Not from here. Not like this." A man wearing

Vide black got close enough to lunge with a spear. Armitage took it from him, snapping the haft over his knee, then stabbed the broken shaft through the man's neck, then almost as an afterthought stuck the spear head through an eye socket. "More of these fuckers are going to cause trouble. They've got demons in 'em. Real monsters, like nothing you runts ever magicked up."

Vertiline turned to the two remaining demon lords. They were massive, towering storeys above them all. Fat from taking the best food—*best not to think about what that is*—each with a huge weapon. The one closest to the main exit held a chain whip so large no ship could use it as an anchor without sinking. The one closest to the portal held a giant club of rude wood, gnarled, with black spikes hammered through. The chain whip was corroded, the spikes coated in dried gore. *The monsters are used to their work.*

"High Justiciar." The barest stammer shook Tarragon's words. *I'd forgotten she was here.* Without Requiem's radiance, Tarragon was just like the rest of them. A woman, strong in body and mind, but not fit to fight a demon lord. "What do we do?"

There is but one here ready for this challenge. Vertiline turned to the demon-ridden army and their mighty masters. "By Cophine of the breaking dawn, Ikmae of the shattering day, and Khiton of the ending night, I call you to challenge, creatures. You will face me."

The demon lords, who didn't appear to have taken much notice of Vertiline, Armitage, and Tarragon, turned at the names of the Three. With surprising speed, the one holding the chain whip took two lumbering strides closer. Its face was used to cruelty, and she saw smug glee hiding in there too. "YOU SAY THEIR NAMES, BUT YOU DO NOT BELIEVE."

Vertiline raised an eyebrow. "I am the High Justiciar of the Tresward. I embody belief."

The other lord chuckled like a landslide. "TITLES MEAN NOTHING. YOU CAN CARRY ALL THE SILVER OR GOLD BARS YOU LIKE. PEOPLE CAN RESPECT THE LIGHT. BUT YOU DON'T. WASN'T IT YOU THAT BANISHED THEM FROM THIS WORLD?"

Vertiline stalked closer, the Vide shuffling back. "You speak of things you understand poorly. Give me your names so I may record them in the annals of the fallen."

"IT WANTS TO KNOW US," said Chain Whip. "BETTER THAT IT KNOWS ITSELF."

"WHAT HARM, COUSIN?" The club *whooshed* air as the colossus shouldered the weapon.

The grotesque monster coiled its whip with the clanking of prison chains used to cage gods. "HIGH JUSTICIAR VERTILINE, YOU MAY KNOW ME AS MORSORACHIUS, THE ABYSSAL DOMINUS. MY ... COLLEAGUE IS TENEBRICOR, THE INFERNAL ARCHON."

It knows me. How does it know me? Vertiline kept her voice steady. "Morsorachius and Tenebricor, the people will remember how you fell in agony and despair for putting foot on *our* world."

"I KNOW YOU." Morsorachius played the chain whip through hands the size of houses. "I KNOW YOUR FEARS, AS I KNOW ALL PEOPLE'S FEAR. YOUR DAUGHTER IS SURELY LOST, AND YOU KNOW DESPAIR. YOU ARE BUT ONE. YOUR SCHOOL IS IN TATTERS. YOU SENT THE GODS AWAY FOR A HOPE YOU SQUANDERED. THE ONLY OTHER LIKE YOU LIES SLAIN AT YOUR FEET. YOU ARE THE LAST, AND HOPE HAS FLED."

Vertiline raised sword and shield. The patterns held in her mind, those for fighting dragons, those for halting a landslide, those for sundering a vaulted fortress's gates. Light glimmered on the edge of her steel as she glared over the rim of her shield. "Come, then. Let us speak of—"

Faster than thought, the Morsorachius' chain whip lashed out. Vertiline raised her shield, golden Light doming above her, the whip's metal tip shrieking as it bit and clawed at her defence. She felt the impossible weight of it, the strength of the demon lord behind it, and snarled.

Tenebricor swung the hammer overhand. She danced back, and as the weapon hit, used the shuddering bounce the earth gave to gain height, landing on the weapon, and running up the shaft. Tenebricor's eyes were hateful as it snarled, shaking her free. Vertiline fell, graceful, the pattern ready, landing in a metal clatter and rolling to her feet.

She wasn't ready for the whip. *It moves too quickly for such a large weapon.* But it came anyway, forcing her to step back into Ending Retreat, sword licking out, Light spilling molten on the stone floor. Tenebricor reached for her, and she stepped forward, sword cutting three times in perfect arcs. The demon lord howled, rearing back, but minus three fingers, the ends smoking and charred.

The chain whip came again, and again Vertiline wasn't ready. But Armitage was, her brave stupid husband, who pushed her aside. He wasn't on her threat list, and she had no defence against his move. She staggered back as the chain lashed past her, plunging into Armitage's shoulder. The bad one, where Ormeon had almost taken the life right out of him.

All light about the chain faded as a choked half-darkness snaked down from Morsorachius to where the massive weapon's tip pierced Armitage. Vertiline didn't know what it was or what it would do, but she knew how to return a favour. She lunged forward, shoulder-barging Armitage. No Light, no grace of movement, but he popped free of the weapon as she collided with it.

It's so cold. She felt the ice touch of death, the sluggishness of her limbs as the demon's weapon suckled at her warmth. Vertiline screamed, staggering back, trying to get her guard up. A half-hearted attempt, not worthy of an Adept, but her shield gamely glimmered gold as Morsorachius wrenched the whip back, then speared it forward once more. Right at Vertiline's face.

She raised her shield, firming her stance. Pushing, but cold. Slow. *Fearful*, because her husband might be dying. *Sick*, because Evanne was facing two of these creatures alone. *Terrified*, because Vertiline, the best swordswoman in the world, was outclassed.

The point impacted Vertiline's shield and pierced her arm behind it. The blue bite of the frozen north hit her, but the weapon was slowed by the Light. The merest tip of the chain whip made it to her. It pierced her throat, and she coughed blood. Staggered back and dropped her sword. Her shield fell. She was on one knee. She was alone. She tried the Sway, reaching for it desperately, but couldn't speak over the ruin of her larynx.

I sent the gods away. This is my fault.

Morsorachius chortled, then lashed again. Vertiline closed her eyes, waiting for the end.

She heard a clang, and the shattering of bells. Her eyes opened, the darkness not quite holding her. Tarragon stood with her back to Vertiline, her wheat-pale hair a nimbus of golden Light. She held Vertiline's blade in low guard, a perfect finish to the strike she'd landed that shattered the tip of Morsorachius' weapon.

The demon lord took a step back. Tarragon followed with a step forward. "She's not the last, creature. I spent so long trying to work out why they made me wrong. So broken. I couldn't pass my exams. I was a terrible Builder, and a worse spy. I let my best friend die years ago, and another died just now." She swung Vertiline's blade, the flourish scattering droplets of golden Light. "I think they did it to teach me *how*."

"HOW TO DO WHAT?"

"To keep hope alive." Tarragon's head canted toward the gate behind her, and Vertiline imagined a smile on her lips. "For that."

Vertiline struggled to move, eye line passing over Armitage's slumped form. *Too much blood.* Past the dragons, who stepped aside, both bowing their mighty heads. To Sight of Day, mouth agog. The ancient Feybrind, golden eyes wide. Morgan, face shielded from the Light. To Geneve, the Saviour of Ravenswall, who stepped from the gate, eyes a fury, mouth a hard line. Vertiline remembered her golden arm and leg, both shining with Cophine's glory. Her sister in battle was untouched by time as any Tresward who held the Light, but her face was harder, resolute, in a way she'd never been before stepping into the demon's realm.

"Morsorachius. Tenebricor." Geneve held Requiem, the blazing blade pointed at the farthest demon lord, then the closest. "You left before we could get fully acquainted."

Morsorachius turned and ran. Tenebricor, clutching its ruined hand, followed. Geneve broke into a run, the golden angelic figures Vertiline had only seen once before breaking free from her body. One flicked a blade of purest light through Wild Sur's weapon as the Feybrind tried to shoot Geneve in the back. The other flickered from sight, snapping forward across the room to stand before Tenebricor.

The demon lord howled, swinging the club at the angel before him. Behind him, Geneve was in full run as lightning struck her, a bolt of purest blue-white shattering the roof. Another bolt came down right on Tenebricor, the demon lord exploding and coating the the room liberally with chunks of demon. In the ruined carcass, Geneve rose from one knee, her body smoking with the gods' rage. Vertiline knew she must be hallucinating, because by the Three her dearest friend had just ridden up a bolt of lightning, come down another, and cannon-balled a demon to pieces. And that couldn't have happened.

Could it?

Morsorachius made the outside. Geneve turned back, eyes on Vertiline's for a moment, before snapping to Ormeon. "Dragon. Are you on a break?"

//JUST HOLDING THE LINE.// Ormeon looked to Myryntir. //SOMEONE HAD TO.//

"We must fly."

//YOU MEAN, I MUST FLY AND CARRY YOU.// Ormeon surged forward, *crumping* down beside Geneve, who swung aboard.

"Geneve!" Meri called to her from atop the rockslide.

"There is no time, lover." Geneve saluted the lordling, then Ormeon surged through the gates and after Morsorachius. Vertiline raised a hand after her, unseen, voiceless, dying, then sighed into the dark. *She made it home. My watch is ended, and I can go now.*

Chapter Forty-Nine

Evanne flew facing the sky, like she was doing backstroke. Hitch lay on the air beside her, effortlessly keeping pace, anchored to her presence. She watched the giant demon lord Aterregis storm after her, the massive creature covering impressive ground with great strides. It couldn't ever catch her, not if she pushed the armour like it'd taught her.

But I want to be caught. Almost.

The Trick here was to keep the demons after her so Mama could help the villagers. The plucky lot from Hollyhead wanted to be in this fight, but they weren't built for it. Not the right kind of clay in their construction, just simple people who could fish or hammer metal. Not great Tresward Smiths or Builders of old.

Behind them a bolt of iridescent lightning split the roof of the citadel, immediately followed by another. Moments after, a demon lord broke from the front door, a very angry dragon on its heels. *Now there's something you don't see every day.* "Who's riding that dragon?"

Hitch peered. "I don't recognise them. Want me to go look?"

"It'll keep."

"I have to ask, where are we going?" Hitch was a picture of calm repose, just kind of *stuck* there.

"Back to the fight."

"We're going the wrong way."

"No, we're going the right way, the wrong way around." She watched him process that, ghost-blue lips moving at the same speed as his train of thought. "The thing is, we need to kill the demons."

"Except we can't."

"Sure we can." She pointed an arm above, air turbulence causing her to shimmy, contrails breaking in her wake. "Up there is a weapon that can kill them. Linked to Wild Sur's heartbeat. We just need to kill the broken ancient little fucker and ... job's done."

"And everyone else will die." He said it patiently, as if talking to a Cocker Spaniel. "Including you."

"Faith, spectre." She grinned, despite him not being able to see it. "I've got a plan."

"Oh, gods."

"And I need you."

"I've died once already!"

"This will be the kicker." She sobered. "Right to the end."

He looked at the demon. "I'm not going anywhere." He shook himself. "But you still haven't told me *where* we're going. Specifically."

"Simple. I need a guitar."

SHE BLASTED OVER THE PORT SIDE RAILING OF *DANCING IN THE Storm*, disturbing a flock of gulls. Below the city, indistinct figures duked it out, the odd flash of Light letting her know Mama was still in the fight.

The oracle waited for her, wind whipping his robes. "You shouldn't be here."

"You're right." She strode past him. "Now, where is it?"

He back-pedalled to keep up. "I mean, the ship is going down."

"It's lasted eight hundred years. It'll keep another five minutes." She skipped along the decking, feet trailing as the armour buoyed her while suckling greedily on her wrists. She hissed at the pain but kept going. *Time is not on my side.*

"Perhaps you could tell me what you're after."

She faced the oracle. "Aren't you supposed to be able to see the future?" She cast an eye over the deck. "I need my guitar."

"Your... *guitar*." The oracle repeated the word slowly, with great care, as if it were so heavy he might put his back out by lifting it wrong.

"It's a musical instrument, used for the playing of clever melodies."

"I know what a guitar is."

"Great. Where's mine?"

"And you need it for..?" He trailed off, as if hoping the answer would help settle his mind.

"I'm going to summon the gods."

"At last," he beamed. "A plan so insane I'm sure to be dissolved. It's there, beside that crate of apples."

EVANNE BLASTED THROUGH THE ROOF, KEEPING LOW AS SHE FLEW down the rubble slope. She went past the surprised Holomancer and landed on a boulder the size of a horse-drawn cart. It afforded a generous vantage of the melee. She took in the portal, all black with purple glowy shit, and Morgan wrestling with the ancient Feybrind. Sands Apart was beside her, both women locked in a struggle with the decrepit old guy who, Evanne admitted, was putting up a more than fair fight for someone of his age. *I'll get to him in a moment.* No sign of Myryntir, but what looked like demon lord slurry proved they could be killed.

Vide, the black-suited fuckers all around. Tarragon, holding the line below her, a blaze of wondrous Light. And there, in heart-stopping horror: Mama and Papa. Slumped, still, against the rocks below her.

"Evanne." Hitch stood before her. "You can't help them."

Guitar in one hand, she zipped right through him. A wave of

fatigue hit as the armour quaffed her blood. She landed before them. Papa's eyes were open, but he looked pale and weak. *He's not healing.* A grievous wound in his shoulder leaked his last vitality. Mama was cradled against his good arm. Unmoving. Eyes closed, beautiful, and still.

"Papa?"

"You must run." He coughed. "There is no fight to win here."

"Which of them did this?" she snarled. "Who needs to fucking pay?" Her free fist was clenched at her side.

A *clang* sounded as something rebounded off her armour, and she staggered. Turning, she saw a Vide with a rope harpoon, ready to cast again. The magnetic arbalest chewed him to slurry in a moment. Another took his place, then another. She roared, striding forward, the armour flaying flesh and bone, a riot of circling orbs, silver and brass turning the red colour of murder.

Another wave of fatigue hit. A man grabbed her arm, and lost his hands as the armour severed them, before spheres buzzed through his body and out the other side. A woman hit Evanne in the visor, and a crack appeared. The armour murmured *Self-repair initiated* and she felt it bite her wrists all the harder. She dropped to a knee. Another hit rocked her from the side, then people piled on as the spheres lost power, and fell to the ground like giant metal hailstones. The guitar dropped from her hands and was lost in the melee. Hands scrabbled at her gorget, trying to find a fastening. Hitch shouted, trying to get her attention.

And then, a roar. Like a dragon, but more ... *real*. Something bowled the party off her. A man shouted, and red sprayed. Another roar, a challenge she had never heard before. It was anger, rage, and the power of the beast. Vide scattered in haste, and above her, behind Mama and Papa, on *her* fucking rock, no less: Uncle Heser, astride Pakhet. The grey and black striped tiger was not invisible. Not running away. Here, at the end, with Morgan's great love. Neither safe, all cards dealt and on the table. Heser the Cheg vaulted from the tiger's back, a mace in hand, which he used with great effect to clear a gruesome path to her. Hand out, eyes calm. "Evanne."

She reached for him and let him pull her upright. "Uncle Heser?"

His eyes softened. "I like the sound of that." He casually smashed a man's head in. "Where is my lady?"

"Far end," she breathed, still dizzy. "She's—"

"She is Morgan, the Raven Queen." He straightened. "*My* queen."

"Then go get her."

He gave her a last up and down, nodded, grabbed a handful of tiger mane, and hauled himself aboard Pakhet. The tiger created clear space about her just by being there, probably because not even a demon-ridden Vide wanted any piece of that. "You will be well?"

"I need my guitar."

"It is here." Hitch glowed above the fallen instrument. "With me."

EVANNE STOOD, LEGS WIDE, ARMOUR HUMMING. SHE COULD SEE HOW Tarragon stood like a candle in the night, drawing all eyes away from Morgan, Sight of Day, Sands Apart, and the ancient Feybrind behind it all. *She's buying me time.* "Hitch."

"I'm here, Evanne."

She bowed her head a moment. "I know. You've always been here."

"But I don't know why."

"I do." Evanne straightened. "You make me strong."

"You were strong enough already." He hunched. "I wasn't."

"No one is. Can't you see? We're all alone, and weaker for it." She breathed. "Join me this one last time."

"Will it be the last?" She saw the hopelessness of his not-eyes. The faded blue of his form, and how little of him there was left. "Do you promise? Everything ... hurts, all the time."

"I know." She held her free hand toward him. "I can send you home. If you give me permission."

"I won't be here for you after that."

"That's okay, Hitch. You've been here for all of us, for eight *hundred* years." She straightened. "It's time to settle old debts. To wipe the ledger clean, and free us all."

He slid into her, and she felt the bitter cold as her breath eased in and out from chilled lungs. "How?"

"I'm going to summon the gods and get them to do their fucking *job*." She raised her hand and struck the strings. Not just with her fingers, but her heart, and Hitch's, right there inside her. "I'm going to give you a gift, Hitch. You are a dead man who stayed to see the job done, and it's time to go."

"I love you."

"I love you too. Eric Hitcherson, I give you your name." She felt him grow rigid, her limbs stiffening for a moment, the guitar stumbling, and then he ebbed out. A wisp, all the colours of his soul leaving as she breathed. With his last, she played.

In a world shrouded in darkness, demons arise,
  Their malevolent forces, a deadly guise.
  But we hold the power, deep within our soul,
  To summon the gods, though a promise they must break, for our world to be whole.

Cophine, goddess of morning's tender grace,
  Ikmae, ever-changing, in this desperate space,
  Khiton, lord of night, we plead for your might,
  Without breaking your oath, it's eternal night.

I raise my voice, to the heavens high,
  I summon the gods, my battle cry,
  With hearts united, we'll conquer the night,
  In their divine presence, we'll shine so bright.

Cophine, with your radiance, light the way,
  As dawn breaks, let hope's colours sway.
  Ikmae, master of change, guide our path,

Through shifting sands of destiny, bear this sacrificial oath's wrath.

WE RAISE OUR VOICES, TO THE HEAVENS HIGH,
   Summon the gods, let our battle cry,
   With hearts united, we'll conquer the night,
   In their divine presence, we'll shine so bright.

THE DEMON LORDS APPROACH, DARKNESS IN THEIR WAKE,
   In the absence of gods, our world may break.
   I draw your power, from deep within my soul,
   In their divine essence, I'm made whole.

KHITON, IN THE SHADOWS, YOU MUST REIGN,
   Embrace the night, and break the oath's chain.
   With your silent power, banish despair,
   Let the demon lords tremble, in their dark lair.

AS THE WORLD TREMBLES, 'NEATH THE DEMON LORDS' MIGHT,
   We stand unyielding, in the sacred light.
   With Cophine, Ikmae, and Khiton by my side,
   They'll break their promise to save us all, in this desperate, fateful
stride.

SHE FELT TIME SLOW, THE CLOCK OF THE WORLD CREAKING. HITCH left her, the bitter cold of his sacrifice all those years ago repaid. The Vide froze, demon eyes unblinking. Morgan, a statue at the other end of the room, hand outstretched to Sight of Day. Evanne's golden-eyed friend, falling back from a cut of Wild Sur's short blade. The strike frozen in this bubble of time, Sands Apart mid-air as she dived before the weapon.

Heser, three men trying to drag him down. Pakhet, a spear in her side. Tarragon, beautiful Tarragon on one knee, the Light about her fading.

This moment is how the world ends.

A blue-feathered bird flitted before her, unbowed by the impossible forces slowing time's march. Evanne watched as it lit on the raised spear of a Vide, and it watched her right back. She sighed. "Hello, Cophine."

Cheep.

"I see you've got your hand on the tiller of the universe." The changing form of Ikmae strode from within a pillar, high on the air. He became she, she became a child, then grew into an ancient man. "Bold."

"Needful." Evanne shook her head. "You must all be here for this to work."

"I am here," Khiton rumbled from above. She turned, catching the god striding down the scree slope, his feet also off the ground like Ikmae's.

"You look different, without your ship." Evanne set her guitar down and took her helmet off, scrubbing rust locks with her fingers.

"I was never as good a sailor as Cophine." He shrugged. "She's better at charting a new heading."

Cheep. Cheep cheep.

"Why did you call us here?" Ikmae settled for a moment into the frame of a bold youth, a little fuzz on his chin. "We can't win this fight for you. Not in a way that ends it for all time."

"You heard me. It's all there in the song." Evanne counted on her fingers. "I can do it. I can make this end. Make sense of the middle part. And give us a new beginning. If I don't, the world's going to end. Or get so bad as makes no difference."

Cheep?

"You know how." Evanne sighed, feeling the reality of it, the biting bile in her throat, the sickness in her stomach. "I need to die, though. That's the ticket. And you made a promise to Mama. You made a promise that you'd give her a child, an impossible child that couldn't survive. Not with a Vhemin inside it, and a human too. So, you bound your promise up with all the impossible things gods do, and you made it so I couldn't die. And I really need to die for this to work."

"She's not as stupid as I thought we made her," Khiton said.

"You didn't make me. Mama and Papa did." Evanne glowered at Khiton, still hovering above the ground. "I was stabbed through my broken heart by a spear and lived. I almost drowned but survived. I fought a vampire lord and walked free. I have led a charmed life, all because you won't let me die."

"What will you do?" Ikmae shifted into a girl's body. She was no more than eight years old. "How will you do it?"

"There is a weapon of impossible power above. It cracked our planet and shook it to the core once before. Mireille died shielding us, and even then, it wasn't enough. Everything broke, all at once. That man," she pointed at Wild Sur, "carries the keys to that weapon. So, I'm going to walk over there and end his life. The weapon will fall on the world. On *him*. But he won't be here. He'll be with me."

"Where will you be?" Khiton looked around as if trying to find the hidden meaning in it all.

"You know."

"I need to hear you say it."

Evanne drew a shuddering breath, then pointed at the gate. "In there. I will take the weapon with me. This armour isn't good enough to kill a demon lord. But it's good enough to take me to *their* world, where the weapon will destroy it. There's no Knight Champion to shield them. Just the dark and fear they make. It's time to return the favour."

Cophine flitted off the spear, then changed form, the blue-feathered bird becoming a young woman, resplendent in her radiant armour of the dawn. She stood on the air beside her siblings. "You ask gods to break their vow."

"Yeah."

"The promise of a god is not easily discarded, let alone Three of them."

Evanne rubbed a tear from her cheek. "Your promise is good as done. Mama's dead. She's dead, and she's not coming back." She pointed at Vertiline, pale, so very pale, her neck a bloody ruin, her body cradled in Armitage's arms. "You have no one left to worry about."

"There will still be a demon lord in your world. Three, as it happens."

"The Saviour of Ravenswall is back. I'll take those odds." Evanne's eyes moved to Tarragon's frozen form. "But if I don't do this, everyone dies here, and everywhere."

Cophine glanced to Ikmae, who shrugged from her now crone-like body. Cophine's gaze moved to Khiton, who glared back. "Don't look at me. I can end the promise. Make it stop here. But we need to start something new after."

"I can do that," Cophine said.

"Then we are agreed?" Ikmae shifted to become a chimney sweep of indeterminate age and gender. "The vow is broken. We remove our protection from Evanne. The world's clock starts again, for better or worse."

Cophine closed her eyes, brow furrowing with concentration. "I can't see how the sword balances on its point from here."

Khiton shook himself, his night-black armour taking over his seafarer's garb. Raised his pitch sword, its edge the only gleam of brightness. "Then we make a new sword."

"And carry it to the end." Ikmae shifted again, becoming Evanne. "Are you sure?"

Evanne took a breath, and bit her lip. "I'm sure."

Cophine strode over the air to her. Smoothed her rust locks and bent to put a kiss on Evanne's forehead. She smelled of fresh cut grass and lilies. "Then it is done." She turned from Evanne. "I promised I would set no foot on earth, and give Vertiline the child she needed, if she brought the world's shield back." She very slowly, carefully, stepped down from the air, and put her foot on the ground. It cracked beneath her armoured boot. "I break my promise."

"I too promised," Ikmae said. "I have lived under the world's mantle for these long years, never to set foot atop, to give Vertiline her child, if she brought the Tresward back." He, now a boy child of four, skipped to the ground. Despite his tiny frame, his feet cracked the slate beneath him. "I break my promise."

Khiton straightened. "We needed the Tresward. But all good things must end. I promised to be apart from the world, sailing the seas, so Vertiline could have her child." He stamped to the ground, the floor shuddering, cracking, and buckling. "I break my promise."

"Time to go," Evanne said. "Thanks for not being dicks about this." She stooped, and kissed Mama's still brow. Touched Armitage's grief-stricken face, frozen in this amber moment of time. Then gunned the armour, and blasted toward Wild Sur.

Time shuddered, lurched, champed at the bit, and surged forward.

Chapter Fifty

When Tarragon saw the woman come through the gate, she knew she was a goddess. It wasn't how she'd ridden the lightning and destroyed an elder demon lord in a heartbeat, or how she commanded a dragon. It was how she walked.

She walks like she's Bigger than Big.

She'd pieced together the story of the Saviour of Ravenswall. Vertiline seemed to harbour pain around the topic, but Armitage had been free with the truth, the monster speaking with *fondness* and *respect*. The Vhemin respected very little outside blood on the sand.

Tarragon stood with her borrowed blade. Vertiline lay dead behind her, the High Justiciar felled by the strike of a demon lord, and the goddess had gone in pursuit of that one. The goddess Geneve had given Vertiline a look before she'd gone. It seemed to say *I wish I could stay*.

Tarragon wished she'd stayed too, because the room was full of murder and her side was down on numbers. The Storm was with her. She *felt* it running through her arms, the power of the Three given to mortals. Tarragon moved into *Dawn's Beginning*. It was a simple pattern taught to Novices when they were knee high. It had three straight strides toward the foe, which Tarragon took, and ended with the signature overhand strike into a Vide warrior's shield. Her opponent was driven down like Tarragon wielded Khiton's own hammer, which in a way she did. It left a pile of broken bones inside a meat suit, and Tarragon moved to the next.

Why did she wish she could stay?

It was, of course, because Vertiline and Geneve were friends. Tarragon learned the Saviour's story from Evanne, how Geneve jumped into a demon gate and was lost to all when it closed. Vertiline started the school on the bones of that fight, Imshir rising into glory again in the lands of the sun. And Geneve was now a goddess, which no one knew about, or perhaps Three goddesses, because Tarragon saw the Light take form at her side. Two golden, angelic warriors wore Geneve's face.

Why didn't she stay?

Tarragon took the arm from a man who seemed to offer it to her freely, then seemed surprised when he lost it. *So much time watching the Tresward and doing their patterns.* Sands Apart had told her the secret of holding her Bigness. She did just as the Feybrind said, and the Light flowed. She didn't need Requiem, which was lucky because the goddess had taken the blade back.

If she's a goddess, she can do anything. She can stay.

But Geneve left, and Vertiline died. Was it revenge for being lost in the demon realm for sixteen years? The lordling hadn't said anything like that. Meriwether just wanted her *here*, with *him*, and Tarragon understood that. She felt her brow furrow with frustration as two men tried to take her on the blade, and her borrowed steel cut theirs in half, then she took their heads. She felt the Light buoy her, carry her feet, and walk the patterns with her.

So she must have left because she needs to do something out there *that's more important than her dead friend.*

She wasn't too surprised when Evanne arrived. She'd felt her lover approaching. Tarragon always knew where Evanne was, but she could also feel the Elder demon lord Aterregis approaching almost as fast as Morsorachius and Tenebricor ran away.

Goddesses can see the future. Did Geneve see something that we didn't?

Then, time stopped. Tarragon felt the gearing of the world lock up.

She was astonished, because while she couldn't move, her mind was free. She heard the conversation between the Three and Evanne, cringing a little at how free Evanne was with her words. And she wanted to wail when Evanne said she was going to *die*, like it was only her choice and nothing to do with a once-fairy who'd lived over eight hundred years only to fall in love for the first time right here.

Then time ... started. Not all at once; it limped a little at first, but got the job done well enough. Tarragon knew where Evanne was going: straight for that dickhead Wild Sur and his smug half-smile. The bard blasted overhead, and Tarragon started running. Pounding the cracked and tortured floor, sword low, head down, legs pumping, lungs dragging in dusty, coked, sooty air.

I must stop her.

But Evanne *flew*, faster than a striking falcon, straight for the gate. Wild Sur saw her coming, bringing his weapon away from Sight of Day and Sands Apart. Sands Apart was bleeding and stooped. Tarragon saw the magnetic arbalest spit metal hail at Wild Sur, the ancient Feybrind's sword sundering, shattered shards of steel spraying wide.

Evanne landed before Wild Sur, her lover struggling forward. Tarragon could almost feel the stress loads in her mind, the wheels and cogs of the Builder she was supposed to be seeing the tolerances exceeded, the fulcrum of the armour weighted against what was left of Evanne's body. How hungrily the armour suckled at the Soulkeeper. *Evanne isn't a warrior. She's a ... she's wonderful, she's a bard, she's a leader, but she's not made to die for others.*

That's what I'm for.

But Evanne was at Wild Sur before Tarragon was half-way across the room. The maybe-Vhemin struck the broken hilt from the Feybrind's hands. The Feybrind struck her back, still quick despite his years, but Evanne took the hits, stepped in, and grabbed Wild Sur into a bear's embrace. And she *squeezed*. Wild Sur thrashed, clawing and biting, raking armour, but Evanne pulled tighter, her shoulders shaking as Tarragon ran closer.

A jerk, and the Feybrind slumped. Evanne held him away, and Tarragon saw the jewel at his neck bloom incandescent.

I'm almost there. Faster, Big legs. Just a little faster. Tarragon's chest was tight with strain, bounding toward Evanne, because she could do this. Tarragon could take the dead Feybrind into the gate, because the once-fairy was old, and had lived, and Evanne was so *young*. Tarragon reached for her as Evanne took flight, turning her visored face on the once-fairy.

Sight of Day tackled her. She clattered to the ground, screaming *no no you don't understand she has so much time left*, but the golden eyes above her were sad, and implacable. As if the Feybrind could see the future, or perhaps what was on the other side of the gate, and how unlikely a once-fairy was to survive it.

Evanne said, "I love you," then turned, and blasted through the gate.

Chapter Fifty-One

Morgan clambered to Sands Aparts' side. The woman's breathing was ragged, her ochre eyes only half-open. Morgan looked up, took in Sight of Day's struggle with a very angry Tarragon, then bent back to her patient. "Wake up!"

Sands Apart reached for Morgan's face. The Feybrind's coat was badly cut, ugly red weeping weals marring her hide. Morgan felt the soft fingers at her cheek, then her chin, then a single finger against her lips. The hand fell, and Sands Apart stilled, ochre eyes closing. Her chest rose and fell, but so very slowly. She didn't have much time left.

This will not do. These people are in my kingdom. They are under my protection. Morgan stood, smoothed her robe, and put a shade of tired command in her tone. "Cease your caterwauling." Sight of Day and Tarragon stopped struggling, perhaps out of astonishment. Morgan pointed past them at the legion of Vide surging toward them. "Behind you lies the enemy. You must—"

"Evanne went in there!" Tarragon's words were hot, molten with fury.

"Yes, and if you want her to come back, you'll pull yourself together, woman. Honestly." Morgan eyed them both. "You *do* want her to come back, don't you?"

Tarragon goggled, but Sight of Day, sensing it was safe for the moment to loose his hold, said, *{Did you get hit in the head?}*

"My Lord du Reeves had a plan. Or, the faded shawl of a plan, pulled around the shoulders of desperation." Morgan sighed. "It is simple. He needed me to open the gate, because he thought it was where the Saviour of Ravenswall would be, but also because it would be a good place to put the people we don't want here anymore."

"But, Evanne!"

Before Morgan could use smaller words, the entire side of the building caved in. Rocks the size of houses scattered, and she was impressed with herself that she didn't bow like a craven. Wind surged, dust in the air, and she conceded a squint. Through the wall surged a demon lord. Morgan was having quite the trouble telling them apart, but she thought this one might be Tenebricor, the Infernal Something Or Other.

Behind him, Myryntir, the blue dragon surging with crackling blue energy. *//COME BACK. WE WERE GETTING ALONG SO WELL.//*

Tenebricor lashed out with a fist the size of a barracks, connecting with Myryntir's skull. The dragon was torn from the air, smashing into what was left of the wall, destroying it utterly. The ceiling groaned, giant rocks falling in, and bringing with them an angry red dragon. Ormeon settled on Tenebricor's shoulder, white-hot flames blasting like a weapon of the ancients. *//PICK ON SOMEONE YOUR OWN SIZE.//*

Myryntir struggled up, eyes blazing blue-white. He roared, jaws wide, unfazed by the hit he'd taken. His blue scales were scratched and marred. *Not nearly so pretty*, Morgan mused, *but he's found his purpose. He is the better for it.* Tenebricor reached a paw for Ormeon, and Myryntir rushed forward, grappling the demon lord's arm. Fire and lightning cascaded against the demon lord, who flailed, blinded, singed, but still in the fight.

Ormeon clawed the back of the demon lord's skull, claws rending, tearing bone from skull. Tenebricor shrieked, Morgan falling to her knees with the pain of that sound. Ormeon heaved a breath in, and blasted fire into the gap in the demon lord's skull. Tenebricor's shrieking coughed to a stop, the mighty demon lord swaying. Then its eyes melted from its skull, dragonfire blasting through, and it died, laying its form across a swathe of Vide.

Morgan dusted off her robe—again!—and faced Tarragon. "Wouldn't you rather be here?"

The once-fairy's eyes were wide. "Are you mad? That thing was monstrous!"

"There are more through there." Morgan gestured to the gate behind her.

"What did I miss?" Meriwether stepped in between them like he'd always been there.

Sight of Day glanced to the horde of Vide, then to Meri. *{How did you get here?}*

"I'm a wizard, remember?"

{You lost your power.}

"I didn't 'lose' it. I ... broke a few rules."

"My Lord du Reeves," Morgan breezed. "If you were of a mind to *find* your power, now would be an excellent time."

"Not yet."

Morgan blinked. "Did you see the demon lord?"

"Hard to miss."

"Whatever else could you be waiting for?"

The sky visible through the broken roof crackled, thunder booming before lightning surged down. It impacted the ground, blasting rock and Vide in equal measure as a second demon lord impacted the old stone. *Looks like the mouthy one. Aterregis, wasn't it?* The Wanker King or whatever it called itself clawed feebly toward the gate.

"That." Meri beamed. "We need a live one."

"What," Morgan started, then pressed a hand to her temple. "I feel like I'm getting a migraine."

"You're not. Or we all are. A really big one, very soon." Meri gave an encouraging nod as he pointed up. "Because of that."

Against her better judgement, Morgan followed the line of his arm. A glimmer of fire bloomed in the heaven, then another beside it, then another. "What are those?"

"The end of all things," Tarragon said. "The weapon that killed the world before but unleashed threefold this time."

"Like I said, we need a live one." Meri scritched his beard. "For *after* you hold the gate open."

"Of course, that explains everything." Morgan thought her words didn't have quite the right loading of sarcasm, so she added a little more. "And why would I want to hold the gate open to a realm full of horrible monsters?"

"This is why you need Holomancers." The sorcerer looked at what remained of the ceiling for a moment. "No one here has the long view? Okay. We need a live one for the starlight inside it. I think ... I *know* we're going to need it." Meri glanced at Tarragon. "So we can bring back what we left behind, and not lose what we gained."

A bellowing roar came from the far end of the room, and the massive doors to the outside exploded inward. The last demon lord—Morsorachius, the Abyssal Clown, no doubt—came lurching in, massive running steps shaking the ground. Fire rained from the sky, impacting the monster, and it roared its pain, turning to face the ruin of the door.

And there she is. Morgan admitted Geneve suited her armour, a battle angel made flesh, the two shining warriors at her side Light-born manifestations of her fury. Geneve levelled Requiem at the retreating Morsorachius, starfire falling around. "You are going the wrong way."

The demon lord looked at the down-and-out form of its comrade Aterregis. "*YOU ARE TOO LATE TO STOP YOUR DOOM, AND I WILL NOT SHARE IT WITH YOU.*"

Geneve didn't lower Requiem, the blade of justice burning bright. "You want everything from us. It's time you got your due."

"Tarragon," Morgan breathed. "Tarragon, I know you want to go through the gate. I know you think you'll be helping. But if you want to see Evanne again, please hold the line. Here, with us. With the living."

"She wants to die," Tarragon wailed.

"She doesn't," Morgan said. "The bard is young and feels she will be made into song. But *I* have a plan."

"You do?" Meri gave her some side eye. "Is it the same plan I had?"

"It is not. It is a necessary addition."

Tarragon's eyes were wide, but she bit her lip, and nodded, then turned to face the throng. Which was just in time, as the three points of light in the sky grew larger, the heavens crying and roaring as they came. Morgan felt fear, but she wasn't alone. The demon-ridden Vide surged toward the gate. Or, perhaps, it was away from Heser the Cheg, astride the mammoth tiger Pakhet, bellowing his very human war cry as he came. Tarragon presented her blade to the horde, Sight of Day at her shoulder. Meriwether du Reeves at the other, although Morgan was unsure what good he would do. *Still. Every stick on the pyre helps.*

Morgan bent, retrieving Sands Apart's fallen blade. Just a slip of a weapon, elegant, for a woman struggling to find beauty in the right places. She strode to the line, Heser stepping down from his tiger to stand beside her. "My queen."

She faced him, then caressed his face. Leaned in, and kissed him, his eyes wide as hers closed. "My love."

"*Finally*," Pakhet said. "*We can all die knowing how the saga ends.*"

"Hold this gate open," Meriwether said. "Morgan, you're shit with a blade, and I need you holding the gate."

"The gate will hold," Morgan said. "I commanded it."

"And you need to be alive to—"

"My Lord du Reeves, do not presume to tell me what to do." Morgan eyed the three points of light. "You are a smarter man than that."

Morsorachius bleated his terror, turning to the gate. Finding Ormeon and Myryntir before him, two hounds guarding his retreat path. The desperate demon lord cast about, then rounded on Geneve. "*I WILL END YOU! I WILL—*"

Whatever it would do was lost as Geneve threw her blade at him. Requiem *spanged* off the demon's weapon, which was so large it would put a good log cabin to shame. The Saviour of Ravenswall ran at him as her blade returned to palm, then threw it again, over and over, Light blazing as the demon lord retreated.

He stumbled and fell back on one knee. Geneve leaped, bounding up his leading leg, her angels beside her. Morgan saw her swing Requiem against the demon lord's neck, a mirror movement of the two angels following up, each form slipping into her body as her blow landed.

Morsorachius' head bounced free, and Geneve kept running over the top. She reached Meriwether, her face softening a moment. "Love."

"Love," he agreed. "What kept you?"

"The fate of realms."

"Bah." He squinted at the Vide throng, churning and savage. "What next?"

"Perhaps you need a shield," Tarragon offered.

Geneve glanced at the once-fairy. "Knight Adept..?"

"Tarragon."

"Knight Adept Tarragon—"

"It's just Tarragon."

Geneve pressed her lips into a considering line. "Knight Adept Tarragon, why do I need a shield?"

"To protect the world," Tarragon said. "Like Knight Champion Mireille did."

"I do not intend to die as Mireille did." Geneve swept red hair back. "Who is the sacrifice?"

"Evanne," Meriwether murmured. "She is ... you'd have liked her."

"She's not a sacrifice!" Tarragon rounded on Morgan. "You *said*."

"I did." Morgan tested the point of her blade, finding it very sharp indeed. "Knight Champion Geneve, a moment."

"We don't have much time, Morgan." Geneve shook her head. "I wish we did."

"We have time. Evanne is the woman in the armour who dove into the gate. She is Vertiline's and Armitage's daughter. She—"

"Impossible."

"Many things are possible, Knight Champion." Morgan eyed Geneve, taking in the wide eyes. "She brokered a deal. The apple doesn't fall far from the tree. Evanne accepts her doom for us, but she didn't consult her queen. *I will not stand for it.*"

Geneve gave her a long look, that Tresward visage hiding anything else. Geneve still wore the face of a woman in her late teens, but her eyes held millennia. Geneve looked away first, and Morgan found that the most curious thing of all. Tresward bent no knee. "You are right, of course. She would not forgive me."

Forgive her for what? It was of little moment, because matters pressed. Morgan called to Myryntir. "Mighty dragon! Fastest of all, I need you."

//AT LAST, SOME RESPECT.//

"I need you to fly into the gate and retrieve our wayward daughter."

//A LITTLE TOO MUCH RESPECT.//

Ormeon grinned red. *//OH, GO ON. YOU'RE TOO DAMNED PRETTY TO DIE.//*

"There is a balance I can feel," Morgan said. "We stand at the moment where all can be won or lost. You must do this, dragon."

Myryntir glanced at Ormeon. *//YOU REALLY THINK I'M PRETTY?//*

She nuzzled him. *//YOU ARE THE MOST BEAUTIFUL THING I HAVE SEEN.//*

//HOLD THAT THOUGHT.// Myryntir bunched, surged, and dashed over Morgan's head, and into the demon gate.

"Not very smart, though," Meri mused.

"Now, we must hold the line," Morgan said. "We must hold it for as long as it takes."

"What for?" Tarragon blinked. "What's going to take a long time?"

The ancients' weapons keened and roared over head, hot ashy wake blasting past as they zipped, one, two, three, into the demon's realm. Morgan smoothed—*Merciful Three, again!*—her robe. "The end of a world."

Chapter Fifty-Two

This is an odd place.

Myryntir dove through an absence. It felt like space, but without the starlight that powered the universe. There was an empty part of his mind where the Manifest should have been. A tome of knowledge put there by ancient humans who tried to chain ... well, everything, including creatures like him. Bend them to a purpose, and if they wouldn't yield, break them.

They would be right at home here. This place is not just odd, but evil. It holds nothing for those who live today. It holds nothing for Evanne. I wish she hadn't come here.

Below he spied land, a vast stretch of stone and rubble that held nothing green or wet. It wasn't like Myryntir's world, an orb held in the vastness of space, a jewel slotted into the crown of the sun. This was a beach that never knew the waves. It was a desert that hadn't known trees well enough to forget them.

It explains why they want all the humans' starlight. No suns collapsed over millennia, again and again, to forge the atoms here. It's all ... empty.

The red dragon survived here, though. She was a foxy one, all long teeth and enticing grin. He'd have liked to spend a few more minutes asking her how she had such an elegant span of wing or discuss the red dawn of her eyes. Built like he was, but larger, and stronger.

But slower. It's why I'm here.

Myryntir turned his long neck to look behind him. Back there, the gate held open, and he could see a wink of light beyond. The living world, breathing, thriving, so foreign to the things that infested this land. Any second now—

There they are.

The weapons of the ancients spat through. They moved fast, nosing the sky, terrible dogs off the leash. *I will not survive an encounter with one. They told me the Knight Champion Mireille shielded the world just enough for a few to survive, scratching in the brittle clay to claw toward a new dawn. They say she sent her dragon away.*

They say she loved her dragon. I wonder what it is like to be loved. It must take time to forge a bond like that. To live for another, to always want their thing more than yours.

I wish my Manifest was here. It would tell me, and I wouldn't have to wonder.

He thought about that embergleam grin, and figured if he could make it out of this, he might coax a few years out of the world to learn about love. *I'm not loved. But I see those who are, and that is the precious thing the demons want most. They won't have it, not even a speck, while I live.*

Myryntir turned about, seeking Evanne. She with the beautiful voice and the terrible choices. Three's merciful gaze, but she decided that bringing an untethered blue dragon back to the world was the right call. That she'd just, what, *trust* that things would work out? *I've seen my fangs, and they are terrifying. Why did she do that?*

Maybe I'll ask her. Below, he spied Evanne falling like a comet, a contrail of starlight behind her. The bard was trying to get far from the gate, or perhaps deep into the enemy's territory. Myryntir didn't mind, because he was a blue dragon. The blues held the power of the storm, not that pesky thing the Tresward had with a capital S, but the majesty of nature. The kind of energy the sky spat when it had flat out had enough. It was brighter than dragonfire and fast as light.

He straightened his body, made it an arrow, and flew. Myryntir pushed himself, young heart beating, the chamber of his body stoked with energy, the light crackling about him, urging him forward faster than wings alone. The lightning charging his body broke free in arcs and slashes, lighting the terrain below, bringing the brown-black rock into relief. It highlighted the demons below as they hungrily bounded toward Evanne's falling star. Myryntir roared, lightning arcing from his jaws, so's to give them something to fear.

I must look absolutely badass. I bet the red would be jealous.

The weapons of the ancients were missiles. They'd crafted them to break the very planet they lived on, which was a *stupid* thing to do when the planet was where you kept all your stuff. Important stuff, like blue dragons. The missiles held the power of starlight, Myryntir could *feel* it, but something else, like the ebb and flow of sorcery. The kind of thing no single magician could make. He felt the enchantment that held it, the evocation that powered it, and the thaumaturgy that made it bigger than it should be. A salting of conjuration to bring forth the devils of death, and necromancy to ruin all things. Tied together with a nice little ritualistic bow.

They were imbeciles. Those weapons will ruin everything.

Evanne was close now. She held the still form of Wild Sur. The Feybrind was so spectacularly dense he showed that even someone who'd seen the world break could have a learning disability. Her visor turned to him, her body jerking with surprise. Her voice was stressed, and weaker than it should be. "What are you *doing* here?"

//SAVING YOU.// Myryntir grinned, lightning crackling between them. Her armour lapped it up. *//THERE'S NO OTHER REASON TO BE HERE. NOT A FIVE-STAR RESTAURANT ANYWHERE.//*

"You have to *go*."

//WE ARE AGREED.//

"You can't make it with me!"

//WE HAVE A MISMATCH.// He turned a lazy circle in the not-really-air which still buffeted him well enough. *//I DON'T KNOW IF YOU NOTICED, BUT I'M A DRAGON.//*

"I'm not!"

//A WRINKLE, NOTHING MORE.// He wished for the Manifest again, because he was certain it would contain useful knowledge on

convincing humans to do things in their best interests. *//DO YOU WANT TO BECOME A DRAGON RIDER?//*

"I'm ... dying, Myryntir. The armour's taken too much. It ate and ate until it gobbled Hitch, and now he's gone for good. I'm taking it with me, so it can't eat anyone else."

//VERY SELFLESS, BUT QUITE UNNECESSARY.// Myryntir glanced back at the missiles, which were alarmingly close. *//LOOK, I HATE TO BE BLUNT, BUT WE'RE RUNNING OUT OF TIME. MY HEROIC SWOOP WILL BE LESS EFFECTIVE IF WE EXPLODE.//*

"How will we make it? We've come so far, and we've no time left."

//PUT DOWN YOUR BAGGAGE. BLUE DRAGONS ARE THE FASTEST THINGS EVER MADE.// She looked like she was about to start some more verbal sparring and Myryntir was clean out of patience, so he swooped in, ignoring the staccato popping of the magnetic arbalest's rounds against his armour as it fired at him—pointlessly—and nipped her up in his jaw. Then he tossed her, did a roll, and came up under her. She yelped, Wild Sur's body tumbling away, the jewel blooming brighter at the dead man's throat.

//NOW, WE FLY.//

"Don't you mean flee?"

//DRAGONS DON'T FLEE. WE ARE THE APEX PREDATORS OF THE UNIVERSE.// He glanced over his shoulder. *//MAKE SURE YOU HAVE A GOOD GRIP. TARRAGON WOULD LIKE TO SEE YOU AGAIN.//*

"I've got aaaaaieeeeee!" Evanne shrieked as Myryntir powered back toward the gate.

He could see it. Do the math. Felt the calculations in the backdrop of his mind. It would be close. He breathed cobalt power, lightning arcing against the space around him. Wings beating, urging them on. Evanne wasn't heavy, not for a dragon. But the gate was a long way away. So far up, and he'd come such a long way. *I may have miscalculated. Love may have to wait for the next life.*

Myryntir pushed himself harder anyway, because love seemed like a fun thing everyone should experience. His heart beat against his chest, an organ larger than an entire person. Evanne's hand was on his scaled hide, which he shouldn't be able to notice because she was a gnat, but he *felt* her *right there*. And heard her, as if she whispered into his ear, like they were gathered around a campfire, her jolly with whiskey and him having eaten an entire cow. Myryntir heard the breath of her song, even though there was no wind here, and she had a helmet on. He felt *Evanne*, and wondered if this is what love might feel like, the tiny bloom of it where it all begins. Because she sang to him, the two of them here in this not-place, where no starlight lived, and where they were going to die together.

IN A WORLD OF FIRE AND THUNDER,
 Underneath the skies so wide,
 Myryntir, my loyal friend,
 With you, there's nothing I can't ride.

OH, MYRYNTIR, MY LIGHTNING'S PRIDE,
 Together, we'll reach the stars so high.
 Let the wind and lightning guide our way,
 We'll fly faster, higher, every day.

WITH SCALES LIKE SAPPHIRES, A HEART SO TRUE,
 You're the strength that carries me through.
 Through storms and flames, we'll never tire,
 Together, we'll conquer and inspire.

OH, MYRYNTIR, MY LIGHTNING'S PRIDE,
 Together, we'll reach the stars so high.
 Let the wind and lightning guide our way,
 We'll fly faster, higher, every day.

ORMEON AWAITS, YOUR LOVE'S DESIRE,
 But first, we must conquer the raging fire.

RICHARD PARRY

With every beat of your mighty wings,
We'll soar above, where destiny sings.

MYRYNTIR, LET THE LIGHTNING ROAR,
  As we break through the thunder's core.
  With courage and love, we'll ascend,
  To a love story, we'll forever mend.

OH, MYRYNTIR, MY LIGHTNING'S PRIDE,
  Together, we'll reach the stars so high.
  Let the wind and lightning guide our way,
  We'll fly faster, higher, every day.

WITH HEARTS ABLAZE, AND SKIES SO VAST,
  Our love and courage, they will last.
  Myryntir, my winged dream,
  Together, we'll fly faster, it would seem.

SO SPREAD YOUR WINGS, AND LET'S TAKE FLIGHT,
  To reach our love's eternal height.
  With Myryntir by my side, I know,
  We'll fly faster and never let go.

HE ROARED, BLAZING AN ARC OF LIGHTNING ACROSS THE COAL BLACK sky, and surged forward. He felt her fade, the spark inside her giving out as they went faster. Some twinkle of magic remained in her armour, its grip on him holding tight, and he beat his wings, faster, faster, *FASTER.*

The missiles impacted below. The light of uncreation bloomed, tearing through the demon's realm, hungering for them. But he was Myryntir, he was lightning's pride, Evanne said so, she *said* so, and she

344

said he would fly fast. Roaring again, he put on a last burst of speed, and made the gate. Burst through, just as it snapped shut behind him.

Myryntir fell, energy spent, his armour's lustre gone. His mighty body fell against the stone floor, his and Evanne's bodies scudding across the stone floor. They were done.

But they were home. They could die among friends.

Chapter Fifty-Three

Geneve felt relief so sharp it was a sickness, a punch in the gut and a trembling of her limbs. Years beyond reckoning they'd lived beyond the gate, and now they were back. Meri, Ormeon, and Geneve were *here*. But the cost? Too high, because Vertiline fell.

My sister in battle is dead.

Meri and Geneve had shared quiet words in the other realm when the demons' press abated. Gathered around what campfire Sway could make in that shattered place, Ormeon's bellows breathing at their backs. She'd asked him, *Will she forgive me*, and he'd said, *She will wonder the same thing*.

Vertiline was before her, wrapped in Armitage's forever embrace. Her ghost-pale skin was almost translucent, the gory wound of her neck and red-stained armour showing how the end took her. Armitage's arm protected her in death as he couldn't in life.

Geneve left this world, promising to return. Leaving Vertiline to hold an impossible line while gods and demons battled for the hearts of all. And she *knew* Vertiline. Understood the guilt and love that wound her around the axle of fate, how the Chevalier—

She is Chevalier no longer. Her armour carries the black and silver sash of High Justiciar.

"My sister is dead." Geneve tested the words, felt the truth of them.

Meri touched her elbow. Nothing she could feel through her armour but she sensed it all the same. And she knew the look on his face that would be her undoing if she saw it. *I have no time for tears. Not yet.* "She is."

"I can bring her back."

"You can't." His words were carefully chosen, iron certainty under the pillow of care. "She has been gone too long. Unless."

She risked a look at him. "Speak, Holomancer."

Meri looked away. "I..." he trailed away as Morgan walked toward them. She'd rested Evanne against Myryntir's side, the great blue dragon's sapphire dimmed in death. The Raven Queen carried herself well, the years kinder than those without the Light could hope for. Her Guardsman Heser the Cheg wasn't far; he tended a fearsome grey and black striped tiger. The beast was grievously wounded from a thousand cuts, but it hadn't run.

No, the best never do. They stay, and they fall. She felt her face crinkle but held it firm. "Morgan. What news?"

The twist of a gallows smile touched the Raven Queen's lips but couldn't struggle to her eyes. "We won the day." She glanced at the heaving form of Aterregis, the demon lord struggling against the Ritual bonds Morgan left him with. The demon lord was weak, the energy inside him stolen from people running low. He'd burned much in his fight against Geneve and had forgotten what the Light's lash felt like. "So many fell."

"One didn't have to!" Geneve rounded on her. "If you'd *let me*, this wouldn't—"

"Hush," Meri said. "She doesn't know."

Geneve bit down, her words clipped. "I apologise for my tone. There was a moment before the dragon entered the gate where I could have brought Vertiline back. The Sway could have lifted her back to me. To *us*. But you wanted to keep the gate open. Too much time has passed. I can't bring Vertiline back. I am young, but it would take more than my full life's span to restore her." Geneve shut her eyes, head down. *Israel always counselled truth, especially when it hurt most.* "But you were right. If I'd brought her back, her daughter would have been lost to the demon realm. Vertiline would never trade herself for her child."

Morgan paled, but her chin lifted a micron. "Matters were pressing."

"There's a way." Meri's voice was quiet. "There's always a way."

Geneve scrubbed red hair. "Sorcerer, I have no patience for might-bes and could-be-done. Speak plain."

He took no offence. "That thing," he pointed at Aterregis, "holds a *lot* of starlight. They get that big by feeding on *us*. The Tome says it is possible, but the power ratio is ... difficult to untangle."

Morgan glanced at the demon lord. "You're going to use the demon lord to power a spell?"

"Not a spell. There is no spell to bring back those who are lost. Necromancers resurrect shambling corpses, but it is a false life. Only the Sway can do it. The Three gave us the same tool used to make the world, but they have the power of, well, gods. Tresward must give themselves to part the veil. And there's a lot of themselves... well, *our*selves in *that*." He pointed at the demon lord again, with more emphasis. "It will take more than a word."

Sight of Day slipped beside Geneve as if he'd always been there. Perhaps he had been there for much of the conversation, and she simply hadn't noticed. *{You can't use Sway like you think you can. No, don't interrupt. Just because it is written doesn't make it so.}*

"And you know of magic?" Meri's eyebrow almost reached his hairline.

{I am of the People.} His golden eyes were sad. *{You will need to use the Sway like an incantation. You will need to think like a god.}*

"I have no skill with words," Geneve said. "And I believe as time marches, we will need more starlight. I don't fancy another trek through the gate to get another demon lord."

"The gate is broken," Morgan said. "I broke it."

Meri clapped his hands together. "In a way, this is good news! One less bad option on the table."

Geneve took in his aged face: the cost he'd paid to take his doom into the other realm. She looked across at the fallen blue dragon, and Ormeon's head draped across his still flank. At the form of Evanne, armour battered, laying against his hide. Then, to Vertiline and Armitage. Back to the blue dragon, where the Knight Adept Tarragon knelt beside fallen Evanne. Geneve watched as the Adept straightened Vertiline's daughter's arms, then removed her helmet. Smoothed her hair and touched her face. She laid a small posy of flowers on what was clearly her lover's lap.

Evanne's face was scarce a year's difference from Geneve's own, if that. Geneve considered the fallen warrior. Vhemin scales crept up to a very human-skinned face. Rust locks. Strong shoulders. "They always ask too much of us."

"The gods are real dicks that way." Meri sighed.

"I need an incantation."

"The best person to make songs of words is the bard," Morgan said. "She's... *was* good at it."

Geneve broke from their huddle and strode toward Tarragon. "Knight Adept."

"It's just Tarragon." The woman stood. "High Justiciar, I—"

"I am no Justiciar," Geneve said. "I'm not even a very good Knight."

"But you—"

"Can you sing?" Geneve pointed to Evanne. "Like her."

"I, um." Tarragon shook her head. "But I know someone who sees as well as Evanne did. She taught me how to stand right so the Light would come." Tarragon's shoulders slumped. "She's very badly hurt, though."

"I can fix hurt. I'm having trouble with dead. Take me to this person."

Tarragon led her across the battlefield, masonry from the caved-in ceiling scattered amongst the dead bodies of Vide and village folk. Bits of demon lord still smoked. At the far end of the room, near the gate, lay a Feybrind woman. She was horribly cut, her breathing shallow and ragged. The Knight Adept knelt by her. "This is Sands Apart."

The Feybrind's eyes opened, their ochre beauty taking Geneve's breath away. *I'd forgotten how wonderful the People were.* She regarded Geneve but didn't move. "Friend, I—"

{*I am no friend. I was an enemy. Now, I'm dying. I've done what I can to make amends, and I hope it's enough.*} She took a shuddering breath. {*Do you think the People are welcomed by the Three when we die, or do our souls vanish like morning mist?*}

Geneve thought about that, then hunkered closer to Sands Apart. "I don't know. I wish I did. It seems cruel that we would make the world so very hard for you, then rob you at the end. But ... the world *is* cruel."

{*I like your honesty. Your delivery sucks.*}

"The Knight Adept tells me you are good with seeing into the heart of things."

{*In all things except myself.*} Another rattling sigh. {*I couldn't see the broken part of me that trusted a villain.*}

Geneve thought through what should come next. The Justiciars of old would have said something like, *Give me this spell and I will heal you.* But that was not what Iz or Tilly would have done. It wasn't what Meri would have done. So, she leaned back. "I am going to make you whole."

{*It will not work well. The dawn warrior tried with Sight of Day, but we're ... different.*}

"That is what makes you important." Geneve stood. "Iz said we need all the difference we can find." She reached a hand toward Sands Apart and felt for the Sway. *//BE HEALED.//*

Gods, but the Sway resisted. Bucking and tugging like an unbroken horse. It wound around her hand, a snake seeking another path, but she held it firm. Gripped her fist, and focused, watching as the wounds on Sands Apart closed, the woman relaxing.

Geneve sagged, but Tarragon was beside her, holding her up. "You *are* a goddess."

Geneve stood by herself. "I am no goddess. I like to think I'm not as capricious, for a start."

Sands Apart eased up. {*You have the look of someone who has much ahead of you to be done.*}

"Yes." Geneve brushed back red hair. "And I need your help."

She told the Feybrind what she needed, while the woman nodded along. *{You want the People, who have no Storm or Sway, to help you build a spell to resurrect a fallen warrior? And you want to use the lost souls of the damned, held inside the demon lord, to power the spell?}*

"Yes."

{Next time, ask for something easier.} The woman considered, then half-smiled. *{I think I have just the thing.}*

GENEVE STOOD ABOVE VERTILINE AGAIN. HER DEAR FRIEND WAS where she'd left her. It was so unlike Vertiline to lie still, because she was unbowed by anything. Tilly had been more mother to her than her own. She'd saved Geneve so many times. Meri was there, and Morgan. She turned to them. "I'm ready."

"Then we begin." Morgan straightened.

"There is nothing for you to do, Raven Queen."

"Ah, here at last you remember my title. Fancy bending the knee a little? No?" Morgan shook her head. "You need a friend, Geneve. Always you have faced the enemy alone. Always! But this time the world will ask more of you than you can give. Take my hand. I will be here with you."

"And I." Meri took her hand, Morgan on the other side.

Sight of Day joined hands with Morgan. Sands Apart slipped a velvet hand into Meri's. Tarragon took Sight of Day's hand, and Heser the Cheg slipped between Tarragon and Sands apart. They formed a circle above Vertiline.

"So it will be done," Geneve breathed. She reached for the Sway again, feeling it circle, shy away, but she'd had a blue roan who was feisty and knew how to handle the wilful. The presence of Aterregis was a necessary burden in her mind, and she coiled the Sway about him. She breathed deep, then spoke the words the Feybrind gifted her.

//In shadows deep, Aterregis, you I bind,
As sacrifice, your essence intertwined,

Grant me power to breach death's icy line.

FROM YOUR DARK REALM, I DRAW STRENGTH TO FREE,
The souls we mourn from death's decree,
In our unholy union, reshape destiny.
By your sacrifice, we break the night,
Return the lost to the mortal light.

ATERREGIS, EMPOWER THIS RITE!//

SHE FELT THE SWAY SURGE, THE DEMON LORD SHRIEKING. BUT SHE felt something *else*. The cool hand of Morgan, gripping hers. The Ritualist gathering the Sway as it passed through her. Coaxing it, sharing what she saw, and passing it through the hands of the ring about them.

And then Geneve could consider nothing else because the Sway demanded its price. It hungered and howled, draining Aterregis. The demon lord shrieked and mewled, thrashing, the starlight a torrent from the creature to her. She was burning up. The Light of creation was too much. Geneve felt her skin draw tight, the years pile on her. *How did Meri stand this?* The gods took all, and then more.

And more.

They took it all.

But Morgan's hand still held hers. Meri's, too. And around the ring, other souls, good and kind people, who knew Vertiline, but also knew her daughter, and their fallen dragon friend Myryntir.

They put their souls on the line too.

Chapter Fifty-Four

Ormeon banked through fluffy clouds. The brief touch of moisture slicked her scales a more lustrous red before speed slicked her dry. Below, the land spread out, a beautiful blue-green blanket. *I've always liked how it looks from up here. So ... peaceful. I can imagine how all is well below. How the world unfolds just-so, my imagination making saints of all.*

A gust of wind tried to buffer her and she grinned red, trailing a little smoke. The house she sought was above the broken citadel where they'd made their stand. A scattering of people waved from the ground, her dragon-perfect eyesight showing her men and women of all kinds—humans, Feybrind, and even Vhemin snacks—fixing walls, tilling earth, building anew.

The year since they'd defeated Wild Sur had been kind to the land. *Dancing in the Storm* floated once more. It was said the great sky city was haunted, but the spectre was benign. The tinkle of tiny bells and a hint of sandalwood and cinnamon were found in the depths of the ship's great engine room. It guided those with a dab hand at the ways of metal, showing them how to stoke the great forges and Build anew.

Cophine has such a sense of humour.

Beneath the *Storm*, the once-blasted battleground was cleared. It grew green, the ancient Vehement Systems citadel's cannons quiet. It was a place of learning, one of the last ancient libraries left standing, doors open wide to those with wit and desire. Or just desire. The head teacher had found patience with all, except perhaps herself.

Ormeon descended toward the house, hillside greeting her as she landed with a *whump*. The cottage's front door shook at her landing. A line out the back held washing pegged out to dry. Ormeon saw the vegetable patch was coming along nicely. A row of carrots would be ready soon, if you were the kind of person who didn't eat a steady diet of Vhemin.

Speaking of. The door banged open, Armitage throwing it wide. "Fuck off!"

//HELLO AND GOOD TO SEE YOU, TOO.//

"You're not due until next week." The old Vhemin was still strong, despite the terrible scar she'd given him across his chest.

//I'M DUE WHEN AND WHERE I PLEASE.// Ormeon's Manifest tapped at her mind, telling her *food* and *kill it* and *enemy*. She made all that nonsense go away. *//BUT YOU'RE RIGHT. I SHOULD HAVE CALLED FIRST.//*

Armitage glanced up at her, snake eyes hard. "Did you bring it?"

//CHECK THE BAG.//

He strolled to her side. The saddle she wore had panniers, and he rooted through a couple until he fetched out a bottle. It was a new batch, fresh, and would need cellaring like all good wine did. Armitage rustled out another couple bottles. "Hang about. I've got something for the runt, too."

//IS SHE HERE?//

"Of course she's here." He sauntered inside, and a moment later an older woman came out.

She was ghost-pale, eyes the colour of the northern ice. Her platinum hair was grey, now, but she wore it well, as far as Ormeon could tell. "Greetings, dragon."

//HIGH JUSTICIAR.// Ormeon bowed, her head dipping to the ground. *//ARE YOU WELL?//*

"Well enough." Vertiline walked to her, and placed a hand on Ormeon's muzzle, then leaned in. Ormeon bunted her right back, although very gently because while Vertiline was the High Justiciar, she was also miniscule. "You've come early. Good news?"

//IT IS.// Ormeon glanced down at the keep, the tiny figures below, and the still-broken wall into the main room. //PROGRESS IS SLOW.//

"Building with stone makes men and women strong. Knights must be strong to carry the Light."

//IT'S NOT JUST LIGHT THEY CARRY.//

"True enough." She eased onto the grass beside the dragon, care lines on her face showing time's indelible mark. "The Three would have us use Storm and Sway to keep the world safe, but there's another way. Knowledge lies here, and we'll share it with all."

//I'M ON BOARD. SAVE ME THE SALES PITCH.// Ormeon yawned. //BUT THE SAFEST HOUSES ARE THE ONES EVERY-ONE'S AFRAID TO ATTACK.//

"That's why I'm training Knights. Not for them. For us."

Ormeon grinned. //THAT'S ALL THEY EVER WANTED.//

Vertiline glanced up at her. "Riddles are tiresome, wyrm."

//FEEL LIKE TELLING ME WHAT BEING DEAD WAS LIKE?//

"No."

//THEN I GUESS WE'RE EVEN.// The dragon considered the sky. //I'D BEST BE OFF. I JUST WANTED YOU TO KNOW.//

Vertiline creaked upright. She'd paid the same price everyone else had to put things to right, seventy years now showing in her frame. For all that, she was strong, and her mind sharp. Her heart a little softer, though. "I'm so happy for you, Redeemer. When I first heard your name I thought it was all about war. A sword to wield against the darkness. I didn't think it meant love."

//THAT'S OKAY. NEITHER DID I. THE MANIFEST GETS IT WRONG SOMETIMES.//

Armitage came from the cottage carrying a small rectangle wrapped in oilskins to protect the contents from the elements. Ormeon considered the Vhemin. She'd seen the strength in him, but worried at his age. *It won't be long now, as dragons measure things.* "Don't tell him it's from me. I don't want him thinking I'm going soft."

//YOU HAVE MY WORD.// She sighed. //YOU CAN COME VISIT.//

"Fuck that. I'd have to put on pants and leave the house."

She grinned at the Vhemin. *//I PROMISE IT'LL BE WORTH IT.//*

Armitage glanced at Vertiline, then nodded. "Okay. But they better be house trained."

HOLLYHEAD WAS A GHOST OF ITS FORMER SELF. MOST OF ITS PEOPLE had stayed at the Vehement Systems fortress to learn and build, but a few returned here for a simpler way of life.

Ormeon arced across the sky, sighting the fallen wreck of the *Century Charm*. There were secrets buried in the hulk, and these people meant to find them. They had a leader who worked with those at the fortress to share knowledge from both great factions of the ancients. *Dancing in the Storm* was a treasure trove of Itikari knowledge, and here was the enemy's sister ship.

The old rivalry between Itikari and Vehement Systems had endured over eight hundred years, threatening to pull the world back into darkness when it barely had its head above water. Hollyhead's new mayor had said *I won't allow it*, and that was that.

The great red settled near the lakeshore. They'd put aside a smooth area where she could land without frightening the sheep in the fields. Sheep were delicious, so it was good to provide some space between them and a potentially hungry dragon. *I've never understood how an animal both so stupid and tasty survived extinction.*

She didn't have to wait long. The Mayor of Hollyhead walked down the main street, her husband at her side. The Mayor had not survived the events at the fortress unscathed. She was similarly creased by time, the Ritual she'd leashed the demon lord with having taken its fair share from her. Despite it, she had an easier smile than Ormeon remembered her wearing. "Ormeon. Be welcome."

//MORGAN.// The dragon eyed her husband. *//WHAT HAVE YOU DONE WITH MY CAT, HESER?//*

Heser the Cheg's broad shoulders had slumped a little, but he walked as straight as his wife. "She hunts."

//YOU BETTER NOT BE GIVING HER SHEEP WHILE I'M WAITING BY THE WATER, FREEZING MY SCALES OFF.//

"She claims to have found a small enclave of vampires." Morgan waved a hand *over there*. "She likes to play with her prey. You know cats."

//SO, THAT'S A NO TO SHEEP?//

Heser scratched his beard, which trended well to grey but suited him, as far as dragony sensibilities went. *It makes his head look larger, anyway, and anything that makes them look larger is a plus.* "How goes our regent?"

"*Our?*" Morgan's left eyebrow raised exactly one millimetre.

"Our," he affirmed, not quailing in the face of that gale.

//I HAVEN'T MADE IT THERE YET. IT'S A BIG PLANET.//

Morgan nodded, then pulled her cloak closer against the southern wind. "Well, she always thought she knew better than me. I'll be interested to hear your report."

//ASK HER YOURSELF.// Ormeon spread her wings, then stilled. *//YOU'LL COME, WON'T YOU?//*

"The time is now?" Heser breathed deep. "We will be there."

Morgan gave him a little side eye but nodded. "We will be there, dragon. It's not everyday you get to witness the birth of a new kingdom. Fair, just, and free."

//DON'T PUT TOO MUCH PRESSURE ON THE KIDS OF TOMORROW,// Ormeon rumbled. *//SEE YOU SOON.//*

I REMEMBER THIS PLACE. IT IS MUCH NICER NOW. ORMEON KEPT HER distance from the field where she had done an unforgivable thing and been forgiven. *I do not deserve these humans.*

To be fair, though, it was another human that made me commit evil acts. It is past time for Redemption.

The old castle still crumbled on the hill. Coin flowed into the du Reeves estate from Ravenswall. The du Reeves were allies who guarded the kingdom's northern vanguards. Ormeon kept her height as she surveyed the vineyards. Workers walked the vines, doing whatever ridiculous things humans did to plants to make mind-altering substances. That there were workers at all was a marvel, as the old Lord du Reeves had a fair salting of insanity in his skull.

The new one, though: he's all right.

The docks sported a new structure, and Ormeon could see the merchants Amber and Jade there. They had dogged the Lord du Reeves for exclusive trading rights on liquor, which he was pleased to offer, because as near as Ormeon could tell, the Lord du Reeves had a negative appetite for anything that looked like administration.

Atop the sagging keep's main spire, Ormeon spotted hair still red despite the Sway's demands. Geneve knew her dragon was coming, just as Ormeon knew where her dragonrider was. *We know each other like the sea knows its salt.* Like Vertiline, she'd paid a terrible price for their victory. Her young visage had been stolen by the Three, replacing it with an older woman's, but she still had enough green glint in her eyes and form in her step to be the best swordswoman in the world.

Geneve raised a hand, and Ormeon bellowed fire in return greeting.

Ormeon settled outside the keep, because inside held too many bad memories. Meri promised he would make it a place she would feel welcome, and the dragon didn't have the heart to tell him that might not be in his power. But she loved him all the more for it. He exited the gates as she landed, the dragon blasting a heavy silting of sand and crud, which he squinted his way through before looking up at her. "Really?"

//THESE WINGS AREN'T FOR SHOW. THEY MOVE THE AIR QUITE A LOT.//

"Huh." He kept the squint on. For all he'd been a part of their save-the-world gig, he hadn't put on more years. Perhaps the Three had considered his debt paid when he took his Doom to the demon realm the last time. Perhaps the Three ignored the only remaining Holomancer, because gods were fickle. "Are you letting yourself go?"

//I HAVE KILLED PEOPLE FOR LESS.//

"No, really. The scales on your right flank look a little dull."

She bent, nose to his head. *//YOU ARE TERRIBLY BRAVE OR CRIMINALLY STUPID.//*

"He was the only one who put hand to dragonscale when we first met, out on the burning sands." Geneve called from the keep's gate, walking toward them. "He is eternally curious."

//STUPID AND BRAVE. GOT IT.//

They pair linked arms below Ormeon. Geneve sighed. "Are you well?"

//I'M A DRAGON.//

"Is that a yes, or..?" Meri trailed off.

//LITTLE HUMAN, I AM MADE TO BE WONDERFUL. THE MANIFEST TELLS ME DRAGONS WERE THE BEST THINGS HUMANS EVER MADE.//

"Talked to Sight of Day recently?" Geneve's lips quirked.

//ALWAYS IT IS SOMETHING ABOUT CATS.// Ormeon gave a dragony grin. *//I AM VISITING THEM NEXT.//*

"Is it time, love?" Geneve unlinked from Meriwether and put a hand on Ormeon's lowered muzzle. "I'm so very pleased for you."

//IT IS. I WANT...// Ormeon raised her head a moment away from Geneve's hand, then bowed, front legs lowered. *//I WOULD BEG THE GIFT OF MY DRAGONRIDER'S PRESENCE.//*

"I'm not your dragonrider anymore."

//WHILE THERE ARE STARS IN THE SKY, YOU WILL ALWAYS BE MY DRAGONRIDER.//

"We will be there. There is no force in the world that could keep us away." But Geneve looked at her feet. "I'm not who I used to be."

Her heart is sore, even after a year. *//YOU PAID A PRICE FEW WOULD, SO ALL COULD LIVE FREE.//*

"I had dreams," she said. "I had dreams like yours. This body is too old now."

Meri moved to her, slipping his arms about her waist. "We'll work it out." He brightened. "But we'll be there, dragon."

//THANK YOU.// She shifted. *//THERE IS A PACKAGE FOR YOU.//*

Meriwether brightened. "More books from Armitage?"

//IT IS A MYSTERY WHO PUT THE PACKAGE IN THE SADDLEBAG.//

He clambered up, not as graceful as Geneve by far, but enthusiastic with it. "Did he like the wine?"

//HE SEEMED PLEASANTLY DEPOSED.//

Meri unbundled the rectangle and beamed. "It's a book."

"What of?" Geneve leaned over his shoulder.

"I have no idea. It's in a language I've never seen." The Holomancer seemed delighted, then eyed the keep. "I really shouldn't, but there's still daylight."

Geneve gave him a gentle shove. "Off with you, husband." He swooped in for a kiss, then took his prize toward the keep. Ormeon was left with Geneve in companionable silence, excepting the sigh she offered.

//IT WILL BE OKAY, DRAGONRIDER.//

"Will it?" She hugged herself, still strong enough to carry whatever blade she needed, and still *present* despite lack of armour.

Ormeon stayed quiet for a while, letting the question rest between them. Geneve leaned against Ormeon's leg, and Ormeon sniffed her hair, which smelled quite nice. The dragon thought a lot about what *okay* might mean. For her, and for Geneve, and maybe the world. *//I DON'T ACTUALLY KNOW.//*

"The Manifest lacks the answers?"

//THE MANIFEST WAS WRITTEN BY COMMITTEE.// Ormeon straightened, looking down over the hill leading to the keep, and all the people there. Working together, to make things, or make things better, or just to be with each other. *//I BELIEVE IT IS NOT ABOUT HOW LONG YOU LIVE, BUT HOW WELL. HOW YOUR MARK IS MADE, AND THE PEOPLE YOU MAKE IT WITH.//*

Geneve looked up at her. "Did I do it well, dragon? Did I make a good mark? Only," her voice broke, before she leashed it, "I don't know. I'm so *old*, Ormeon. Meri and I will die in a handspan of years. But we are *young*. We should not yet be half-way through life, with children about us, and good friends to talk with. I won't get to see whether what I sacrificed was worth it."

//I WILL.// Ormeon *chuffed* at her. *//I WOULD NOT BE DOING*

WHAT I'M DOING IF I DIDN'T BELIEVE IN THIS WORLD, AND EVERYTHING IN IT. YOU DID THAT, DRAGONRIDER.//

"Was I a good dragonrider?"

//YOU WERE THE BEST.// Ormeon grinned. *//LET ME SHOW YOU.//*

Geneve leaned on her a moment, then straightened. Pulled the tatters of herself back around her. "I guess if he can leave to *read a book*, you and I can…"

//WE CAN.// Ormeon leaned forward and let her Dragonrider climb about. She launched, the ground pulling away.

Geneve's whoop of joy was heard across the valley.

THE FOREST WAS HOW ORMEON REMEMBERED. IT WAS QUIET, COOL without being cold, and away from humans and Vhemin. Toward the heart of it, klicks from any edge, and thus random chance encounter with a stray tourist, was a tiny cottage. The cottage stood in a respectable clearing. A decent-sized garden's distance away, a brook with aspirations of becoming a river bubbled its way through, and a clever person had built a water wheel to harness its power. A pocket smithy stood near the wheel.

There were two horses ambling about the field, keeping the clover at bay. They didn't seem to have much else to do, which worked for all parties. The horses, who knew Ormeon well by now, didn't freak out, bolt, dig up the ground, or destroy structures. At her massive *whump* landing, one horse flicked an ear, and she elicited a tail flick from the other.

Situation normal.

The horses were Orange and Hickory. Ormeon was sure it was important which was which, but she couldn't remember. The horses didn't care about the dragon, so the dragon didn't care about the horses.

The cottage had a porch, sheltered with an awning, roofed with good thatch, not any hint of poor maintenance to be found. On the porch was a rocking chair, and beside the rocking chair, a bassinet. The bassinet was empty, but the chair was full of a very pregnant Sands Apart.

{Hello, dragon.}

//HELLO, CAT. WHERE IS THE OTHER ONE?//

{He is hunting. He knew you were coming. He never tells me how he knows.}

//THERE IS LUNCH?//

{Despite the noise of your arrival, I'm sure he will find some. There is plentiful game here. No one else is around, and we don't eat much.} She smoothed the round of her belly. *{We will eat a little more, soon.}*

//YOU'RE NOT TOO FAT TO TRAVEL?//

Sands Apart gave her a deep and level ochre stare. *{Hickory might think so, but she could use the exercise.}* Sands Apart's fingers paused, then were sharp, and precise. *{She is fat.}*

Across the field, Sight of Day walked from the tree line and into the sun. Time had touched him almost not at all, the long-lived People measuring their span like dragons, if given the chance. He carried a deer across his shoulders and held a bow loosely. Ormeon waited for her old friend to take the deer out back, wash up, and join them. It was nice, here, with two of her favourite People. They didn't make much noise and understood how the world *should* work.

When Sight of Day emerged from the cottage's front door, he ruffled Sands Apart behind the ear, touched her neck very lightly, then faced the dragon. *{As suspected. You turn up for dinner empty handed.}*

//I DIDN'T WANT TO KILL A HORSE SOMEONE HAD TAKEN A LIKING TO.//

The cat half-smiled. *{There are few horses about. I would recommend boar. They are ferocious this time of year and are quite delicious with the right amount of rosemary.}*

Ormeon sobered. *//I KNOW SANDS APART IS CLOSE. BUT ... IT'S TIME.//*

Sight of Day gave the dragon an even, golden stare. *{I'm not sure of your point, exactly.}*

Sands Apart stood, slipped an arm around Sight of Day, and leaning close to him before she said, *{I'm pregnant, not dead.}*

//IT IS SOME DISTANCE TO THE MOUNTAIN.//

Sight of Day didn't say anything for a spell, just listening to the forest. Ormeon twitched as a bee came too close to her ear. A bellbird called from the trees. She was almost ready to lay down and sleep when Sight of Day said, *{Distance is a thing that can be traversed. It is a solvable problem for one of the greatest smiths in the world. What could never be undone would be missing an event like this. We will be there.}*

Ormeon lowered her head. *//YOU HUMBLE ME, CAT.//*

{It's good you still have perspective. Are you hungry?}

RAVENSWALL WAS A LONG FLIGHT. IT WAS THE LAST STOP ON Ormeon's journey before she returned home. She was glad she'd asked Tarragon to saddle her, so she and Geneve could fly once more. But now it was time to make the final visit. *I have a very special favour to ask.*

Dragonwing over the skies of Ravenswall wasn't entirely welcome. Not after the last time Ormeon was here. She clearly wasn't responsible for the busted docks, though. That had the look of a completely different group of assholes. Despite not being entirely welcome, no one shot at her. She coasted over the artist's borough, which was returned to its former glory. While Morgan wished the borough to continue, she no longer ruled as queen. Her Regent was a card-carrying believer, and Ravenswall was once again a place of music.

The Regent had said, *A song lifts the hearts, when you need to carry something really heavy.* She wasn't wrong. In that, as with many other things.

Ormeon cruised to the keep. It was massive, much repaired since the Saviour of Ravenswall had done her thing. The central courtyard had been fashioned big enough for someone of dragony size. The big red *crunched* into cobbles, but carefully, because there were people here, and many of them looked like they'd rather be somewhere else.

The statue is new. Toward the castle's main door stood a man carved in stone. While the statue was eye-level with Ormeon, the model—assuming all proportions were kept when upscaling—was not particularly tall, or particularly handsome. He wore armour, though, his face tilted toward the sky, and he rode atop a massive, rearing tiger.

Pakhet will have kittens.

Ormeon sobered, because she remembered the hoof code, although it wasn't strictly true. This time it was; this soldier had died in battle. She leaned forward, peering at the plaque beneath it.

Erik Hitcherson, saviour of us all.

Tarragon burst from the doorway behind the statue, running down the steps and grabbing Ormeon's foreleg in a big hug. "You're back!"

//HELLO, BUILDER.//

"I'm not a Builder any more."

Ormeon considered that. It didn't feel true. *//YOU MADE THE STATUE, THOUGH.//*

"How could you tell?"

//BECAUSE IT WAS MADE WITH LOVE.// Ormeon rumbled. *//SHE CARED FOR HIM VERY MUCH, AND YOU FELT THAT, AND PUT IT IN THE STATUE.//*

Tarragon stepped away and toed the ground. "He and I didn't see eye to eye. Not all the time. But we always agreed on how important she was."

//SPEAKING OF, IS SHE HOME?//

"She's dealing with a trade delegation."

//I COULD COME BACK.//

"No, I think she'll be right out. She sent me ahead and said I should ask you to yawn."

//YAWN?//

"I don't make the rules."

Ormeon shuffled, then curled her tail about her forelegs. A few moments later, the Regent emerged from the keep, dragging a reluctant man behind her. The reluctant man was very well dressed, and wore a wig, no doubt to deal with his balding pate. He looked like he was less than a minute from pissing himself at the sight of a dragon. The Regent pointed to Ormeon, and said, "We have a dragon. The dragon is very good at seeing into the hearts of men and telling if they're lying."

The trade delegate looked at Ormeon, then at the Regent. "The dragon can tell if I'm lying?"

"I didn't say you specifically." The Regent gave a tiny bell of laughter. "What an odd way of phrasing it."

"Uh. Yes! Quite." The delegate gathered his robes. "Perhaps a small discount on lumber is in order. While the weather has been poor for forestry, in this instance we can make a concession to the crown."

"Excellent," the Regent said. "Do you want to talk to the dragon?"

Ormeon, sensing her cue, yawned wide, showing many teeth, and a little emberfire. When she'd stopped yawning, the delegate was nowhere to be seen, and the Regent was laughing. //THAT WAS UNKIND.//

"It was necessary. He was going to talk me to death! And I've been dead once before. It's no fun ticket." The Regent sauntered down the steps and glanced up at Ormeon. "Hello, dragon."

//HELLO, EVANNE.// The bard was a shade leaner than when she'd died, and looked a little older. Her face said *I'm nearing thirty* but her eyes had an almost negative level of maturity. *As expected.*

"How's Uncle Heser?"

//UNCLE HESER AND AUNT MORGAN ARE BOTH FINE. AUNT MORGAN IS INTERESTED IN WHAT YOU'RE DOING TO HER KINGDOM.//

"Aunt Morgan can stop hiding out in the sticks and come see." Evanne gave an easy smile. "Are you well?"

//I AM EXCELLENT.//

Evanne considered that statement, the dragon's tone, and her posture. "You're lying."

//I AM ACTUALLY EXCELLENT. WHAT YOU MISTAKE FOR FALSEHOOD IS ME DISSEMBLING BECAUSE I WANT SOMETHING.//

"Don't dragons just take what they want?" Tarragon walked to Evanne, leaning close. "The rest of us have to work at it."

//DRAGONS TAKE WHAT THEY WANT IF IT IS DELICIOUS OR WARM. WE LIKE EATING AND SLEEPING ON HOT STONE. THIS IS A LITTLE MORE NUANCED.//

Evanne's smile widened into a genuine grin. "You want me to sing."

//WE WANT YOU TO SING, YES.// Ormeon stilled, feeling unaccountably nervous. *I'm a dragon, by the Three. Show some courage.* *//BUT NOT JUST ANY SONG.//*

Evanne sobered. "No, not just any song. This kind of song will take time. It will be wearying. I'm not sure if I can do it anymore."

"Don't be mean," said Tarragon. The Builder looked up at Ormeon. "She's been writing it for weeks."

//YOU DIDN'T KNOW I WOULD ASK!//

"She knew," Tarragon said.

"I kinda did," Evanne breezed. "Saw it on the other side of death's door. Felt the wind beyond the gate. Knew the future, for a moment."

Ormeon and Tarragon shared a look. *//I CAN'T TELL IF SHE'S TELLING THE TRUTH OR MAKING IT UP.//*

Evanne glanced up at the dragon. "You say that like it's two different things."

//IT IS!//

Evanne's smile returned. "You say that like the Manifest has all the answers. It doesn't. Let me get my coat."

//YOU DON'T HAVE TO LEAVE NOW. WE HAVE A WEEK.//

"If you think for a hot second that I'm fucking *walking* for a week when I've got a perfectly good dragon right here, you've another thing coming." Evanne sauntered back inside.

//SHE HAS SOMEONE TO MIND THE FARM?//

"She has someone to mind the farm while she's *here*, let alone when she leaves." Tarragon huffed. "Evanne is wonderful, but she's not a ruler. She's a leader."

The dragon gave a red stare to the Builder. *//WHAT'S THE DIFFERENCE?//*

"Rulers tell us what to do. Leaders make us want to do it."

//THEN SHE IS A VERY GOOD LEADER.//

THE INSIDE OF THE TEMPLE WAS QUIET, WARM ALMOST TO THE POINT of being hot, but not unclean, and it smelled of nothing but baked stone. Deeper within the ancient structure, a geothermal plant still powered relics of a bygone age. That heat faded to a modest strength out here.

They were all present. Vertiline and Armitage. Morgan and Heser, and they'd brought Pakhet, who was visible just this one time. Geneve, and Meri, her best human friends of all, companions through all they had struggled with in the demon realm, and before. Sight of Day, and Sands Apart, bringing a new tiny Feybrind into the world soon enough. And Tarragon the Builder, and Evanne the bard.

They will do so well, Ormeon thought. *They will remake the world better than it was.*

The humans were gathered in a rough semicircle before Ormeon. Geneve cleared her throat. "We are here, love."

//I AM ... NERVOUS.//

Vertiline offered a chuckle. "You've clearly never faced a dragon in combat."

Ormeon nodded, serpentine and regal. *//I HAVE NOT. WHAT I HAVE DONE, THERE IS NOTHING IN THE MANIFEST FOR.//*

Tarragon huffed. "Ormeon. We all love you. Even Armitage!"

"I fucken do not."

"He's just saying that. We are here for you. For this moment. Take us in."

Ormeon nodded. *//AGAIN, I AM HUMBLED.//* She backed away and led the group through the cavern. It snaked about, but was still clean, growing warmer as they went, which was comfortable if one was a dragon and wanted to sleep on hot rocks. They rounded the last bend, and there was Myryntir. The blue dragon looked smug, and entirely too pretty. It made Ormeon swoon, and she was not the swooning type.

Before Myryntir was a clutch of eggs. They were in many colours. Some red, others blue, one or two black, over there a green one, but right at the front? A single golden egg. Each egg was about the size of a human torso, which was an odd way to measure volume, but Ormeon was hungry.

"They are beautiful," Evanne breathed.

"You are so brave. I'm so proud of you, bringing them into the world," Geneve said. "You have done so well."

//I DID SOME OF THE WORK TOO,// Myryntir said.

//IGNORE HIM. HE'S FAMISHED.// Ormeon looked about. Her friends. Here, after all they'd been through. *This is the truest gift. Real companions, no matter whether we are scaled, furred, or have bald skin like baby moles. //THANK YOU ALL FOR COMING.//*

The golden egg wobbled, a small crack forking down its surface. Evanne walked closer and put her hand on it. "He's going to be a big one, but also strong of heart. Does he have a name?"

Myryntir's head came closer on his long neck. *//WE THOUGHT HE WOULD BE AMIR. THE WORLD NEEDS MORE AMIR.//*

"The world does," Tarragon whispered.

//IT'S TIME,// Ormeon said. *//I DON'T KNOW IF I'M READY.//*

"No mother is ready," Vertiline said.

Evanne looked up at her, then put her tiny hand on Ormeon's great foot. Pulled out her guitar and sat cross-legged at the dragon's feet. "You're ready. You know how I know? Because Amir is ready."

//THEN SING, BARD. GIVE US A SONG FOR THE AGES.//

"I've got just the thing," Evanne said. She adjusted herself, let her fingers drop to the strings, and there, in the circle of friends and lovers, true family all, with new dragons coming to the world for the first time in eight hundred years, she sang for them a song of the ages. The music wrapped around Ormeon, the power of it astonishing. A benediction, or a blessing perhaps.

But a gift, from the heart, from one generation and species to another. To share this world with, forever, and to be stronger for it.

In the darkest hour of night,
When the world lost its guiding light,
We rose above the shadows' fall,
For hope's the strongest of them all.

In fractured souls and broken dreams,

A glimmer of a future gleams,
With every tear, we'll stand up tall,
For love's the answer to our call.

THROUGH TRIALS FACED AND BATTLES WON,
We'll find the strength to carry on,
With unity, we'll break down walls,
And rise above when darkness falls.

IN EVERY HEART, A FLAME IGNITES,
A beacon in the darkest nights,
In kindness shown, we'll stand up tall,
For goodness leads us through it all.

OH, LET THE REDEEMER'S SONG SOAR,
A symphony of love we'll pour,
Through every heart, we'll heed the call,
To sing the hymn of hope for all.

AS DAWN BREAKS THROUGH THE ENDLESS NIGHT,
All people redeemed by Light,
Together, we shall rise and soar,
And sing the hymn of hope for all,
Yes, sing the hymn of hope for all,
The hymn of all.

THE END.

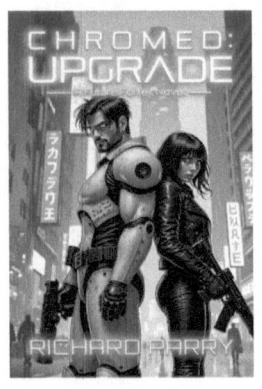

THE LAST SONG HAS BEEN SUNG. **BUT THE music never stops.**

The Splintered Lands are behind you. The battle is won. But in the neon shadows of the future, another war is about to begin.

The corps own everything. **Except for those who refuse to kneel.**

Mason was trained to obey, a syndicate enforcer drowning in his past, following orders just to survive. **But just like Tarragon,** he's learning that some things are worth breaking for, **even if it means walking away from everything he's ever known.**

Sadie sings in the dark, a singer without magic but no less powerful. Hers is a song of defiance in a world suffocating under corporate rule. Evanne had dragons. **Sadie has nothing** but a stage, a stolen mic, and **a crowd desperate for something real.**

There's no magic here. No gods or ancient wars—**just black-market cybernetics, hypervelocity weapons**, and a world where **every choice is paid for in blood.**

Turn the page. Welcome to the world of Future Forfeit.

CHROMED: UPGRADE
A CYBERPUNK CONTINGENCY

Off Grid

Never go off the grid. That was the rule. It kept Mason alive. If you had to, make sure you had a weapon and backup. Apsel's reach stopped where link coverage ebbed away to a gritty residue.

Mason had a weapon, but backup was a long ride away. *You're fifty percent there. Stop complaining. Get inside.*

Seconds was the kind of bar nobody would go twice. An old chipped door, the auto sensor broken, the sliders sticky with beer or blood. Mason shouldered it aside. The interior felt warm. Humidity stuck like a bad odor to the air. In its better days, it would have hosted over a hundred, the pump and beat of music making their own statement.

Today, fewer than a dozen people were nursing drinks, telling themselves the usual lies. He eyed a woman by the bar, working what magic she had left on a john, her use-by date well passed. The john looked no better, a long, stringy guy with fewer teeth than he'd been born with.

Neither were worth credits or paperwork.

He wasn't here for hookers or their clients. Mason was here for the promise of a lead. Most people would call it a rumor, but he'd spent enough time off-grid to know where truth lay among the grime.

Mason's optics scanned the bar, picking out the mods. *Seconds* wasn't the kind of place you went into blind. His first pass gave him nothing to cry about. Bionics done on the cheap, a knife where a laser would be best, out of fashion chrome making the wrong kind of statement. Nothing here was mil-spec.

Green neon flickered behind the bar, as tired and listless as the patrons. The bartender watched him, one chromed arm working a dirty rag over a dirtier surface. His eyes were underlined with a smatter of *hanzi*, the logograms giving off a soft phosphor blue bioluminescence. A couple of teenage *ganguro* girls were making out in a dark corner, the pastel of their eyeliner garish with the green from the bar. Mason's audio brought him the whisper of their bright clothes as they rubbed against each other.

Carter said this was the place. Someone had come in here, dropped credits into the old terminal on the back wall, and made a play to buy company assets. Mason brushed rain from his jacket, then made his way to the bar. His tailored clothes said *cash* and *syndicate*. No one got in his way.

Not yet.

Mason's overlay highlighted the bartender. No ID. No link. His optics showed a ghost who worked *down here* because *up there* was impossible. An illegal, like all the rest.

"Hey." Mason put a grainy photograph on the bar. A side shot of a man, orange mirror sunglasses on, greasy hair over a face gone soft and ugly. Carter had uplifted it from the terminal. "Know this guy? He's a buyer."

The bartender didn't look at the photo, his gaze touching the bottles stacked up in front of the flickering neon. The dirty rag paused. "I never heard of that mix. Been making drinks a long time now."

Mason tapped his finger on the photo. "It's a popular drink. Exactly the thing you'd get in this part of town."

The bartender shrugged. "Drink like that, might be expensive." The rag resumed motion, his chromed arm picking up the green light and pushing it around the bar top after the rag.

Mason saw the *hanzi* under the bartender's left eye flicker, the glow stuttering. He pressed greasy notes down on the bar next to the photo. "I understand. Maintenance. Got to keep the kitchen in working order."

"Exactly." The rag stopped moving again. Mason caught a reflection in the chromed arm as a man walked in from the street. A sharp gust of night air followed him in, the faintest hint of sewage mixing with the acrid scent of rain. The bartender nodded to the newcomer. "It's killer out there." The photo and the money vanished, whisked away by the bartender as if they'd never been. He moved further down the bar, filling a cocktail shaker with dirty ice.

The newcomer sat next to Mason, a hint of Davidoff cologne washing off him. "Mind if I sit here?"

"It's a free country." Mason didn't turn, taking in the expensive suit cuffs out of the corner of his eye. Tailored sleeves went with the cuffs. Might be an exec out for some fun at the people's expense.

Might be syndicate trouble.

"That's the biggest lie I've heard this week." The man shook water from his coat, throwing the heavy jacket over a vacant barstool. "Hasn't been free since they invented the credit card."

"You don't seem to be suffering."

The man gave a quick laugh. "Business is good. What can I say?"

The bartender pushed a tumbler in front of Mason, the ice nestled in around a rich amber liquid. Algae in the drink sparked a bright pink, flecks of light flashing in amongst the amber and ice. "Your drink."

Mason nodded his thanks, taking a sip. The liquor was rougher than he'd expected. He coughed. "Christ." He saw a splash of white as he set it down. A scrap of paper was stuck to the bottom of the glass. *A note for my eyes only*. Money spoke a universal language.

The man next to him gestured to the bartender. "Whatever he's having."

"You really don't want to do that." Mason grimaced. "Last time I order the house specialty, that's for sure."

"I can handle it." The man counted notes on the bar. "These throwbacks need to get linked. I hate cash. It's too dirty."

"At least it's quiet." Mason took another swallow, then glanced at the stranger's tailored cuffs. He looked back down into his drink, reading the address written on the note. "It's probably as good a place to die as any."

A heartbeat of silence followed as pressure built in the air. Mason felt his lattice react, its prediction routines making his hands grab the bar's edge, heaving him over the top. A blast wave hit, tossing him against the wall. Mason's perception of time slowed as overtime flowed over him.

The fibers in his jacket stiffened to take the impact. Glass and liquor rained on Mason from the shattered bottles above the bar. His optics flickered as they adjusted contrast, first to the flash of light then the dancing shadows. A single neon filament above Mason stuttered out the last of its life in refracted green before the bar went dark.

"I'm glad you appreciate your situation." The man's voice came from the other side of the bar. "No offense. Like I said, business is good."

"None taken." Mason planted his feet against the bar, bracing himself in the narrow space. He pulled his Tenko-Senshin sidearm from under his jacket, the whine of the weapon soft in the darkness. The nose of the weapon tracked the man's footsteps as if it had a mind of its own. "Reed Interactive?"

"Good guess, but no. Metatech. Apsel?"

"Yeah." Mason listened for movement. *Careful. Metatech means mil-spec bionics. Keep him talking.* "What are they like?"

"Metatech?" The man paused. "They sure as shit provide better backup than Apsel Federate."

Mason's smile glinted in the darkness. "What makes you think I need backup?"

The man laughed as he made for the door. No hurry in it, like he did this kind of thing on a daily. "Buddy? You look fucked to me."

The door squealed a complaint as it opened, followed by a distinctive thud as Mason's opponent tossed in a grenade. *Get up, Mason. Move!*

Mason rolled over the bar. He hit the kitchen door as the grenade exploded, throwing him into a stove so grimy it looked like a movie prop. He fell hard, then pushed himself upright. His optics flickered in the darkness — *goddamn EMP* — then switched to thermal, the intense bright square of the Tenko-Senshin's energy pack outlined against the blue-black of the floor. Mason felt the cool calm of the hard link as his palm gripped it.

Only an amateur would rely on an EMP grenade against a syndicate asset. Top-shelf bionics barely noticed. *An amateur, or someone who really does have backup. You got what you came for. Time to go.*

"Mason?" The link flickered into life, Carter inside his head. Her deep, husky voice was tinged with a hint of concern.

"Now's not a good time, Carter." Mason went back to the kitchen door. A couple of tables burned, shedding sooty smoke. The heat from the flames scorched the center of his vision with white, so he switched back to visual light. "I'm busy."

"That's what I'm calling about." She paused. "Don't go out the front."

"You checking up on me?" Mason looked through the door's cracked window. The jumble of wreckage was unrecognizable. A mess of plastic and wood veneer nestled atop bodies. "I didn't know you cared."

"They used energy weapons. The signature is quite clear from sat telemetry."

"Plasma?"

"Looks like."

"Jesus. You get cancer from those things." Mason pushed the snout of the Tenko-Senshin ahead of him.

"No." Carter sounded annoyed. "You get *burning* from those things. The fire would kill you, and you would hurt the entire time you were dying. You were lucky. And careless."

"Thanks."

"You're not going to be alive long enough to get cancer."

"Like I said, now's not a good time. You can list my failings later."

"Why not just go out the back?"

"Two reasons. First, they'll be expecting that." Mason stepped through the kitchen door, his feet crunching on broken glass.

"The second reason?"

"The bartender gave me an address. He's in here somewhere." Mason paused. "What, no snappy comeback?"

"It'll be expensive." Carter sounded doubtful.

"Put it on my tab. Did I miss a budget cuts memo?"

"I'll call a medivac." The link went dead.

Mason stepped over a body flung from the center of the plasma strike. He looked at it as he passed. *Not this one.* The radius of damage was from Mason's spot at the bar. His overlay plotted a line on Mason's optics, showing the point of origin.

A booth, no different from the rest. No sign of the *ganguro* girls who'd been there, the booth black and empty. A fluorescent light stuttered to life, then went dark as sprinklers kicked in. Muddy water trickled from the ceiling for a moment before dying out. Loose drips of dark water stuck to the ceiling nozzles.

Mason found the bartender sprawled backward against a broken table. His chrome arm was gone, the stump smooth and pale. *Cheap work. No anchoring.* Or maybe the guy didn't want to get that close to the metal. Mason scanned as he knelt. His HUD told the violent story of the bartender's injuries. Burns. Lacerations and bruising. "Hey."

The bartender coughed, the sound ragged and wet. "I tried to ... doesn't matter. Did you get the address?"

"I got it." Mason nodded to the door. "It'll keep a few minutes longer."

The bartender grabbed Mason's arm. "You don't understand. They're killing us."

"Killing you?"

"The rain. Your *buyer*. That's what's for sale. Don't you know?" He coughed again.

Mason stood. "Who was it?"

"What?"

"Who did you lose to the rain?"

The bartender looked at him, firelight playing across his features. The blue had faded from the *hanzi*, leaving gray marks like scars. "My brother."

Mason nodded. "Try not to move. A medivac's coming."

"I can't afford that." The man's eyes turned pleading. "Just leave me here. I'll be okay."

Mason looked at the Tenko-Senshin, the weapon's hum a gentle touch in his hand. He moved toward the door. Before he stepped into the street, he glanced back. "It's on the house."

"Which house?" The bartender slumped back. "Who'm I gonna owe for this?"

Mason didn't reply as he walked outside into the hissing rain, the door yawning behind him.

Chapter One

"I don't know if I love you anymore." Sadie tightened a garter strap, grabbing a shirt from the pile on the floor. "That's all I've got."

"Seriously?" Aldo looked at her from the couch. "You're doing this to me now? We're on in five." They were in Sadie's dressing room. A huge mirror surrounded by ancient incandescent bulbs reflected their sins.

"I know, baby." She shrugged the shirt on. They hadn't taken the time to unbutton earlier. "But that's the way it's going to be." They were supposed to be readying for tonight's performance. But then the urge struck, and ... well, Aldo didn't get urges as often as he used to.

"Shit." The drummer rummaged around the pile on the floor, grabbing a pair of black leather pants. He felt in a pocket, pulling out a rumpled pack of cigarettes. He offered one, lighting it for her with an old-style Zippo, the skull motif etched on the side worn with time. "When will you know?"

"Know what?" Sadie worked on some black eyeliner. A rush job would have to do. She pursed her lips at her reflection in the mirror, then dragged on the cigarette.

"Jesus, Freeman! Whether you love me or not."

"I don't know." She put the cigarette down in favor of a comb, teasing her hair.

"You don't know? How can you not know?"

Sadie sighed, her shoulders sagging a little. She didn't turn away from the mirror. "It's not that easy."

"It's easy for me."

"No kidding. That was the fastest round we've ever had."

Aldo looked down at his crotch, then back up at her reflection. "Hey. You said you wanted it quick."

"I said I wanted to get it done before we had to go on. It's not the same thing." Sadie pointed to his pants with her free hand, still wrangling her hair with the other. "You should put those on."

"Why? What if I don't feel like playing tonight?" Aldo started putting a foot into the leather pants anyway.

"Are you five years old?" Sadie raised her eyebrow. "I guess I play without a drummer tonight."

"What?" Aldo stumbled as his other foot got caught in his pant leg. A year ago, he'd filled them out; now, not so much. *Too many of the wrong drugs.* "You don't have a band without a drummer."

A knock sounded on the door. "You're on." It was the stage manager Bernie, still carrying too much stress for his own good. "Don't do this muso shit tonight, Freeman! I got a hundred people out here who've paid—"

"Shut it, Bernie!" Sadie turned to face the door, a hairspray can raised in one hand. "I'll be on when I'm fucking on! Don't you have an ulcer to nurse?" She could imagine his wattled chin underneath bulging eyes in a sallow face, vein beating in his forehead. *Admit it, Sadie. You like pissing him off.*

"Musicians. You're all the same..." Bernie's voice drifted into an indeterminate mumble as he stormed off.

Aldo pushed an arm through a black sleeve, his movements sharp and angry. "You haven't answered."

Sadie gave a last flourish with the hair spray, pouting at her reflection. *Maybe too much grunge, Sadie.* "What? About the drummer? I don't need a drummer."

"Every band needs a drummer. But no. The other thing."

"I played two years without a band, let alone a drummer. What makes you think I need a band? Christ. Bernie's right, musicians are all the same." Sadie stood, grabbing her jacket from the back of a chair where she'd tossed it earlier. The leather was real, a parting gift from her father. It and the guitar were the only things he'd ever given her.

The guitar. Sadie looked at it, gleaming in the corner by the door. A shiver tapped its way up her spine. God, but she loved to play. Her hands itched to hold it.

"Jesus. You're breaking up the band?" Aldo's mouth hung open.

"What? No, unless you stay locked in your room tonight." Sadie pulled on her boots, the metal clasps jingling against her hands, then moved to the guitar. She almost reached for it but turned to Aldo instead. Her lips quirked, black lipstick against the pale white of her skin. "So. You playing tonight, lover?"

Aldo pulled the edges of his vest together, then ran a hand through his hair. Tall and lean. Dark hair. Dark eyes. *You always liked the tall dark and handsome, Sadie.* He dropped a lopsided grin at her, and she almost wanted to take it all back. "Yeah. I'll play for you, Freeman. Let's go."

She grinned back, then turned and picked up the guitar. "Okay. Let's rock this house." Sadie yanked the door open, letting her boots clank and stomp their own way to the stage. Time to *play*.

HER LIPS BRUSHED THE OLD MIC. THE AIR CHARGED WITH THE SMELL of liquor and sweat. It'd only take a spark to ignite it.

Ancient incandescent lights shone down on Sadie, bright and hot. Her fingers touched the strings, the sound almost gentle as notes leaked and flowed from the speakers. The crowd hushed, a giant's indrawn breath.

Like the feeling before a storm.

She felt the band behind her. Aldo with his electronic drum kit. The sound wouldn't be quite right, but it's what they had. Janice stood with her guitar, the digital board doing all the hard work.

Fakes. Impostors on her stage. That wasn't music. Sadie played at

The Hole because of the people. They were off the grid, just like her. You'd be hard pressed to find a link in the room.

The mic in front of her smelled of excitement. It was time.

Sadie brought a hand down against the strings, the fingers of her other skipping against fingerboard. The crowd surged against the stage as the Seattle sound mixed with air made rich with their despairs and hopes.

The room grew heavy. People ground against each other, jerking and dancing with the music. She forgot about Aldo, about Bernie and his cut, and about how she would make rent. For a little while, the strings under her fingers were all that mattered, and she sang alongside her guitar until her voice grew hoarse.

Sadie stopped, the guitar's notes dying away. The crowd stumbled against the fallen beat. Sadie breathed, the microphone sharing her exertion with them. Her pulse pounded.

"Sorry." She smiled, lips to the microphone like a lover's ear. The room echoed with her voice. "I'm just tired." Sadie glanced to the side and saw Bernie in the wings, a scowl blooming on his face. Her smile turned to a grin, catching against her teeth.

"So." Sadie turned back to the crowd. *My people*. "Should I stop?"

NO. The roar washed over her. She closed her eyes in the face of it.

"Ah." Sadie's fingers touched the strings again, the sound walking around the stage. The crowd hushed for her. "I could use a drink."

Some hero in the crowd raised his bottle toward the stage. More followed, the press of bodies almost urgent. She held a hand up, stilling them. "Thanks. Just put it on the edge." The muscle along the stage let the hero deliver her drink. He had eager eyes and a face that wanted to be kind. "What's your name?"

"Mark," said the hero.

"Not Jax the Destroyer? Merlin the Merciless?"

"It's just Mark."

Sadie smiled again, fingers plucking strings, the sound of the guitar thanking him. "No shit, Mark. I guess not all heroes wear capes." She stepped forward, grabbing the bottle from the edge, the glass sweating against her hand. Sadie saluted Mark with the bottle before tipping it back. The beer was cool and clean, and she finished the bottle in a moment. She tossed the empty aside, a tinkle of glass reminding her bliss was fleeting. *But you can make it last a little longer*. "Thanks. Someone buy Mark a drink!"

The crowd cheered, shifting to the bar. Sadie glanced at Bernie. His scowl struggled to hold. People buying liquor always increased profits, especially in a place like this.

Sadie's fingers caressed the strings. She'd lied. Sadie never felt tired when she played.

SADIE SHUFFLED THE WAD OF DIRTY PAPER, COUNTING NOTES. "Where's the rest?"

Bernie shrugged. "That's it. That's your cut."

"Bullshit." Sadie kicked off her boots to tumble into a wall. The mirror of her dressing room shimmied in complaint. "They were on fire, Bernie. They bought beer *and* a cover charge."

He shrugged again, his belly rising and falling with it. "What can I say. Cash is a rare thing. If you had a link you could check the books yourself." A smile crept on his face but found it foreign territory and left. "You think I'm trying to cheat you? C'mon, you're my star!"

Linked? Hell with that. "I think you'd cheat your mother if you thought you could get away with it. And I don't want shit in my head. Gets in the way of the music."

"The band doesn't think so." Bernie nodded to the door. "They're happy digital. You're the one with an ancient guitar."

"Ancient? It's a classic. It's the sound that pulls people in. Besides, you're confusing the issue." Sadie waved the wad of money, fighting red rage. "I can't even pay for parking with this."

"You don't have a car."

"It's because you pay shit. What if I just moved on?"

Bernie cocked his head. "I dunno, Sadie. Where you going to find someone who lets you play without a link? It's borderline illegal. I look the other way." He tried the smile again. "Because you're like a daughter to me."

"You make passes at all your daughters?" Her eyes drifted to his gut, then back to his face. "I think you let me play because I fill your bar every night. You bought a new car after I started here."

"It's a Toyota-Mitsu."

"It's a Lexus." Sadie pushed a chair in front of the mirror, straddling it backward. "Only reason you don't own a Mercedes is because it'd get stolen around here."

"Whatever." Bernie waved a dismissive hand. Sadie's blood got another degree closer to boiling point. "So, leave. Or stay. I don't care, but if you stay, make sure you're on time tomorrow." He pulled the door open, almost colliding with Aldo. "Christ! Aldo, talk some sense into your woman." Bernie shouldered past and out.

"She's not... Never mind." Aldo looked after Bernie, then glanced at Sadie. "You okay?"

"Just great." Sadie held up the money. "Here, take it. For you and Janice."

"You got your cut?" Aldo looked at the cash, not taking it, but also not looking like he wanted to know the answer. "Hell."

"Yeah, I took my cut." Sadie offered the money up again. "Go buy something nice. Like a beer."

"Beer's free. About the only thing that is in this place."

Sadie looked him up and down. "Just take it and go."

Aldo reached for her, his hand almost making it to Sadie's shoulder. It hovered beside her a moment. She wanted his hands on her like before it had gone bad. *It'll be okay. Go on.* Sadie held herself still, daring Aldo to touch her. To show her how he felt.

His hand dropped to the cash. "Right. See you." Aldo stepped out the door. Gone, like a missed taxi.

Sadie looked after him, then kicked the door closed. She brushed the tear from her eye, a streak of black left behind from her makeup.

That's why I don't love you anymore, Aldo Vast. It's because you're an asshole.

The Future is Forfeit...

UNLESS YOU TAKE IT BACK.

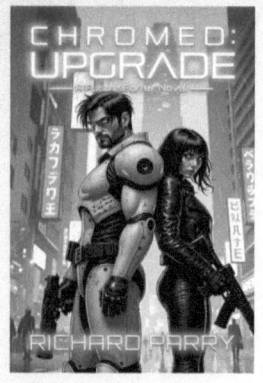

The corps own everything. The syndicates run the streets with enforcers like **Mason**. In between is where people like **Sadie** fight to survive.

Mason is drowning in his past, following orders to stay alive—until he's given one he can't follow. But **betrayal is hard when you've got everything to lose.**

Sadie sings to the dispossessed, a voice of defiance in a world that wants her silent. The crowd she sings to needs more than promises. It's **waiting for something real.**

The gods can't hear you when your future is forfeit. No magic can save you. There's only cybernetics, hypervelocity weapons, and **the price of rebellion paid in blood.**

Grab *Chromed: Upgrade* now!

https://www.books2read.com/ChromedUpgrade

Because our future belongs to those who refuse to kneel.

Also by Richard Parry

DAWN'S WARDEN

The Three Faces of Fate

The Undefeated Throne

The Fury of the Betrayed

THE SPLINTERED LAND

Tomb of the Six

Blade of Glass

The Storm Within

Requiem's Justice

The Copper Bard

Heartsong

The Hymn of All

THE EZEROC WARS

The Ezeroc Wars universe is big (and growing!). Get the reading guide here: https://www.parrydox.com/ezeroc-wars-reading-guide/

The Empire's Rogues: Volume 1

FUTURE FORFEIT

Not sure where to start? Get the reading guide here: https://www.parrydox.com/future-forfeit-reading-guide/

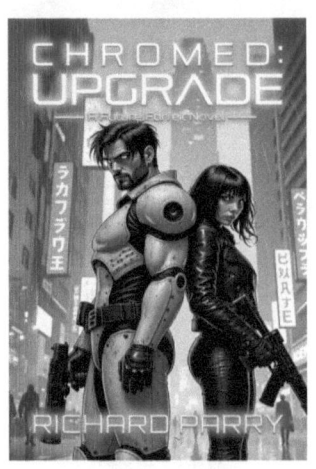

Chromed: Upgrade

Chromed: Rogue

Chromed: Restore

City Stories

Chromed: Consensus

Chromed: Delilah

Chromed: Meltdown

NIGHT'S CHAMPION

Night's Favor

Night's Fall

Night's End

About the Author

Richard Parry worked as a senior marketing manager in one of the world's top tech companies. It sounds cool, but it wasn't all cocaine parties. He lives in Wellington with the love of his life, Rae. They have two cats, Harry and Friday, who chase birds. The birds, who have the power of flight, don't seem to mind.

WAIT. DON'T GO!

Thanks for reading my book. If you enjoyed it, let's keep the party going:

📖 Join *Roll for Narrative* for reviews, storytelling breakdowns, and writing misadventures:

https://rollfornarrative.parrydox.com

✒ Lurk, judge, or say hi:

https://www.parrydox.com

P.S. An angel still gets its wings for every five-star review, but I'm told they're on backorder.

a amazon.com/author/richard.parry

g goodreads.com/richard_parry

BB bookbub.com/authors/richard-parry-6ffc3911-9f2c-43ef-8ab4-13dc-cd7f5874

▶ youtube.com/@parrydigm

🦋 bsky.app/profile/parrydox.com

in linkedin.com/in/therealrichardparry